THE LION AND THE NURSE

Best Wishes,
Patty Apostolides

Also by Patty Apostolides

Lipsi's Daughter
Candlelit Journey: Poetry from the Heart

The Lion and the Nurse

A Novel

Patty Apostolides

iUniverse, Inc.

New York Lincoln Shanghai

The Lion and the Nurse

iUniverse books may be ordered through booksellers or by contacting:

iUniverse
2021 Pine Lake Road, Suite 100
Lincoln, NE 68512
www.iuniverse.com
1-800-Authors (1-800-288-4677)

Because of the dynamic nature of the Internet, any Web addresses or links contained in this book may have changed since publication and may no longer be valid.

This is a work of fiction. All of the characters, names, places, incidents, organizations, and dialogue in this novel are either the products of the author's imagination or are used fictitiously.

ISBN: 978-0-595-46793-8 (pbk)
ISBN: 978-0-595-91083-0 (ebk)

Printed in the United States of America

In Loving Memory

To my nephew Nikitas (1986–2006)
You were a ray of sunshine
That brightened up our days.
You are dearly missed—
In so many ways.
May your memory be eternal.

Love is patient; love is kind; love is not envious or boastful or arrogant or rude. It does not insist on its own way; it is not irritable or resentful; it does not rejoice in wrongdoing, but rejoices in the truth. It bears all things, believes all things, hopes all things, endures all things.—**1 Cor 13:4–7**

Make a habit of two things; to help, or at least to do no harm.
—Hippocrates

ACKNOWLEDGEMENTS

I'd like to give my sincere thanks to the following people who contributed valuable information or useful comments that helped shape the novel into what it is: Chris Bartel, Gerald Braude, Rob Evans, Mary Jo Gileno, Kathy Lambros Matrakas, Helen Reddylane, Louise Skendrovic, and the Kos United Tourism Board.

I'd also like to thank the Greek churches and organizations I participated in, my Greek-American friends and relatives, and the numerous libraries and bookstores in which I spent a significant amount of time; you all contributed in some fashion.

I'm eternally grateful to my mother, Anna, for being the best Greek mother one could have, and my father, Christos, who is up there in heaven, keeping an eye on everything; and to all my sisters and their families, who have shaped me into what I am. I love you all.

With deep love and admiration I'd like to thank my wonderful husband Tony, who is the inspiration behind my writing, and last but not least, to our son Tony, Jr., who reminds us of how young and joyful we can be.

PROLOGUE

June 1972

Cassiani trudged alongside her mother down the dusty, unpaved road, away from Mrs. Lukas' house. It was the end of June, a lazy, warm summer day that allows time for the senses to discover the beauty of nature as it unfolds petal by petal. The hill sloped down the side of Dikeos Mountain, allowing picturesque views of Kos Island with its pine trees, olive tree orchards, and walnut tree groves. The sweet scent of mountain peppermint that drifted their way and the cattle grazing below the nearby pasture were all ignored as the heat of the summer sun beat a slow tempo on Cassiani's sweaty forehead. The black dress she was wearing with its long sleeves didn't help much in this heat.

"I'm glad we didn't stay long in that house," Cassiani said. "I didn't feel comfortable with Mrs. Lukas."

"She's all right once you get to know her," Vera said absentmindedly.

Cassiani pulled her long, silky mane of raven black hair together and quickly braided it. She felt a sense of relief as they passed under the shade of a pine tree. A trace of a breeze paused briefly to cool the sweat on her neck, then playfully leapt away, rustling the leaves on the trees. "Does she have family? She was all alone up there in that large villa."

"She's been a widow for years. She has no children," Vera replied. "I did hear she has a brother in America. He's married and has a son."

An aching feeling inside Cassiani's chest formed when she thought about her deceased father. His untimely death three weeks ago had shocked them all. Her whole world had turned upside down since that fateful day. Her youthful assumption that life would go on forever in its idyllic simplicity had been shattered and in its place was the knowledge of one's fragility in this unpredictable world. Her Christian belief mercifully numbed the pain of her loss; to think that her father was up there in heaven somewhere looking down on them was a consolation.

Cassiani's jaw tightened as she recalled the conversation they just had with the sour faced Mrs. Lukas. "I couldn't believe it when Mrs. Lukas said she found another pharmacist to replace Father. It's only been a few weeks since Father …," She paused, not wanting to say the word. "I don't understand why she didn't let us keep the pharmacy. Weren't we paying her a monthly mortgage? Wasn't the pharmacy supposed to become ours one day?"

"Yes, but we cannot maintain the mortgage and besides, I cannot manage the pharmacy by myself," Vera retorted. "We know nothing about the business. Your father was the pharmacist." A loud cry escaped her and her eyes filled with tears. She stopped and took out a handkerchief from her pocket to blow her nose. "Oh, my Marco! Why did you have to leave me?"

Cassiani put her arm around her weeping mother, trying to comfort her. She felt her mother's grief and a sob escaped her. "I'm so sorry. I'm so sorry."

Vera wiped her tears away, sniffling. "It's no use crying." She shook her head. "It is not going to bring back your father." She stuffed the handkerchief in her pocket. "I must think about our future, including your dowry. Mrs. Lukas was kind enough to offer me the job."

"What happened to the money earned from the shop? Didn't we save any?"

Vera sighed. "Athena's marriage, including her dowry, drained us of our savings. How were we to know this would happen?"

Cassiani quietly digested the information. "I'll get a college education and work hard so you won't have to work. You'll see. I'll become a nurse!"

"You're eighteen going on nineteen. You should be thinking about marriage," Vera said. "Besides, where will you find the money to go to college? Money doesn't fall from the tree!"

They reached the intersection. Ahead, the winding road eventually led down into the village of Zipari. To their right, beyond the orchard studded fields lived her grandmother.

"Let's visit your *Yiayia*. She's been eager to see us and I want to talk to her about something," said Vera, a determined look on her face.

"Is it about our house? We can't afford to keep it, can we? Will we have to move in with her?" asked Cassiani. She could see strong emotions playing on her mother's face.

"You are a very bright girl, Cassiani, and I can't hide anything from you. Yes, we will be moving in with Mother. She is expecting us."

CHAPTER 1

———————— ❦ ————————

April 1979

Truth exists, yet often times we don't see it. Elusive, like a deer in hiding, it waits, revealing itself only when the beholder stands still, ready to accept it unconditionally. Such a moment of truth exposed itself on this spring afternoon to Cassiani, but was she ready for it?

Cassiani stepped out on to the sunlit balcony carrying a bucket of dirty soap water in one hand and a wet mop in the other. Her mind was miles away at the University Hospital in Cleveland, Ohio, where she worked the past five months as a registered nurse. Today she would have been taking blood pressure readings at seven o'clock in the morning or popping thermometers into patients' mouths. Or she would have been reading charts and administering medications. Instead, she was here on the Greek Island of Kos, mopping Mrs. Lukas' upstairs apartment.

A week ago, when she and her sister received the telephone call from the doctor at Kos Hospital telling them that her mother experienced a heart attack, it had come as a shock. Athena couldn't come because she was pregnant with her second child, so it was decided that Cassiani would come. Cassiani rushed to get here, dropping everything she was doing with no other thought but to nurse her mother. When she arrived three days ago, little did she know that today she'd be cleaning and mopping Mrs. Lukas' house.

Cassiani lifted the bucket and poured the soapy water over the side of the balcony, watching the water disappear down the slope of the lime-green hill below.

Further observation revealed flecks of color among the hill; clusters of white cyclamen, bunches of daisies, and bright red poppies that swayed with each caress of the wind. She took a deep breath, enjoying the fresh mountain air.

Two wooden chairs and a small square table sat on the balcony. She sank into one chair, plopping her slender legs up on the other chair, enjoying the sun-drenched panoramic view of Kos Island below. She could see far on this clear day; the whitewashed houses scattered here and there, the sandy beach of Tigaki with its salt lake, and in the horizon, the small island of Pserimos.

Her gaze settled to her left, beyond the row of Cypress trees that marked the property's boundary, on the winding road leading to the house. She remembered the walk she had with her mother years ago down that very same road. It was dusty and half the width; suited more for pedestrians and donkeys than for cars.

This morning her mother said, "You'll find the road paved now, so don't miss the way. It was done two years ago when Mrs. Lukas bought a new Mercedes."

Cassiani glimpsed the dark shade of a lonely automobile driving up the road, but lost track of it just as quickly; probably her imagination at work. Mrs. Lukas was napping downstairs and wasn't expecting anyone. She yawned, rubbing her eyes, enjoying the feel of the warm sun on her face. Her eyes fluttered shut as she fell into a light sleep.

Thud.

Cassiani jumped up from her chair, knocking it over, her heart beating wildly. She anxiously peered through the balcony's glass door into the darkness of the apartment. Could it be that Mrs. Lukas had walked up the stairs looking for her and had slipped on the newly mopped floor? She opened the door for a better look. Then she caught sight of the man. His movements were slow and cautious, as if he had sensed another presence ... *her presence.* "A burglar," she whispered. She quickly made the sign of the cross. "Dear Lord, have mercy on me."

He was lean and dressed in dark clothes, and was heading purposefully towards her.

*   *   *   *

"What are you doing here?" Leo demanded. Just as he was about to reach the balcony he slipped on the wet floor and landed on his back.

At that very same moment Cassiani sprinted past him, then slid on the wet floor, her arms flailing about her until she regained her momentum. In her haste to leave, she blindly ran into the luggage lined up at the door. She lost her balance and grabbed the doorframe managing to keep from falling. She shakily pulled the two large suitcases upright. Were these the cause of the sound she heard from the balcony? She glanced at the nametag. "Dr. Leonidas Regas," she whispered. Why did the name sound familiar? Her eyes flew open. "Oh, no!"

The *burglar* was none other than the much-awaited nephew of Soula Lukas. How could it be? He was supposed to arrive tomorrow. Ashamed at her behavior, Cassiani turned around and stared at the fallen man. She inched her way towards him, careful not to slip on the wet floor. Although his eyes were shut, to her relief she could make out the faint movement of his chest rising and falling rhythmically. Yes, he was alive, and undeniably handsome. His tanned face was lean, with a strong chin and a prominent, straight nose. She bent down, ready to check his head for bumps when his eyes fluttered open, staring upwards to gaze at the ceiling.

She caught her breath when his eyes settled on her. Magnificently large in size, their golden hazel color, speckled with emerald and saffron, glowed like a cat's eyes … *no … more like a lion's eyes.* It was unnerving, the intent way he studied her.

"Ouch," he said, touching the back of his head. Apparently satisfied with the result, he raised himself in a sitting position. He studied her once more.

She could feel the warm rush of his breath against her face. Suddenly aware of how physically close he was to her, Cassiani moved back, trembling. A minute ago she was nursing a vulnerable, weak patient. As soon as he spoke, as soon as he was a man again and not a patient, society's norms, her Christian principles, and her parents' sound upbringing joined forces, sending warning signals up her spine. *You're alone in this apartment with a man.*

"Don't worry, I won't bite." His teasing voice was low and husky. She smiled. He smiled back. "What were you doing here?"

Cassiani was very conscious of his stare. "I, I was …" For some odd reason, she couldn't speak. Instead, she stood up and pointed towards the balcony where she had left the bucket and mop. She made the motion of mopping.

In one swift movement he was up on his feet, his agile body moving cautiously to the balcony. His eyes rested on the mop. "That explains the wet floor."

Cassiani was about to introduce herself when she heard a faint call coming from downstairs. She turned her head to hear better. "It's Mrs. Lukas. She is calling." She ran towards the door, knocking the luggage over.

"Wait!" Leo shouted.

Cassiani flew down the steps. This time there was no turning back. She sprinted through the large kitchen with the peppermint tea scent, across the narrow hallway with its paintings, and into the bedroom. She found Soula Lukas sitting upright in her bed, propped up by several large pillows. The pink satin robe covering her thin frame, meant for a much younger woman, captured the eye first before settling on her olive-skinned, wrinkled face. Her fluffy white hair circled her head like a misplaced halo.

Maybe it was the way her brown eyes, clouded and unfocused, looked up at Cassiani, or the dazed look on her face, as if she had just seen a ghost; whatever it was, something had caused her to call out.

Cassiani leaned over and touched her shoulder. "Mrs. Lukas, is everything all right?" she asked, feeling breathless. "I heard you calling."

"What? Oh, yes," Soula muttered. Her hand fluttered over her eyes. "I had a dream. Yes ... a dream. That Leo was here."

"Actually, Leo did—" Cassiani began, then stopped when she saw Leo.

In a few strides Leo reached his aunt's bed. "Aunt Soula!" He bent down and kissed his aunt tenderly on the forehead, then eased his body on the edge of the bed

Her face lit, Soula gripped his hand as if she were testing the reality of his presence. "So you weren't really a dream after all." Her voice trembled with joy.

Captivated by this new development into Mrs. Lukas' world, Cassiani watched with surprise, witnessing the caring look on Leo's face and the gentle way he touched his aunt's arm. There was sensitivity in that gesture, one that conveyed a soul that had experienced love and knew how to show it and this spoke louder than words to Cassiani's fine-tuned heart. She was mesmerized.

The tender way in which Mrs. Lukas gazed back into her nephew's eyes revealed no coldness or hardness that Cassiani had glimpsed in the past, but a startling show of affection resembling the love of a mother towards her child.

"I stopped by earlier, but you were asleep."

"Ahh, so that was what happened!" Soula said, touching Leo's face fondly. "Weren't you supposed to come tomorrow?" She scrunched her face. "Is today Thursday or Friday?"

Leo patted her on the hand. "We had arranged for me to come today, Thursday."

"Oh, my," Soula replied, appearing apologetic. "For some reason I thought it was tomorrow." Her fingers brushed her forehead. "I'm becoming rather forgetful."

Cassiani quietly removed herself, not wanting to interfere with the reunion. As a nurse, she had learned not to pry into people's affairs. She paused at the door and looked at them. "I must be going."

Leo stood up. "I'm sorry if I frightened you. I wasn't expecting to find anyone upstairs in the apartment."

I wasn't expecting anyone either. "That's all right. I'm the one that should be apologizing," Cassiani replied.

"What happened?" Soula asked Leo, her eyes narrowing.

Leo told her about his fall. He chuckled, gingerly touching the back of his head. "There isn't even a small bump for a souvenir."

"I have to go now," Cassiani said, feeling awkward under Mrs. Lukas' scrutiny. "My mother hasn't been feeling well. I need to be with her."

"Say hello to her for me," Soula said, her face softening. "Oh, and don't forget to take the payment for cleaning the upstairs apartment. The money is on the kitchen table."

Cassiani blushed at the patronizing manner in which Mrs. Lukas had just spoken. *I helped because I wanted to, not because of any payment.* Instead of replying, she fled from the room.

*   *   *   *

Leo watched with amusement at Cassiani's flustered exit. His mind had been preoccupied all day with business deals and his aunt's health. Cassiani's brief entrance into his life had been a refreshingly beautiful diversion. *I wonder whether I'll see her again. I wonder where she lives.* "Who is she?"

"She's the daughter of my hired companion, Vera Meletis. Vera had a heart attack recently. I needed help, so she sent her in her place." Soula motioned to Leo. "Come, take my arm so I can get up."

Leo held on to his aunt as she arose out of bed. "I didn't see her car outside. Does she need a ride—"

"Don't go thinking too much about her," Soula interjected.

"What makes you think that?" Leo asked, shrugging his shoulders.

"Oh, an old woman's intuition," was his aunt's tart reply.

CHAPTER 2

———————————— ❦ ————————————

Cassiani hurried home, wondering how her mother fared without her. This was the first time since she arrived from America that she had left her alone so long. As soon as she entered the house, she looked for her. "Mother! I'm home!" Her mother was nowhere in sight. On the counter she discovered a little note from her mother stating that she would return soon.

Feeling thirsty, Cassiani searched for the jug of water in the refrigerator. It was not there. She sighed as she went out into the back verandah. She had forgotten how rustic this mountain home was. Even the kitchen sink did not have a faucet, but only a pipe that ran through the wall and outside, draining the dirty water. She had gotten used to having piped water in America. *Mrs. Lukas had running water, sinks and faucets, and real bathrooms.*

An old wooden square table with four chairs sat in the middle of the stone-paved verandah. The overhead grapevine, with its tendrils woven through the trellis, formed a comfortable shade from the sun. The empty glass jug and old, wooden pail sat on the table; it was a sign that they needed to be filled.

With jug and pail in tow, Cassiani marched past the outhouse, heading towards the well. The house was situated on a small ridge of the mountain and the expansive back yard sloped gently downward. Along the way, she stopped by the herb garden. The rows of basil, thyme, sage, oregano, and spearmint were showing early signs of growth. She snipped several spearmint stalks, enjoying their fragrance. Behind the herbs was the vegetable garden with green onions ready for picking. She plucked a few. She continued down the hill to the well.

She thought about the events of the day. Leonidas Regas was the last person she expected to see at Mrs. Lukas' house. He was not at all like his aunt. He did not even resemble her. He not only was handsome, but kind … two characteristics that were somehow lacking in Mrs. Lukas. Just thinking about him made her feel better.

In what seemed like no time, Cassiani had filled both the jug and pail with well water. She heard the sound of birds chirping from the branches of the nearby lemon trees and laughed. "You'll get your share!" She poured water into the nearby bird bowl before she left.

Once inside the house, she placed the spearmint and onions on the counter, then poured the water into a ceramic washbasin. With a bar of homemade olive oil soap, she scrubbed and washed her face and hands.

"Ahh, you're back." Vera entered the kitchen, carrying an apron filled with brown eggs. In her mid fifties, remnants of her youthful beauty were still apparent. Although her large eyes, small nose, and full mouth spoke of another era when men would rightfully sneak an admirable glance her way, widowhood had changed all that. Her rotund face, and gray hair combed back into a bun, sent a strong signal that she did not care to be available to anyone. "I went next door and gave Mrs. Kalotsis some yogurt. Look what she gave me." Vera lifted up the apron filled with the eggs. "I need to put these somewhere."

Cassiani grabbed a bowl from the cupboard. "Here, use this." She helped her mother place the eggs in it. She could hear her mother's heavy breathing. "You are out of breath again."

Vera took a deep breath, placing her hand on her chest. "I tried to get here as quickly as I could when I saw you from Mrs. Kalotsis' window." She counted the eggs. "*Krimas,* in my haste, I must have dropped an egg along the way."

"I hope you had a chance to rest."

Vera nodded emphatically. "I took a nap in the afternoon." She made the sign of the cross and rolled her eyes upward. "The pills Dr. Vassilakis gave me have helped. *Doxa Ton Theo.*" She stared at Cassiani. "What is that on your face?"

"Oh, I forgot!" Cassiani rinsed the dried soap from her face, laughing. "You came in while I was washing up."

Vera handed her a towel. "How did everything go with Mrs. Lukas?"

Cassiani told her mother what happened, including the unexpected arrival of Leonidas.

"Ahh. So he came today. Soula's been known to be a little forgetful these days." Vera peered at the liturgical calendar on the wall. "Leonidas' name day was just a couple of days ago, April 15."

Cassiani wasn't about to comment on Leonidas' name day. She knew if she did, it would give her matchmaking mother cause to talk more about him.

Vera took out the small coffeepot from the cupboard, then looked around.

"Are you looking for this?" Cassiani gave her mother the jug of water.

Vera thanked her, then reached for the bag of coffee. She prepared the thick brew of Greek coffee. "Now that the subject came up ... I don't remember seeing Soula's nephew. She always went to him every year. What does he look like?"

"Now, Mother! Honestly! Do you think I'm going to fall for that? Every room in her house practically has a picture of him. Every time an eligible young man comes along, you have to—" Cassiani warned.

"All right. All right. I'll stop," Vera interjected. She took a spoonful of sugar, poising it above the vessel. With a contrite voice she said, "Do you want yours sweet?"

"Yes," Cassiani watched her mother stir the coffee. "You should slow down on the coffee. It'll make your heart race. Maybe some spearmint tea would be better for you."

"This is my first cup, honestly," Vera said. "Even Mrs. Kalotsis was surprised when she offered coffee and I declined." She began humming a Greek tune. "By the way, did Soula remember to pay you for cleaning her house?"

Cassiani was puzzled at her mother's question. There had been no mention by her mother that there would be payment. Cassiani had assumed that she was doing a good deed. "Yes, but I didn't take the money."

"This is no time for charity! We need the money!" Vera waved the spoon in the air, then dunked it back into the brew, stirring vigorously. "I don't know how I'm going to get through this," she muttered.

Cassiani was speechless for a moment, unable to interpret what she just heard. "What do you mean?"

"I haven't worked in almost two weeks. We just have enough in the bank to last us a couple of weeks."

Cassiani was dumbfounded by her mother's admission. It was not like her mother not to have money. She recalled the two million drachmas that her mother received several years ago from selling the land she inherited. A portion of that amount helped to pay for Cassiani's education. The balance should have been enough to sustain her mother all these years. *What happened to the rest of that money?* "I thought that you had quite a bit of savings, from selling the *iko-pedo,* and from working for Mrs. Lukas," she said.

Vera nodded. "Last summer, when your grandmother passed away, I spent the remaining money to pay for her cemetery plot. God rest her soul." She made the sign of the cross. "Since February, I've been living off of the weekly earnings I make from Mrs. Lukas, and she paid only two hundred drachmas a day."

Cassiani paced the room, thinking about what she just heard. "Why that comes to just over three dollars a day! I earned ten times that much when I worked last summer as a cashier!" She stopped and stared at her mother. Up until now she knew very little about her mother's finances. *Maybe it was because she had never asked me for money or shown signs of needing money before.* "Why didn't you tell me it was that low?"

Vera shrugged her shoulders. "If I told you, you wouldn't have finished your schooling. You would have stopped so you could work. I didn't want that to happen ... not after all that money invested in your education."

Cassiani was silent, mulling things over in her mind. Her mother was right. She would not have finished school, but would have worked to help out her mother.

Vera poured the frothy coffee into the small cups and handed a cup to Cassiani. "Come, let's have some coffee." She appeared tranquil and peaceful as she sat down to drink her brew.

Cassiani joined her, amazed at her mother's quick transformation. This showed Cassiani how easily her mother could separate her problems from the pleasures in daily living. *Let's admit it, Greeks do enjoy their coffee, like the British enjoy their afternoon tea.* She inhaled the rich aroma of the coffee and proceeded to sip it quietly. Maybe there was more to coffee than just being a stimulant. It brought people together.

"I'm also thinking that your airfare ticket must have cost you a fortune. You probably used up all your savings to get here," Vera said.

"The ticket was a little high," Cassiani admitted. She paid nine hundred dollars for a last minute ticket, which was two month's worth of salary. "I still have four hundred sixty dollars left in the bank." She sighed. "It would have come in handy." She took another sip from the hot brew. *I wonder whether Athena sent the airplane tickets as she said she would? Even so, with limited funds, how are we going to manage until we leave for America?*

Vera removed two glasses of yogurt from the refrigerator. She handed a glass to Cassiani. "Try some of my yogurt."

"Mother, I'd like to get a hold of Athena. How can I telephone her?"

"We'll go to Kostas' store, in the village," Vera replied, "but we'll have to wait until Monday when the bank is open. There isn't enough money for the call."

Monday seemed too far away to call Athena. "Isn't there anyone else that has a telephone?" Cassiani asked. "We can pay them back on Monday."

Vera gazed out the window, her eyebrows furrowed. "Mrs. Lukas has a telephone. Do you want to try her?"

Cassiani bit her lip. How could she talk on the telephone in front of Mrs. Lukas or her nephew? They would overhear her conversation with her sister telling her about their financial problem. It would be too embarrassing. "I'll wait until Monday."

"Oh, don't frown. We aren't that desperately poor. Mrs. Lukas will make sure we get the payment. She's very good on that score." Vera fanned herself with her hand. "Now that you have a free moment, why don't you check my blood pressure, dear?"

Cassiani retrieved the stethoscope and blood pressure monitor and began taking the measurements. "Good, one hundred thirty-three over seventy-five." She removed the strap from her mother's arm. Her fingers found her mother's wrist. She looked at her watch. "Your pulse is seventy two." The stethoscope was then placed on her mother's chest. "Now breathe slowly." Moments later, Cassiani removed the stethoscope. "Everything looks good. It seems as if your medicine is working." She put her instruments away. "You also have to watch your diet so it doesn't get worse."

"Now that you are here, you can tell me what to eat. The doctor just gave me pills, acting as if that was all I needed."

"You need to slow down on the meat and fats. Eat more fruits and vegetables. Also, eat less sweets. I remember you always liked the pastries," Cassiani lectured.

Vera chuckled. "I have Mrs. Lukas to blame; she loves her lamb and rich pastries. What could I do but cook her food and keep her company?" She patted Cassiani fondly on the arm. "I'm so glad you are here. It's nothing like having family close by."

"If it weren't for my nursing classes I would have come sooner," Cassiani said, hugging her. "Now I'm going to try some of your yogurt." She sat down and spooned some of the creamy concoction in her mouth.

"Tell me daughter, how is your new job at the hospital?" Vera asked. "You are working there as a nurse now?"

Cassiani was not surprised by her mother's question. The past few days since she arrived they had been intent on her mother's health; this was the first time they sat down to chat about something other than her mother's health. She told her about her job, how she liked it there, and about the people she worked with.

"Ahh," Vera said, sounding pleased. "Since you've been there only a few months, will you lose your job because you left so unexpectedly?"

Cassiani shrugged her shoulders. "I told them it was a family emergency. My nursing supervisor said that the job would be waiting for me when I got back."

They continued their conversation. Cassiani told her about how Athena got her to join the local Daughters of Penelope. "We just had a benefit luncheon and raised several thousand dollars for the local children's hospital."

Vera appeared thoughtful. "Someone's bound to have a brother, or a son, or even a nephew."

Cassiani smiled. Her mother's comment did not surprise her. She was known to be a good matchmaker in the village and had earned quite a reputation in helping marry a few local girls, including her sister. She spooned the last bit of yogurt into her mouth. "By the way, the yogurt is delicious. Everything you make is good, even cooked dandelion greens."

"Good that you reminded me." There was a gleam in Vera's eyes. "Could you do me a small favor?"

"As long as it's not to clean anyone's house," Cassiani warned.

Vera laughed heartily. "I wanted to get *horta* before they were all gone, but now with my heart, I'm afraid it will be too much for me. Could you go?"

Cassiani nodded. When she was young, her mother and grandmother would take her and her sister every spring to the nearby fields to pick dandelion greens. She enjoyed the idea. "I don't mind going. Is it where you used to pick the greens?"

"Yes. Follow the same road you took this morning to go to Mrs. Lukas' property, then turn left just before reaching the new road that leads to her house. You'll see that hill to your left." Vera made motions with her hands.

"I'll go first thing tomorrow morning."

"Good." Vera looked at her with a smile. "Now, I have a suggestion for you. Why don't you play the violin for me, just like your father used to? Let's sing our worries away. All right?"

Cassiani was amazed at her mother's ability to cope with hardship through the power of music. Both of her parents had musical talent; her father was an avid part-time violinist, who jumped at the chance to perform at musical events in town, and her mother would sing along with him. Cassiani knew she acquired that musical talent; at the age of six she became an eager pupil under her father's tutelage, and in America, while studying nursing, she took violin lessons and played in local orchestras whenever she could. "Where is Father's violin?"

"Let's see, where did I put it?" Vera's plump body stirred out of its complacent stance and swooshed out of the room.

CHAPTER 3

Friday

Cassiani awoke to the sound of her mother's singing. She yawned and stretched, shifting her sore body, looking for a soft spot on the small, old bed. She shut her eyes again, drifting back to sleep, feeling the morning breeze from the open window wrap itself around her. Scents from the gardenia bushes outside her window filled the room with a sweet fragrance that held promises of summer.

Moments later, Cassiani was again awakened by her mom's piercing soprano voice. She wasn't going to get anymore sleep. She rubbed her eyes, then stared into the cramped room. All their furniture had come with them when they moved here seven years ago, and it was crammed into every available space in this small house, including this room. Her eyes settled on the clock; it was almost seven thirty.

There was a rap on her door. "Cassiani, get up! This is a good time to go for the *horta!*"

A half hour later, Cassiani marched through the rocky fields, dressed in an old, checkered, summer smock that was long, and billowed forth from the teasing wind. Her hair was braided and tucked underneath a large straw hat. Her eyes combed the slope until she found what she was looking for. Marching towards the region, she caught a glimpse of Mrs. Lukas' white villa farther up on the mountain, nestled behind the towering cypress trees. She wondered what Mrs. Lukas and her nephew were doing. Her mother had told her that Mrs. Lukas was a late riser and didn't wake up before nine thirty. It was a few minutes past eight. They were probably sleeping.

The morning mountain breeze felt fresh against her skin as she worked steadily among the outcrops. There was a rhythm to her movements as her left hand sliced the pliant earth with a knife and the other hand yanked the dandelions from the ground, stuffing them into the brown, burlap bag.

Her thoughts wandered from America to Kos, going back and forth, as she tried to solve her mother's financial problem. If only she could get a hold of the money in her savings account. That would surely help. *Maybe I could write a letter to the bank, allowing Athena authority to withdraw it for me.* It would take at least two weeks before they got the funds. Cassiani shook her head. They needed the money much sooner. She wondered whether there was another way to make some money.

An hour later she held a bulging bag of green trophies. She inched her way down the rocky terrain towards the main road, ready to leave, when she saw a few more tempting greens in front of her. She bent down and yanked a plant. "Eeeehh!" She shot up in disgust when a plump worm wiggled out of the dirt-encrusted roots of the plant, dangling in front of her. She could never get used to worms. *Here you are a nurse, dealing with all kinds of traumatic situations and you get squeamish over a little, silly worm.*

"You look like you're having a fun time."

Cassiani twirled around to face a smiling Leo. She felt her face flush, wondering how long he had stood there watching her make a spectacle of herself. He was leaning against a cedar tree, handsome in his casual attire of khaki pants and white polo shirt. "Dr. Leo! Yuk! I mean … good morning."

"What do you have there?" He strolled towards her to have a look.

Cassiani giggled nervously as she held the offending plant with outstretched arm. "I was picking dandelion greens for my mother and I saw a worm." She tried to see where the worm went. "I never did like them."

Leo gently took the plant from her hand. "Here, let's put the worm back where it belongs."

Cassiani watched in wonder at his calmness as he kneeled, took a twig from the ground and teased the worm out of the dirt-encrusted roots. There was a surgical precision about his movements that reminded her of the assuredness and skill she had witnessed in surgeons performing operations. The pink worm quickly disappeared into the grass.

Leo rose, glancing around him with a satisfied look on his face. "It was here somewhere that I played as a child. I remember an area filled with wildflowers, particularly the bright, sunny daffodils. I would cut the daffodils to give to my mother." He smirked. "But by the time we reached the house, they were wilted."

Cassiani's eyes widened as she felt the stirring of something deep inside her. There was something endearing in the image of Leo as a boy, giving flowers to his mother. "Daffodils are beautiful flowers, even if they are wilted," she said. "I found a spot filled with flowers today."

"Oh? Where is it?"

"Let me show you." She pulled up the hem of her dress slightly and led the way. Just then, the bag tipped a little and she pulled it up, grabbing the ends before anything fell out.

Leo lifted the bag from her dirty hands. "I can hold this for you." He peered inside. "Hmmm, someone's going to have a nice meal tonight."

"There's plenty in there. I can give you some to take back with you."

He was thoughtful. "That is kind of you, but I'm headed down to the village and I can't be carrying these with me."

Cassiani was very conscious of him by her side as they climbed the stony territory, heading towards the ridge. Large boulders and tall cypress trees marked the boundary to their right. When they reached the lime-green, grassy field, she stopped and pointed to the colorful display of lilies, cyclamen, and wildflowers. "There they are."

"Yes, this brings back many memories." Leo turned and gazed to their left. "There used to be a trail there that led towards the flowers." He pointed in that direction. "I must have been five or six, playing ball in that area."

"Did you have any brothers or sisters?"

Leo's eyes twinkled. "I was an only child … and you?"

Cassiani told him about her sister. "We used to race in the fields when we were young, to see which one would win." She smiled at the memory as she pulled back a few stray strands from her face. "For some reason, I always won. Sometimes I would slow down intentionally to give her a chance to beat me." She stopped when she noticed the intent way he was looking at her.

Leo followed her quietly back to the edge of the property. He handed her the bag. "I hope you and your mother enjoy these greens in good health. *Horta* are supposed to be good for you."

Cassiani wrinkled her nose and giggled. "I admit I never acquired a taste for them. They always seem so bitter."

"A lot of things are good for us, but we have choices and don't always do what is good for us," Leo said. He removed an envelope from his pocket. "This is payment for cleaning my aunt's house yesterday." He placed the envelope in her hand. "I took the liberty of adding a little more to it. Maybe the payment she left you wasn't enough?"

Cassiani stared at her name written on the envelope. "No, it wasn't that," she mumbled. How dare he think that it wasn't enough? She was ready to give it back to him. *Don't let your pride take over. We need the money.* She stuffed it into her pocket in silent misery. "Thank you."

"I must be going now. Good-bye." Leo sauntered down the road with his hands in his pockets.

Cassiani stood motionless, unable to tear her gaze away from his retreating body. Hot and weary, she trekked home, dirty arms laden with the bag of wilting greens.

✳   ✳   ✳   ✳

Vera peered inside the bag, her eyes opening wide. She chuckled. "You have my blessings, daughter. This is more than I expected. Did you go where I told you?"

"Yes. To the other side of the hill, facing Mrs. Lukas' house." Cassiani washed her grimy hands in the water basin.

Vera looked expectantly at her. "Good. Was anyone else there? I mean, was anyone picking greens?"

"No, but I did see Dr. Leo." Cassiani dried her hands. "He must have seen me working in the field and stopped to talk to me."

"Ahhh." Vera's eyes lit up.

"And guess what he gave me," Cassiani said. Before her mother could respond, she plucked the envelope out of her pocket and handed it to her.

"What's this?" Vera asked. She fingered the wad of bills, separating and counting the money. Her eyes flew open. "Eight hundred drachmas!"

Cassiani stared at the money, surprised by the amount. It was more than she expected. *Now I have enough money to telephone Athena tomorrow.* "It's for cleaning his aunt's house," she replied shakily. "He thought I hadn't taken it because it wasn't enough money."

Vera laughed heartily, kissing the bills. "Thank the good Lord! Whatever the reason, it doesn't matter. You got paid, and that's what counts. He's a good man, this Leo Regas."

The rest of the day her mother was in a jovial mood. At first, Cassiani thought her mother's jubilance was because they had received the money. Then, a nagging thought came to her that maybe it wasn't the only reason. Maybe it was because Leonidas Regas personally made it a point to single her out and pay her the money himself. Whatever the reason, she did not resist when her mother asked her once again to play the violin.

Cassiani retrieved her father's violin from the closet and brought it into the kitchen while her mother stood over the stove, stirring the boiling greens in the large pot. With feelings of reverence, Cassiani coated the strings with rosin, then tuned the instrument. She poised the violin on her shoulder. "What song would you like to start with?" Her mother began to sing a romantic Greek song. Cassiani recognized the tune and joined her.

After an hour of playing, Cassiani went into her bedroom to put the violin away. Just then she heard knocking at the door followed by her mother's greeting; Mrs. Kalotsis had arrived. Cassiani quickly finished her task and hurried into the kitchen, eager to greet the older woman.

Kalliopi Kalotsis was a small-boned, tanned woman in her mid-seventies. She was dressed in black, with a black scarf covering her white hair. "I heard Cassiani's wonderful playing and had to stop by." Kalliopi handed a covered plate of food to Vera. "My grandson caught these fish today. I already fried them."

"Mrs. Kalotsis!" Cassiani rushed to her side and exchanged hugs with the older woman.

For some reason, Mrs. Kalotsis' kind face reminded her of her grandmother. The last time she had seen her grandmother was seven years ago at the harbor; it was the day Cassiani was leaving for America. Mrs. Kalotsis had also come. The picture of her mother and the two older women, all dressed in black, holding on to each other as they waved goodbye to Cassiani's departing ship was imprinted in her mind forever.

Mrs. Kalotsis clutched her hand as her bright green eyes gazed back at her. Filled with love, they shimmered with unshed tears. "My dear, you grow prettier every time I see you. You look just like your grandmother Athena, tall, with those large eyes and beautiful hair. She was my best friend, and the loveliest woman on this side of Kos!" She tightened her grip. "Oh, how I *do* miss her!"

Caught off guard by strong emotions, Cassiani felt the tears flow down her face.

"You've been gone, what, seven years? Seven years can make a difference to an old woman like me." Mrs. Kalotsis pointed sadly to her weathered face. "See how I aged?"

"You're exactly as I remembered you ... a friendly, kind woman!" Cassiani gushed.

"Ahh." Mrs. Kalotsis smiled as she patted her on the hand. "You were always my favorite. I often asked your mother about you and she would tell me your news."

"I hope it was good news!" Cassiani said, laughing. She began to set the table.

Mrs. Kalotsis sat down at the table. "Oh, yes." Her face beamed. "From what I hear, you took after your grandmother. Athena had a healing touch. Whenever someone had a stomachache or a cold, or whatever ailment, she would help treat them."

"Cassiani came to take care of me when she heard about my heart attack. She doesn't want me to do anything," Vera said proudly. "She even went and picked *horta* today."

"Really?" Mrs. Kalotsis' eyebrows rose. "Usually they are all picked by now." She spoke with the wisdom of someone who had years worth of picking greens.

Vera nodded. There was a gleam in her eyes. "I know. That's why I sent her. She came back with a bag filled all the way to the top. Everyone else thinks the same thing and leaves the fields alone." She winked, chuckling.

Cassiani laughed along with Mrs. Kalotsis.

"We'll give you some to take with you," Vera said. "Cassiani, let's get dinner ready."

Cassiani added olive oil and freshly squeezed lemon to the bowl of boiled dandelion greens. The pan-fried fish, a loaf of homemade bread, and bowl of olives and cut green onions completed the supper.

When they sat down to eat, for some reason, the bulging eyes of the fish stared at her from her plate and that was enough for Cassiani to put her fork down. Ever since she was young, the bones always seemed to get in the way, and now the eyes. She stared woefully back.

"Eat, it's good for you," Vera said, her mouth full.

Cassiani swallowed, then nodded. "Yes, it is good for me." She picked up the fork and began eating.

CHAPTER 4

That Friday morning Leo's taxi arrived in Psalidi, a quiet town located two Kilometers east of Kos Town. The shape of Psalidi was like a triangle that jutted out into the sea, with a clean, sandy coast that appeared untouched. In the center of the triangle were salt marshes and wet meadows. The cab rolled to a stop in front of a hotel. Palm trees lined the paved path to the door. Leo studied the address on the envelope; it was the same address as that of the hotel's address. He shook his head. *This couldn't be Nicko's residence. Maybe there's a mistake.*

The last time Leo saw his childhood friend, Nicko Xenoudis, was when he was still in college. He took a college summer course in Greece and visited Kos during that time. In those days, Nicko's family lived near his grandparents' house up in the mountain. They owned a small gift shop in the mountain village. Nicko wrote him a letter a couple of years ago, telling him about their move to Psalidi. *He didn't mention the hotel.*

With misgivings, Leo entered the large lobby. It was teeming with fair-haired tourists speaking a foreign language. From his many travels abroad, he recognized they were speaking Swedish. Feeling out of place, he turned to leave.

"Leo!"

Leo turned and saw Nicko striding towards him. The boyish grin and long, straight bangs gave him a youthful, appealing look. He was of average height, stocky, and dressed casually in blue jeans and a blue shirt. Other than a little weight gain, Nicko hadn't changed a bit.

Leo hugged his friend joyfully. He waved Nicko's letter in the air. "I didn't realize the address you gave me was a hotel until today."

Nicko laughed. "We live in one of the suites upstairs. My uncle sold it to my parents, and the whole family works here, including some of my cousins." They talked for a few minutes. The din in the lobby had risen and it was difficult to carry on a conversation.

"I know a place where we can talk," Nicko said. He led the way to the back door, then outside to the next building. "We built this addition two years ago."

"It appears that your business is doing well."

Nicko grinned. "It looks that way. We signed up last year with an international travel agency. We provide the lodging, food, and entertainment for their tour packages." He opened the door and looked inside.

Leo's ears picked up the rippling sounds of a bouzouki playing a solo. Moments later it was accompanied by a chorus of men and a band. "Sounds nice."

"I forgot that Louis, our bouzouki player, would be practicing with his band," Nicko said. He paused as if thinking. "Follow me." He waved to the band as they entered. "*Yia-sas Pedia!*" Sounds of the band's greetings followed them.

They sat down in the far corner of the room. Leo told him about his business and his aunt. He then learned that Nicko was getting married in early September. "Congratulations!" Leo said.

"Leo, I'd really like it if you were my *koumbaro* at the wedding," Nicko said.

The request caught Leo by surprise. He stared at Nicko, wondering how he was going to fit his friend's request into his busy schedule. Jack Finch, his boss, placed business over pleasure, and if there was any business dealings that coincided with Nicko's wedding day, Leo knew that the business deal would take preference. To make a commitment to this request, so many months ahead when his work was so unpredictable, was almost impossible. *But it is once in a lifetime that this happens, and what better excuse to come to Kos than for this?* Leo's lips slowly curved into a smile. "Thank you for the honor. I'll be there."

Nicko's happiness was obvious as he grinned back. "Thank you my friend."

The music stopped just then. "The band is taking a break." Nicko gestured to Louis. "Louis!"

Louis' rangy body ambled towards them. He had a long, beak nose and stringy, black hair that reached down to his shoulders. He wore the wide bottom pants that were in fashion, with an open shirt that revealed a scrawny neck encircled by a thick, gold chain. Long side-burns completed the picture.

"*Pos pame?*" Louis Kotsidas greeted Nicko with an anemic slap on the shoulder. He sat down in a chair and bobbed his head towards Leo, his strands of hair dancing on his thin shoulders. "*Sprechen zie Deutsche?*" he asked, with a thick Greek accent.

Nicko chuckled. "No luck this time. He's an old Greek friend of the family." He introduced Leo. "Louis tries to figure out what country the tourists are from."

Louis guffawed, slapping his thin leg. "Sorry about that! I thought you were German."

"The fair looks come from my mother's Irish side."

"Ahh. Do you have any sisters?" Louis winked.

"No," Leo said, smiling tightly. *Even if I did, I wouldn't want them to meet you.*

Louis took out a pack of cigarettes from his shirt pocket and offered it to them; both men declined. He lit a cigarette. "What do you think, Nicko? Did we sound good today?"

"Your music always sounds great!" Nicko said. "Ready for those tourists tonight?"

"Of course!" Louis smiled slyly. "It's those female tourists that make it fun, if you know what I mean."

Nicko laughed nervously. "My cousin is riding next week in Pyli's horse race. What have you decided, are you riding again this year? Maybe you'll come in first this year."

Louis' eyes glittered, indicating a show of interest. "I've been thinking about it."

"What is this horse racing about?" Leo asked Nicko.

"Every year on April 23rd, the village of Pyli celebrates St. George's name day with horse racing, singing and dancing. It's quite an event."

"Louis, are we going to sit here all day, or are we going to play?" a band member called out.

Louis took a last puff before putting out his cigarette. "Can't even take a break," he muttered. He got up and stretched lazily, then sauntered towards the band.

*   *   *   *

Later in the day, Leo found his aunt in the parlor. She was sitting in her favorite gold velvet armchair with the white trim, reading a book. A cup of chamomile tea and a small plate of cookies sat on the table next to her. Strains of classical music could be heard in the background.

Aunt Soula placed her book down on her lap and gazed at him proudly. "Each time I see you, I feel like a young girl again. You probably broke a number of young women's hearts."

Leo smiled in response. He knew what would happen if he answered. She was fishing to find out if he had a girl. "I have no time for a relationship. I'm too busy."

"Tsk.tsk ... tsk," she said, waving a knobby finger at him. "You need to take time, so you can have a family of your own one day. Look at me. I chose not to marry until I was in my forties. Now I'm by myself ... no husband and no children. You're my family."

"I don't mind being single. I enjoy the freedom and the flexibility. Besides, my job doesn't allow me time to stay in one place long enough to meet anyone."

"You're a workaholic, just like your grandfather!" Soula chortled.

Leo grinned as he sat down on the chair next to her. "Better that than a bum. Weren't you the one extolling the virtues of money all these years?"

"Yes. I know the value of money too well!" Soula replied tartly. "Father was very good at reminding me of it." She had a far away look on her face. "It wasn't always like that, you know. When I was a child, Father was a farmer, working the land." She paused, looking at Leo, as if she was gauging his reaction, as if this was the first time she was telling him this story.

Although Leo had heard her recount the story several times before, he realized that she had forgotten that she told him; he knew it was important to her. He nodded, prodding her on.

There was a gleam in Soula's eyes as she continued. "I remember him coming home every evening with sweat on his brow, his hands dirty from working the land all day. He worked hard and was a smart man, so that by the time your father was born, Father had enough savings to buy more land and some buildings. But his heart was into shipping. I remember that he would always talk about one day owning a ship. '*That is where the money is,*' he would say."

She paused to take a sip of the tea. "When I was a teenager, Father's rich uncle from America passed away and left him an inheritance. With this newfound wealth, Father had enough money to buy his first ship. That marked the beginning of a new life for us. But he was always traveling back and forth from Piraeus, managing his shipping business. We rarely saw him."

Leo realized that even though his aunt loved to talk about his grandfather, it always seemed to leave her with a nostalgic sense of longing. He decided to change the subject. "How about a little lively music?" He went to the record player and chose Vivaldi's *Four Seasons*.

Leo mentioned his morning visit to Nicko's hotel.

"If I had known you were going down there, I would have told you to take the Mercedes. I don't use it anymore. It just sits there."

"Thank you, but I didn't mind the walk to the village. Besides, you were still asleep when I left this morning," Leo explained. He continued his conversation, describing the tourists, and Nicko's family's hotel business, making it a point not to mention Nicko's upcoming wedding. "There were some exotic vases in the hotel lobby. I forgot to ask Nicko where they got them from."

Soula leaned forward excitedly. "You should have asked."

They had a lively discussion on vases and vase dealers that Soula had found for Leo. Around three o'clock, his aunt began to yawn. "I need to get my beauty rest," she said. "Why don't you go rest also? We can catch up on our news later."

This afternoon respite was a daily ritual for all of Greece; something that had been passed on from generation to generation. It was as if Greeks had it built into their genes to rest each day and to be refreshed for the evening.

*   *   *   *

Leo sat at the round table, facing the open kitchen window. He ignored the sunlight and the spring breeze that rustled his papers; he was intently examining the report. Several papers were pulled from his briefcase and reviewed. He redid the numbers. He rubbed his eyes. Carl's numbers did not match his. Coordinating the export of steel from the U.S. to Europe with Carl Huber, a Princeton graduate hired two months ago was not going to be an easy task. Carl worked late hours and weekends, trying to meet the deadline. He also was quick to pick up the different facets and international regulations of this complex business, but did he know enough to get the job done properly without Leo overseeing things? He would have to telephone Carl.

Leo needed to take a break first. He sauntered out to the balcony. The resplendent sun painted everything in vivid colors ... from the rugged green hills and emerald forests below to the crystal blue sea beyond. This relaxed feeling defied and denied the worldly pursuits he had been immersed in: the discussions with colleagues and business associates; the continual awareness and updating of global politics; and the monitoring of a country's fluctuating exchange rates. He sat down to enjoy the panoramic view. His arm bumped something. It was the mop, still sitting in the bucket where Cassiani had left it yesterday.

Leo pictured her delicate features, small straight nose, creamy skin, large, innocent black eyes and long black hair. Earlier this morning, when he gazed out the balcony, he had spied the lone figure picking the greens on the hill below the house. So he took the opportunity to take a walk down that way. This time, Cassiani did not rush away. Her company was quite refreshing and pleasing. He remembered her embarrassed reaction as he gave her the envelope with the money. She did not act like someone used to being paid for cleaning a house. *But she did take it.*

Then he remembered the mistake on the report. He glanced at his watch. It was six thirty. Leo slipped back into the apartment to make the telephone call.

CHAPTER 5

Jack Finch entered his New York office that morning. A widower in his early sixties, his ruddy, tanned face, plaid shirt and blue jeans gave him an appearance of a cowboy rather than the owner of an import-export firm. The only thing missing was the cowboy hat. His import/export firm Finch and Associates employed ten full time staff and nine part-time employees stationed in various parts of the world. The business made close to five million dollars gross revenues annually.

A mug of hot coffee and a banana-nut muffin were his source of nutrition for the morning along with the daily dose of The Wall Street Journal. A few minutes later he smacked his lips in satisfaction; his stocks were doing well.

There was a knock on his door. Sally, his secretary, peeked into the room. Still unwed, she appeared younger than her fifty-one years. She held a stack of papers. "These need to be signed."

Jack placed the newspaper aside and studied the documents. He began to sign them.

A few minutes later, Sally buzzed him. "Ben Doukas is on line one."

Ben owned a shipping agency in Greece; Leo had been working with him on different European business deals. Last year, the rising oil prices affected their export business in a detrimental way. Lately, Russia had been having poor harvests of grains, so Leo researched different companies that produced grains. After he found a wheat company in Italy willing to do business with them, they bought an aging bulk cargo ship called *The Lion* from Ben for that purpose. The company used up almost all of its cash reserves and Leo even dipped into his inheritance fund to help buy the twenty-four year old ship. Their business did well, even with the soaring oil prices.

Jack picked up the telephone. "Ben, how are things there in Greece?" They talked pleasantries before getting down to business.

"Jack, I have a business proposition for your firm." Ben told him that he found a buyer in Greece for wheat. "Leo had shown some interest in it."

Jack discussed it further with him. "I'll let Leo know about it," he said before hanging up. He sipped his coffee, feeling pleased. Seven years ago, Leo came to the firm as a fresh doctoral graduate from Yale. Leo did very well, helping expand the business to include grain and steel exports to Europe; his knowledge and hard work helped triple company revenues. *Things are looking good.*

∗   ∗   ∗   ∗

Leo telephoned Carl. "Carl, Leo here. I'm calling from Greece. How are things there?" After they talked for a few minutes, Leo brought up the subject of the numbers. "Could you please check the third column, fourth line down? Your numbers are lower than mine." He read aloud his numbers. He could hear the shuffling of papers in the background.

"Yes, you are right, mine are lower," Carl said.

"Did you remember to use the new price list? Since the oil prices went up, our shipping costs went up also, and they need to be added into the final cost. Check with Jack for the updated price list."

"All right," Carl said. "I will do that right away."

Leo could hear Jack's voice in the background.

"Can you hold on a minute?" Carl asked. "Jack wants to speak with you."

"Leo!" Jack said. "How are things there in Kos with your aunt?"

Leo filled him in. "Right now she is napping," he finished.

"What a life!" Jack said, laughing. "Sometimes I want to take a snooze in my office and close the door, but I'm always being interrupted!"

They both laughed.

"I know you're on vacation, but Ben just called. He has a proposition for us." Jack told him the proposal. "You're the expert on these commodities. What do you think?"

"I am very interested."

"Good. Ben thinks it's a good opportunity and he's willing to fly you to Athens on Monday to discuss it. Can you make it?" Jack asked.

"I'll find the time," Leo said, realizing the importance of this deal.

"You'll need to telephone his office to schedule the meeting. As you know, he's a busy man. Do you have his telephone number?"

"One minute." Leo leafed through his small telephone book and checked for Ben's number. "Yes, it's here. Meanwhile, can you do me a favor and give Carl the new price list for the steel? He's using the old one and his numbers don't match mine for the Sifon contract. I want to make sure everything goes smoothly so we can export the steel on time."

"Sure, sure. Keep me posted."

Afterwards, Leo placed a call to Ben Doukas' office. The small airplane was to pick him up at ten o'clock Monday morning at the Kos airport. After he hung up, Leo flipped through the pages of the telephone book, then telephoned Vince, his contact person in Italy. They talked for a few minutes. He jotted a few numbers down, then telephoned a couple of other wheat companies in America and went over some figures and dates with them.

*   *   *   *

That evening Leo joined his aunt downstairs. *I must remember to tell her about the trip.* He helped her set the plates and silverware on the cherry wood table in the dining room; it was able to seat ten people, and seemed just as large as when he was five years old. The room exuded an air of affluence, boasting of marble columns, exotic vases, a large Oriental rug, and a crystal chandelier.

"Why don't you pour the wine? You know where it is," Soula said, pointing to the liquor cabinet. "I'll go get the food." She left for the kitchen.

Leo pulled two crystal glasses out of the cherry cabinet and filled them with red Mavrodaphne wine. Nothing had changed materially. Even this imported liquor cabinet was the same as he remembered it. Only the utter stillness of the empty room was a reminder that neither his grandparents nor his parents were here.

He reflected upon his years spent here, filled with laughter and joyful times. He was born here and he lived here with his grandparents the first several years of his life. His parents worked in the medical office and were gone most of the day, yet he did not want for anything. Those carefree childhood years were mostly spent with his grandmother and later, his aunt.

His grandfather was often away on business and would bring back souvenirs from the different places he visited. Leo would sit on his lap and listen to stories about his trips.

They stayed in Kos until the year Aunt Soula's husband passed away. No one foresaw the chain of events that were to come after Aunt Soula came to live with them in the house. Newly widowed, she was dressed in black, subdued, and in mourning.

Leo quickly found himself the center of attention for his aunt. She showered him with gifts and fondly read stories to him. However, tension mounted, as his aunt did not get along with his mother. His grandparents began the building of the upstairs suite to accommodate his aunt. The construction was slow and at one point, his parents argued with Aunt Soula. That was when his family left for America. Leo remembered crying through the whole trip. He never saw his grandparents again.

Now, years later, his parents were somewhere on the other side of the world. All that was left of the memories of his past life in Kos was an aging aunt who lived here alone. He tried to shake off the morose feeling that descended upon him.

"Here we are." His aunt entered the room slowly, carrying a large bowl. "Can you help me, Leo? The bowl is too heavy and might slip out of my hands."

Leo rose immediately to offer her assistance. He took the bowl filled with stuffed grape leaves and placed it on the table next to the tomato and cucumber salad.

"I had these dolmades made just for you," she said. "I knew you liked them."

Leo thanked his aunt. It had been a long time since he had a home-cooked Greek meal. Either his parents had been away on missionary work or he had been traveling.

"How is your father?" Soula asked, sitting down. "Is he still doing missionary work?"

Leo nodded. "Father says they're helping to build a Greek Orthodox Church in the Dominican Republic. They also continue to provide medical services to the natives whenever it is needed." He munched his salad.

"I have to hand it to George," Soula said dryly. "I never thought my younger brother would be doing that kind of thing in his retirement years." Then she paused, thinking. "But then again, he was always into helping others. That is why he went into medicine. He took after Mother. She had a compassionate soul."

Her rare compliment towards his father touched Leo. "Father was concerned about you when you said you weren't well enough to visit. He urged me to visit you, and mother did also."

Soula snorted, pushing her plate away. "Don't try that on me, Leo. You can't make people like each other if they don't!"

Leo knew she was referring to his mother. His aunt never accepted his mother into the family, ever since that argument. His aunt sent two cards each year to his family; one for Christmas and the other for his father's name day, and that was it. Leo was her link to the family.

"Come, Leo, don't look so gloomy," Soula said, patting his hand. "Let's focus on the here and now. You're here with me and that's all that counts to me. I'm so glad you came."

Leo smiled at her. "I'm glad I came also. It's been years since I visited Kos. The walk this morning was very refreshing." He lifted his glass and took a sip. "By the way, I forgot to tell you earlier that I took the liberty of paying Cassiani Meletis for her services yesterday."

Soula's eyes flew open. "How did you manage to do that?"

"Simple." He flashed her a wide smile. "I saw her picking greens from my balcony this morning and remembered you mentioning that she did not take the money for her services. So when I went for my walk, I stopped to give it to her."

Soula chewed her meal silently for a couple of minutes. Her face suddenly perked up. "I have some news for you." Her twinkling eyes and wide smile signified something important. "I spoke with Mrs. Xenoudis this afternoon on the telephone. I just learned that your friend Nicko is getting married and the bride to be is Manolis Pantelonis' only daughter. Anyway, I invited them along with Nicko's parents and some other friends for a lunch party tomorrow."

"That's nice," Leo remarked, his eyebrows raised. "What's the occasion?"

"Your name day, of course! Isn't that a wonderful idea?" Her normally guttural voice had risen, filled with excitement.

Leo smiled at his aunt's kind gesture. This was the first time he would be celebrating his name day with her, and it appealed to him. It also meant that his aunt was feeling well enough to throw a party. *Maybe this not the best time to tell her about the trip. It can wait until tomorrow.*

CHAPTER 6

Saturday

Cassiani awoke to the sound of pots clanging in the kitchen. She jumped out of bed when she heard the loud crash. She hoped her mother hadn't fallen. She ran towards the door blindly, ramming her right large toe into a piece of furniture. "Ouch!" she yelled, hopping up and down, holding her foot. How could such a small thing like a toe have so much pain? She walked more carefully out the door, her large toe sticking up in the air.

Vera's ample body was bent over as she rattled the pots around in the cupboard. Her well-padded operatic voice sprang forth with incredible strength, interrupted by a chuckle or two. "Ah, there you are! Hah!" She yanked out a large pot, waving it triumphantly in the air, unaware that her bun had unraveled and long strands of hair had escaped all around her head, or that the noise she made had awakened her daughter and probably the whole neighborhood.

Cassiani planted a kiss on her cheek. "Good morning. It seems like you are better today."

"Yes. It must be the medicine!" Vera sang out, placing the pot down and patting her on the arm affectionately.

"I was thinking of telephoning Athena later today," Cassiani began, then she saw the meat on the counter. "What are you fixing?"

"Lamb," Vera said proudly, picking up the large slab of meat and placing it in the pot, singing gustily. She added the chopped garlic, then rubbed the lamb with spices. Next, olive oil and lemon were slathered on top. The covered pot was thrust into the oven. She wiped her hands on a towel and moved the oven's knob to a magical place on the dial that didn't have numbers.

"Where did you get it?" Cassiani asked.

Vera cleaned the counter top, avoiding looking at her. "Mrs. Spanos dropped it off."

"What's the special occasion? We never had lamb except for a holiday."

"It's not for us. It's for Mrs. Lukas. She's expecting company today. It's for Leo's name day."

Cassiani's mouth dropped open. "Mrs. Lukas asked you to cook this?"

"No, no. First she asked Mrs. Spanos to cook it for her," Vera explained. She began to wash the dishes in the sink. "But she couldn't do it, had to go down to see her grandchildren. So, Mrs. Lukas asked her to bring the lamb to me."

"How could Mrs. Lukas do this to you? You're still recovering from a heart attack!"

"Now please don't look at me that way," Vera said, appearing flustered. She reached for a towel. "I'm feeling so much better these days. Besides, it's really not that much work. It just cooks itself. More importantly, we need the money."

We need the money. It was beginning to sound like a mantra. Her mother was trying to survive the best way she could. Cassiani's shoulders slumped forward. "Is someone going to drive you there, or are you walking up that hill with that pot?"

Vera didn't answer right away; she finished wiping the dishes, then neatly folded the towel and placed it to the side. "I asked Mrs. Kalotsis if her son was coming up this way at all, but she said he was working today."

"What about a taxi?"

"Hah! Do you know how hard it is to find one up this way?" Vera retorted, gesturing in the air. "Besides, why should I pay just for a few minutes walk?" She shook her head. "No. I'll just walk. I'm used to it. Do you know how many times I've walked up that hill?"

"Twenty minutes up that hill in your condition ..." Cassiani warned.

Vera was quiet. "Maybe it wouldn't be a bad idea for you to help me then."

"What time do you have to be there?" Cassiani asked.

"The luncheon starts at one. I should be there around twelve."

"I'll carry the pot up the hill and help you with the meal."

"Thank you, my dear. That will be a great help!" Vera gushed. "Would you like something to eat?"

"No, I'm not very hungry."

*   *   *   *

Cassiani wore her white cotton blouse, long flowery skirt, and flat walking shoes for the climb up the hill. Her mother had insisted that she wear a more formal attire, but she had resisted. She carried the pot of lamb while her mother carried the bowl of greens. It had been Cassiani's idea to bring the boiled greens.

"Let's stop here under the shade so I can catch my breath," Vera said, leaning against a tree, panting.

"Why didn't Mrs. Lukas' nephew visit her all these years?" Cassiani asked.

"He was either too busy studying, or too busy working. Mrs. Lukas would visit him in America instead. This year, she said she was too sick to travel, so he's visiting her."

Cassiani was intrigued by what her mother said. She remembered the affectionate exchange between Leo and his aunt that day in the bedroom. Leo's visiting his ailing aunt because she was too sick to travel was another positive mark to his character.

Vera took out a folded handkerchief from her pocket and wiped her perspiring face with it. "I don't think Soula is sick. She's getting on in years and wants to see Leo married before she passes away. Someone told me that she found a girl for him. Nina Vassilakis. She's Dr. Vassilakis' only daughter. She's beautiful and smart, and her father built a villa on the beach for her dowry."

Cassiani was curious about this Nina. "How old is she?"

"Twenty-eight. Older than you, but she doesn't look it, the way she dresses and takes care of herself." Vera cocked an eyebrow. "I hear she dies her hair blonde and wears fake nails. Her shoes come from Italy and her dresses—"

"What else does she do besides dress up?" Cassiani interjected, recognizing her mother's veiled jab.

"She studied interior design with some of the best teachers in Europe. I tried matchmaking her once, but Nina's got her nose up in the air," Vera said. "She has broken so many engagements, tsk … tsk. Do you know how many girls are unwed because of her? Practically all the men here have chased after her. Anyway, I wouldn't be surprised if she and her family were invited to the meal today."

"Oh?" Cassiani asked, wondering if she wanted to meet such a person. "Does this Leo know that?"

"Of course not!" Vera said, chuckling. "He's thirty-four and a confirmed bachelor. The last thing you want is for him to know. He would catch the next plane to America if he knew."

"What does he do?"

"So you finally care enough to ask about Mrs. Lukas' nephew," Vera teased, wagging her finger.

"It's, it's different when you actually see him face to face," Cassiani stammered.

"He is a doctor; not the medical kind. He has a doctor's degree in finance or something like that. Mrs. Lukas says he studied at a very good university in America. Yaeeal, I think."

"Yale," Cassiani said, looking thoughtful. "That's supposed to be a very good school."

"Anyway, he works for a business that buys and sells thing to different countries." Vera tucked the handkerchief in her pocket. "*Pame.* We'll be late if we stay here talking all day."

They resumed their journey. The row of cypress trees at the end of the street was the signal that they had arrived; a gentle breeze and the shade from the trees brought a welcome relief from the hot sun. They reached the stone path that led to the house. A couple of cars were parked on the road near the path. To their left could be seen the large, whitewashed, two story villa with its majestically landscaped surroundings. They walked slowly towards the house.

"Do you know who else has been invited to the luncheon?" Cassiani asked, breaking the silence. She was beginning to feel nervous about the whole thing.

"I asked Stella when she brought the lamb over, and she didn't know. You'll see for yourself when you help me serve. You might even recognize some of them."

"Mother, you talk as if I enjoy doing this!" Cassiani blurted. "I didn't spend all these years in America, getting a college education, only to serve food to these people."

"Then stop right here and I'll take it!" Vera demanded, tugging at the pot. "Do you think I want to do this? I have no choice. You see these swollen hands? They dusted and mopped so you could travel to America and become a nurse. Now I ask you to do something for me once, and all you do is whine. Your father would have scolded you the way you talk to me, young lady!"

"I'm sorry. I guess my pride gets in the way sometimes." Cassiani hung her head. "You are a good mother and I do appreciate all you've done for me, and if I didn't have this pot, I'd hug you."

"That's all right, daughter," Vera said, her voice softening. "You'll understand one day when you have children of your own."

They resumed their walk. "Oh look, the door is open," Cassiani said. "Do you mind if I go ahead so I can put this down?"

Vera nodded her approval. Cassiani walked briskly forward, leaving her mother behind, intent on relieving herself of the heavy pot. As she approached the door, she spied Leo Regas standing in the hallway. He was dressed in a casual beige suit and white shirt and his back was turned to her. He appeared to be studying the oil paintings on the wall.

CHAPTER 7

Cassiani stopped abruptly at the doorway, not knowing whether she wanted to be the first to greet Leo. He turned and saw her; a spark jumped between them as their eyes locked.

Leo stared at her, apparently surprised to see her. "Cassiani, what brings you here?"

"Dr. Leo, hello. My mother cooked the lamb for the luncheon." Cassiani lifted the pot.

"Here, let me take that. It looks heavy." His fingers softly brushed hers when he took the pot, making her acutely aware of his closeness.

Cassiani stood there, about to thank him when she was abruptly pushed forward by her mother's clumsy entrance.

"Sorry, dear," Vera said, trying to right herself. "You stopped right in front of me."

"I was talking to—" Cassiani began.

"Dr. Leo!" Vera boomed, sidestepping her daughter. "*Chronia Polla* for your name day! I'm Vera Meletis. I'm happy to have finally met you."

"Thank you. The same can be said for me." Leo smiled as he bowed his head. "May I ask how your health is doing these days?"

Vera beamed. "Much better, thank you." She showed him the bowl. "We also brought you a nice bowl of greens. Cassiani said you like them?"

"I do!" Leo warmly thanked Cassiani.

The walk down the hallway was slow and leisurely. They passed the parlor; its double glass doors were partly opened, and Cassiani glimpsed a few people standing there. They reached the kitchen and Leo placed the pot on the counter top.

"How is your aunt?" ventured Vera. "I haven't seen her in weeks."

"She is in the parlor with some of the guests. It seems like she's feeling well today," Leo said.

"That's good," Vera said. "She always liked giving parties."

"I think it's more than that," Leo said, his eyes twinkling. "We Greeks are a social people, and relish getting together for a meal; for not only do these times serve the purpose of nourishing the body, but also the soul."

Just then, Soula entered the kitchen. She walked slowly with a measured gait, wearing a dark blue suit, a pearl necklace, and several large rings on her fingers. "I am so glad you are feeling better," she said to Vera, hugging her. She then turned to Leo. "Leo, dear, why don't you go back to our guests? I don't want to leave them alone too long."

"Yes, you are right." Leo excused himself and left.

Vera reached into a drawer and pulled out two clean aprons. "So tell me, Soula, how many guests do you have?" She gave Cassiani an apron, then tied the apron around her waist.

"Dear, I invited eight guests. So that totals ten altogether," Soula said. "Let me show you what there is." She inched her way around the kitchen, pointing to everything. As she left the room, she said, "Please have the food ready by one o'clock. Some people have to leave early."

Cassiani helped her mother with the preparations. The black olives, sliced feta and kasseri cheeses, and marinated peppers were arranged in circles on a large tray. She could hear the increase in voices as she steadily worked.

"I wonder who she invited." Vera peeked curiously out the door. "More people have come. I don't recognize them. Hurry."

Sliced cucumbers, yogurt, and minced garlic were whipped together into a creamy tzatziki sauce. Cassiani spooned the sauce into a large bowl. She pointed to the large tray of spanakopitas on the counter. "I wonder who made these."

"It looks like Mrs. Spanos dropped these off," Vera said, popping a crisp spinach pie in her mouth. "Hmmm. Good. I know her cooking anywhere. Here, have one."

"No thanks. Are there enough for everyone?"

"Don't you worry," Vera said, tittering. "There's plenty here. I'll just take these into the parlor. I'll pass the tray and be back shortly for the rest of the appetizers. You take care of the tomato and onion salad."

Cassiani cocked an eyebrow at her mother's seemingly effortless comeback. "Are you feeling up to it?"

Vera waved an arm in the air. "I'll stop if I'm not feeling well." Her plump body disappeared before Cassiani could say anything else.

As Cassiani sliced the tomatoes into a large bowl, she thought about her mother; she was a walking paradox. One minute, she was a heart attack victim, and the next, she was tackling chores that would have tired a younger person. A worrisome thought surfaced; her mother had never been sick before and did not know the extent of her new physical limitations. She was like a caged animal, used to being free; each time she would come up against the bars of the cage—in this case, her ill heart—her body would let her down. *Life will never be the same for Mother.*

The noise grew louder. Laughter was sprinkled like confectioner's sugar on the festive occasion. By the time her mother returned, the salad was tossed, the bread sliced, and the lamb and potatoes were being warmed in the oven.

Vera leaned against the counter to catch her breath. "Guess who's here? Aspasia and Manolis Pantelonis! I had no idea Soula knew them."

Cassiani's eyebrows went up. "Mary's parents are here?" Memories of her childhood came rushing back. Mary Pantelonis was her best friend throughout grade school. Their families got together often and Cassiani and her sister would play with Mary. They had lost touch after Cassiani and her mother moved to the mountain.

"They were just as surprised to see me as I was them," Vera gushed, appearing flustered. "I told them that I was helping Mrs. Lukas out, you know, as a *friend.*"

Cassiani bit her lip. *They probably didn't expect to see Mother serving them, and she was probably too embarrassed to say she was working for Mrs. Lukas.* "Why do you suppose they are here? I mean, how would they know Mrs. Lukas, all the way on this side of Kos?"

"I'll find out soon enough." Vera glanced at the clock on the wall. "Oh, dear, we must move quickly! The dining room table needs to be set."

"Why don't you rest a little? I'll do it," Cassiani commanded.

Vera followed her into the dining room and plunked herself down in a chair, fanning herself with a folded piece of paper, giving her directions. "You need to change the tablecloth. There is one in that cabinet. You'll find its matching napkins. They're already ironed."

Cassiani replaced the old tablecloth with the more decorative white tablecloth. She spread her hands along the edges of the cloth, smoothing the small creases against the table. The border caught her attention; it was made of delicate cross-stitched flowers on a winding green vine. "Oh, these little flowers are lovely," she exclaimed, touching them.

"I stitched them," Vera said proudly. "What do you think I was doing all those days when I sat and kept her company? Took me a year to finish. She only uses it for special occasions."

Cassiani folded the cloth napkins, noticing the matching flower pattern with the tablecloth. "I suppose these are your *kentimata* also?"

"She wouldn't have it any other way," Vera replied smugly.

Cassiani worked quietly, placing everything in order.

The parlor was across the hall from the dining room and the noise had risen significantly. Vera looked in the direction of the parlor. "By the way. I was right. Doctor Vassilakis came with his wife and daughter. He was surprised to see me."

"I don't blame him," Cassiani muttered under her breath. "Who are the other people?"

"There's Louis Kotsidas, a bouzouki player from Kos Town, and another couple. Their last name is Xenoudis, but I don't know them. They seem to be friends with Manolis and Aspasia."

The crystal glasses came out of the cabinet and were dusted with a napkin. Cassiani placed them carefully on the table.

"Come, we only have a few minutes. The china set and silverware are located in the cabinet." Vera pointed towards it. "It will be a sit down lunch, so set the table for ten people."

"A sit down lunch?" echoed Cassiani, wondering if her mother could handle the task. She was afraid to ask the next question. "Are you supposed to serve them?"

"I tried to talk Mrs. Lukas into making it a buffet, saying that I wasn't in any condition to be serving the meal, because of my health. See, now that I'm talking to you, I feel tired and out of breath. Anyway, she didn't want a buffet. She asked if you could serve instead. What could I do? I said yes."

"Oh, Mother!" Cassiani exclaimed. This had gone too far. There had to be a better way to earn money. Her mother had unwittingly placed her in an awkward position and she resented it. She didn't want to be serving people, especially her old friend's parents.

At the hospital she performed well under pressure; her cool-headed ability to think and move swiftly had been recognized by the staff. She did very well because she enjoyed her work, and it showed. This was turning out to be a situation that was testing those abilities. "I don't have any experience serving people! What if I spilled something? I'm going right in there to tell Mrs. Lukas that we are going to have a buffet!"

Vera slid down the chair, her hand pressed on her chest. "Oh! I'm feeling weak all of a sudden, as if I'm going to faint."

Cassiani rushed to help her mother, feeling guilty. Maybe she had been too hard on her. She touched her wrist. It felt clammy and her pulse was racing. "I'm sorry, Mother. I didn't mean to yell at you."

"That's quite all right, daughter. I think we're both feeling a little nervous."

Cassiani helped her up. "Come, let's go into the kitchen so you can get some rest."

"Shall I go tell them about the buffet?" Vera fanned herself with her free hand.

Cassiani sighed, trying to find sense in all of this. "I'll serve them." For some odd reason, her knees were feeling soft and her hands were clammy as she took her mother's hand.

Vera smiled weakly at her. "You have my blessings."

They reached the kitchen. "Sit down here. I'll go get Dr. Vassilakis."

Vera shook her head. "No! No!" she said, almost choking. "Don't interrupt him. I don't want to ruin their lunch. They're having a good time. A little rest is all I need. Just let them know that the food is ready."

Cassiani squared her shoulders as she began the trek down the hallway to the parlor. This was one of the few times she wasn't going to listen to her mother. This morning her mother was feeling well enough to cook the lamb and later, to walk up the hill, acting as if she were going to her own wedding. Everything changed once they got here. Her mother needed medical help and that was more important than earning money.

Cassiani stopped when she saw Leo standing in the hallway conversing and joking with a blonde-haired woman who was laughing teasingly back at him. The woman was slim and petite. Her black dress fit her snugly; the hemline was above the knees, which was the fashion of the day. She held a wineglass in her well-manicured hands. It had to be Nina Vassilakis.

Leo turned around and looked at Cassiani, as if he sensed her presence. "Yes?"

Cassiani pointed towards the kitchen. "My mother is not feeling well. Her heart is racing." She felt Nina's eyes upon her. "I was going to get the doctor."

"I'll bring him to her," Leo said. "You should go back and keep an eye on her."

CHAPTER 8

Dr. Vassilakis' short, thick frame breezed into the kitchen alongside Leo. The doctor walked with the assurance of a man who was used to handling patients for many years. His dark rimmed glasses made him appear studious. The strong smell of cigar smoke hung on his clothes. "Mrs. Meletis, what is the problem?" He lifted her hand, then looked at his watch as he measured her pulse.

"I'm very sorry to bother you, doctor," Vera tittered, appearing nervous. She fanned herself. "One minute I feel all right, and the next, I feel so weak and tired."

"Have you been taking the medicine just as I prescribed?"

"Yes, doctor," Vera said, her eyes widening. "But, to be honest, every time I take it, I notice that it bothers me here in my stomach." Her hand rested on her stomach.

"Did you take your medicine today?" Cassiani asked, afraid what the answer would be.

Vera blinked. "Now that I think about it," she said, then paused. She flung her hands in the air. "I was so busy preparing the meal that I completely forgot to take it this morning!"

Cassiani sucked in her breath. She should have known better than to trust her mother to faithfully take her medication. Her mother had no idea of the negative impact that a missed dose would have on her heart. *From now on, you should monitor her medicine.*

"Naughty woman!" Dr. Vassilakis snorted and shook a thick, stubby finger at Vera. "How can I help you if you don't follow my orders? First, you don't take the medicine the way you are supposed to, and second, you are here working! You are in no condition to work. I will express my concerns to Mrs. Lukas!"

Vera appeared embarrassed. "I'm sorry."

"Mrs. Meletis is not to blame," Leo said firmly to the doctor. "We are at fault. She should not have been asked to help in the first place. What is done, is done. Meanwhile is there anything that you can do to help her?"

"I have something in my medicine case that might help her for now," Dr. Vassilakis said, his voice calmer. "I always carry the case in my car."

"If the heart medicine is bothering her, then her dose should be adjusted or her medicine changed," said Cassiani, defending her mother. "Heart medicines have serious side effects and have to be monitored closely. Not every patient tolerates the medicine the same way."

"Young lady, your mother is very ill and she should not play games with her heart medicine. If she doesn't take her pills properly, how can we see whether or not they are helping her? She could even have another heart attack or even a stroke, and she won't be so lucky next time," Dr. Vassilakis said before leaving.

"I'm afraid he is right, Cassiani," Leo said. "Doctors can only do so much. They are like a teacher who can only succeed when their students cooperate and take the time to study; in this case, a doctor can help only if the patients take their medicine faithfully."

Cassiani was quiet. For some reason she was feeling miserable.

Soula entered the kitchen slowly, appearing anxious. "Leo, is everything all right? Nina told me you were here."

Leo explained the situation.

"Oh, dear," Soula said, looking at Vera. "I wasn't aware how much work you had done. Please, don't do anymore work today. Cassiani, I will need your help. Quickly. Begin with the salads first. Once they are served, then serve the main meal. Leo, I need you to take care of the wine."

Cassiani's back straightened up. She was about to throw in the towel and leave with her mother. She never did like taking orders, but when she saw Leo watching her, she swallowed her pride. Her mother had promised that she would help, and it wouldn't be fair to leave them in the middle like this. *Besides, we need the money.*

*   *   *   *

Cassiani carried the large silver tray of roasted lamb and potatoes into the dining room. The talking was boisterous and laughter was rampant. Mrs. Lukas sat at the head of the table. Dr. Vassilakis sat to her left, conversing with her. He had removed his eyeglasses, revealing a pair of thick, bushy brows.

"Mrs. Lukas, you must listen to me." Dr. Vassilakis wiped his glasses with his napkin as he talked, then used the napkin to wipe his sweating forehead. "You need to have tests done so we can diagnose the problem better."

Cassiani quietly scooped the lamb and potatoes on to Mrs. Lukas' plate.

"I don't like getting poked by needles," Soula said flatly.

Cassiani filled the doctor's plate next. He was talking in earnest and ignored her.

Cassiani moved on, wondering about Mrs. Lukas' health; it seemed as if Dr. Vassilakis felt she needed to be tested for something. Leo sat to the right of Mrs. Lukas. He looked as if he was deep in thought. She caught him gazing at her as she filled his plate.

Leo thanked her, then pointed to the empty seat next to him. "Nina is sitting here. She'll be right back."

Cassiani placed the food in the empty plate. Next to Nina's seat was Louis Kotsidas, smoking a cigarette. It had to be him. Somehow he looked like a bouzouki player with his long hair. When he saw her, he handed her his plate, winking. "*Yiasou, Koukla mou.*"

Cassiani blushed at the compliment. She was sure everyone at the table had heard him. He had said it loudly enough. His words were hard to shake off; they were sweet like honey and sticky enough to be irritating.

Next to Louis, at the end of the table, sat Manolis Pantelonis. He was talking to his wife, Aspasia, who sat across from him. A man in his late sixties, with a gray mustache, he was dressed in a dark blue suit, a white shirt, and wine-colored tie. Although he made and sold shoes, music was his real passion. His receding gray hairline, large ears, and twinkling eyes that sloped downward gave him an endearing, puppy-dog look.

"Cassiani, is that you?" Manolis asked, greeting her with his typical sloppy grin and gentle pat on the back.

"Hello, Mr. Pantelonis." Cassiani placed the food in his plate, feeling her face flush. She didn't know whether to be happy to see him or to cry for being placed in such an embarrassing situation.

"Ahhh, Cassiani. How time flies. Your old friend, our little Mary is no longer little. She is getting engaged."

"Mary is getting engaged? How wonderful!" Cassiani exclaimed, surprised at the good news of her old friend.

Aspasia rose to greet her. "Cassiani, my dear, how are you?" She was plump and short, with an attractive, friendly face and a ready laugh; a sign of an easy life. The gold bracelets on her tanned arms jingled as she moved. "It's been years, hasn't it?"

Cassiani moved the tray to the side to avoid collision as she was embraced in a cloud of perfume. "Hello, Mrs. Pantelonis. I just heard about Mary's engagement. I think that's great!"

"Isn't that wonderful? The couple sitting next to me, Mihalis and Betsy Xenoudis, will be her future in-laws." Aspasia gestured towards the well-groomed couple on her right side. They were joking loudly with Louis Kotsidas. Cassiani noticed Leo's seat was now empty, and so was Nina's.

Aspasia patted her on the back. "I know you're busy. We'll talk later."

Cassiani thanked her. She resumed her task. After she finished filling Mrs. Xenoudis' plate, she proceeded to fill her husband's plate. Mihalis Xenoudis was deep in conversation with the doctor's wife and apparently didn't see Cassiani as he lifted up his arm in a gesture, holding a glass of wine. Cassiani swerved to avoid him but it was too late as his glass collided with her arm, spilling the red wine all over his lap. She apologized, reaching over to get a napkin to clean the mess. Just then, the tray slipped from her hands and landed with a loud crash on the marble floor. The food from the tray spilled on to the floor, splattering everything around it, including her skirt, the tablecloth, and the clothing of everyone seated nearby. Mr. Xenoudis and his wife jumped out of their seats, talking excitedly and dabbing their stained clothes with their napkins.

"Oh, dear!" Soula said, obviously disturbed. "Cassiani, clean up the mess! Quickly, and bring some food for Mrs. Vassilakis!"

Cassiani shoveled everything back on to the tray, wiping the floor as much as she could with the napkins offered to her by the couple. She marched into the kitchen, angry and humiliated. She felt as if she had been tested and had failed the test.

"Mother!" she called out. Her mother was nowhere in sight. She trashed the dirty food from the tray into the garbage pail, then washed her hands and skirt. She found a little food still in the pot and scooped it on a plate. She marched it in to Mrs. Vassilakis. Back in the kitchen, she washed the tray, grumbling to herself. This was not a good day for her.

Her mother came into the kitchen a few minutes later.

"Where were you?" Cassiani asked. She blew a stray strand of hair away from her face.

"The parlor, to tidy it up," Vera said absentmindedly. "I saw Dr. Leo and you-know-who outside the window as I was cleaning the parlor. They were walking in the garden."

Cassiani gave her mother a puzzled look. "You-know-who?"

"Nina! Who else?" Vera said, appearing exasperated. "Anyway, she was smoking, but I noticed he wasn't. That's good. It looks as if he's got some brains on him."

"Mother, I hope you weren't spying on them!"

"Who? Me?" Vera asked, with an innocent look, shrugging her shoulders. "They were right there in front of me, in full sight. I couldn't help seeing them."

Cassiani suppressed a giggle. If the couple wanted any privacy, the garden was the last place to be. The windows in the parlor spanned the whole side of the wall facing the garden. "You shouldn't have been tidying up the parlor. Not in your condition."

"It wasn't that much work, really. Come, you must be hungry. Hunger always does that, make us angry. That's why I always kept your father well-fed." She peered inside the empty pot. "What happened to the rest of the food?"

"There isn't any left." Cassiani informed her about the spill and how she used the remaining food to fill Mrs. Vassilakis' plate.

"Oh dear," Vera said, sighing. "Then we'll just have to eat the spanakopitas I saved for later." She pulled out a couple of flattened spinach pies from her pocket. They had been wrapped in a handkerchief. "Come, let's sit."

Cassiani munched on her spinach pie, feeling better. Images of the scene in the dining room replayed themselves in her mind. "Mrs. Lukas was quite upset about the accident."

"Those things happen. You aren't the first or the last. Soula can be a grouch sometimes, believe me! When she barks, you better listen!" Vera crowed, waving her hand in the air.

"Hello."

Cassiani's head swerved upward to the sound of the female voice, her mouth full of food. Behind Nina's small frame stood Leo's tall frame. Cassiani swiped at her mouth, conscious of the crumbs there. She felt her face flush.

Vera's body careened awkwardly forward as she stood up quickly. "May I help you?"

Nina's eyes aimed insolently at Cassiani's plate. "Do you have any spanakopitas left? I don't eat lamb."

Cassiani gulped down the last morsel of food, almost choking.

"Dear girl," Vera said, rushing towards Nina. "You don't eat lamb? Why didn't you tell us?"

"I hadn't had a chance to. I came back and the food was already on my plate," Nina said. Her voice was tight, matching her annoyed look. "Anyway, I'm not that hungry. Leo, let's go back outside for some fresh air. It's stuffy and warm in here."

CHAPTER 9

"You go ahead, I'll be right with you," Leo said, watching Nina leave. He turned and looked at Vera. "Mrs. Meletis, I am aware that these past several years you have done a wonderful job providing companionship to my aunt, as well as other duties, and I'm grateful for it." He began to pace the room, his hands behind his back. "However, as you know, Dr. Vassilakis strongly recommends you take a break from the work due to your heart condition. It can be strenuous at times and detrimental to your health. I agree with him."

Vera appeared remorseful. "Yes, he is right. I should do what he says."

Cassiani glanced at her mother, surprised at her meek, complacent tone. It was not like her mother to be so conforming.

Leo appeared relieved. "Then it is settled. You will no longer work for her until the doctor says you can," he said. "He recommends that my aunt have a nurse watch her for a few days."

"Dr. Vassilakis said she needs a nurse?" Vera asked, her eyes wide.

Cassiani tensed, anticipating what her mother was going to say next.

"Yes." Leo pursed his lips, looking thoughtful. "I also think it's a good idea for her to have a personal nurse, but from what I hear, they are hard to come by." He dug his hands in his pockets, looking off into the distance. His face wore a worried expression.

"I would like to suggest something," Vera said sweetly. "Why not have Cassiani nurse your aunt? She has a nursing degree from America and has even worked in a hospital."

Leo looked at Cassiani in surprise. "Cassiani?"

Cassiani was slow to respond, feeling mixed emotions. Her mother's resourceful request did not surprise her. *We need the money.* What bothered her was that one minute she was acting like a servant to his aunt, cleaning, cooking, and serving; the next minute she was supposed to be a nurse. What must Leo think? No wonder he looked surprised. *It seems as if Mother is pulling strings, and like a puppet I am moving wherever she wants me to.* She was going to have a long talk with her mother afterwards. She turned to Leo and said, "Yes, it's true. I am a nurse." She told him about her degree and where she worked.

"She went into nursing because she has special abilities," Vera said, beaming. "When she was twelve, she helped save a three year old boy who had fallen into a well. Everyone thinks it was a miracle that she was able to revive him. I thank the Good Lord for blessing her with the healing touch." She looked up towards the ceiling and made the sign of the cross reverently.

Cassiani was silent. Yes, she had been blessed, hadn't she? Even at the hospital, she had a knack for helping patients heal better than what the doctors predicted. *But did her mother need to say all that about her?*

Leo nodded. "I like the idea. I will suggest it to my aunt. What do you think, Cassiani, could you do it?"

"I came here to help my mother," she said flatly. "I don't know how I'll find the time to nurse anyone else, let alone Mrs. Lukas."

Leo was about to speak, then paused, looking expectantly at Vera, as if he were watching a chess game.

"Yes, she did come to help me," Vera admitted. She folded her plump arms neatly on her lap, looking down at her dry, reddened hands. "She can work half the day with your aunt, then take care of me the other half of the day."

Leo gazed at Cassiani. "That suits me. What do you say Cassiani? Why don't you come tomorrow and we'll discuss it with my aunt?"

Cassiani noticed the obvious display of relief on her mother's face. The constant reminder that they needed money was humbling. She nodded, feeling numb all over. "That will be fine with me."

"Tomorrow is Sunday," Vera said quickly. "I prefer for her not to work on Sundays. It is the Lord's day of rest."

A troubled look passed over Leo's eyes, then left just as quickly. "As you wish." Then he said as an afterthought, "Could it be possible for Cassiani to pay a social visit to my aunt tomorrow? You're invited also. She'll start work officially on Monday."

"Cassiani can come, but I probably will not. I'll be resting tomorrow," Vera said.

"Cassiani?" Leo asked. There was a twinkle in his eyes.

Cassiani appreciated that he overrode her mother's decision and asked her instead. She also liked his inviting her to pay a social visit to his aunt. *This shows that he elevated me from the servant status to an equal status.* She smiled at the thought. "All right."

"Good." Leo smiled back. He was about to leave, then paused. "I believe my aunt hasn't paid you for today." He pulled out a wad of bills and proceeded to put several in Vera's hand. "That includes payment for Cassiani's help."

Cassiani's momentary lapse of happiness plummeted as she was reminded of the reason why she was there in the first place ... to work, and no matter how wishful her thinking about Leo inviting her tomorrow, the bottom line was that Leo was paying them. Her stomach also made a nosedive at that moment, grumbling loudly; she hadn't eaten anything but a spinach pie all day.

Just then Nina re-entered the kitchen, her mouth set in a firm line. "Leo, your aunt is asking for you. Cassiani, please serve the coffee and desert. We have to leave soon."

"Will you excuse me?" Leo asked as he left the room.

Vera shoved the pot of coffee in Cassiani's hands. "Cassiani, the coffee."

Cassiani hurried through the motions of pouring the hot, dark thick coffee into the small coffee cups for everyone. She returned to the dining room with a tray full of honeyed baklava, koulourakia, and finikia. Everyone was talking and laughing as Cassiani served the refreshments. Leo was conversing with his aunt and the doctor. He paused when he saw her approach with the tray. He chose the elongated honey-dipped finiki. "Thank you."

Louis was chatting animatedly with Nina when she reached his seat. Cassiani bent down and showed them the tray of pastries.

Nina shook her head, a smirk on her face. "I don't eat sweets."

Louis leaned towards Cassiani. "There's my *Koukla* again." He stared at the tray, then pointed at the baklava. "Sweet as this pastry you are serving."

Nina laughed raucously at his remark, as if enjoying some private joke. "Louis you're so funny!"

Louis winked slyly at Cassiani. "Are you free tonight? I'm playing bouzouki at the Xenoudis club in Kos Town."

Cassiani clenched her teeth. She dropped the baklava in his plate. "No, I'm not." She could feel Louis' eyes on her as she flounced out of the dining room.

*　　　*　　　*　　　*

The guests left one by one, and Cassiani steadily cleaned the dining room. She could feel the sweat on her brow trickling down the sides of her face and an ache in her back as she worked quickly. She had only one intention, to finish so they could leave. Raised voices in the hallway caused her to look up; her mother was conversing animatedly with her old friends, Aspasia and Manolis. It appeared as if they were catching up on their news.

As she worked, Cassiani went over the happenings of the day, remembering her feelings of resentment at being placed in this particular situation—something she had no choice in. It was not that she did not like to work. She had always been a hard worker. It was the fact that her mother's inability to do the work and the need for money was forcing Cassiani to do things she would never have done. Maybe there was a lesson to be learned here.

A half-hour later, Cassiani returned to the kitchen, ready to leave. It was almost four thirty. She stopped abruptly when she saw the pile of dishes on the counter. She had forgotten them. She quickly went to work, washing all the dishes and silverware, then wiping them dry with a towel. She carried the pile of cleaned dishes back to the dining room cabinet and moments later, returned with the clean silverware.

Vera entered the kitchen, a grin on her face, just as Cassiani finished taking off her apron.

"I'm all done," Cassiani said tensely. She did not want to stay there one minute longer. "I'll tell Mrs. Lukas that we're leaving."

"Thank you, daughter," Vera said, kissing her. "By the way, I noticed that Dr. Vassilakis is still here. Could you ask him to drop us off at the intersection? I don't think I have the energy to walk down the hill."

The large, airy parlor showered Cassiani with sunlight that streamed in from the large windows. Through the windows, she witnessed Leo sitting outside with Nina. For some reason, Cassiani had a sinking feeling in her stomach when she saw the couple in the garden. *Why does it bother you?* She secretly wondered if he would have offered to drive them home if Nina hadn't been there. She deliberately ignored them and focused her attention instead on the conversation in the parlor. Dr. Vassilakis was seated with his wife on the creamy beige French-style sofa near the fireplace. He was talking to Mrs. Lukas.

Dr. Vassilakis stood up, appearing slightly flustered. "Too bad you don't want to sell me the pharmacy," he said to Soula.

Cassiani's attention was riveted to the conversation when she heard him speak about the pharmacy. *Father's pharmacy.* Was Dr. Vassilakis trying to buy it?

"Look, I have an idea. George owns the second floor of the building. He used to have his medical office there. I'm pretty sure it's not for sale, but maybe you can rent the office space upstairs. I'll have Leo check into it," Soula promised.

Dr. Vassilakis nodded politely. "That's a possibility." He took her hand. "Thank you for a wonderful lunch, but we need to be going. I know we must have tired you."

"Oh no. I'm not tired," Soula replied.

Tessie Vassilakis rose and went to hug Mrs. Lukas. "Dear Soula, thank you so much for your hospitality, but we do need to let you rest."

"My sweet, where is our Nina?" Dr. Vassilakis asked his wife as he went to the window and peered outside.

"Leave the children be. Leo will drive her back," Soula ordered.

"Excuse me, but we must be leaving." Cassiani stepped into the room. "Is there anything else you'll be needing?"

"No. That will be all," Soula said, motioning towards the door.

"Cassiani, everybody was pleased with the meal," Tessie said, smiling at her. "Louis Kotsidas said the nicest things about you, I'll have you know."

Cassiani didn't know what to say. Although she did not particularly care to hear what Louis Kotsidas said about her, she did appreciate Tessie Vassilakis' comment about the meal. She smiled lamely. "My mother should take all the compliments. I just helped her." She was about to leave when she remembered her mother's request. "Dr. Vassilakis, my mother wanted to know if you could drop us off at the intersection."

"Surely."

So it was settled. They piled into the car and Dr. Vassilakis drove wildly down the steep road, with one hand toting his stubby cigar, while his wife sat next to him chatting about the latest fashion. Cassiani's head was stuck out the open window all the way down the hill, trying to avoid the trail of smoke that seemed to do a beeline to her nose.

"You can stop here," Vera bellowed, leaning forward and tapping the doctor's shoulder. The car's tires squealed to a stop. She thanked the doctor as she tottered out of the back seat.

"Remember to take your medicine!" Dr. Vassilakis trumpeted, waving his cigar at them as he sped away.

CHAPTER 10

As soon as the car disappeared, Cassiani bent over and coughed soundly, clearing her lungs.

"Are you all right, dear?" Vera asked, patting her on the back.

Cassiani took a deep breath and straightened up, gazing towards the direction of the retreating car. "I feel like I'm having an asthma attack whenever I'm around smokers."

"Yes, you're right. I couldn't wait to get out of the car." Vera wrinkled her nose, waving her hand in front of her face at the imaginary smoke. "His cigar was quite smelly."

They strolled down the sunlit lane towards their house. Although the dirt path was dusty and only wide enough to fit one car, it revealed a breathtaking view of the island and sea to their left. To their right, the mountain sloped steeply upward, and to their left, steeply downward.

The road wove around a bend, then straightened. It wasn't long when they had reached flat open space. To their right were the boundary stones of the Lukoumis family; their sizeable property sloped gently upward. It included several olive trees and grape orchards, a cow, some goats and chickens. A narrow stone path led to the front of the two-story whitewashed house with its blue shutters. Cassiani could see the heavy-set Mrs. Lukoumis sweeping her front courtyard.

Mrs. Lukoumis waved to them. *"Elate yia café!"* she called out.

"Next time, Mrs. Lukoumis. We have work to do," Vera called, waving back to her. She turned and whispered to Cassiani as they walked past the house. "She's a nice lady, but if we stop now for coffee, we'll be here all evening. Once she starts talking, she'll *never* stop."

They continued walking. Cassiani's ears caught the tingling sounds of bells coming from her left. She gazed down the rolling hill, looking for the source of the sound and spied a group of sheep grazing below. A short man wearing a baggy hat and shapeless trousers was carrying a cane and walking briskly towards the sheep.

"There's Barba Yannis," Vera said. As they walked past his house, she paused and gazed at the front door. "His wife, Meropi, must be in the back. I can't see her. I wanted to introduce you to her. Maybe next time."

"Does she have a nephew or grandson?" Cassiani asked impishly.

Vera chuckled. "And if she did?"

They approached an immense olive orchard to their left. Nestled in the midst of the orchard was a large white villa with two smaller houses nearby. Cassiani remembered visiting the villa a few times.

"I don't know if you remember, but all this property belongs to Mrs. Kalotsis' cousin, Katina," Vera informed her. "She has two sons and a daughter. They make the best olive oil in town."

Cassiani nodded. She remembered the family. The sons were married and lived on the property with their families. They all helped make the olive oil and sold it in the village. She quietly gazed at the bucolic scene before her. "I became friends with Maria, Katina's daughter. What happened to her?"

"Oh, Maria?" Vera made a gesture in the air. "She's married and lives in Athens."

Cassiani's eyes flew open. Maria was probably twenty years old by now. She remembered her as a bright-eyed thirteen-year old girl with braids and freckles. It was difficult envisioning her as being married. "Oh!"

There was a gleam in Vera's eyes. "I helped marry her to Mrs. Lukoumis' cousin two years ago. He's a successful businessman from Athens and he's fourteen years older. They met when he was visiting his cousin," she said proudly. "If you would have been here then, he would have been a good match for you."

Cassiani was quiet. She recalled how her mother kept telling her to visit her that summer, but she was too intent on finishing her schooling.

"By the way, speaking of a good match, I spoke with Aspasia and Manolis," Vera said. "Mary's fiancé's name is Nicko Xenoudis; his parents were the couple at the luncheon." She continued her discourse, telling her how Mary met Nicko at the Xenoudis hotel last year, during a wedding reception. "Now they're getting engaged." She paused, just enough time to take a breath, then continued. "Manolis and Aspasia invited us to the engagement party tomorrow night, but I said I wasn't sure if I was up to it—you know—with my heart and everything." Vera gestured towards her heart as she spoke.

Cassiani felt a sense of disappointment. Her old friend was getting engaged and it would have been nice to attend the party. "Your health comes first."

"Wait, there's more," Vera said. "Manolis said how much he missed having your father play. So, I asked him if he'd like for you to play the violin with him at the engagement party."

"You did?" Cassiani stopped in her tracks, eyeing her mother warily.

Vera's eyes glistened with unshed tears. "I told him how you play just like your father and how you even play in an orchestra in America." Her voice trembled. "Anyway, after he got over his surprise, he agreed, saying you can play in memory of your father. Do you want to do it?"

Cassiani had mixed feelings. On the one hand, she liked the idea of playing the violin at the party. *What about having that talk with Mother about pulling your puppet strings?* "Mother. I...." She paused, trying to find the proper words about how she felt her mother was controlling her life since she returned, but they didn't come when she saw the tears in her mother's eyes. This wasn't the time to say no. She nodded instead. "I'll do it for Father, and for Mary."

Vera patted her daughter on the shoulders. "You have my blessings, daughter. He said for you to be there by seven."

Up ahead was their one-story whitewashed house with its large front yard. Beyond, she could see Mrs. Kalotsis' house and then the bend to the right that led to the other side of the mountain where there were a few more houses nestled among the tree-lined hills. Cassiani's right foot had formed a blister. She bent down to examine it, slipping her foot out of the shoe. Her mother looked curiously at her. "Just a little blister," Cassiani explained. She stood up, replacing her shoe.

"I have a cream that I can put on it when we get home," Vera offered.

A hen sprinted past them, clucking loudly. She stopped farther down the road, her white neck bobbing up and down as she pecked at some speck on the dirt ground. Then she lifted her head proudly, staring at them as they approached.

"Cluck, cluck," Cassiani said, laughing at the hen's behavior. "One of Mrs. Kalotsis' hens is loose again. Oh, and there's her rooster!"

The rooster dashed past them, his legs kicking dust as he chased the hen farther down the road. His head bobbed up and down as he tried to overtake her.

Cassiani laughed. "We better tell her."

"Don't worry, she knows," Vera said, chuckling. "Says it's better for the eggs. All that running and such. Hehehe ..."

The scent of the gardenia bushes greeted her as Cassiani opened the gate and walked into the yard. Sunlight bathed the abundant flowers that bordered the stone pathway that led to the front door; there were gardenia bushes, purple irises, rose bushes with pink and red rose buds, white lilies, and red and white geraniums. Grapevines climbing the white trellis in front of the house provided the stony courtyard with shade. The vines were already bursting forth with a colorful display of purple berries.

To their right, tied to the nearby lemon tree, stood their two goats, Tiri and her baby, Tiraki. They were bleating nervously. The tingling of their bells could be heard as they pulled on their ropes.

"Oh! I forgot to take them to the back after milking Tiri!" Vera said. She looked towards Mrs. Kalotsis' house. "Normally Kalliopi takes them for me if I forget. Maybe she was busy."

"I'll take them." Cassiani ignored her exhaustion as she untied their ropes and led them down the well-worn path to the open field in the back. A stall stood on the far right corner, surrounded by a fence. She opened the gate to let them in, watching the kid frolicking around its mother playfully. When Cassiani returned to the front, she found her mother going around the garden, tending the flowers.

"The lilies are beautiful," Vera said, smelling them. "This year, since Easter came early I wasn't able to donate the lilies for the *epitaphio*. They weren't in bloom yet." Then she moved over and touched a red budding rose from a large rose bush that grew against the house. "This was your grandmother's favorite rose bush because it was the first to bloom. Soon, we will have beautiful roses. Ahh, life. One day we are in our prime like these flowers, and the next—we are gone. Look at these. Even these have to go one day."

Cassiani stood watching her mother move around the garden, touching the plants. She appreciated her mother's nurturing trait; everything she touched that was living, plant or animal, thrived well under her care. Cassiani's thoughts traveled to the engagement party tomorrow. "I still can't believe that Mary's getting engaged."

Vera nodded. "Can you imagine? We always thought she'd remain a spinster, with her plain looks and being so shy. How old is she now?"

"Six months younger than me, so that makes her twenty-four," said Cassiani. She didn't like the fact that her friend had been referred to as a spinster. "Back in the United States, being twenty-five, I mean twenty-four, is not considered too old to get married. Why I've seen women getting married in their thirties."

"Let that not happen to you!" Vera retorted. "Once you hit your thirties, it's harder to find Mr. Right!"

They slowly entered the house. It was dark inside.

Vera switched on the light. "We'll stop by the cemetery after church tomorrow. I must remember to take new candles for your father and grandparents."

"I do miss them," Cassiani said, feeling sad all of a sudden.

"So do I, but what can we do? Life has to go on for the rest of us left behind. At least where they are, they don't suffer or have any want."

Cassiani took her shoes off and rubbed her feet.

"Let me get that ointment," Vera said, hurriedly pulling on her apron and going into her bedroom.

A few minutes later, Cassiani's blistered foot was propped on the chair and slathered with the ointment. She watched as her mother bandaged it. "You would have made a good nurse," Cassiani said. "You have grandmother's healing touch."

Vera finished bandaging the foot. "Hmmm. Your father always used to tell me that," she said proudly. "Your grandmother Athena taught me all I know about herbs."

Cassiani bolted up, her foot forgotten. "Athena! I completely forgot to call her today. I was so busy, and tomorrow I'll be at Mrs. Lukas' house." She sank back down in the chair, feeling disappointed.

"That's all right, dear," Vera said, patting her on the back. "I'm sure whatever you need to tell her can wait. There's always Monday. You can call her then."

*   *   *   *

Later that evening, after resting and eating dinner, Cassiani practiced her music while her mother sang along. She tried to anticipate the songs that Manolis would pick tomorrow night. Her mother helped by offering some suggestions. Cassiani continued practicing until she felt comfortable with her playing. Afterwards, she and her mother sat on the back verandah, watching the stars shine like diamonds in the black sky.

"It was nice of Dr. Leo to agree to have you work as his aunt's personal nurse," Vera said. "Did you notice how he made it a point to invite you over tomorrow for a social visit?"

"Please don't make too much of it. He invited you also," Cassiani said. "I think he wants me to get to know his aunt a little better before I start working for her."

"Maybe you're right," Vera said, appearing thoughtful.

"By the way, I thought you mentioned earlier that you didn't think she was that ill. What made you change your mind and offer my services?" Cassiani asked.

"Sometimes, my dear girl, one has to do what is best for oneself," Vera said. "Now that I can't work, how would we manage with our bills? She needs a personal nurse, and we need the money. So now everyone is happy."

"I don't know how she is going to feel having me as her nurse."

"Don't worry. If she liked me all these years, she'll like you."

Cassiani disagreed silently. She and her mother were so different. Her mother was a pragmatic, extroverted, middle-aged woman who had raised a family of two girls, loved domestic work, and accommodated Mrs. Lukas' every whim. Cassiani was an introverted, college educated, single woman, who liked to read books and play the violin, and was probably too sensitive for Mrs. Lukas' biting words.

CHAPTER 11

Later that evening, Leo sat in the parlor conversing with his aunt. It appeared that she was in good form. She was sitting in her favorite high-back armchair, with its gold velvet fabric, appearing to enjoy his undivided attention. Their conversation flowed on a number of topics, from his trips overseas, to the latest news in politics, to the people on Kos Island. The sunset was evident through the glass doors that led out into the garden, giving the room a cozy, golden glow.

"Did I tell you that Dr. Vassilakis wanted to buy the pharmacy for his medical practice, but I told him it wasn't for sale?" Soula asked.

Leo's eyebrows went up. "Is that right?"

A smug smile hovered on Soula's lips. "Imagine that. After all these years, Socrates is interested in it." Her face became businesslike. "Leo, I think it wouldn't be a bad idea for the doctor to rent the upstairs, since neither you nor your father are using it."

Leo's aunt was not only known for her artistic bent, but for her business sense and helped rent the upstairs suite of the pharmacy in the past. But Leo knew that his father preferred doing things on his own. "I'll check first with Father and see what he wants to do with the upstairs."

"Why bother with your father? He would trust whatever you say. Socrates is coming here tomorrow to talk about my health, with Nina. You can talk to him then."

Now that the topic of health came up, Leo decided to tell her about hiring a personal nurse.

"You hired a *nurse?*" Soula asked, her normally guttural voice rose shakily, ending in a high pitch. Her unsteady hand leaned against the table, pulling her thin body up to its full four foot nine inch height. She stood there staring at her nephew straight in the eyes. "There is *nothing* wrong with me!" Signs of indignation were stamped all over her body; from her straight, rod-like back, to her withered, tanned arms folded tightly across her small chest.

"Aunt, it's all right. Please calm down," Leo said. He realized he touched a deep chord. By bringing in a nurse, he was declaring to her that she was ill and could not function independently. It was not something she was ready to face. To someone else it would have been a welcoming gesture, but to her it was humiliating. He stood up and touched her arm gently. "I'm doing this because I want to help you."

Soula's clouded eyes found Leo's warm, caring eyes; the hurt and indignation seemed to vanish as she gazed into his eyes. Her body relaxed and she sighed. "I'm already feeling better now that you are here," she muttered.

"Here, why don't you sit back down," Leo said, helping her into her chair.

"Whose idea was it anyway to get me a nurse?"

"I felt that you needed someone to take care of you. Since Mrs. Meletis cannot work for you at this time, she suggested Cassiani's services."

"Cassiani?" Soula's eyes flew open. She was thoughtful. "Come to think of it, Vera did tell me once that one of her daughters was studying to be a nurse."

"You did say nurses were hard to get. Didn't you?" Leo's eyes teased his aunt's.

"Yes, I did," Soula said, tapping her fingers nervously on the side of the chair. "But—"

"I want to make sure you are all right so you can visit us in the United States in the near future. It's not like you to skip your annual trip to America. What would we do without all those statues and vases you bring each year, if you were sick? The buyers depend on you."

"I did miss the trip this year," Soula said, "and I had picked out some nice vases to bring with me." Her face mellowed. "But it wasn't because I was sick. I mean, there were several reasons why I didn't come."

"Name one other reason," Leo said, teasingly.

"Well," Soula began. "For one, Nina Vassilakis returned this year from Paris and when she told me of the latest interior designs, I asked her to redecorate my house. She agreed, and it's taken longer than I expected to finish the project. She hasn't even begun on the upstairs apartment. Anyway, I couldn't just leave her in the middle of it, now could I?"

"That's not what I heard when you telephoned me a month ago," Leo said, crossing his arms. He was a little puzzled at his aunt's prattling explanation. "All I heard was that you weren't feeling well."

"Yes, at that time, I wasn't. For some reason I'm feeling a little better now that Nina's been coming, and now that you are here." Soula attempted a weak smile, patting him on the hand.

"Hmm. I'm beginning to understand." Leo stood up. "I feel like some coffee. Would you like some?"

"Thank you, dear. Coffee would do just fine."

Leo walked into the kitchen, feeling a little uncomfortable. There was something about his aunt's explanation why she did not come to America that did not ring true. He knew from his father's medical practice, that when people were ill, they weren't up to starting any new projects, like decorating a house. Their energies were spent trying to overcome the illness. On the other hand, he knew his aunt was an artist, and an eccentric one at that, and inclined to doing things that often didn't make sense. Was it possible that her "illness" was a psychological one, stemming from loneliness, or even depression? Maybe she felt that redecorating her house would help her more than by visiting America.

He returned with two cups of the hot brew. "Here you go." He handed her a cup, then took a sip of coffee. "How about a little music?"

"Ahh, music. You sure know how to push the right buttons," Soula said, cackling. "I've been too lazy lately to get up and do it myself. It's over there."

He looked through the records, then turned to her and said, "What do you say for some Strauss?"

"Suits me." A few minutes later, strains of a lilting Strauss waltz could be heard. "Good," she said, smiling. She took a sip of coffee.

Leo joined her. "So, dear Aunt," he began. "I still think you need a nurse, and Cassiani is as good a nurse as any. Besides, you said they are hard to come by here."

"I thought we were done with that topic!" Soula sputtered, appearing exasperated.

"I thought we were just getting started," Leo replied, chuckling at her expression. There was more resistance here than he imagined. "I'm doing this for your own good, you know."

"I can't picture Cassiani as a nurse." Soula stared into space as if she were thinking. She clasped her fingers tightly. "She's too clumsy. Did you see how she dropped that platter of food and got everything dirty? Why, my favorite tablecloth is ruined because of her."

Leo shook his head. He must have been outside looking for Nina when that happened. "I don't know how that has anything to do with whether she's a good nurse," he insisted. He knew how his materialist aunt could get irritable over the slightest mistake. She had a propensity for wanting everything perfect. "I hope you weren't too harsh on her. She was working quite hard today."

"I just told her to clean up the mess!"

Leo was silent, contemplating what he would say next. This was not going to be easy, and he needed a little time to regroup his thoughts. The Strauss waltz just finished and he arose to change the records. This time he chose a lively Brandenburg Concerto. *That's what I need, a change in tactics.*

Years of negotiating deals and working with difficult customers had taught him not to give up, but to try different tactics. He went to the sofa and sat down. "You know, I was quite shocked to see Mrs. Meletis today, after her recent heart attack. If I remember correctly, heart attack patients need bed rest for at least two weeks. I am convinced that she came because she needed the money, and furthermore…." Leo paused, trying to find the right words.

Soula cocked an eyebrow, as if she were interested. "Yes?"

Leo continued. "Even for Cassiani to clean your house—given that she is a nurse—this is something she doesn't normally do. Those are signs that they are in dire straits."

"If they needed the money, then why didn't Cassiani pick up the payment I left for her that day on the kitchen table?" Soula retorted, crossing her arms.

"Probably pride, or even embarrassment. Who knows," Leo said, shrugging his shoulders. "When I paid Cassiani yesterday morning, she did not resist."

"Hmmmff!" Soula mumbled. "What young woman could resist you?"

Leo laughed. "By the way, now that Mrs. Meletis will not be working, I was wondering how she'll manage without any income coming in." He paused, seeing the interest in his aunt's eyes. "Does Greece have a welfare system for those who do not work?"

"A welfare system? Do you really think she's that poor?" Soula stared at Leo. "Leo, I can't see beyond my nose! Vera kept thanking me for allowing her to help with the luncheon, the poor thing, but I was so busy. I forgot to pay her!"

"Don't worry. I took the liberty and paid her."

Soula was silent, picking nervously at her collar. "Oh, all right! If it's to help Vera pay her bills, I'll let Cassiani be my nurse!" she grumbled.

Leo smiled. *She does have redeeming qualities.* "Good. Cassiani begins officially on Monday. Oh, and I've invited her to come by tomorrow, to spend a little time with you."

"I don't see why," Soula said, appearing perplexed. "I'll have Nina and her father over, and you, of course. I don't need her company."

Leo's eyebrows went up. His aunt's response puzzled him. "She also needs to feel comfortable with you," he explained. "What better way than in a social setting?"

"It looks as if you've thought of everything," Soula said dryly.

"Dealing with people is part of my job description," Leo said, smiling. "I was hoping to take a break from all of that, by coming here, but it looks as if I am needed here too."

"I'm glad you came. At least I'll get to see you for a few weeks."

Leo sucked in his breath. *I forgot to tell her about my trip.* "There's been a recent change in my plans." He noticed the puzzled look on her face. "I need to be in Athens on Monday for an important business deal."

"Monday? You just got here!"

Leo explained the situation to her. "I'll try and return as soon as I can."

"In that case, be sure to stay in my apartment. You remember where it is." She rambled off the address.

Although it had been fourteen years ago when he stayed in her apartment in Athens, he still remembered it clearly. It was a four-story building with two apartments on each floor, located near Panepistimiou. "Yes, I have it written down in my phone book."

"You remember Mrs. Galatsis, my rental manager; she is still on the first floor. She has the key to the apartment. Don't forget to tell her you're my nephew."

Leo arose and kissed her lightly on the forehead. "You know that you're my favorite aunt."

Soula chuckled, appearing pleased. "Yes, that's because I'm your only aunt."

*   *   *   *

Later that evening Leo telephoned his parents. They were staying in temporary housing situated in a rural area of the Dominican Republic. He tried several times before he reached them. His father picked up the telephone. They exchanged greetings.

"How are things there with your aunt? Is everything all right?" George asked.

"She's still her gutsy self, although she seems a little pale at times and is doing less around the house. The doctor was talking about running some tests on her. Anyway, I hired a personal nurse to watch her; Cassiani Meletis is her name."

"Cassiani. That's an interesting name," George said. "How did you find her?"

Leo explained the situation to his father. "She studied nursing in Cleveland," he finished.

"I did my internship at the Cleveland Clinic, before working at the hospital in Parma. That's where I met your mother." George paused. "I still keep in contact with my old colleagues there, in case this Cassiani ever needs anything."

Leo was surprised at his father's offer. "Thanks. I'll keep that in mind. By the way, Aunt Soula gave me a lot of resistance when she learned about Cassiani being her nurse. I had to work twice as hard to convince her to go along with the idea."

His father's hearty laugh made Leo smile. "Your mother should hear this. I think your aunt has an aversion to nurses. Period."

His father's disclosing remark surprised Leo. Maybe there was some truth in what he said. "I also think part of her problem is psychological. I had a talk with her today." He told him about the doctor's daughter, Nina Vassilakis, and the reasons why his aunt did not come to America. "She felt she could not leave her in the middle of the project."

"So, Socrates Vassilakis married after all!" George said. "When we lived in Kos, he was still a bachelor at the age of thirty-eight. We thought he'd never marry."

Leo was surprised to learn that about Dr. Vassilakis. "I almost forgot to tell you." He told his father about the doctor's interest in the pharmacy and renting the upstairs.

"Why don't you take care of it, now that you're there? I trust your judgement," George said. He paused. "So, Socrates has a daughter. Very interesting."

His father's open-ended comment begged for an explanation. "She is blonde, single, and specializes in interior decorating, and she looks nothing like Socrates."

George laughed. "Good! Soula is not well enough to travel, but it appears she is well enough for decorating, and I wouldn't be surprised … in matchmaking. That's Soula for you."

Leo decided to change the subject. "How is Mother?"

"She's fine. Keeps me busy. Colleen, come to the telephone. It's Leo."

"Happy name day, dear. We miss you," Colleen said.

Her soft voice was soothing to Leo's ears. He told her about the name day party that Aunt Soula gave for him. His mother was pleasantly surprised.

"Your father wants to say something," Colleen said.

"I heard your mother wishing you a happy name day," George said. "Sorry we forgot about it, what with so many things to do. *Chronia Polla kai na ta ekatostisis.*"

Leo thanked him for the name day wishes, then told him about his business trip. "I feel confident that with Cassiani by her side, Aunt Soula will be fine."

"By the way, we'll be returning to Washington in two weeks. The building of the new Greek church has been delayed," George said.

"I'll probably see you then."

"Have a safe trip," said George. "Give our love to your aunt. Oh, and regards to Socrates and his family."

The distant sound of his father's chuckle could be heard as Leo hung up the receiver.

CHAPTER 12

Sunday

Vera rapped on the bedroom door. "Cassiani!" she sang out, then swooped into the room, carrying the incense burner. She made the sign of the cross with the burner, whisking the fragrant smoke around her. "Time to get up! We're going to church. Service will start soon!"

When her mother spoke in that tone, Cassiani knew it was best to listen. The Sunday ritual had begun. Like clockwork, she arose and went through the routine. This was one time she was thankful that her mother liked to hoard things. The clothes she left behind years ago were still in the closet. When she opened the closet door, a distinct smell of mothballs emanated from the closet. She sniffed the clothes in dismay; they all smelled like mothballs.

Not having any other choice, she dressed into her favorite outfit, a white dress with a small pink jacket, hoping that the odor would eventually go away. The strong smell hung around her as she washed her face in the basin. Cassiani met her mother in the kitchen.

Vera was dressed in black; a sign she was still in mourning for Grandmother Athena. Her hair was pulled neatly back this time, and not a single silvery strand was loose. "You look lovely with your hair down, but that jacket seems a little tight on you. They don't wear that style anymore," Vera said, shaking her head.

"I rushed to get here and didn't bring any Sunday dresses with me," Cassiani explained. "Besides, I like this dress, even with its smell."

"Smell?" Vera said, coming to her and sniffing. "Oh, that. It helps keep the moths away. It'll go away in time." She went into the bedroom and returned with a bottle of cheap perfume. She sprayed the perfume all over Cassiani. "This will get rid of it. You're twenty-five now. How are you going to find anyone if you don't dress up like all the other girls?"

"I'm not looking for *anyone*," Cassiani said, crossing her arms.

Vera continued, ignoring Cassiani's remark. "Look at your sister, Athena. She liked to dress up and she was married when she was twenty, like me. There's a nice beige dress in your closet that was hers. It's still in fashion. Why don't you try that one on?"

Cassiani pressed her lips together. "This dress is the last birthday present Father bought me before he passed away, and I'm wearing it."

*   *   *   *

The fragrant scent of incense greeted Cassiani and her mother as they entered the Greek Orthodox church. Orthros had already begun. Cassiani followed in her mother's footsteps, first lighting her candle and placing it in the sandbox that held several lit candles. She then made the sign of the cross and went to venerate the icons that were stationed there. Other villagers that filtered into the church greeted them with solemn nods, then went through the same candle-lighting ritual.

As Cassiani and her mother walked to a pew next to the wall, she noticed how several heads turned as they passed by. She realized that the perfume her mother had sprayed on her had mixed with the mothball smell and a new smell was emanating from her. It was quite rancid.

It was customary for the elderly to have priority in the seating. Cassiani stood while her mother sat. They received nods and smiles from the women near them. The men were segregated from the women and children. By the time the Divine Liturgy started, the church had filled up. The smell of incense and the droning sound of the two chanters lulled Cassiani into a meditative state. It was peaceful and relaxing, as she quietly kneeled and prayed.

When the liturgy ended, she waited in line to take the proffered holy bread. Her eyes combed the church, looking for a familiar face. It had been years since she was last here. Stella Spanos, a friend of her mother, waved to them from the back of the church. Cassiani smiled back. Behind Stella she caught a glimpse of a tall man. *Could it be Leo?* Other people got in the way, obscuring her view. She focused on her task before her, kissing the priest's hand and taking the *antithoro*.

They walked outside into the courtyard. Groups of people decked in their Sunday clothes were standing outside talking. Stella and Panos Spanos waved to them, coming to greet them. Panos Spanos was short and stocky with straight brown hair and a pleasant smile that never wavered. He resembled his wife so much that the first time Cassiani saw them years ago, she thought they were brother and sister. Today, they were both dressed handsomely in their matching beige-colored Sunday suits.

"Mrs. Lukas said she needed someone to cook for her now that I'm no longer there. I mentioned your name," Vera told her old friend. "Has she talked to you about it?"

"Yes, she did." Stella waved her hand in front of her face as if she had just smelled something rotten. "Thank you for recommending me. I'll begin tomorrow. She asked me to cook for her in the mornings."

"My Stella is the best cook!" Panos announced proudly. He sniffed, then made a face and pulled out a handkerchief from his pocket and placed it on his nose. "There's some kind of smell here. I don't know where it's coming from." He looked around him.

Cassiani cringed when she heard it. She knew it was the mothball and perfume combination from her dress. She was thankful that her mother did not offer any explanation, but instead continued chatting with Stella as if she didn't hear Panos.

"Oh dear, we must be going. The children are expecting us," Stella said, waving at her nose and glancing at her watch. "You know how it is, with our new grandson."

"He's five weeks old and we can't get enough of him," Panos finished.

The couple hurried away.

*   *   *   *

As soon as Cassiani and her mother were alone, she asked her not to put mothballs in her closet again. "All the dresses smell like mothballs."

"I don't smell anything," Vera said absentmindedly. When they entered the house, she hastened to the oven and pulled out several glasses filled to the brim with creamy yogurt. "I forgot to take them out this morning." She dipped a spoon into the thick yogurt and tasted it. "Good. It turned out nice, with just the right tartness. Come and have some."

After finishing her yogurt, Cassiani went to her bedroom to change. She was feeling a little nervous going to Mrs. Lukas' house for a social visit. What would she say to her? A few minutes later, she heard her mother conversing with someone. It sounded like Mrs. Kalotsis.

"I'm not going today, but Cassiani is going. Yes, around noon. She can take it to them."

Her mother's voice dropped to a whisper and Cassiani couldn't hear anything else. She brushed her long, wavy hair, twisting and wrapping it up into a bun at the nape of her neck. She heard her mother's bedroom door close, followed by operatic singing. Cassiani smiled. Her mother always sang while changing her clothes.

The white button-down silk blouse and straight black skirt were pulled out of the luggage. She sniffed them. There was no smell here. This was one time she was thankful that the clothes she brought with her from America were still left in the luggage because they didn't fit in the overstuffed, mothball-ridden closet. Her nylons were left on and her scuffed walking shoes were buffed.

A half-hour later, Cassiani's breathing was brisk and her gait equally fast as she walked the stone pathway to Mrs. Lukas' house. Her watch showed twelve o'clock. She admitted that she did not enjoy the idea of spending time with Mrs. Lukas, let alone taking care of her. "Dear Lord, help me cope with this woman," she prayed aloud.

Leo answered the door. He was freshly shaved, with his hair combed back, and he was dressed in a light blue suit. He looked as if he were dressed for church. "Good morning, Leo."

"Cassiani, welcome," he said, grinning. "I saw you in church this morning, but you left before I could greet you."

So Leo had been at the church after all. "It was quite crowded today," Cassiani replied.

"I have good news for you," Leo continued. "I've already talked to my aunt about you. She has agreed for you to be her nurse."

Cassiani thanked him. They walked slowly down the hallway towards the parlor. He moved rhythmically with her; his stride was sure and steady as he talked.

"I don't know how long she'll need you. It all depends on what the doctor says, but for now, you can work Monday through Saturday," Leo said.

Cassiani nodded. "What time would you like for me to be here?"

"She's a late riser, so it's best to come around ten and leave when she naps in the afternoon." He looked at her. "Probably around three or four. If you feel she needs more care, you can work out the times with her. By the way, how long can you stay today?"

Cassiani noticed his business-like tone, as if he were talking to an employee. *I am an employee. But he invited me for a social.* "I'll be able to stay until three."

"Good. I will pay you weekly for your services, of course. Let's say, three American dollars per hour. Is that suitable?"

Cassiani nodded. Although it was less than what she made in the United States, she knew that on the island, this was considered a generous amount. *That would really help.* "I do think she first needs a doctor's diagnosis. I cannot prescribe any medication on my own."

"Dr. Vassilakis will be stopping by this afternoon. Hopefully you'll still be here to talk to him," Leo replied. They reached the parlor. "Please, why don't you go in. I'll be back shortly." He headed towards the direction of the stairs.

Cassiani smelled the mint tea as soon as she entered the parlor. Soula Lukas sat in an armchair next to a small round table, sipping her tea. She was dressed all in blue, from her short-sleeved blouse to her long blue skirt. Cassiani greeted her.

"Cassiani," said Soula, putting her cup down. It rattled slightly as it settled in the saucer. "What brings you here?"

Cassiani's eyebrows rose. Mrs. Lukas' comment took her by surprise. *Remember, she has a tendency to forget.* "Leo invited me to spend a little time with you," she said, "now that I'll be your nurse."

"Oh, yes. I forgot," Soula said, knitting her brows together. "Leo thinks I need a nurse." She squinted at her. "Are you really a nurse or a nurse's assistant?"

Cassiani winced, trying hard not to be affected by Mrs. Lukas' doubtful voice. She confirmed her initial assessment that Mrs. Lukas was not going to be an easy person to work for. She explained her nursing degree and the work she did at the hospital.

"Ahh." Soula appeared thoughtful as she gazed at her.

Cassiani was about to put her handbag down when she remembered the cheese and yogurt. She pulled out the bowl of yogurt and loaf of cheese and showed them to Soula. "The yogurt is from my mother and the *mizithra* is from Mrs. Kalotsis."

"Very good. Please take them in the kitchen. Put some yogurt in a small cup and slice some cheese up for me with some toast. I haven't eaten anything yet except for this tea." Soula gestured towards the door, shooing her away.

CHAPTER 13

Cassiani cut the white cheese, making distinct whacks each time the knife hit the plate. *I am a nurse and this is not what Leo invited me for.* She found some biscuits in the bread bin, but no fresh bread to toast. *The paximadia will just have to do.* They were plunked down on the plate with the cheese. She tried to justify the reason why Mrs. Lukas would ask her to do this. Was it because she wasn't feeling well enough to do it herself and had no one else to cook for her? Was it because she did not like her?

"Thank you for helping my aunt," Leo said.

Cassiani swung around when she heard his voice, caught off guard. Leo was standing at the door, dressed in a white shirt and beige pants. She was surprised that she hadn't heard his footsteps. His smile was gone and a perplexed look shadowed his face.

Leo leaned against the frame of the door, crossing his arms. "If that's for my aunt, she typically gets her own food."

Here was her opportunity to speak, to say how she felt about the way she was bossed around, but the words could not come out. She turned her back to him, resuming her task in stoic silence.

"Is everything all right?" he asked softly.

She looked down, blushing. Her voice wavered, "She needed something to eat and I'm just helping out."

"Come, you can tell me," he persisted.

This time when she looked up at him, her eyes were full of tears. Like a dam that overflowed, she could no longer hold her emotions at bay. "Did you ever have the feeling that you weren't wanted, and no matter what you did to please the other person, it wasn't appreciated? I was invited here for a social, and, and ..." She hiccuped, pulled a tissue from her pocket and wiped the tears from her eyes. She hiccuped again, then blew her nose. *How embarrassing for him to see this outburst! You're acting like a child, feeling sorry for yourself!*

"I'm glad you told me." He placed a hand on her shoulder. "To be misunderstood and unappreciated is an unfortunate thing, and sometimes one can do nothing about it." He turned her around to face him. He gazed intently into her tear-ridden eyes, then slowly lowered his face towards hers. "And sometimes one can," he whispered.

Cassiani instinctively stiffened, holding her breath, shutting her eyes. *What is he doing?* It was finished just as quickly as it began ... a feathery light kiss on her left cheek.

"Please don't cry. Everything will be all right." His husky voice was filled with compassion.

Cassiani opened her eyes. Confusion set in, her crying forgotten. She felt warm and tingly all over and very much aware of the closeness of his body. His beautiful eyes tenderly gazed into hers. "What was that kiss for?" she whispered.

"I think you needed it. Besides, it made you stop crying, didn't it?"

She looked down, unsure of her feelings. Why did she feel disappointed in his answer? Did she expect a declaration of love?

"A kiss on the cheek is a customary sign of greeting between friends, isn't it? We are friends now, you and I."

She nodded slowly, as he moved away. He had been so close, so intimate, so quickly. Too quickly. Her hands shook as she spooned yogurt into a small cup, trying to keep busy, trying to behave as if this act of friendship was normal. *But it didn't feel normal.*

Leo took the pot of coffee and poured the hot brew into a cup. "I just made this a few minutes ago," he said casually. He tasted it. "Good. Not too strong." He found a spoon in the drawer and spooned some sugar into the cup. "My aunt preferred drinking tea today. There's plenty left. Would you like some?"

"No, thank you." Cassiani watched silently as he stirred the coffee. She appreciated his offer. She was about to place the yogurt and cheese in the refrigerator, when she remembered her manners. "I brought some yogurt that my mother made. Would you like some?

"Thank you. I'll try some later," Leo said. He took the plate and cup. "I'll take these to my aunt."

When they entered the parlor, Cassiani was greeted by a snoring sound. Soula's head was buried in her chest; she was obviously dozing. Cassiani was humbled by the image before her—of an old woman trying to stay awake. In that moment, Mrs. Lukas' vulnerability dissolved the invincible façade she evoked in Cassiani's memory, of a larger-than-life ogre of a woman who took away their pharmacy seven years ago.

The sunlight that streamed into the room highlighted Leo's features as he placed the cup of yogurt and the plate down. He strode purposefully towards a large collection of records that sat near a record player. With slow and leisurely movements, he placed a few records into the record player. He turned and looked at Cassiani. "A little music to stir the soul."

Soft strains from a section of the Brahms fourth symphony filled the room. Just the sound of the stringed instruments made Cassiani relax a little bit. She sat in the armchair next to the sofa, her mind traveling miles away to the orchestra in Cleveland. *We played that piece last year.*

Soula was awakened by the music. "Yes, it was getting a bit dull in here."

"Did you know that Cassiani plays the violin?" Leo asked, settling into the sofa.

Cassiani's eyes flew open. She was surprised to hear Leo declare something she hadn't told him. How did he find out about her playing?

"Cassiani?" asked Soula, staring at her. "I guess I shouldn't be that surprised. Your mother used to tell me about your father's playing; she also sings quite well, I might add."

"Manolis told me Cassiani played violin ever since she was a young girl," he added, his eyes twinkling. "Maybe she could play for you. I hear that music is therapeutic. Am I right, Cassiani?"

Cassiani nodded shyly.

Soula eyed the yogurt and nodded with satisfaction. She scooped a spoonful into her mouth. "Leo, aren't you going to join me?"

"I think I'll pass. The food I ate yesterday was enough to last until supper," Leo replied, touching his stomach.

Cassiani's ears picked up the new tune that was playing. "Mozart's fortieth symphony. That's one of my favorites." She hadn't realized that she spoke aloud until Mrs. Lukas responded.

"You *do* know your music. I like that one also," Soula said, nodding appreciatively. "There's one thing I admire, and that is the fine arts. I love art—any type of art—sculpture, painting, music." She lifted her hands and spread out her fingers. "See these hands? My piano teacher used to say they were just the right size for playing the piano. Now my fingers are stiff and full of arthritis."

Soula talked about her youth and how her family originated from humble beginnings, but her father worked hard and they became so wealthy that she and her younger brother never wanted for anything. She studied piano with the finest teachers, traveled all over the world, and studied art history in an elite college in Paris. "With an emphasis on Greek art, of course," Soula finished, her one eyebrow cocked. She paused to catch her breath.

Cassiani realized that Soula Lukas liked being the center of attention. She was a natural performer, and she was doing it now in her own eclectic way. "Mrs. Lukas, don't forget to eat your food," Cassiani reminded her. She watched her lift her hand, holding the biscuit.

"See how my fingers curl up like that? It's from the arthritis," Soula said.

Leo smiled. "My aunt plays piano excellently, even if she says she has arthritis."

"Yes, the piano is back in Athens. I do miss it." Soula dipped the biscuit into the coffee.

Leo glanced at his watch. "I need to be down at Kos Town to meet with Nickos. Cassiani said she will be here for a few hours, so you won't be alone." He kissed his aunt lightly on the cheek, then flashed a smile at Cassiani before leaving.

"Don't forget. Dr. Vassilakis and Nina are coming at two," Soula said.

CHAPTER 14

———————— ⸙ ————————

Cassiani gazed out the parlor window while soft strains of classical music filled the room. She could never have imagined that she would be taking care of Mrs. Lukas as well as her mother, or that she'd be meeting someone like Leonidas Regas. Then she remembered his kiss earlier today. He said that they were friends, but her female intuition had told her it was something deeper, something more than a friendship. Cassiani glanced back at Mrs. Lukas; she was snoring and her head lowered, signaling she was still asleep.

Leo was a nice contrast to his aunt; Cassiani felt comfortable with him. After he left, Mrs. Lukas fell asleep, leaving Cassiani alone. Cassiani felt like a fish out of water. *What am I going to do now?* A loud snore startled her out of her reverie. She turned and looked at Mrs. Lukas, trying not to giggle.

"What?" Soula sputtered, aroused by her snoring. She gazed down at her plate.

"Mrs. Lukas, how many hours do you sleep each night?"

Soula yawned. "If I get four hours of sleep, I'm lucky."

"It seems that you catch up on your sleep during the day."

"I *barely* get enough sleep," Soula said, sounding offended. "By the way, do you have a shorter name? Maybe Cassie or something?"

"They call me Candy in America," Cassiani said.

"Candy?" Soula asked, then tittered. "I'll stay with Cassie."

Cassiani needed to find a common element, something Mrs. Lukas liked. "I was looking at the garden," she said, her voice a little shaky. "It's very nice. Do you take walks outside?"

"Not by myself. I'm afraid of falling. I fell once, about a month ago. Luckily your mother caught me. Now that you're here, I might try; although you don't look too strong. We might fall together."

"Don't worry about that! I've been told by several patients that I'm quite strong," said Cassiani, laughing. "Shall we go outside for a stroll then?"

Soula smiled. "I like the garden." She slowly arose, gesturing to Cassiani. "We'll go this way."

They walked outside to the verandah. Cassiani could see her mother's handiwork in the flowerbeds and the numerous rose bushes. It was a sizeable garden, with pebbled pathways, several gardenia bushes, a couple of lemon trees, a water fountain in the center, and a bench nearby. "This is a very nice garden," she said.

"Your mother took care of the garden for me," Soula said proudly. She gazed around her. "Now I have to find someone else to do it for me."

They continued their stroll, passing the fountain. To her left, Cassiani could see Tigaki beach below and the stretch of blue water beyond.

"Up ahead is another bench. We can sit there." Soula pointed towards the line of trees that seemed to border the perimeter. Underneath the sprawling shade of a large tree sat a bench.

Cassiani's curiosity made her ask, "Do you have family in America?"

"My brother George, Leo's father, lives in Washington, D.C. with his wife," Soula said. "But I haven't seen them in years."

They reached the bench; a simple sheet of marble rested on top of two cement legs. Clay pots filled with red and pink geraniums were positioned on each side of it.

"Does Leo live in Washington with his parents?"

Soula appeared exasperated. "My dear, Leo lives in New York, where his job is." She planted herself down on the bench.

Cassiani joined her. "My mother told me you go to Athens in January?"

"Yes. It's too cold for me to stay here, so I go for a month, then visit Leo in February for a couple of weeks. I'm lucky if I see him every day. Leo's a wanderer. He travels all over the world. Can't sit still. Just like his grandfather." She waved her arm in the air with a flourish.

Cassiani was silent, digesting the information.

"I've been trying to marry Leo off for years, but he's slippery as an eel." Soula cackled. "But this time, I think he found his match with Nina Vassilakis."

Cassiani didn't respond to Mrs. Lukas' confiding remark, but gazed ahead, feeling miserable. Yesterday afternoon Leo and Nina were strolling in this very same garden together. *Maybe there is some truth in what Mrs. Lukas just said.*

"They do make such a handsome couple," Soula said, appearing smug. "I wouldn't be surprised if we'll be hearing wedding bells soon."

*   *   *   *

They would have stayed longer in the garden but Soula complained of being bitten by mosquitoes. She clutched Cassiani's arm as they inched their way back to the house. "I feel one here, underneath my arm." She lifted her right arm and slapped it. "Did I get it?"

Cassiani noticed purplish bruises underneath Mrs. Lukas' right arm. "Mrs. Lukas, did you bump your arms? There are some bruises there."

"Probably from those hungry, bloodsucking mosquitoes," grumbled Soula, smacking her arm. "I'll get you yet!"

They entered the parlor and Mrs. Lukas settled herself back into her favorite armchair.

"*Yiasas!*" Nina called out.

Cassiani tensed when she saw her. Nina wore a white mini skirt and black, sleeveless blouse with a low neckline. Her pearl-clustered earrings hung like large globes from her ears and jingled as she walked.

Nina went and kissed Mrs. Lukas on the cheek. "The door was open." She sat down next to Soula. "Father's on his way."

Just then the doctor entered the room. The rank smell of cigar emanated from his chunky body as he greeted Soula. He nodded politely to Cassiani. "Cassiani is your name. Am I right?"

"Cassie is Vera's daughter. You remember her; she served the lunch yesterday. Now Leo has hired her to be my nurse," Soula explained.

Dr. Vassilakis' eyebrows went up. He appeared surprised. "I didn't know you were a nurse. Where did you study? Athens?"

Cassiani told him.

"I visited Cleveland many years ago for a medical conference. I remember watching a Doris Day movie then. She had a lovely voice." There was a gleam in his eyes.

Cassiani nodded. "I also enjoyed her singing, but my favorite actress is Aliki Vouyouklaki. She has a lovelier voice."

Soula turned and patted Nina's hand. "Nina, dear, why don't we go over the decorating ideas?" They began to chat softly.

Dr. Vassilakis lit a cigar and began puffing on it, asking Cassiani questions about her nursing school in Cleveland. Cassiani coughed nervously as she answered. They continued for a few minutes before she rasped, "I'm sorry, the smoke gets into my throat."

He chuckled, waving the cigar around. "I'll go outside. My wife says it's the only place I should be when I'm smoking cigars."

"Use that door," said Soula, pointing to the French glass door.

He excused himself and left.

Cassiani stood there, unsure of what to do. Should she sit down and join in the conversation? Neither of the women looked her way. As if reading her mind, Soula turned and stared at her. Cassiani felt hopeful. *Maybe she'll ask me to sit down and join them.*

"Cassie, go and prepare some coffee and refreshments for our guests," Soula said. "There are *koulourakia* and *finikia* in the refrigerator. Add an extra plate and cup for Leo. We can have them in the dining room."

Cassiani felt a lump form in her throat. She hurried out the door. *What have I gotten myself into?* Fifteen minutes later, with shaky voice, she announced to Mrs. Lukas that the refreshments were ready.

Soula walked with Nina to the dining room. "Please tell the doctor we'll be in the dining room. He might want to join us," Soula told Cassiani.

Dr. Vassilakis sat on the bench puffing away on his cigar. As soon as he saw Cassiani, he snuffed the cigar. She told him about the refreshments in the dining room. Cassiani walked with him towards the dining room. "I also wanted to let you know that I saw a few bruises on Mrs. Lukas' arm and she seems a little pale and tired. She might need to be tested for anemia."

"Hmm," Dr. Vassilakis said. "I'll have a talk with her." He entered the dining room and sat down at the table. "Mrs. Lukas, Cassiani told me that you have some bruises on your arm. We will need to run some tests on you to find out what is causing them."

Soula appeared doubtful. "Why go through all the trouble to be tested just for a few bruises?" She swiped at something in the air, then slapped her arm. "I may have bumped myself for all I know. Why make a big case out of something so small?"

"You cannot put your head in the sand like an ostrich and expect the problem to go away, because it *won't*. You've also complained of fatigue and weakness. These symptoms might be caused by an underlying disease, like anemia; if it is left untreated, who knows what this may lead to?" Dr. Vassilakis' bushy eyebrows knitted together. "You *do* want me to help you, don't you?"

Soula's voice wavered as she said, "When do you want to see me?"

"Have your nephew bring you first thing tomorrow morning to the hospital to get blood tests done. Don't eat anything after midnight tonight."

"He can't bring me. He's leaving for Athens tomorrow morning for a business deal," Soula announced almost too triumphantly. "He'll be gone for a few days."

"No need to wait on him. Nina can take you tomorrow," Dr. Vassilakis said.

Cassiani glanced at her watch; it was just before three o'clock. *I need to get ready for the engagement party.* "I need to be going," Cassiani said to Mrs. Lukas. "What time should I come tomorrow?"

"Nina should have her back by noon," Dr. Vassilakis said, nodding his head as if dismissing Cassiani.

CHAPTER 15

Cassiani walked down the sunlit road away from Mrs. Lukas' house. Although her gait was brisk, there was a slight limp as she favored the foot with the blister. It was still a little sore. She was glad to be out of the house and eagerly looking forward to the engagement party tonight.

The sound of tires and the whir of a motor interrupted her thoughts. A car was turning the bend quickly. She skipped to the side of the road, her heart beating fast. The car came to a halt. It was Leo.

"Cassiani!" Leo exclaimed. "Are you leaving so soon?"

"I needed to leave. Besides, Dr. Vassilakis and Nina are there." She paused, trying to find the proper words. "Your aunt is in good hands."

"You don't sound very convincing."

Cassiani's stomach fluttered and her knees felt weak. Could he read her that well?

Leo got out of the car and took her hand, his eyes twinkling. "Come on, I can tell you have something to say. Remember our pact of friendship?"

Cassiani's heart fluttered. *There he went again, saying we were friends and making it difficult for me to believe it.* He stood too close, making her feel warm all over. The sun's rays bounced off his golden locks, displaying a golden radiance about him. She blinked, trying not to be lured by the irresistible image. "I found purplish bruises underneath your aunt's arms. Dr. Vassilakis and I think she might have anemia."

Leo was silent. "How did she react to the news?"

"I think she's uncomfortable with the whole thing." Cassiani told him about the tests that were scheduled for the next morning. "Dr. Vassilakis said that Nina could take her, since you have a business trip to make. I plan to be at the house tomorrow by the time she returns."

"Good."

"Well, I must be going." Cassiani began to walk away, mindful of the blister on her foot and his accompanying stare. She heard the car door slam and the revving of the engine.

"Would you like a ride to your house?"

Cassiani turned. Leo was driving in reverse, following her with the car. She suppressed a smile. "Thank you, but your aunt, and the others are expecting you."

"Come. I'll take you," Leo said whimsically. "I saw the way you were limping."

Before Cassiani could respond, he had opened the passenger door for her. She eased herself thankfully into the car. "It's just a small blister."

"Those are the ones that are the most painful." Leo slowly turned around and went down the hill.

Cassiani gave him the directions to their house. She told him about her childhood, her father's death, and how they moved into her grandmother's house a few months before she left for America. "It's nice there, but can be quite rustic at times."

"That must have been quite a change for you, in more ways than one," Leo admitted.

Cassiani was quiet as the memories of that difficult transition came flooding back. Up ahead was the intersection. "Oh, turn right there." Moments later, they reached the house.

"This is quite a pastoral setting," Leo said, stopping in front of the gate. "This whole area feels like that, doesn't it? Peaceful and restful. I quite enjoy it."

Cassiani nodded, not knowing what to say. Although there was some truth in what Leo said, after her father died and they moved to this place, she had felt it too constrictive, too depressing. When her sister offered for her to go to America, she had been eager to accept.

"I hope to be back Tuesday afternoon." Leo smiled. "Do you have a telephone number in case I need to get a hold of you?"

"No. We don't have a telephone." Cassiani got out of the car. She noticed Leo's thoughtful look. "Thank you for the ride."

"If we didn't have company, I would have stopped in to say hello to your mother." Leo waved to her as he turned the car around and drove away.

*   *   *   *

Cassiani entered the house, humming, and thinking about Leo's departing words. What would she have done if he had stopped in for a visit? Just the thought of it made her feel giddy and happy. "Mother!" she called out. Her mother wasn't anywhere to be found. She guessed that she was next door at their neighbor's house.

After changing into more casual clothes, Cassiani searched in the closet for a dress to wear to the engagement party. She stopped midway when the strong odor of mothballs assailed her nose. She sighed, resigned to the fact that she was not going to get any rest today.

After she threw the mothballs into the garbage, she chose a few dresses from the closet. She washed the clothes in soapy well water, thinking about Leo and the ride back home. A yearning formed, deep inside her heart. She paused, feeling the longing embrace her; she wanted to be held and touched, to feel loved. Whatever negative thing happened with Mrs. Lukas was replaced with Leo's image. Cassiani resumed her task. After several minutes, she dumped the dirty wash water, then rinsed the clothes with fresh well water. It was four thirty when she finished hanging the last dress on the clothesline.

Without stopping to rest, Cassiani pulled out the violin from its case and began to practice her music. She was intent on giving a good performance at her friend's engagement party.

Several minutes later Vera entered the kitchen, short of breath. "I was next door with Mrs. Kalotsis, enjoying some … tea, when Mrs. Lukoumis came over. She talked and talked, and before I knew it the time passed so quickly," Vera said, fanning herself. "When I heard you playing, I rushed over here."

"Let me check your heart." Cassiani took her mother's vital signs. "Everything is a little elevated. I think you should get some rest."

"I do feel a little tired," Vera said, yawning. Her fingers pulled stray strands of hair from her face. "I didn't sleep well last night. I'm going to take a nap."

"Should I stay with you? Do you think you'll be all right?"

"No, no. You be a good girl and go. They are counting on you. Dress nicely, especially since you'll be playing with Manolis. What about that nice beige dress?"

Cassiani sighed. She could no longer ignore the fact that lately her mother made it a point to tell her how to dress. "This is Mary's party, not mine. The last thing I want to do is to take the spotlight away from her."

"Yes, you are right, but don't go looking like a mop either. The people they'll invite there will all be dressed nicely." Vera pulled out an envelope from her pocket and opened it, counting the money. "The bus doesn't run this late, so you'll have to walk down to the village to catch a taxi. Here is some money for the taxi."

Cassiani thanked her.

"This money came at a good time," Vera said, putting the remaining bills back into her pocket. "Oh, and don't forget to take the gift. It's wrapped in white tissue paper, sitting on the living room sofa."

"What is it?" Cassiani asked, her curiosity piqued.

"Something I made; a white linen tablecloth with a border of roses. It also has matching napkins, just like the ones I made for Mrs. Lukas."

Cassiani smiled. "You always liked to cross-stitch."

"It was intended for your dowry. Now I'll have to start another one. Took me almost a year to do it. I don't anticipate you'll be marrying soon anyway."

Cassiani ignored the challenging comment as she went outside to check on the dresses; most of them were still damp. To her relief, an old blue cotton dress had dried and there was no lingering smell on it. After ironing the dress, she put it on and gazed into the mirror. It had a square open collar, with short sleeves and an accompanying sash that she tied around her small waist. Although the blue had faded a bit from several washings, she felt that it was appropriate for the occasion. *You mustn't be better dressed than the bride-to-be is.*

Cassiani rummaged inside the wooden box that held her old trinkets and found her gold cross with the necklace. The original gold chain necklace was broken and had been replaced by imitation gold. Constant wear had tarnished the necklace and Cassiani stopped wearing it for fear that it would break and she would lose her cross. She fastened it around her neck. For some reason she wanted to wear it today.

Knowing that she'd probably be standing on her feet for a long time, she slipped on her old, loose sandals. She expertly twisted her mane of hair and pulled it to the back, then whisked it into a bun at the nape of her neck. A few hairpins were inserted just to be sure nothing got loose.

A few minutes later, she passed by her mother's bedroom and noticed the door was shut. She was probably asleep. Cassiani grabbed the small gift from the sofa and left for the party. She couldn't shake off the feeling that the tablecloth had been intended for her own wedding someday.

*   *   *   *

The ride to Kos Town was uneventful and it gave Cassiani a chance to relax. The taxi passed through a stretch of flat road lined with scenic views of blue water and sandy beaches to her left, and small shops and whitewashed houses scattered here and there on either side. The tourists were everywhere, with their loose, colorful attire, and fair looks, toting cameras and bags, walking or biking. She compared her life with theirs. So many people from other countries came to visit this island, while natives like her, moved elsewhere. Were they here to capture a glimpse of magic, or to escape from their lives for a few festive days? Were they here to dance to the lively music and taste a part of Greece and its culture? Or were they here to find love?

A feeling of excitement enveloped her once she saw the Knights' Castle in the distance. Its dignified stance, hundreds of years old, marked their arrival to Kos Town. The Castle was still in good condition, built during the 1400s by the Knights of St. John in order to protect Kos Island.

They turned left on Ethnikis Antistasseos road. Happy memories of her childhood flooded her thoughts; the walks to the harbor, the games she played with her sister and Mary, and the times she attended her father's musical events. She thought about Mary and her engagement. She was happy for her; she had found love. Now that Cassiani had her mother's ill health to contend with and their finances to worry about, there was no time for love in her own life. She would be too busy working.

The taxi stopped in front of the two-story house. It was a large property filled with fruit trees and plush landscaping. Cassiani knew that the Greeks were notorious for not keeping time and would stroll into an event a half-hour or even an hour late, and she was right. She was the first guest to arrive. Manolis greeted her with his typical sloppy grin. "I'm glad you could make it," he said. He turned and shouted into the hallway. "Aspasia, come!"

Aspasia came to greet her. The gold bracelets on her hands jingled as she removed her apron. "Welcome, my dear. I was just in the kitchen, finishing up."

A scent of female perfume surrounded Cassiani as Aspasia embraced her. Cassiani handed her the wrapped gift. "This is a gift for Mary."

Aspasia thanked her. "I'll go find her." She left excitedly with the gift.

Manolis looked at Cassiani keenly. "Do you remember when I used to play music with your father? You were just this high, no more than five or six years old. You'd sit in the corner pretending to play your own violin, trying to mimic him."

Cassiani giggled. "He taught me his songs after I pestered him to let me play."

"I know. That is why I wished to have you play here tonight. I wanted you to play in his memory," he said, wiping his reddened eyes briefly.

"Mary, look who's here," Aspasia said, entering the room with her daughter behind her.

Cassiani stared at the young woman, not recognizing her. *Is this Mary?*

CHAPTER 16

———————— ❦ ————————

Mary was dressed in yellow, from the appealing creamy yellow chiffon gown that showed off her tiny waist to the matching yellow high heels. She boasted an hourglass figure that appeared to be tanned from head to toe. Her hair was streaked blonde and her makeup completed the picture. The mousy, overweight Mary had evolved into an attractive, modern day woman.

"Cassiani!" Mary exclaimed, hugging her. She stepped back to take a look at her. "It's been years, hasn't it? You haven't changed a bit! Why that dress ... I remember it! You wore it to my graduation party, didn't you?" Without waiting for a reply, she gracefully stepped to the side, pulling on Nicko's arm. "This is my fiancé, Nickos Xenoudis."

Cassiani blushed at her friend's tactless remark about the dress. With effort, she focused on Nicko. He smiled as he shook her hand. He wore a white suit that was a little too tight, with gold buttons that were ready to pop off. One thick arm was draped possessively over Mary's shoulder.

"The party will be out in the verandah. It is too warm to have it inside." Aspasia led them into the house, through the nicely furnished rooms and towards the kitchen.

The kitchen was warm from all the baking. There were trays of food everywhere, on the table, on the counter, and on the stove. The rich smells of freshly fried squid filled up the space, giving it a cozy feeling. Cassiani recognized Mrs. Xenoudis, who was dressed in an expensive looking dress, mixing something in a bowl.

"Betsy, let me help you," Aspasia said, picking up another bowl. "We'll finish faster."

Betsy Xenoudis nodded at Cassiani recognizing her. "*Yiasou,*" she said. "I remember you from the party yesterday. See, now it's my turn to cook!" She held up her bowl, chuckling. "We all take turns, my dear!"

Cassiani laughed in return. She followed the young couple outside to the back verandah. Several round tables, tastefully decked with white tablecloths and flower filled vases, occupied the space. A buffet table, set to the side, displayed trays filled with fluffy pilaf, cinnamon topped moussaka, hearty pastitsio, and creamy skordalia dip. In the center of the table was a large Grecian vase filled with bright yellow and white lilies.

"I remember you wrote me a letter once, but I lost your address. How is your sister Athena doing?" Mary asked Cassiani.

"Fine. She is pregnant with her second baby. Her first child, Vera, is four years old now."

"Oh, how wonderful! Tell her to send me pictures!" Mary said.

Cassiani's eyes flew open. Mary had never shown interest in her sister before. Was this enthusiastic reply a superficial expression of the moment, intended to appear popular in front of her fiancé or did she really mean it? Whatever the reason, Cassiani liked it; she nodded appreciatively. Shy, awkward Mary had changed.

"I heard from Mother that you finished nursing school. You were always talking about becoming a nurse," Mary said smartly.

Cassiani chatted about her schooling and her job at the hospital. "It's quite demanding, but I love working with the patients," she finished.

Nicko's eyes twinkled. "There is always a need for nurses."

"There's also a need for wives who cook well," Cassiani replied quickly. "Mary's cooking was always the best."

"Oh, you're being too kind," Mary tittered.

Cassiani persisted. "I still remember that chocolate torte you made for your sixteenth birthday. It was delicious."

Betsy came out of the kitchen carrying a tray of food. She placed it on the buffet table. "Children, please come," she said. "We must go and greet the guests that arrived. Hurry." Mary and Nickos followed Betsy into the house like two obedient puppies.

Aspasia came out to the verandah just then, holding a tray of food. She placed it down, then hovered around the buffet table, rearranging the trays of food. She gave Cassiani a plate. "Help yourself to the food, dear," she said, as she breezed back into the house.

Cassiani chose a spanakopita, a scoop of garlic dip, and a serving of rice, then walked to a table in the far corner of the verandah. It felt good to sit and do nothing. She nibbled on her food, watching the guests arrive. First there was a group of people in formal dress; their outfits were splashed with vivid reds, blues, pinks, and yellows. They were talking and laughing with Mary and Nicko. Cassiani didn't recognize anyone from that group. They appeared content and happy, as if they had no worry in the world.

A group of tourists arrived. They were blonde and tanned, speaking a foreign language among themselves. Their laughter raised the noise level even higher.

Cassiani watched as the verandah swelled with people. It felt odd, experiencing her friend's happy moment and at the same time, not being able to share it with anyone. Mary and her family were busy conversing with their guests. *This is Mary's happy moment. Stop being so selfish.*

"Cassiani! Come!"

Cassiani looked up. Manolis was smiling and waving to her. He had removed his jacket and tie, and his sleeves were rolled up. He was ready to play. He placed a couple of chairs at the far edge of the verandah and sat down. There was a microphone in front of him and behind him was the amplifier. Several tables had filled up with people, while other folks stood in small groups, holding wineglasses filled with wine, talking and laughing.

Toting the violin case and handbag, Cassiani sat down next to Manolis.

"I heard from your mother that you played in an orchestra in America," Manolis said. "That is quite an accomplishment. How did you manage it?"

Cassiani told him that her violin instructor recommended she join the orchestra. "So I auditioned and was accepted." She pulled the bow out of the violin case.

Manolis' eyes shone with pride. "You have talent, just like your late father. I wish my daughter could have taken after me." He bent his head and strummed the bouzouki softly. "But she can't carry a tune, let alone play an instrument."

"I believe the Lord has blessed everybody with different talents," Cassiani said, swiping the bow's white horsehair with the rosin. "I remember Mary liked to cook."

"Well said. She does have a knack for cooking, but it all went here." He pointed to his stomach, laughing heartily. "She's been on some diet lately. Lost a lot of weight. Nicko likes to eat, though. So we'll see how long she can stay on her diet once they are married."

He focused on tuning his bouzouki, his ear cocked towards the instrument. One hand plucked the string while the other hand turned the knob at the top.

Cassiani rested the violin on her shoulder. "I also need to tune the violin to your bouzouki. Could you play the "la" note for me?"

He willingly obliged her, plucking the string a few times as she tuned. With a small nudge of the peg and a twist of the fine tuner, she was in business.

"We'll begin with a love song. *Filise me*," he said, with a twinkle in his eyes. "This one was your father's favorite. He used to play it for your mother, and she would sing along. Let's see if you recognize it. I'll play first, then you follow after the first stanza."

Manolis' long fingers stroked the bouzouki expertly, evoking memories of Cassiani's past, dipping into the recesses of her mind. The music brought back joyful memories of a time when everyone dear to her was alive and there was no sorrow. She knew this song well. She began to accompany him. From Manolis' pleased expression, she knew that she and her violin were giving a good performance. Everything and everyone melted into the background as the music took a life of its own, claiming the right to be heard.

Aspasia joined them; her throaty alto voice crooned a love duet with Manolis' bass. As the last traces of the song finished, Cassiani didn't have time to look up to the clapping of the bystanders, for Manolis had already sprung another song on her. This was his happy day and he was showing it. This time, Mary and her fiancé got on the dance floor. People cheered when others joined the couple on the dance floor.

At one point, the blonde hair of the back of a tall man's head came briefly into Cassiani's view, and then disappeared just as quickly as he retreated into the crowd. For a split second, she entertained the idea that it might be Leo, but she brushed the thought away. There were several fair-haired men here tonight. Cassiani could barely see beyond the bodies of the people swaying and dancing in front of her.

Someone threw money in the air, showering the couple with drachmas, a symbol that they wished them prosperity. Two little children, a boy and a girl, darted between the dancers like monkeys, grabbing the paper money that floated towards the ground. They handed them proudly to Aspasia, their faces filled with wide grins.

"One for you and one for you," Aspasia said cheerfully, giving each child a bill. "The rest is for the couple." She excused herself and flounced into the house, her arms full of money.

The songs flowed together, one after another, easily, joyfully, and with spirit. Manolis chose dance songs that were easy for Cassiani to follow. First came the lively kalamatiano, followed by the heavy zembekiko, which a few young men got up to dance. They leapt into the air, kicking their heels in happy abandonment, waving white handkerchiefs, while everyone clapped in unison, cheering them on. The hasapiko was next, danced to by a few girls who giggled a lot as they tried to remember all the intricate steps.

It was getting dark and several overhead lights were turned on; their white beams shining down on the heads of people. An ache had formed in the middle of Cassiani's back as she played. She stopped after they finished a song to wipe her wet forehead with the back of her hand.

Manolis looked up at her curiously, then rested his bouzouki on his lap, a queue for a break. He stood up and picked up a small glass of ouzo and lifted it up in the air, waiting for the people to get their glasses. "Please, let's have a toast for our daughter, Mary and her fiancé Nicko. Aspasia and I, and Nicko's parents, Betsy and Mihalis, are very proud of their engagement today. To your health and prosperity, and many blessed years together."

People cheered, while peppered sounds of clinking glasses followed the toast. Cassiani licked her dry lips, tasting the salt from her sweating face. She was feeling undeniably thirsty. Her eyes desperately combed the crowd, looking for Mary or Aspasia, wondering how she could get a hold of a glass of water. Before she could do anything, Manolis started another tune. Cassiani played dutifully along, secretly wondering when they were going to stop.

Aspasia came a few minutes later, thanked Cassiani, then whispered noisily into Manolis' ear. He peered down at his watch, looking doubtful, then nodded as if convinced.

"Cassiani, it is nine o'clock. It is time to stop." Manolis slowly wiped his sweating forehead with a handkerchief, then rolled down his sleeves and put on his jacket. "Your playing brought back wonderful memories. I felt as if your father was here tonight. I enjoyed it."

"Thank you. I enjoyed playing also." Cassiani's lips felt dry as she talked.

Aspasia tugged on Manolis' jacket. "Come, Manolis."

Manolis winked at Cassiani. "I'm afraid I need to play the host now."

Cassiani watched as he followed Aspasia into the crowd. She suddenly felt very alone. She peered at the crowd anxiously, trying to find Mary. Maybe she could talk to her, but she didn't see her. Resigned to the fact that her friend was not going to be available, she wiped the rosin off the violin with a small cloth, then tucked the violin back in its case and shut it. It was time to leave.

Clutching the violin case against her chest, Cassiani was resolved to go home. To her dismay, she felt a wave of exhaustion overcome her. She tried to fight the faint feeling by taking a deep breath. Just then, she sensed a presence. Someone was standing next to her. She swung around.

CHAPTER 17

"Hello, Cassiani."

Cassiani's heart soared when she heard the enticingly deep and mellow male voice. Leonidas Regas stood in front of her, his eyes glowing brightly in the soft darkness of the night. His dark blue shirt, open at the collar, gave him a surprisingly rakish look. There was no trace of the professional image of the afternoon. "Dr. Regas." Her voice was raspy, his name catching in her dry throat. She nervously tucked the loose tendrils of hair behind her ears, painfully aware of the faded dress, the tarnished necklace, and the old, tattered sandals.

"You can call me Leo." He gestured towards the far end of the verandah. "I was watching you from that corner over there. I didn't know you'd be playing here tonight."

His eyes were begging for an explanation. She complied and told him about her father's playing. "I learned the songs from him, so they asked me to play tonight, in his memory, and...." She felt a dark wave descend upon her as her legs gave way. She slumped into the seat. "Whew! I am a little wiped out, and thirsty. It's been a long day."

"Take deep breaths. I'll go get you something to drink," Leo said, quickly leaving.

Cassiani inhaled deeply, afraid of fainting. She must have been holding her breath when he was talking to her. She made the sign of the cross, then touched her cross as she whispered a short prayer.

Leo returned with a glass of water and a pitcher. "Here," he said, pressing the glass to her mouth. "You must have been dehydrated."

She thanked him, gulping the water down, almost choking.

"Go slow this time," he warned, filling the empty glass with more water. He placed it to her lips and watched as she drank it more slowly. "Would you like some more?"

"No thank you," she said, putting her hand up. She smiled. "I'm fine now. Really."

Leo relaxed. He placed the glass and pitcher aside. "I know the groom's family," he offered. "Nicko has been a good friend since grade school. We kept in touch all these years."

"Old friendships are rare to find. You did the right thing by honoring this special event."

Leo nodded. "It would have been an insult not to come to his engagement party. How about you?"

Cassiani warmed to his question. "I've known Mary since we were children. My family used to live a few blocks from here and we spent much time with her and her family, but when we moved to the mountain, we lost touch with them." She looked around for Mary. "I feel I have so much to talk about with her, but I realize she's very busy today."

"Come to think of it, I also haven't had a chance to talk to Nicko yet. He's also been very busy with his fiancé." He turned and gazed at Cassiani. "By the way, that's a very nice cross."

"It's helped me many times," she began, then stopped.

"Is that right?" Leo asked, appearing curious. "In what way?"

"Two years ago when I was attending courses at college, I lost it. Three days later was September the fourteenth, the day of The Exultation of the Holy Cross. That day, as I was walking on the campus, a dark-skinned girl approached me holding my cross. 'Is this yours?' she asked. I was so happy to see it. After she gave it to me, she disappeared, never to be seen again." Cassiani was about to continue when she was interrupted by the sound of a high-pitched female voice calling out Leo's name.

Cassiani turned to see whom it was; she tensed when she saw Nina Vassilakis standing at the back door to the house. She wore a black sleeveless dress with a low v-neckline. Loud, round earrings and heavy makeup completed the picture. She called Leo's name again. This time it was not a sweet, innocent call. This sounded like a command. Cassiani glimpsed Mary standing behind Nina, gesturing to him. "Nina and Mary are calling you. I think you are wanted in the house."

Leo chuckled. "I forgot how strong your ears were. I didn't hear anyone calling me." He turned to have a look.

Nina approached them, her heels clicking on the verandah. "Leo! Nicko is looking for you. He's out in front. We'll be going to hear Louis play."

Leo bent towards Cassiani's ear and whispered, "Would you like to come with us?"

Although the invitation was agreeable to her ears, Cassiani resolutely shook her head. "Thank you, but I must be leaving. My mother is by herself."

Cassiani watched his tall, lean body join Nina's petite body. Nina leaned against him, laughing and looking up at him. He laughed with her. It seemed as if Nina had staked her claim.

A few minutes ago, Leo's presence made her feel as if an angel was in her midst, getting her water to drink; and now, as he walked away, she felt as if the darkness of the evening had just swept over her. She stood there, wondering if she should go inside and bid everyone goodbye. It was too much of an effort. It was time to go.

She walked shakily to the side of the house, her eyes combing the area for the small stone path, the same one she used to skip on when she was young. The moon cast an eerie glow, just enough light to outline the stones as she made her way down the path. To her right was a large field filled with the dark shapes of fruit trees, and to her left, strains of spirited Greek music blared out from the open windows, probably from the stereo system. The party had moved inside.

She stopped when she arrived at the front of the house. Leo and Nina were conversing with Nicko and Mary on the front sidewalk, along with three young men and a couple of young women. Cassiani stood there, not wanting them to see her. Maybe if she stood still long enough, they would leave. Her strong ears picked up part of the conversation.

Nina's voice was loud and abrasive. "Did you see that peasant girl, what's her name, playing in that old dress? Her mother is Soula Lukas' maid."

"Oh, no," Cassiani whispered, not wanting to hear anymore. She felt her face flush with anger, or was it humiliation? She huddled behind the large gardenia bush that rested against the wall, trying to find some comfort in the hiding place.

Nina didn't stop. "She played so loud she practically drowned Manolis with her playing."

Her laughter was joined by others.

"Who invited her anyway?" asked one other woman.

"My father. Her father used to play in the band with him," Mary explained, shrugging her shoulders apologetically.

"What happened to Yannis, the violinist?" someone else asked.

"He is away on a trip. They couldn't find anyone else to replace him," Mary said.

"I thought she played *quite* well," Leo said. "I haven't heard that kind of playing in a long time."

Cassiani's case scraped the wall as she turned to have a better look at him. The sound must have carried over to the group, for Leo glanced her way as if he heard her. She immediately moved back, out of sight.

Nicko nodded. "I thought she played well also. Let's go to the nightclub. Louis is expecting us."

The group quieted down and piled into the two cars parked there. Cassiani waited until the cars left. She turned and walked the other direction, her legs aching and her heart heavy. Was she showing off in her playing? She didn't realize it. Nina referred to her not only as a peasant girl, but a maid's daughter. The twisted knot in her chest became stronger when she focused on Mary's response to Nina. Mary was not the old friend that she left behind; she had changed.

Slowly, mechanically, Cassiani walked into the darkness of the night, numb from exhaustion. Where was she going to find a taxi at this time of hour? Even more importantly, she wondered whether she had enough money.

*   *   *   *

It was ten thirty when Cassiani flagged down a taxi at the main road. She had resisted getting a taxi sooner so she could have enough money to pay for the ride home. As she entered the car, she spied Leo and Nina driving by. She ducked her head quickly so they wouldn't see her. She was surprised to see them leaving the nightclub already. He probably was taking Nina home. She told the driver her address. She dozed off in the taxi, exhausted.

"Miss, we arrived."

She groggily got out of the taxi, not remembering the amount the driver had said. She dug into her pocket and gave him the little money she had with her. "Is that enough?" she asked anxiously. She watched as he counted the coins. "My mother is Vera Meletis. I can get more change from her."

The driver shook his head. "That's all right, Miss Meletis. I know your family. Your father was our pharmacist. You go home now. It's late." He drove away.

The cool, mountain air and short nap revived her a little, giving her the boost of energy she needed for the journey up the sloping road. The lonely sound of a hoot owl could be heard in the distance. She entered the yard. The light in their house was on.

Her mother was sitting at the kitchen table gazing sadly at a photo album. "No matter how long your dear father is gone, I still miss him." Vera wiped her wet eyes. "He was such a good man. Ahh, you left me dear husband, just when I needed you the most!"

"I miss him too," Cassiani said, hugging her. The photograph showed a young, thin man wearing a beige suit and hat. Her mother stood next to him, slim and attractively dressed in a well-tailored suit and hat. "You know, you made such a handsome couple."

"Until this day, I still wonder how he died so suddenly. One minute he was a man in his prime, only fifty-five. The next minute, he didn't wake up from bed," Vera said, making the sign of the cross. "The Lord works in mysterious ways. I can't understand it."

Cassiani just sat there. She didn't have the energy to cry, nor to talk. Just to listen. But she knew that her mother's sadness was more than the loss of her father. Her mother was also mourning the loss of her health and the loss of a live-lihood; all hope wiped away because she was too ill to work. Her mother was experiencing a crisis. Something had to be done about it. She yawned. *It would have to wait until tomorrow.*

"Enough about me. How did it go tonight?" Vera asked, looking at her daughter. "Did they like your playing? Did you remember to give the gift?"

Cassiani nodded, too tired to talk.

"I was beginning to get worried about you. It's past eleven, do you know that?"

Cassiani tenderly removed her sore feet from the sandals, then stood up, ready to go to bed. "Manolis didn't stop playing until just after nine. I ended up walking on the main road before I could find a taxi."

"Oh, you poor girl. Wasn't anyone at the party able to drive you home? I'm sure someone could have taken you if you only asked."

"I didn't ask." Cassiani paused, wondering if she should tell her about Leo and Nina. Her mouth tightened into a straight line. *Why not tell her the truth?* "Leo and Nina were there, but they went to the nightclub after the party, with the others. I saw Leo driving Nina home."

"Ahh, so they were there together," Vera said, her eyes narrowing.

"Now if you'll excuse me, I'm really tired." Cassiani walked away, her shoulders slumped. She was glad her mother didn't say anything about her dress.

"You wore that old dress! I can't believe it!"

Cassiani's shoulders straightened. She kept walking. "Good night, Mother."

CHAPTER 18

Monday

Soula arose at eight o'clock to the sound of the alarm clock. "Too early for my standards," she thought. She washed herself in the bathroom; each motion premeditated and not wasted. She must preserve her energy since she was not allowed to eat before the tests. A half-hour later she made her way back to her room. She searched the closet for something to wear. There were so many clothes, so many choices. "Something that I can role the sleeves up," she muttered, feeling bewildered. Then she saw the blue silk dress. She stared at it.

The image of Sotiris, the handsome medical student she fell in love with, came to her mind. She was nineteen when she met him at a dinner party; she was wearing this same dress, with a white satin sash tied around her small waist, dainty white gloves, a pearl necklace and matching pearl earrings. He complimented her on her attire and that sparked the beginning of her first love.

After that day, every chance she could get she would try to see him. His departure for Athens a few weeks later left behind a love-struck young woman. She had to find a way to be near him. The solution presented itself. She was going to study nursing in Athens. She approached her father with the idea.

"There is no reason for you to become a nurse. You are wealthy. Marriage is your career," her father scoffed, crossing his arms.

Soula then confessed her feelings about Sotiris and how she was in love with him. "I want to marry him," she announced.

Her father was adamant. "You are going to marry a rich man, not a doctor."

Soula cried and stomped her feet, but to no avail. Her father would not budge. She became ill after that and he compromised by sending her to Paris instead, "To learn the arts." The young doctor vanished from her life and so did the dream of becoming a nurse.

Soula stared at the dress. It had never been worn since then.

"Mrs. Lukas!" Stella called, just as she entered the room.

Soula jumped; she had forgotten all about Stella coming this morning. "You gave me a fright!"

"Sorry," Stella said, appearing flustered. "I just got here and didn't see you in the parlor, so I came looking for you." She stared at the blue dress. "What are you getting dressed up for?"

Soula explained that she was going to the hospital for tests. "Something unexpected," she said, waving the blue dress in the air. "I will be leaving shortly and will return later in the day, probably after twelve. You can come back then."

Stella's face turned red. "I'm sorry, but I made other arrangements for the afternoon."

"Then come back tomorrow morning. There is some food in the refrigerator for today."

Stella regained her cheerful composure. "By the way, that's a nice looking dress," she remarked as she left.

Fifteen minutes past nine, Soula sat in Nina's car. She wore the blue dress, complete with white sash and white gloves. A sense of satisfaction that she was able to wear this outfit after all these years made her feel like a young girl again.

"Do you suppose Leo will like the changes I intend to make to the upstairs suite?" Nina asked.

"What kind of changes are they, my dear?"

Nina talked about converting the neutral colors into more contrasting colors, "like a black lacquered table and white sofa." She mentioned adding black and white tile in the kitchen. "I was also thinking of adding a splash of red, like red sofa pillows on the white sofa, to give the room some color."

"Don't worry, he'll like anything you do."

As soon as Soula entered the hospital, her agreeable demeanor was replaced by a stubborn, mulish look. They were the first ones in the waiting room. Nina left, saying she had some chores to do and that she'd be back soon. Soula sat quietly, her hands clamped together, as if she were praying; she was trying not to fall asleep. She wanted to see everything that was going to be done to her. The technician came shortly and took her into the room.

Soula never did like needles and her eyes bulged when she saw the syringe coming towards her arm. She shut her eyes, feeling a wave of nausea hit her stomach. *Why is she taking so long?* Soula peered from the corner of her eye as the technician reached out to get a second tube. "That should be enough, don't you think?" she asked.

"We're not done yet. We need to take two more."

Soula's eyes flew open. "*Two* more?" she protested. "It's bad enough I have anemia, and now you want to take *all* my blood?'

"Please relax. There now, it won't be long before we're finished."

A man and woman were sitting in the waiting room when Soula returned. She looked around, wondering what happened to Nina. "I never saw so much blood being taken out of my body!" she grumbled as she sat down.

The two patients nodded in silent understanding. They opened up and shared their own stories. More people came into the room. Time passed and Soula dozed off.

"Mrs. Lukas. Mrs. Lukas."

"Yes?" Soula said groggily. She opened her eyes to find Nina tapping her on the shoulder.

"Mother wants you to come over after all this is done, for a bite to eat. She says you'll probably need it after they take your blood," Nina said.

"Oh, is that right? I do feel light-headed. What time is it?"

"Eleven thirty."

✴   ✴   ✴   ✴

On this same sunny morning, at eight o'clock, Cassiani had arisen and was getting dressed. She ignored the sunlight and spring breeze coming through the window; her mind was focused on last night's event, particularly what Nina and the others said about her afterwards. Although it was a small consolation that Leo had been at the party and did invite her to go with them to the night club, she could not erase the fact that he had driven Nina to the party and taken her home afterwards. Cassiani felt strongly about going back to America after yesterday's event. She didn't want to stay here. She would have to have a talk with her mother.

"Breakfast is ready!" Vera sang out. She began to sing a familiar tune, her voice a pure and silky smooth soprano, full of compassion.

Cassiani entered the kitchen, smelling the fresh aroma of coffee. The coffeepot she had brought with her from America was brewing the coffee. This was the first time that her mother used it to make coffee. She kissed her mother, then helped set the table. "I noticed you made American coffee. Thank you!"

"I thought since you brought the pot and coffee all the way from America, why not make something that you like." Vera lifted up her cup. "See, I made myself some tea."

After a simple prayer, they began to eat breakfast.

Cassiani took a sip of her coffee. It was extremely bitter. "Ooh!" she sputtered.

Vera's eyes flew open. "What's the matter? Is it too strong?"

"That's all right." Cassiani went to the refrigerator. "I'll just add a little more milk." She poured some of the coffee from her cup into the sink and replaced it with milk. "Mother, before I left to come here, I spoke with Athena. She misses you and wants you to come back to the United States with me. Now with her second pregnancy, she feels you can help her."

"I'd like to help her, but how could they manage feeding us? Her husband is already feeding three mouths. Besides, do they have room for another person?" Vera dunked her paximadi in her tea.

"I helped share in the cost of the food when I was living there. Besides their house is big enough for both of us, and we can share the bedroom I was using."

"Every six months I have to return to Greece. That will cost us money," Vera said.

Cassiani sighed. This wasn't going to be easy. She remembered how they'd try to talk her mother into coming to America in the past and she would always be full of excuses. Initially, her justification had been that she needed to take care of Grandmother. Now her mother was saying she didn't want to be a burden to them. "I will be making enough money. I could pay for your trips," she persisted.

"Ba-a-a-ah!"

"I forgot the goats in the front. I brought them there so I could milk Tiri this morning," Vera replied. "Please go and check up on them. They may be tied around the tree again."

Cassiani bounded outside. She laughed when she saw Tiri and Tiraki tangled up together. Tiraki's little body hugged her mother's body and her head was perched on her mother's back. A bleating chorus greeted Cassiani as she approached them. She bent down, trying to remove the rope that was tightly wrapped around the stubborn goat's body, but she was unsuccessful.

Cassiani laughed. "I have a better idea." She hurried into the house and returned with the shears. In no time, she had the goats loosened. They ran towards the back where their stall was. She followed them and opened the gate to let them in. She leaned against the fence and watched the baby goat frolicking around her mother.

As Cassiani walked slowly back to the house, she realized that the goats liked it better here than in the front, where they were tied up. She realized that Mother was in a similar situation. Mother preferred living here than in America. *You want Mother to come to America because you're only thinking about yourself, about your career. What about her? This is her life. Yes, but she needs help now, and it's better if she were close to family.*

When she returned to the kitchen, her mother had just finished eating. "The goats are in the back." Cassiani washed her hands. *Tell her now about how you feel.* "As I was saying, it's not only for Athena that I want you to go to America, it's because *I* also want to go back."

"I guess you don't want to live here, do you? This place isn't big enough for you. You were meant for bigger things," Vera said wistfully.

Cassiani swallowed her guilt feelings. It seemed as if her mother had picked up her unspoken feelings and put a voice to them. "Mother, don't get me wrong. If I could stay here I would … but I worked hard to get my nursing degree and I don't want to stop now." She gazed at her mother's strained face. "I'm also planning to sign up for classes in the fall; I'll be working towards a masters' degree in nursing."

Vera appeared puzzled. "Didn't you get your degree? Why do you want another one?"

"I can become a nursing supervisor," Cassiani persisted. "And then I'll make more money. If you have money, then you won't have to depend on other people for a livelihood, like Mrs. Lukas, or have people looking down on you."

"*Who* is looking down on you?" Vera asked, her eyes flashing with angry pride. "Don't *ever* let anyone make you feel that you are lower than them." She paused, thinking. "You are ashamed that I am working for Mrs. Lukas, aren't you?"

Cassiani was silent, her eyes glued to her plate. Her mother had an uncanny way of getting straight to the truth. *Do I feel ashamed?*

"No one should ever be ashamed for honest work!" Vera said, not waiting for Cassiani to respond. She waved a spoon angrily in the air. "Tell me something, my daughter, did anything happen at the party last night that I should know about? How were Mary and her family towards you?"

"Why do you ask?"

"Because some little bird is telling me that you were comparing your life to theirs, and were probably wishing that your parents had a house, clothes, and money, and that you were the one getting married."

"I did compare my life to theirs," Cassiani admitted.

"Something also tells me that she said something to hurt you. Am I right?"

Cassiani nodded, the tears welling up in her eyes. She arose and hugged her. *Mother understands me.* "Oh, Mother! She looked and acted so different. She's not the Mary you remember. She acted as if she was doing me a favor for being there."

"Ahh, my daughter." Vera wagged her head. "Mary thinks she is too good for us now that she is getting married to a wealthy family." She paused, her eyes narrowed as if she were thinking. "Unfortunately, at your age, finding a husband here can be a problem."

Cassiani's body bolted up. "*She* found a husband!" Her hand flew up to her mouth as soon as she said the words. She realized how her mother had teased those words out of her mouth. *Do you really want to have what Mary has? To get married and live here, like Mary?*

"She's an only daughter," Vera said, "with a sizeable dowry to speak of. Before your dear father passed away, we had a very comfortable and good life. Just like them. But things changed after that. That is the reason I let you go to America; I felt you could have a better life there with Athena than with me here." She paused to brush the tears from her eyes. "Besides, you shouldn't compare yourself to others. You don't know what fate is in store for them down the road."

Cassiani nodded, feeling guilty for her outburst. "You're right, Mother." She realized that her mother was doing the best she could under the circumstances. "You know, in America, they don't ask for dowries, and being twenty-five is not considered too old for marriage. There, I could easily find someone to marry, if I wanted to." She gazed wistfully out the kitchen window. "If I were to stay here, I may just end up being a spinster for the rest of my life!"

Vera's eyes flew open. "Don't say that! You are a beautiful girl! Someone will come along." She stacked the dishes noisily on the counter. "Let me ask you one more thing. What do you think about this Leo Regas?"

"Leo Regas?" Cassiani echoed. She was thoughtful as she cleaned the table. "I think he's a nice, friendly sort of person. He's educated and handsome, and he did come to help his aunt." She sighed. "But he's seeing Nina Vassilakis."

Vera was silent. "Why don't you go and get some water to wash the dishes?" She watched her daughter take the jug and go to the doorway. "Maybe America is not such a bad idea after all," she muttered.

Cassiani went and hugged her. "Oh Mother, you won't regret it!" Minutes later, she returned from the well with the water and started to wash the dishes.

Vera wiped the dishes with a kitchen towel, humming. "I need to put the money that Leo gave us into the bank in Kos Town. It'll go too quickly if I keep it here. I also need to do some grocery shopping." She placed a clean dish in the cupboard. "What plans do you have for today?"

"I was thinking about going to Tigaki beach for a quick swim; then after I return from Mrs. Lukas in the afternoon, I want to telephone Athena. It'll be morning their time."

Vera's eyebrows rose. "It's a little cool for a swim this time of year."

"I don't mind going. It's been years since I've been to the beach."

Vera smiled. "You always liked to spend time there when you were young." She glanced at the clock, then removed her apron hurriedly. "We better get ready. We need to catch the bus." She hustled out of the kitchen.

CHAPTER 19

Ten o'clock, Vera entered the bank in Kos Town. This was the bank she had done business with all these years; even when banks opened up closer to where she lived, this was the one she came to. After she deposited the money in the savings account, she checked the balance. It showed nine hundred fifty drachmas. She then checked the balance in the other account. She walked away with a smug smile.

When she sold the land several years ago, she opened the second account and deposited the two million drachmas in it, with the intention of providing both for Cassiani's education and her dowry. The moneys for Cassiani's education were already withdrawn and the remaining balance was nine hundred thirty-three thousand drachmas. *But Cassiani must not know about this account. Not until the proper time.*

As Vera left the bank, she bumped into Vassiliki Anthis. "Fancy meeting you here after all these years!"

"Vera! It's so good to see you!" Vassiliki kissed her friend on the cheeks. "Bobby just started work here. This is his second week." She lifted up a paper bag. "I brought him some food."

They stood outside the bank, catching up on their news.

A few minutes later, Bobby joined them. He kissed his mother fondly on the cheek, then took the bag of food. He squinted at Vera behind his thick glasses. "Oh, hello, Mrs. Meletis." He smiled. "How is Athena? I remember she married some Greek-American engineer."

"Yes, and now she's living in America. They're expecting their second child soon," Vera said proudly. She took out photos of Athena and her family from her purse and showed them. She studied him as he looked at the pictures. Even though he wasn't blessed with looks, he was an affable young man. *Too bad it didn't work out with Athena.*

Bobby's eyebrows went up. "Didn't you have another daughter?"

Vera smiled, then told them about Cassiani, her education, her hospital job, and her dropping everything to come and help her. "I feel *so* much better now that she's here."

Vassiliki invited her for a cup of coffee at her house, which was within walking distance of the bank. "So we can catch up on our news," she said, patting Vera fondly on the arm.

"Thank you dear Vasso, I would really like that, but I still have several chores to do," Vera replied. *Don't let this opportunity slip out of your hands.* "Why don't you and Bobby come over for dinner later tonight? It would be nice for Cassiani to meet you, after all these years."

*   *   *   *

Eleven o'clock, Vera placed her call to Athena from the village coffee shop. "Athena, Athena? Your mother here!" she shouted into the telephone. She looked behind her in the kafenio. A couple of tourists had lined up behind her to use the telephone.

"Mother? Is everything all right? It's four o'clock in the morning here," Athena said.

"Oh, I must have awakened you. I'm sorry. How are you all doing? How's David and my Verula?" Vera shouted.

"We're all doing fine! I'm six months pregnant now and getting a little tired. The good news is that David has a new job and it pays well. How are you doing?"

Vera's eyes glanced furtively behind her. Two older women that she recognized had now joined the line behind the tourists. They waved to her. Her voice dropped and her shoulders bunched forward as she moved closer towards the telephone, mindful of the attentive listeners behind her. "I'm better now that Cassiani is here. I bumped into Mrs. Anthis and her son, Bobby. Remember him?"

"What? I didn't hear you! Speak up!" Athena interrupted.

Vera shouted back into the telephone, repeating her news. She finished with, "Bobby works in the bank and is still unwed! I invited them over for dinner so he can meet Cassiani!"

Athena laughed. "Ahh, haha. You tried to match him with me years ago, but it didn't work. What makes you think it'll work with Cassiani?"

"Yes, because you had already met your husband who was visiting from America. He snatched you up before anyone else could," Vera replied tartly.

Athena laughed again. "I'm glad he did. Anyway, I don't think Bobby is her type. He's too soft. She needs someone smarter. Someone who can take charge." She paused. "Oh, before I forget. Someone called from the hospital asking for Cassiani. His name is Andy Andrakis and he says he works with her. I gave him your address in Greece."

Vera was surprised to hear that. Cassiani hadn't mentioned him at all. *But she did say that she could get married in America if she wanted to.* In her excitement she forgot to lower her voice. "Do you know this Andy? He sounds like a Greek boy."

"What did you say?" Athena asked, sounding puzzled

"Is this Andy a Greek boy?" Vera shouted excitedly. There was silence on the other end. She stared at the phone in disgust. "This is a bad connection."

"Mother, don't hang up! I sent you the airplane tickets. Did you get them?"

"Airplane tickets?"

"We got a very good deal on them and they're nonrefundable. They should be arriving there any time now."

"I hope you didn't do anything rash! Anyway, you have my blessings!" Vera said, with tears in her eyes. "Cassiani is going to call you later today. Don't tell her that I called you. I don't want her to know."

They said their good-byes. As Vera passed the two Greek women at the end of the line, she nodded a polite greeting. They asked her if she was planning to leave for America.

"My daughter Athena wants me to go live with her in America. She is pregnant," Vera said, smiling proudly, her arms ballooning out over her stomach.

"Ahh," were the pleased sighs of the women.

*   *   *   *

Vera poured the hot brew into her neighbor's cup, then in her cup. "I don't know what I would have done carrying all those grocery bags to the house."

Kalliopi Kalotsis' pleasant face broke out into a smile as she took her cup of coffee. "What did I do? My son was taking me shopping anyway, and we saw you there. It wasn't much effort for us to bring you back."

"You should be proud of your Pavlo. He is a good boy."

"I am very blessed." Kalliopi's wrinkled face broke out into a broad smile. "He has a good job, a good wife and their children are healthy and doing well in school. What more could a person want than to see their children doing well?"

Vera fingered the edge of her collar nervously. "I feel the same way about my Athena, but I still have Cassiani's future to think about."

"Yes, I understand," Kalliopi said solemnly.

Vera stared out the kitchen window. She sighed. "Meanwhile Cassiani and Athena want me to go to America."

"How many times have I told you," Kalliopi said, leaning forward, "it is good to be near your family."

"But what about the house? Who will take care of it for me?"

"Don't worry about your house!" Mrs. Kalotsis said. "Go for a few months. See how it is. I will keep an eye on the house and the goats for you. Then you can decide later what to do."

"God bless you and your family," Vera gushed. "You are like a mother to me."

"Your mother and I were very close, like sisters." Kalliopi smiled fondly. "Now tell me, what is the news with Cassiani? Have you found anyone for her?"

"There's an old friend of the family. They live near Kos Town. She has a son named Bobby. He is still unwed and works in the bank."

Mrs. Kalotsis' eyebrows went up. "Oh, that is nice. A banker."

Vera pursed her lips. "I don't know if Cassiani would be interested. He's not the handsomest boy. Even if she were interested, it would mean she would have to stay here, and her heart isn't for it." She leaned towards her friend excitedly. "There might be someone else. I called Athena this morning and she told me a man from the hospital was asking for Cassiani. She gave him our address."

"What happened to that Leo that you were talking about?"

"He's been seeing Nina Vassilakis, you know, the doctor's girl—the one with the nose up in the air." Vera made a gesture with her hand, flipping it near her nose. "She is like a magnet, zooming in on any man visiting the island. Her family came to the luncheon Saturday at the Lukas residence and she wasted no time in getting close to Leo. My daughter even saw them together at Mary's engagement party yesterday evening."

"Cassiani is prettier than Nina, with her tall height, those beautiful black eyes and fine complexion. What does Nina have? She's got small eyes, a small mouth, and a small body. It's the way she dresses and all that makeup that makes her look attractive!" Kalliopi retorted.

"That's right," Vera said, smiling smugly. "But Cassiani doesn't want to dress up and show off her looks. She is very, how do you say it, simple. Nina is much more sophisticated, and her parents have money." Her eyes opened wide. "They built a very expensive villa for her. My daughter has no such dowry to speak of."

"Cassiani has her education! Being a nurse is not something to make light of. You should be proud of her!" Mrs. Kalotsis persisted.

"I am. Don't think that I'm not." Vera replied. "But Soula Lukas is also interested in Nina, and if Soula wants Nina for Leo, then my daughter doesn't have a chance."

CHAPTER 20

Cassiani strolled along Tigaki's long, narrow sandy beach, going west towards the salt lake. She enjoyed the scenic view of the crystal blue water ahead, feeling the tug of the wayward breeze. Although it was not yet ten o'clock, there were a few open umbrellas scattered on the beach, signaling that others had arrived before her. When she reached a more private area, she placed her towel down and sat on it.

A seagull flew overhead, its graceful wings greeting her as it sounded its poignant call. Cassiani felt a surge of happiness, thinking how wonderful it was to be sitting here enjoying this natural moment. The blissful moment flew away just as quickly as the bird, replaced by the nagging worry about her mother's health. She frowned as she thought about her mother's heart condition.

Cassiani knew that heart medicine, or any kind of man-made medicine for that matter, was not natural to the body. If her mother's disease progressed, she would probably end up taking more pills. Cassiani remembered the elderly cardiac patients that she would see in the hospital. Some were taking fifteen or twenty pills a day. She shuddered at the thought. *I'll get her checked by a good cardiologist when we go to America.*

Feeling some relief about her decision, Cassiani decided to go for a swim. She peeled off her clothes, revealing her old one-piece bathing suit, a birthday present when she was sixteen years old. It was a little snug on the top but otherwise in good condition. She shivered in anticipation as she walked to the edge of the beach. The saltwater enveloped her blistered foot, causing a slight stinging sensation. *The minerals from the water will be good for the blister.*

The rhythm of the flowing and ebbing tide enticed her. She ran boldly forward, dunking her body into the water's icy embrace and swimming forward. She turned, and with her face towards the sun, serenely floated along. It was as if time stood still and she was wrapped up in the sun's rays, bundled up, drifting like a log. When the sun began to feel hot on her face, she knew it was time to go back.

She dried herself with the towel, then wrapped it around her waist. Her watch showed ten thirty, there were still a few minutes left. She strolled along the beach, going west towards the salt lake, gathering seashells. A beautiful conch shell rolled in with the waves and landed at her feet. It glistened from the sun's rays as she picked it up, admiring its beauty.

"Get out of the way!"

Startled, Cassiani jumped back, plunging into the water. A flash of something large and brown flew dangerously close by. She stood up, shaken and drenched by the incident. All the seashells she collected had sunk into the water. She glared at the retreating brown horse and its rider as they vanished around the salt lake's bend. She was certain of one thing—it was downright dangerous to ride a horse on the beach.

Cassiani ran back to her resting spot, carrying her wet towel, determined to leave. Just then she heard a horse neighing. She looked around, feeling apprehension. This time the rider was walking alongside his horse and they were coming towards her. To her surprise, the rider was none other than the bouzouki player, Louis Kotsidas. Cassiani slapped the wet towel protectively in front of her body. This was one person she didn't particularly want stares from.

"I'm sorry, *Koukla mou*," Louis said, ogling her. "I hope I didn't frighten you."

"Did you know that horses are not allowed on the beach?"

Louis patted his horse. "I brought him down here to exercise. Swimmers usually don't come in this area. You should stay closer to the other swimmers and don't wander off too much."

"I wasn't paying attention," Cassiani said lamely, realizing he was right.

"You live around here?" He lit a cigarette and offered it to her.

Cassiani shook her head at the proffered cigarette. "Up in the mountain, near Zia," she replied. She watched warily, as he puffed on his cigarette, suppressing an urge to cough.

"So, why haven't you come to see me play sometime? I am very good, you know," Louis drawled, smiling at her, lazily waving the lit cigarette in the air.

The breeze shifted, carrying the smoke from the lit cigarette straight into Cassiani's face. She bent over, coughing soundly. "It's my asthma. Kuughh, kuughh. It acts up whenever I'm near smoke," she explained. "I have to go get my medicine." She grabbed her handbag, slipped on her sandals and strode down the beach, away from Louis.

Cassiani kept up an incessant cough until she reached the shade of a tree. Once there, she stole a glance behind her. Apparently, Louis got the message, for there was no sign of him. Relieved, she threw on her dress and began her trek back home. She was not about to stay around Louis, in her bathing suit. *It was not proper, and besides, he made me feel uncomfortable.*

The house was empty when she arrived. She barely had time to wash and change into a clean set of clothes. Even with all her rushing, she arrived ten minutes late to Mrs. Lukas' house. To her surprise, the front door was locked and no one answered her knocking. She paced nervously for several minutes, her eyes continually searching the road for signs of Mrs. Lukas. She walked around to the back of the house and knocked on the parlor's glass door. No one was there. Different thoughts haunted her as she pictured Mrs. Lukas either inside the house, fallen and helpless, or so ill that they had to hospitalize her. As she left, she could hear the distant sound of a telephone ringing in the house. She had the odd feeling that it might be Leo calling his aunt.

Cassiani returned an hour later feeling anxious and worried, but Mrs. Lukas was still not there. It was two o'clock as she walked home, muttering to herself. "If she doesn't want me to take care of her, then I won't!"

✳   ✳   ✳   ✳

"You're back already?" Vera looked up from her cross-stitching. A large white tablecloth was laid out in front of her.

Cassiani told her what happened. She grabbed a glass and poured water into it. "I thought she'd be finished with her tests by now." She gulped down the water, quenching her thirst.

Vera frowned. "They've probably gone somewhere to eat," she replied. "I wouldn't worry about her! She's not as fragile as her nephew makes her out to be."

Cassiani's eyes zoomed in on the cross-stitch. The bright red stitches were tight and even, forming a rose; the color contrasted well with the pure white of the linen. "How beautiful! A white tablecloth with roses," she said. "Did you just start it?"

"I bought the cloth and threads today. I am making it for you. I wanted it to be a surprise, but you caught me."

Cassiani sat and watched her mother's fine stitching. "I wish I could stitch like that."

"Years of practice, my daughter. You do quite well with the needle. Remember the white table napkins you stitched before you left for America? I still have them."

Cassiani blinked. Those carefree days when she had free time on her hands to stitch napkins were gone. That easygoing life vanished after her father passed away. She felt as if another person had stitched those napkins. "I had forgotten all about them."

Vera stopped and stared at her daughter. "Tsk. Tsk. Did you know that your face is red? Just like this rose that I'm stitching!" she said, rising. "I'll get you something for it."

Cassiani touched her face and winced.

Vera returned with a small jar of cream. "Here, rub some on your skin." She studied her face and bared shoulders. "I don't think you'll get blisters, but you should be more careful next time. You burn easily like me."

Cassiani dabbed some cream on her face. She told her about her encounter with Louis Kotsidas on the beach. "The nerve of him to keep smoking even after I coughed!"

"What do you expect from a bum like that!" Vera said, snorting. "Look where he works, at the nightclub, and you know everyone smokes there. Smoking is like air and water to him."

"Yes, and in a few years, *he'll* be the one coughing," Cassiani said grimly.

"What a crime for such a good-looking man to go to waste," Vera said. "He does nothing but play bouzouki, drink, and smoke. I asked around and heard he's a womanizer. He chases the tourist women, but won't settle down. He probably has all kinds of diseases by now. You keep clear of him."

"Oh, don't worry about me!" Cassiani said, crossing her arms, feeling uncomfortable under her mother's veiled scrutiny. "I've never allowed any man close enough to even kiss me. Louis Kotsidas is no exception."

"Good!" Vera said. She focused on her stitching, humming. After a minute of concentrated work, she looked up. "By the way, I bumped into Mrs. Anthis today at the bank. She was so happy to see me, after all these years. Bobby her son works there, and ..." Vera paused, finishing a stitch on a rose; she cut the red thread and tied it with careful movements.

Cassiani eyed her mother warily. She couldn't help notice the gleam in her mother's eyes and the wide smile; her mother was up to something. "And?" she prompted.

"I invited them over for dinner tonight."

Cassiani blinked. She remembered that family vaguely. "Tonight?" she asked. "What is there to serve?"

"Don't worry about that. I did some grocery shopping today and bought some chicken. I'll bake it in the oven with potatoes. We'll throw a little salad and bread together, and that'll do fine."

"Is Bobby still single?" Cassiani asked, challenging her mother, her eyes narrowed. "I remember him when you were trying to get him together with Athena. He used to be *stout*."

"Yes, he is single. He should be thirty years old."

Cassiani crossed her arms. She remembered how her sister shunned Bobby's advances. "What does he look like *now*?"

"Well, you wouldn't call him handsome, but he is a nice boy. Because of his height, one might call him … a little overweight, but if he were taller, he would look just fine. Although he is losing a little hair on the top and combs it to the side to cover the bald spot—"

"That's all right," Cassiani interrupted, waving her arms in the air. "You don't have to continue."

Cassiani left for the village at three thirty to telephone Athena. Her mother did not come with her, saying, "I need to rest before the dinner." A half-hour later, she had reached the row of stores that marked the boundary. Most of the shops were closed for siesta. Luckily, the one she wanted was still open. She was thankful that there was no one else in the shop other than the owner; he waved to her from the back as she walked to the telephone.

Her sister answered the telephone. They chatted for a few minutes before Athena told her about Andy's telephone call a few days ago. "I gave him your address," Athena finished.

Cassiani was surprised to hear that. This was the first time he had shown her any personal interest. "He's my supervisor. I told him I had to leave for the island. I guess it's something about work." Cassiani's voice dropped a notch. "Athena, did you get a chance to buy the tickets?" She listened as her sister told her the news. "Good. I'll keep a lookout for them. I also wanted to tell you about Mother's financial situation."

*　　*　　*　　*

That evening, Cassiani helped her mother prepare the dinner. At some point, her mother disappeared into the living room to look for her old china set. Cassiani knew her mother was deliberately going out of her way to have her meet eligible men. This invitation tonight was proof that she'd prefer her daughter marrying a young man from Kos and staying here rather than go to America. But how could she? The other day, her mother seemed to accept the idea of going to America. Cassiani was so confused; she didn't know what to believe anymore. *If you don't look at it as a matchmaking effort, but as a friendly gesture on your mother's part, then you'll feel better.*

"Cassiani, please check the chicken and potatoes in the oven," Vera called out from the living room. "We must not let the potatoes bake too long!"

Cassiani dutifully did as she was told. She noticed her mother was taking a long time. She peeked in the small living room. "Do you need any help?"

Vera's head was buried in the cabinet of the china dresser. A pile of different shaped dishes and plates were stacked next to her. "They're here somewhere. It's been years since I used them." She pulled out a stack of large china plates. "Here they are!"

Cassiani went back into the kitchen. By the time the table was set with the expensive china plates, Vassiliki Anthis and her son arrived. Mrs. Anthis was a pale, thin woman with large eyes, a thin nose, and thin lips. She was considered a beauty in her youth. Her son did not take after her; he was overweight and had a bulbous nose, and his small eyes peered at her from behind thick glasses.

"What a beautiful young woman you have become!" Mrs. Anthis kissed Cassiani on the cheeks. "Do you remember me, Cassiani?"

CHAPTER 21

The twelve-seat airplane that Leo traveled in landed at the Athens airport at ten o'clock, Monday morning, amidst the downpour of an unusually heavy rain. It was a slow haul to downtown Athens. The taxi's windows were fogged up, making it difficult to see. An accident ahead caused much traffic on the road. It was almost noon by the time they arrived at Athens.

"Here we are," said the taxi driver.

Leo dashed through the rain and into the shipping mogul's building. The secretary who greeted him as he entered the office was new. She was young, well groomed, and wore glasses. He introduced himself.

"Mr. Doukas was expecting you this morning, but unfortunately, he had to go to the dentist for a toothache. He will try and meet you back in the office by four o'clock."

Leo glanced at his watch, nodding. He could do that.

The rain had stopped altogether by the time Leo arrived at his aunt's apartment. He obtained the key from Mrs. Galatsis. The suite was larger than the one in Kos, with two bedrooms and two bathrooms. It was a quiet oasis from the busy, noisy streets he had just left. It was elegantly furnished with expensive French provincial style furniture, and exotic vases and lamps. The marble floors were covered with richly decorated oriental rugs. He smiled when he saw the unavoidable presence of the grand piano. It filled up the whole living room and made a strong statement about the artistic and eccentric style of his aunt.

After showering, he rested on the bed. His arms behind his head, he stared at the ceiling, his mind on a number of issues. Typically, a missed meeting didn't bother him, but he had a sick aunt waiting for his return. *At least Cassiani is watching her.*

He dialed his aunt. No one answered. *She probably hasn't returned yet.* He then dialed his firm's phone number. Although the office wasn't open yet, he wanted to leave Jack a message on the answering machine. He had made it a habit to always check into the office and let Jack know his whereabouts. "Jack, Leo here. I'll be at Ben's office in Athens at four. The meeting was postponed until then. I'll keep you posted on developments." Before he hung up, he gave the telephone number at the apartment.

Leo slipped out of the apartment, looking for a restaurant. Around the corner, he sat and ate a hearty Greek luncheon of stuffed tomatoes, salad, bread, and wine. Afterwards, he strode through the shopping district of Monastiraki. He stopped occasionally to examine vases and other items. After two hours of inspecting goods, he returned to the apartment carrying two bags filled with several items that appealed to him in uniqueness, low price, and quality. He also had acquired several business cards for contact information.

*   *   *   *

Around three thirty, Leo telephoned his aunt; this time he spoke to her. "Aunt Soula, how did it go with the blood tests?" he asked, trying not to let the worry he felt show in his voice. "I called you a couple of times before but you didn't answer." *I was beginning to get worried.*

"They poked me with needles, pricked my finger, then had me wait for a while before they told me what they already knew. I have anemia but they don't know what is causing it."

"Anemia?" Leo asked. "What does Cassiani say about all this?"

"I haven't seen her today."

Leo was surprised to hear that. He had trusted that Cassiani would be there for her. "What do you mean? Wasn't she supposed to come at twelve?"

Soula told him what happened. "I ended up staying at Tessie's house for several hours. It was quite distressing because Nina left with her car, and didn't return to get me. I had to take a taxi back. I'm exhausted. I have to go back tomorrow for some x-rays."

Leo's mouth formed a straight line at what happened. Cassiani was not to blame. Even if she had come to the house, she would not have found his aunt there today.

"Where are you? Weren't you supposed to be back this afternoon?"

Leo winced. His aunt's question sounded more like a plea than a question. "My meeting was postponed for later today. I'll be back tomorrow as soon as I can. Why don't you have Cassiani take you tomorrow?"

"Cassiani?"

The surprise in his aunt's voice showed an obvious resistance to Cassiani's care. There was one thing that would help change her mind, and it was money. "We are paying her as a nurse. She can drive you there and back. This way you can also be sure you'll get home on time." He deliberately inserted the word "paying" into his sentence, knowing it would strike a chord with his aunt. She was not one to waste money needlessly. Paying a nurse to sit around would not fare well with her.

There was a pregnant pause. "Yes, you are right," Soula responded.

*   *   *   *

It was nine o'clock on this cold, rainy Monday in midtown Manhattan. Jack Finch had just arrived in his office on the tenth floor. He held his briefcase in one hand and a bag with a muffin in the other hand; his newspaper was tucked underneath his armpit.

Sally, his secretary met him at the door, appearing agitated. "A diplomat just called from Turkey. His name is Matt Doran. He said it was urgent."

"Could you get me coffee, then dial the number for me?" Jack went into his office and settled in his seat. Sally promptly came in with his mug of coffee. He sipped on the hot brew, wondering what the call was about. Moments later, Sally buzzed him; he picked up the telephone. "Jack Finch here."

"Mr. Finch, I called earlier from the American embassy in Turkey. This morning we were notified that the freighter *The Lion* ran aground at the Dardanelles strait while trying to avoid collision with an oil tanker. We understand that your company owns the ship."

Jack bolted up, knocking the mug of coffee over and getting splashed in the process. "What?" He yelled, then yowled "Wow!" when he felt the hot coffee seep through his pants. He ran out the door yelling, "Sally! Get me some napkins. Sally!"

Sally entered the room a minute later and swiped at the director's desk with a few paper towels before grabbing the telephone. "Mr. Finch spilled some hot coffee on him. He'll be right back," she said to Matt, then left hurriedly.

A few minutes later Jack returned to his office. He picked up the telephone. "Er, yes. So what happened exactly?"

"At five thirty this morning, due to bad weather and poor visibility, the *Nisse*, a Romanian oil tanker floundered from its path in the Dardanelles strait and almost collided with *The Lion*. *The Lion* swerved last minute to avoid the collision, causing it to run aground," Matt said.

Jack sank down in his chair. "What happened to the crew?"

"They are all right, but the ship needs to be addressed. We were hoping that when the tide came in, it would get back on track, but it hasn't. It is blocking the flow of ships in the strait."

"Was there any damage to the ship?"

"We don't know. Anything is possible, especially with older ships. The captain said because of her age, the ship might crack any minute and go under. Although the engineers from your ship are checking it, we need a responsible party from your company to come and take charge of the situation."

"Yes, we'll get to it right away." Jack glanced at his watch and did a quick calculation in his head. "How much margin of time do we have?"

"The sooner your people get here the better. The ship is costing everyone money."

Jack hung up the telephone, a thoughtful look on his face. His eyes rested upon the large framed picture of *The Lion* hanging on the wall; a sinking feeling in his stomach followed. His hand trembled slightly as he wiped his sweaty neck. He looked out the window at the dreary gray scene before him. This was *not* going to be a good day.

He glanced at his watch. It was nine thirty. Leo left him a message that he would be at Ben Doukas' office this afternoon. He dialed Ben's office.

CHAPTER 22

Leo entered Ben's elegantly furnished office. Ben was speaking on the telephone. Although he was in his late fifties, Ben appeared much younger. He was fit and slim, above average height, and with graying hair impeccably combed back. One side of his face appeared swollen, as if he had a wad of cotton inside his mouth.

Ben got off the telephone, arose and shook hands with Leo. "Leo! I apologize for any inconvenience our missed appointment may have caused you."

Leo smiled at Ben's temporary lisp. "I heard you had some dental work done?"

"Yes. I've been on liquids all day because of it. It's too painful to bite on." Ben pointed to his swollen jaw, then winced. "Please, have a seat."

"Thank you." Leo sat down in a tanned, leather chair. "Your generous gesture in providing a private airplane is greatly appreciated."

"My pleasure. I understand you were on vacation and were called away on my account?"

Leo recognized the small talk. This interest in his personal life was a way to ensure a comfortable atmosphere. He nodded. "I am visiting my aunt in Kos."

"Ahh, Kos Island with the crusaders' fortress, the beautiful harbor, and the Hippocrates tree. I knew a man from there once." Ben had a gleam in his eye as he leaned forward, appearing interested. "He was a good businessman. With his common sense and business savvy, he was able to scrimp and save to buy his first cargo ship. Ten years later, he owned four cargo ships."

Leo didn't know of any other ship-owner from Kos except his grandfather. He remembered the tall, regal man with the white mustache and captain's hat.

Ben continued. "I learned everything about shipping from this man. When he retired from the business, he sold all his ships and moved back to Kos. One of those ships he sold to me at a very cheap price. I was young and eager to have my own business, and that ship was the beginning of a successful career. His name was Leonidas Regopoulos."

Leo blinked when he heard the name. "Leonidas Regopoulos was my grandfather."

"Your grandfather?" Ben's jaw dropped. He winced in pain, and touched his jaw gingerly. "You caught me by surprise. Isn't your last name Regas?"

"Yes. My father changed his name to Regas when he moved to the United States, and this is the name I go by." Leo was intrigued by the connection between the two men. "How did you meet my grandfather?"

"I was a young captain looking for a job in Piraeus. He hired me to captain one of his ships. Before the trip, I remember him saying to me, Ben, one thing I rely on my crew most of all is to keep their eyes and ears open, for when you least expect it, that's when things happen." Ben paused, looking out into the distance. "He wanted to make sure we ran a tight ship. You see, we only had one boiler in those days, not two or three as they have today and if that went, there went your ship."

Leo nodded. "He used to tell me stories, when I was young, about how he made sure the crew maintained and cleaned the ship from top to bottom."

Ben appeared thoughtful. "You need to know one more thing." He stood up, his hands in his pockets. "Your grandfather didn't like being retired, and it wasn't long before he returned to Piraeus and bought a new cargo ship. He named it *Leonidas*. The ship ran different types of freight for a couple of years before he passed away."

"I had heard about the ship."

Ben nodded expectantly. "After your grandfather passed away, the ship sat in the dock for over a year, unattended, until the lawyers settled the papers of the estate. Shortly after that, your grandmother, through the insistence of her daughter, consulted with me. She said that she didn't have the experience to run a shipping business, and offered to sell the ship to me. I agreed. After I bought it, I named it *The Lion*."

Leo was stunned. He did a quick calculation in his head to verify the numbers. *The Lion* was twenty-five years old. His grandfather passed away twenty-three years ago, when Leo was eleven. So that meant only one thing. "*The Lion* is the same ship you sold to us a year ago."

Ben nodded. "It's not a young ship, but it's definitely a workhorse."

"And it's back in the family." Leo was quiet, contemplating on what he had just heard. Now that he knew this ship was originally his grandfather's, it held even more meaning to him. "We work hard to keep it well maintained. We haven't had any problems of it breaking down."

Ben nodded. "It's good to see his grandson following in his footsteps."

Leo smiled at Ben's sentimental use of words. That was another reason why he liked working with him. He was very personable.

"*Yiasas.*"

Leo looked up. The man that entered the room was small and wiry, yet his head was disproportionately large for his body; he sported large ears, a black mustache, and a balding head. Ben greeted his brother-in-law and introduced him to Leo.

Ben shuffled some papers together on his desk. "Now, let us get on to business." He looked at Leo. "Grain has been leaving Greece for Russia in large numbers, and consequently, there is demand for it here. We are looking for wheat from America to be supplied to the Sitaris Company here in Greece. My brother-in-law, Kostis, owns the company and will deal with the necessary paperwork and customs issues here."

"I'm beginning to see." Leo nodded, looking at Kostis. "If the Russians need the grain, I don't see why Greece can't supply it to them, and if the Greeks need grain, I don't see why America can't supply it to them. But first, we'll need to check out a few basic things. How much grain are they looking for? Will this be one shipment or several?" He continued his discussion.

Leo found out that due to the heavier cargo, they needed to go with a larger ship than *The Lion*. Ben had a five-year old bulk cargo ship that was 65,000 dwt. It was called the *Bali* and was available for Leo to charter for six months. Ben would supply the crew.

"You would ship the wheat to Kostis starting in September. Once the grain arrives, then we send our own goods back to the United States. We both get our shipments in, so this way the ship isn't empty," Ben finished.

They discussed prices, banking, and legalities. Leo wrote some numbers down and made some quick calculations. Just then the telephone rang.

"Yes?" Ben said. He listened, then gave Leo the telephone. "It's Jack. It's urgent."

"Leo, I have some bad news. It's about *The Lion*," Jack said. He told him the news.

Leo was astounded. "*What?*" It took him a minute to find his composure.

"We don't know if the ship will make it. Due to the force of the winds, the weight of the load, and the ship's age, there is a possibility that the ship may crack unexpectedly and sink."

Leo ran his fingers through his hair nervously. "How did you find out?"

Jack told him about Matt Doran's telephone call. "The captain and two engineers are assessing the situation. Meanwhile, the ships in the straits are backed up and waiting for our ship to be moved out of the way. The longer we wait the more the cost for everyone. I'm making arrangements to come as soon as I can, but since you're already in Greece, it would be faster for you to fly over there to oversee everything until I get there."

"All right. Could you give me Matt's phone number?" Leo scribbled the number on a piece of paper. Jack also gave him another number for the port authority before hanging up.

Leo glanced up at Ben and Kostis as he stuffed the paper into his pocket. "I'm sorry, but I have to leave immediately." He told them the news.

"Thousands of ships pass through the narrow Turkish straits every year, and there's bound to be a situation like this. Those are very narrow channels and there are some sharp bends," Ben said knowingly. "I had something happen to one of my ships a few years ago and a few tugboats were all that it needed to pull it free. Nothing happened to it. But if you need any help, feel free to call. *The Lion* is like family."

"Thanks." Leo smiled tightly at Ben's kind offer. He looked at Kostis. "I liked what I heard today. I'll get some prices for you and we'll go from there."

"Good," Kostis said, smiling. "You take care of your ship first."

Three hours later, Leo landed in Turkey. With no other thought than to reach the ship, he headed straight for the port authority. They took him by boat to the location where the ship was grounded. A few tugboats were already there and positioned to pull the ship. It was a laborious effort to free the ship from its spot; it wouldn't budge. When Jack arrived at midnight, Leo thankfully let him take over. At two o'clock in the morning the ship finally inched forward; Leo gave a triumphant shout when it happened. But the danger wasn't over. The ship's captain and two engineers said that it had sustained some damages. "The ship needs to be repaired before it can continue its journey," they reported. "There are too many cracks."

Slowly, *The Lion* was moved to a safe location for repairs.

A tired and exhausted Leo checked into a hotel in Istanbul at five thirty Tuesday morning. Sleep was the farthest thing from his mind.

CHAPTER 23

Tuesday

On this sunny spring morning, Cassiani could hear the birds chirping outside her window, causing her to smile as she slipped into her black skirt and white blouse. Feelings of anxiety intruded her thoughts; she wondered what she would find at Mrs. Lukas' today. The only comforting thought in all of this was that Leo would be coming back soon.

The gold cross and chain were put on next. There was a sense of security whenever she wore the cross. She pulled up her hair and formed a bun, then reached for the hairpins on the counter. To her dismay, she found only two hairpins; there usually were four. She got on her hands and knees and searched the floor for the lost pins.

"What are you looking for?" Vera asked, standing at the door.

Cassiani stood up, wiping her hands. "My hairpins. I lost them." She stopped when she saw her mother's face. "You're breathing heavily again. Did you do something you weren't supposed to?" she asked.

"I was watering the garden, then I saw some weeds and started pulling them."

"Come, let's take your readings." Cassiani's hair was forgotten as she left the room to check her mother's vital signs. A few minutes later, she confirmed that everything was within the normal range except her mother's pulse. "Why don't you rest while I get breakfast ready?"

Cassiani prepared breakfast. "Do we have any fruit, like apples?" she asked. She missed eating fruit. She had them year round in America. "You should eat more fruit. It is good for you."

"They're not fresh, and too expensive. They bring them in from a long distance during this time of the year," Vera said, shaking her head. "We get plenty of cantaloupe and watermelons in the summer, but now, it's too early for anything."

"You need to eat fresh fruit. You either invest in your health now, or end up going to doctors later." Cassiani made tea for both of them. After a brief prayer, they ate their toasted bread, goat cheese, and boiled eggs.

Vera looked up at her intently. "So what did you think about Bobby?"

"Bobby?" Cassiani stared at her mother. She had forgotten about yesterday's dinner with Bobby and his mother. He seemed to be interested in her, giving her his undivided attention, but she could not picture herself forming a relationship with him. "Let's say that he is nice, as a friend, but no more than that."

"You didn't like the way he looked. I could tell."

"Not only that, it was also what he said and did. He laughed too easily over nothing, and all he talked about was wanting to go to America and wanting to know what it was like."

"I noticed," Vera said, nodding. "I also didn't like his table manners. Did you see the way he wolfed down his food and ate up all the bread? He'll eat you out of house and home!"

Cassiani laughed. She teased her mother. "You didn't have to offer for him to visit us on Wednesday, his day off, just as they were leaving!"

Vera appeared apologetic. "It was just an automatic gesture on my part, you know, a formality. I didn't expect him to say yes so quickly! That shows he's interested in you."

Cassiani didn't want to pursue that topic. "Mother, before I forget, I wanted to talk to you about my conversation with Athena," she said. "She sent us airline tickets that she bought at a discount price, which means they are nonrefundable. We should be receiving them anytime now. We're scheduled to leave in a few weeks, which doesn't give us much time to prepare."

A heated discussion ensued. Her mother kept focusing on the negative impact of the move while Cassiani kept stressing the positive side. At one point, Cassiani glanced at her watch. Her eyes flew open. "Oh no! I'm late for work!"

*   *   *   *

Cassiani ran up the hill wondering what she would find today at the Lukas residence. Panting, she reached the front door. To her relief, the door to the house opened this time.

Mrs. Lukas was sitting in the parlor. Cassiani noticed Mrs. Lukas' disheveled appearance, from her unkempt hair, to her long, beige robe that hung loosely on her small frame, as if she had just awakened and hadn't yet changed into her clothes. Cassiani greeted her cheerfully.

"What took you so long?" Soula snapped, peering at her. "What happened to your hair?"

Cassiani's hand flew to her hair. "Oh, I forgot to put it up!"

Soula studied her. "It's becoming that way. You should wear it down more often."

Cassiani blinked, surprised by the rare compliment. "Thank you."

"How's your mother doing?"

"She has a hard time sitting still."

"I know what you mean. When she was here, she was constantly moving around, doing things for me," Soula said, cackling. "She never could sit still."

Cassiani noticed Mrs. Lukas' softened expression. It appeared as if she liked her mother.

"How is everything with you today?"

Soula yawned. Her features slipped back into a disgruntled look. "Not so good. Stella came seven thirty this morning. Too early! Would you believe it? Her husband honked the horn as if he had nothing else to do but wake up the whole neighborhood; it was so loud." She gestured into the air. "I didn't feel like going back to bed, so I sat here. I'm waiting for Stella to bring my breakfast."

Cassiani nodded. "I came twice yesterday, but you weren't here. How did it go?"

Soula shared the information about her anemia. "Now they want me back today at eleven, for an X-ray. I don't know why they want me to have all that done," she grumbled.

"X-rays are sometimes included in physical exams if the doctor feels it is necessary," Cassiani explained. "Is Nina going to take you again?"

"No. You will. Leo wants it that way, and I agree with him."

Cassiani was surprised to hear that. "All right." She removed her equipment from the handbag, and with deliberate gentleness, wrapped the cuff around Mrs. Lukas' thin, wrinkled arm. "Let me check you then, until Stella brings the food." She measured her vital signs. "Except for your blood pressure being a little low, everything appears the same as Sunday."

"Good morning, Cassiani!" Stella called, entering the parlor carrying a tray of food.

Cassiani greeted her cheerfully. Stella's presence brought her a sense of comfort. She radiated love and goodness wherever she was, even here, with Mrs. Lukas.

Stella placed the tray on the table and gazed at Soula with a broad smile. "Here you are, Mrs. Lukas, some nice, fried eggs, buttered toast, a slice of cheese, and milk. Now you enjoy it." She watched Soula bite into the toast. "I brought you a nice size *tsipoura* today. I can make the fish plaki style for dinner. Would you like that?"

Soula appeared pleased. "I like fish. I seem to eat lamb all the time."

"Good. Did you need anything else?" Stella asked, clasping her hands together.

"Please have the dining room table set for three people. Oh, and from now on, don't come earlier than nine o'clock. I don't get up until then."

Cassiani was thoughtful as she watched Stella leave. She liked Stella's cheerful and good-hearted nature. Maybe what Mrs. Lukas needed was a relaxed, comfortable environment and a cheerful employee. "Mrs. Lukas, how about a little classical music?"

∗   ∗   ∗   ∗

Mrs. Lukas had taken her time to dress, not allowing Cassiani to help. So they were already late when they drove down the winding mountain road. At the Zipari intersection Cassiani turned right, heading towards Kos Town. Cassiani relaxed momentarily under the sun's rays and slow pace of the island. However, the closer they got to the city, the more Cassiani was wracked with uncertainty.

"Stay on Asklipiou," Mrs. Lukas muttered before dozing off.

Careful and cautious, Cassiani drove down the main road that led into the city with its many streets. She didn't notice the cars and motorcyclists zooming past her as she slowed down to a crawl. Somehow they ended up on Megalou Alexandrou, heading west. It wasn't long before the Grigoriou intersection loomed up ahead, signaling that they were going back to where they had started. Cassiani sighed. "Mrs. Lukas, I think we are lost."

Mrs. Lukas sputtered herself awake, then peered around. She gestured into the air. "To the left, turn to the left before you pass it! The hospital is down *that* way!"

CHAPTER 24

They arrived back at the house a few minutes past three. Cassiani nudged Mrs. Lukas. "Mrs. Lukas," she said, waking her. "We're here." She held on to her as they walked into the house.

"Hmmm. It smells good," Soula said groggily. "It's nice to come home to a well-cooked meal." They entered the parlor. She gestured towards the armchair. "Help me move the chair around. I want to face the garden today. It relaxes me."

Cassiani turned the armchair around to face the window and helped her sit down. She moved the small round table closer to Mrs. Lukas.

Soula yawned, then squinted at her watch. "I'm expecting Nina at three. Why don't you go and see if Stella set the dining room table."

"You also need to take your iron pill. Would you care for a snack to go with that?"

Soula nodded. "Some toast is fine, with tea."

Cassiani peeked into the dining room. The table was set for three and in the middle of the table sat a large, covered bowl, a plate of sliced bread, and a bowl of kalamata olives. Once in the kitchen, Cassiani busied herself preparing the toast and tea. As she poured the hot peppermint tea into the cup, she felt her arm and body tremble; she almost spilled the tea. *That's odd.* She placed the pot down. Just then she felt the floor shaking. She gripped the edge of the counter to balance herself. Feeling uneasy, she waited, wondering if that might have been an earthquake. To her relief the tremors did not return. She hastened towards the parlor with the food.

"Here you go, Mrs. Lukas," Cassiani said, placing the food in front of her. "Did you feel the tremors?"

"What tremors?" Soula asked. Her hand was poised in the air, holding an open pill bottle.

Cassiani didn't have a chance to reply, for just then a loud pounding noise came from the front door. "Excuse me." She hurried towards the door wondering why they couldn't just open it. She got her answer as soon as she opened the door. It was Nina.

Nina wore a sleeveless white blouse, black miniskirt, and high heels. In one hand was a covered bowl and in the other, a large bag. Just then the ground shook forcefully, causing her to lose her balance. She lurched forward.

Cassiani grabbed her to keep her from falling. "Are you all right?" she asked. "It seems as if we're in the middle of an earthquake."

"Yes," Nina said, appearing annoyed. She pulled away. "Is Mrs. Lukas here?"

"She's in the parlor." Cassiani replied. "She's been expecting you."

"Please take this into the kitchen. It's for tonight's meal."

Cassiani took the covered bowl, feeling her face flush at the woman's condescending tone. She sped to the kitchen and placed the bowl down. The earth shook again and she grabbed the counter. Then she heard the scream.

Cassiani rushed to the parlor, her heart pounding. Mrs. Lukas was lying crumpled on the floor and Nina was bent over her, crying hysterically.

"She's, she's not breathing!" Nina wailed.

In one swift movement, Cassiani kneeled next to Mrs. Lukas, opening up her airway passage by pulling her head gently back. She knew what to do and went to work. She probed her neck, trying to find a pulse. There was none. Gently, rhythmically, steadily she performed CPR on Mrs. Lukas while Nina sobbed uncontrollably. *Dear Lord, please let her live.*

She pressed on her chest several times, then breathed into her mouth, trying to resuscitate her. After what seemed like a long time, Mrs. Lukas' chest heaved and she gave a loud gasp. Then she started to breathe deeply. Cassiani gulped back her cry of joy as the giddy feeling of saving her life threatened to overwhelm her.

"Mrs. Lukas, can you hear me? Mrs. Lukas!" Cassiani cried.

Soula Lukas opened her eyes slowly. Cassiani noticed that her eyes were a light brown color, and one pupil was dilated, while the other wasn't. That worried her.

"What happened?" Soula whispered. "What? Why? What happened?"

"She's alive?" Nina said, her face appearing as if she just saw a ghost.

"Shh. Just rest for now," Cassiani said firmly to Mrs. Lukas. "You fainted. I need to check you, to see you didn't break anything when you fell."

Cassiani touched her right leg. "Do you hurt here?"

"No."

Cassiani touched her other limbs, asking her the same question and receiving the same response. There was nothing broken. Just then, Mrs. Lukas began to cough, moving her head from side to side, appearing agitated.

Cassiani recognized the woman's distress. "Here, let's move you to the side so you can breathe better." Cassiani positioned her so that she was semiprone on the floor. That seemed to help, because Mrs. Lukas stopped her coughing. Cassiani stroked her forehead, talking to her gently, trying to keep her from sleeping.

"My head, it hurts," Mrs. Lukas whimpered, her voice slurring, her eyes shut.

Cassiani was beginning to feel frustrated. She didn't have any equipment to work with, like in the hospital. She was on her own and she had to use her wits quickly. "Nina can you call the ambulance? I think it would be best for her to go to the hospital."

Nina went to the telephone that was on the coffee table. She dialed the number. After what seemed a long time, she hung up. "No one answered," she said petulantly.

"Please try again," Cassiani insisted.

Nina tried twice, but to no avail.

Cassiani noticed that Mrs. Lukas had fallen asleep. "Mrs. Lukas. Mrs. Lukas," she said, her voice raised. There was no response.

*   *   *   *

Cassiani knew something was terribly wrong when Mrs. Lukas didn't reply. Her fingers massaged Mrs. Lukas' white-haired head, searching for some clue. To her amazement, she discovered a large bump in the back of her head. "Oh, no!" She stood up, her mind racing.

"What's the matter?" Nina asked.

"There is a bump in the back of her head, maybe a hematoma. If it's what I think it is, this is serious. We need to get her to the hospital quickly. Can you call your father?"

Nina flashed her an angry look before she dialed the number. "Father, Nina here. There's an emergency. No, not me. It's Mrs. Lukas. I found her lying on the floor. She wasn't breathing. Yes, Cassiani was here. I don't know when this happened, just that I found her on the floor."

Cassiani realized how it must sound to the doctor, to hear that the nurse was in the house but wasn't there to keep an eye on Mrs. Lukas. *If I had been in the room, I could have gotten to her quicker. How long was she like that ... a minute or two?*

"Cassiani made her breathe, but now she won't wake up," Nina said. "We already called the ambulance and they didn't answer. All right. I will tell her."

Cassiani gazed at her expectantly. *Maybe her father could get us an ambulance.*

"Father said we should try calling the ambulance again," Nina said. "He will telephone the hospital to be ready for her."

Cassiani felt a sense of disappointment. This wasn't going to be easy. "We can't wait for them. It might be too late! We have to take her ourselves!"

"But—"

"Please keep an eye on her while I find some sheets." Cassiani rushed out of the room. She scrounged in the bedroom until she found clean sheets. She grabbed them and ran back.

Nina was sitting in the chair, her legs and arms crossed, appearing upset.

Working quickly, Cassiani opened a sheet and slipped it underneath Mrs. Lukas. Should she attempt to drive to the hospital with the car, or have Nina do it? The answer came quickly. "Nina, could you bring your car up to the door? It's too far to take her to the car."

"My car? But there's no driveway. It's just a small path!"

"You'll make one *now*. Please go!"

Cassiani heard the door slam as Nina ran out.

CHAPTER 25

Cassiani continued working methodically, pulling the sheet from under the woman's body to the other side. She kept her in the semiprone position to ensure that the respiratory passages were clear. As she waited for Nina's return, she checked Mrs. Lukas' pulse. It appeared normal and she was still breathing. "Mrs. Lukas. Mrs. Lukas." She pinched her arm. There was a faint response; a fluttering of eyelids were followed by a low moan. Good, but still no reply. "Please, Lord, show me what I need to do. Please do not let anything happen to her."

Then she thought about Leo. He was supposed to arrive later today. She took a piece of paper from her purse and scribbled a note to him, hoping he would see it. She placed it on the round table next to the breakfast plate. Just then she noticed the bottle of iron pills. It was lying on its side, opened; several pills had spilled out on the table. Her glance on the floor confirmed her suspicion. A few pills were lying there. Mrs. Lukas must have opened the bottle of pills during the earthquake and dropped them, then bent down to pick them up. That's when she lost her balance and fell to the ground.

The sound of Nina's footsteps on the marble floor alerted her. She looked up. "I need your help, Nina. Please take the other end. We're going to carry her with the sheet."

"Isn't she going to fall out?"

"Not if you roll it up like this." She showed her. "One hand will hold the sheet upward near the head, and the other around her knees. Her weight will keep her inside the sheet. Just hold on tight."

Slowly, they lifted the woman, but she was too heavy for Nina. Cassiani was able to hold her end up, but Nina was too weak. They lowered Mrs. Lukas to the floor.

"Now what?" Nina asked, looking exasperated.

"I think we'll have to drag her. We'll wrap her up in the sheet. You hold her legs up."

"What?" Nina seemed disgusted.

"Do you have a better idea?" Cassiani retorted. She was getting tired of Nina's resistance. Cassiani slipped her arms underneath Mrs. Lukas' armpits, then wrapped her hands tightly around her chest, lifting her upper body. Nina positioned herself near her legs.

"All right, here we go," Cassiani said.

They pulled the woman inch by inch out into the hallway and through the front door. Just then the telephone rang. They stopped and looked at each other. "We can't leave her now," Cassiani said, panting. They continued their tortuous journey as the telephone continued to ring in the distance

Getting Mrs. Lukas into the car was an equally difficult task but Cassiani slid into the back car seat and hoisted her up from the shoulders. They laid her carefully down in the back seat. Cassiani held on to Mrs. Lukas while Nina drove them to the hospital. They were going at a fast pace down the winding mountain road and the ride was exceptionally bumpy. Cassiani tried to keep from bouncing while holding on to Mrs. Lukas at the same time. Once they reached the main road, it was a smoother ride. Cassiani thought about her mother, wondering how she was doing and hoping she wouldn't worry too much about her. Her watch showed four o'clock.

*   *   *   *

The tremors from the earthquake frightened Vera. She scurried outside, making the sign of the cross and saying a prayer. She headed for the stall, removed the goats and brought them to the front yard. The goats were jittery and she had a hard time tying them around the lemon tree. Just then she felt another tremor. Her heart beat rapidly as she tied the last knot. She leaned against the tree, breathing heavily, her hand pressed to her chest.

Mrs. Kalotsis waved to her from her front courtyard. "Is everything all right?"

"My heart is going a little fast. I think I exerted myself too much." Vera replied.

They stayed outside until the tremors stopped. Mrs. Kalotsis' chickens were milling around them, clucking nervously all the time. After a while, the hens calmed down. It seemed as if the earthquake had stopped.

When Vera went back inside the house, she anxiously checked for damages. A few framed photos had fallen from the wall and a newly formed crack was evident on the side of the living room wall. Other than that, she saw nothing else damaged from the quake. With trembling hands, she took the tablecloth outside to stitch, hoping it would calm her down. She would sit and wait for Cassiani's return.

An hour later, she became worried. *Cassiani should have been here by now.* She placed the tablecloth to the side, then glanced down the lane, hoping for a sign of her daughter.

It was a fifteen-minute walk down the hill to Mrs. Spanos' house. Vera's breathing was labored by the time she arrived. Stella was in the kitchen, busy sweeping some broken pieces of a vase. "*Kalispera*, Stella! How is everything? Did you feel the earthquake?"

"We just got back from our daughter's house." Stella paused and sighed. "We were there when the ground shook terribly, but we were all right." She finished sweeping up the pieces from the floor. "Thank God, there was no damage to the house other than a few things that fell and broke, like this vase." She stared at her. "Come, have a seat. You look quite flushed."

Vera thanked her as she sat down. "Stella, it's four thirty and my Cassiani hasn't come home yet from Mrs. Lukas' house. I'm worried that something may have happened to her. She should have been home by now. Do you know anything?"

"I saw her this morning when I went to the house. They were supposed to go to the hospital for some test around eleven or so."

Vera wiped her sweaty brow. "They should have been done by now. You never know what will happen when one of those earthquakes decides to strike. God forbid you're in the wrong place." She made the sign of the cross.

"Yes, across the street from my daughter's house the neighbor's roof collapsed!"

Vera's eyes flew open. "*Christos kai Panagia!*" she exclaimed.

"Luckily everyone was outside and no one got hurt."

"Oh, Stella! Maybe something terrible happened to my daughter! Oooh, I don't know what to do!" Vera wailed. She placed her hand on her heart, sobbing.

"Please, calm down. You're not going to help anyone by getting hysterical. The best thing to do is to go to Mrs. Lukas' house and see!" Stella said. She went to the back door and called her husband. "Panos, my love, come quickly! We need you."

Several minutes later, Panos parked on the boundary line of Mrs. Lukas' house. "Look, tracks were made from a car." He pointed to the tire marks that ran along the path to the house.

The door to the house was wide open. They searched the rooms and found no one inside.

"Here is a note!" Stella called out from the parlor. "Your daughter wrote it!"

Trembling from excitement, Vera rushed to her and read the note aloud. "Dr. Leo, your aunt fell and hurt her head during the earthquake. Nina and I took her to the hospital. She is unconscious. We will probably be there when you arrive. We hope to see you there. Cassiani."

With shaking fingers, Vera took the pen that was nearby and added a few more words to the note. She looked at the couple. "Could you do me one more favor?"

CHAPTER 26

Dr. Vassilakis examined Mrs. Lukas. She was still unconscious. The oxygen tubing was hooked up to her nose and an intravenous line was supplying her with liquids. There was a concerned look on his face as he gently touched and probed the patient. His stethoscope hung like sausage links around his thick neck. He turned and looked at Cassiani. "Would you happen to have Leo's telephone number? He should be notified about his aunt's precarious situation. With the earthquake, it's very chaotic now and it would be difficult to transport her to Athens."

Cassiani shook her head. "I'm sorry, but I don't know it. He's supposed to be returning later today. I left a note at the house for him."

"We'll just wait then, won't we?" Dr. Vassilakis said, as he walked away.

Those first few moments, waiting, wondering what the outcome was, with no one to talk to, were excruciatingly slow for Cassiani. She silently prayed for Mrs. Lukas. The nurses were scarce, having spread themselves thin doing different tasks, leaving her alone.

When a nurse finally showed up, Cassiani excused herself and went to the emergency waiting room. The small room was still filled with people. She walked to the door and stood outside for a moment. People were walking down the street and the sun was still shining, as if the earthquake a few hours ago had never happened. A tawny colored cat wandered by, its tail in the air, meowing at her. The cat circled her legs, purring. Cassiani bent down and stroked its head, smiling. "Hello, kitty." When the cat looked up at her with its kaleidoscope eyes, their brilliant hues reminded her of Leo's eyes. A distant honk caused the cat to vanish around the corner.

Cassiani re-entered the waiting room. Knowing her mother, she would probably be worried sick by now. *If only we had a telephone, I could contact her.* Just then, an older couple entered the hospital. They both appeared disheveled and disoriented. The old man moaned, then teetered as if he were going to fall. His wife grabbed him. Cassiani rushed to help steady him.

"He's in a lot of pain," said the man's wife. She clutched his arm tightly. "We think he broke his leg when he fell during the earthquake. I don't know what to do."

"Here, I'll get some help." Cassiani immediately helped him sit down, then searched for a wheelchair. Moments later she returned with one. "Let's get him in this and I'll wheel him to the back. The nurses are all busy." As they searched for an empty bed, the woman introduced herself as Georgia Pappas, and her husband's name was John. They eventually found an empty bed and Cassiani helped his wife put him in the bed.

Cassiani found a middle-aged nurse who was busy giving medication to a patient. She was tall and thin, with short, gray hair, and a kind face. Cassiani waited until she finished her task, then introduced herself. The nurse's name was Fanny. Cassiani pointed to Mr. Pappas lying in the bed. She explained his situation and the possibility of a broken leg.

"Are you his daughter?" Fanny asked, walking briskly toward the old man's bed.

Cassiani followed her. "No. I'm a nurse, visiting from America. I felt that he needed urgent care after I checked him."

After Fanny took charge of the man's care, Cassiani excused herself and went to the waiting room. She busied herself helping newly arrived patients; most of the injuries were from the earthquake. The hospital nurses thanked her for her help.

As Cassiani worked steadily, she thought about her mother and prayed that she was not injured by the earthquake or had another heart attack from the impact. At other times she thought about Leo. Even if he tried making it today, she heard from several people that the flights were delayed due to the earthquake. How would he take it if his aunt didn't survive? She knew he loved his aunt very much. She saw it by his actions.

She was beginning to feel a sense of pity for Mrs. Lukas who had become suddenly so vulnerable and frail. *You chose to be a nurse, to help people, and it is better not to get emotionally involved with your patients. Prepare yourself for the worst.* She touched her gold cross. "May the Lord forgive me and please watch over Mrs. Lukas," she whispered.

Just then, Fanny came looking for her. "Cassiani, Dr. Vassilakis wanted you to know that Soula Lukas just woke up and is alert. He says you brought her in just in time."

Tears of joy welled up in Cassiani's eyes. "Can I see her? I'd like to be with her."

Fanny touched her arm. "He ordered a few tests for now, so afterwards would be better. She'll be up on the second floor when she's all done," she said as she left.

Cassiani said a silent prayer, thanking God for his help. A big weight of responsibility resting on her shoulders these past few hours was just lifted. She wanted to burst out and share this victorious moment with her patient, her mother, or Leo. She returned to the waiting room. It was partially empty and there were no new patients. She sat down in a chair.

After she was allowed to see Mrs. Lukas, what should she do? Should she stay with her all night? Should she go home? How was she going to get back home? She brought no money with her, and her pride would keep her from asking for money from the nursing staff. The sound of a door slamming startled her.

"Cassiani!" Vera shouted. Her excited voice resounded through the waiting room. Close behind her were Mr. and Mrs. Spanos. She rushed forward and hugged Cassiani. "I was so worried about you. Tell me, my daughter, what happened?"

Cassiani told her the news. "Luckily, Nina was there to help me take her to the car and drive her here," she finished.

"And Mrs. Lukas?" Vera asked, her eyes expressing concern.

"The nurse just came a few minutes ago and said she is awake and alert. The doctor is checking her and running more tests."

"Oh, good!" Vera exclaimed, along with everyone else. She made the sign of the cross.

"You saved her life," Stella Spanos said, her face showing admiration. Panos, her husband agreed.

Cassiani smiled back. "God was with her." This was one part of nursing that she liked; to see miracles happen. *And Mrs. Lukas' recovery was definitely a miracle.*

Vera studied her closely. "You look a little tired. Have you eaten anything?"

"I was too busy helping patients. Several were injured from the earthquake."

"Panos, please go get something for us to eat. There's a shop down the road," Stella told her husband. "Bring something to drink also."

"May the *Panagia* and *Christo* bless you and your family," Vera told him as he left. She sat down, then patted the empty seat next to her. "Come, sit down."

Cassiani sat down and Stella sat next to her.

"Cassiani, are you all right? You look troubled."

Cassiani was surprised by Stella's perceptive remark. This woman had a good heart. She brought her mother here and cared enough to ask how she felt. "I do feel guilty for not being next to Mrs. Lukas when she fell. Maybe if I was there, she might not have—"

"Cassiani, you don't take enough credit for your actions. You saved her life!" Stella said. "Mrs. Lukas was very lucky to have you by her side. Otherwise, who knows what may have happened to her?"

Vera turned to her friend. "Ever since she was a child, my Cassiani had the gift of healing. See how she saved this woman's life? Nina would not have known how to revive her."

"Yes, your mother is right," Stella said, patting Cassiani fondly on the arm.

"Now that we're talking about Nina," Vera said, looking around. "Where is she?"

"Nina went home. She said she was tired," Cassiani said.

*   *   *   *

Panos returned quickly with food and drinks, and they all sat down to eat. Cassiani munched her food, listening to the conversation between her mother, Stella, and Panos. The topic centered on the earthquake. The other people in the room joined in the conversation. A young couple sitting nearby said their courtyard had split in two and their house also suffered some damages. A heavy-set woman sitting farther away said that her mother was sitting outside cleaning some beans when the tremors occurred. "She fell and hurt herself, so I brought her here," she explained.

Cassiani had heard these stories earlier, when she was taking the patients to the back to be treated. It was intriguing to note how an unfortunate and traumatic event like the earthquake brought these people together. It seemed as if they found comfort in sharing their stories and in each other's company, even if for a short time.

Cassiani checked her watch. It was six thirty. She was beginning to worry about Leo. *Maybe he didn't see my note. Maybe something happened to him. Maybe the airport was closed due to the earthquake.*

A half-hour later, the Spanos couple arose to leave. "We need to go to our daughter. She still needs help with the baby," Stella explained to Vera. "It's like being a mother all over again."

Cassiani told them how grateful she was for bringing her mother and for getting the food.

Stella smiled back. "What are friends for?" she replied. She kissed Cassiani on the cheek.

Cassiani waved to both of them as they left. Outside it was already beginning to get dark. The couple vanished quickly down the dimly lit street. Cassiani walked back to where her mother was sitting. Her mother was having a conversation with the couple sitting to her right. *Mrs. Lukas' tests should be finished by now.* Cassiani patted her on the shoulder.

Vera looked at her daughter. "Yes?"

"I'll be back soon. I'm going to check up on Mrs. Lukas." Cassiani headed towards the back, thinking about Mrs. Lukas and wondering about Leo's whereabouts. As she was about to take the stairwell, her thoughts were interrupted by her mother's loud voice.

"Dr. Leo!" Vera bellowed her greeting.

Cassiani turned around, her heart racing. Her eyes zoomed past the seated people to the man standing at the entrance door. *Leo is finally here to take charge.*

CHAPTER 27

Vera rushed to greet Leo at the door. "Your aunt is awake!" she exclaimed.

"I called the hospital from the house and they told me she was still unconscious," Leo said. "Thank you for all that you've done."

"I didn't do anything," Vera gushed. "Cassiani saved her life."

Cassiani noticed her mother waving for her to come. She approached them.

There was a relieved look on Leo's face as he greeted her. "Cassiani, can you tell me what exactly happened, from the beginning?"

Cassiani dutifully told him, trying to sound as professional as she could.

"Did she have to wait long before the doctor saw her?" Leo asked.

"Actually, they took her in right away," Cassiani said. "The waiting room was filled with people injured from the earthquake, but I made a strong point about her dire situation."

"Thank you for everything," he said huskily. "Your efforts saved my aunt's life."

Cassiani flushed at the intense way that he looked at her. "I was only doing my duty."

"I knew that I can rely on you." Leo gazed around the room expectantly. "What happened to Nina?"

Vera sniffed. "She was tired and went home." She pulled out a wrapped souvlaki from inside her purse. "Would you care for some food? We had some left over."

"Thank you, but right now all I want to do is to see my aunt." Leo turned to Cassiani. "Would you be able to show me where she is?"

Cassiani led Leo down the corridor. She noticed for the first time that his eyes were bloodshot, his face was unshaven, and his shirt was wrinkled. Yet even in this unkempt state, he walked with the assurance and confidence of a worldly man.

They walked up the stairwell.

"I would have been here much sooner but I had to go to Turkey for an emergency." Leo rubbed his eyes. "I had to represent our company until my boss arrived." He was about to continue, then paused, as if taking time to think about the next words. "I appreciate that you stayed with my aunt until my return." He smiled warmly at Cassiani.

Cassiani gazed back. "We didn't know in what direction her injury would take. I felt responsible for her until you came." They entered the second floor and continued walking. The smell of disinfectant assailed her senses.

"I tried calling my aunt to tell her I'd be away at least another day ... but ..."

"She didn't answer the phone, nor did anyone else," Cassiani finished.

Leo nodded. "After I learned about the earthquake in Kos, I became worried that something may have happened to her." His fingers combed his bangs back nervously. "I tried to get here earlier, but the airplanes flying in were delayed because of the earthquake."

"Your aunt is fortunate to have a nephew like you who cares so much about her," Cassiani blurted. She flushed when she saw him staring at her. "Although she passed through a difficult time today, the good Lord was with her."

Leo smiled. "Let's not forget your part in this."

Cassiani smiled at the compliment. They entered a large room with several rows of beds, partitioned by curtains. She caught sight of a young nurse tinkering with the medical equipment on a cart. Cassiani introduced herself and Leo, then asked her where Mrs. Lukas was.

Fifi, the nurse, gazed back with wide, blue eyes. "She is my patient. Come this way."

They passed the bed that held Mr. Pappas. He and his wife waved to Cassiani.

"They'll take good care of him, Mrs. Pappas," Cassiani piped back. A couple of other patients greeted her as she passed them. In another bed, lay an old woman that Cassiani had helped earlier. Cassiani stopped to find out how she was doing.

The woman thanked her. "Please, let my daughter know I am here."

"I surely will," Cassiani replied to the woman. She resumed her walk with Leo.

"It looks like you helped quite a few people get situated," Leo remarked.

Mrs. Lukas was at the far end of the room. She appeared to be sleeping peacefully. Fifi nudged her awake. "Mrs. Lukas, can you hear me? It's Fifi, your nurse."

"Ehh?" Soula said groggily, her eyes half-open, attempting to smile.

Leo bent over her, talking softly to her, holding her hand.

"Leo, is that you? How did you find me, you old rascal?"

"When Cassiani and Nina brought you to the hospital, they left a note for me at the house that you would be here. Guess who is here with me?"

"Nina?"

"No. Nina went home," Leo said, pausing. "Cassiani is here. Would you like to speak to her?"

Soula gestured feebly into the air. "That's all right." She shut her eyes. "I'm very tired."

Just then, Dr. Vassilakis came into the room with another doctor. He introduced him as Dr. Kafetsoulis. Dr. Vassilakis bent over the patient. "Mrs. Lukas, wake up. It's Dr. Vassilakis." he commanded loudly. "Do you know where you are?"

Soula opened one eye, then the other, then blinked as the doctor shined a light into her eyes. "Of course I do! I'm in the hospital!"

"Your aunt is very fortunate." Dr. Vassilakis shoved the small flashlight into his white coat pocket. "She had us worried, but she pulled through it. Isn't that right, Dr. Kafetsoulis?"

"Yes," Dr. Kafetsoulis said. "If her condition was worse, she would have had to be flown to a major hospital in Athens, and there's always a risk involved during transport. We do not have the capability to perform the surgery on her, which would have required opening a section of the head to drain the fluid that had accumulated and was pressing against the brain."

Leo winced. "What do you propose she do now?"

"I'd like for her to stay a couple of days in the hospital, to be observed," Dr. Vassilakis said. "To make sure she is completely out of danger."

The two doctors and the nurse left shortly after.

"*Yia-sas.*"

Cassiani looked up to the sound of the familiar female voice. Nina's voice had changed from the annoyingly scratchy whine of a few hours ago to a soft purr. She was carrying a bouquet of roses. Her mother was right behind her.

Nina and her mother literally took over Mrs. Lukas' care. Cassiani moved out of the way, watching from the side at all the fuss and commotion made over the sick woman.

Fifi came into the room. "Mrs. Lukas," she said cheerfully. "I'm back."

"What do you want from me *this* time, Fufu?" Soula asked.

Fifi giggled nervously. "My name is Fifi." She held up a syringe in her hand. "Dr. Vassilakis wants me to give you a shot." She looked at the group gathered around Soula. "You *don't* want to see where she's going to have it, either."

Everyone cleared the room quickly, then returned when she notified them that she was finished. Fifi proceeded to prop Mrs. Lukas up on her pillow. "If you need anything, let me know, Mrs. Lukas," she said. "I'll be your nurse tonight."

Leo asked Fifi questions about his aunt. A discussion ensued.

Cassiani waited a few minutes, listening to their conversation. It looked as if she wasn't needed. Cassiani excused herself and left the room.

"Cassiani!" Leo came out into the hallway. "Thank you again for all your help." He touched her arm. "I'd like for you to continue nursing her. You know my aunt better than anyone else."

"Oh?" Cassiani was surprised to hear him say that. A few minutes ago, he seemed to have been quite content talking with Fifi. "What about that nurse, *Fifi*?"

Leo sighed. "I'm having some doubts about her." He gazed into her eyes intently. "Could you return in the morning?"

Cassiani was surprised by his request. It seemed as if Mrs. Lukas had several people watching over her already. *But he wants you to watch over her.* She nodded. "My mother didn't get a chance to see her. Will it be all right if I brought her with me tomorrow?"

"Of course." His gaze briefly fell on her mouth before settling on her hair. "By the way, your hair looks nicer when you leave it down." He went back into the room before she could respond.

Cassiani felt as if she were walking on clouds after hearing his compliment. She had forgotten about her hair all this time. She also realized that Leo entrusted her with the person that he loved, even when there were hospital nurses by his aunt's side.

She found her mother conversing with the couple that sat next to her. Cassiani greeted her mother. "Mrs. Lukas has too many people visiting her right now," she said. "Dr. Leo has asked us to come back in the morning."

"Shall we leave then?" Vera stood up, ready to bid her farewell to everyone.

Cassiani touched her arm. "I need to do one more thing before we leave." She gestured to a heavy-set woman. "Your mother asked for you. Let me take you to her." When they reached her mother's bed, the young woman's show of appreciation was evident as she hugged Cassiani, then thanked her profusely.

It was ten o'clock when Cassiani and her mother finally arrived home.

CHAPTER 28

The next morning Cassiani wanted to wear the black skirt and white blouse, but her mother insisted she wear a more proper dress.

"There will be doctors there. You don't want to go looking like a peasant girl!" Vera exclaimed. She returned with a beige silk dress and a matching belt. "Wear this. It used to be Athena's but it was too tight on her, and she wore it only once." Vera placed it on the bed, then swooshed out of the room. "She wore it the night she met her husband. She captured his heart."

"Mother!" Cassiani watched her mother's retreating figure. After careful scrutiny, she finally slipped into the dress. Although it fit nicely on her, it made her look a little pale. As if thinking the same thought, her mother returned with a pearl necklace.

"This'll give it a little color near the face," Vera said. A few minutes later, she returned with a pair of beige pumps, waving them in her face. "These go with it." She stopped and stared at her. "You should put your hair up. Here, let me get you the hairpins I found the other day." She returned with three hairpins.

For some reason, Cassiani felt good dressing up. *Is it because Leo is going to be there?*

They waited for the bus, but it did not show up. They walked to the village. "The shops are closed," Cassiani announced, as they passed the closed doors of the stores.

"Ahh!" Vera said, appearing flustered. "Today is St. George's feast day. What with the earthquake and Mrs. Lukas' condition, I completely forgot."

They flagged a taxi to take them to the hospital. They learned from the taxi driver that the horse race in Pyli was to take place today. They arrived at the entrance of the hospital around ten o'clock, lugging bags bulging with food. It was difficult for Cassiani to appear professional and polished when carrying bags of food. Like a racehorse on a tight bridle, she wanted to stride forward, but her tight dress and high heels restrained her. She had to settle for tiny steps.

Mrs. Lukas was not in her room. They learned from a nurse that she had moved to a private room. When they arrived to the new room, Leo was sitting by his aunt's side, talking to her. Cassiani noticed his tousled appearance, unshaven chin, and wrinkled shirt; these were signs of having slept the night before in the hospital chair next to his aunt. He rose to greet them; his lean body moved agilely in one fluid motion of muscle and sinew. *Like a lion in a cage. He's not used to being cooped up in a small hospital room.*

Cassiani and Vera greeted them.

Vera kissed Mrs. Lukas' weathered cheek, then planted herself down in the chair Leo had been sitting on a minute ago. "I was here yesterday, but you were sleeping. Look what I brought you … homemade bread, your favorite cheese, fresh eggs, and honey to sweeten you up."

"I'll bring some extra chairs," Leo said, leaving the room.

"Vera! Would you believe it, here you were in the hospital a few weeks ago, and now look at me, it's my turn," Soula said, cackling.

"Thank God, my Cassiani was there to help you," Vera chortled.

Soula's lips formed a thin line of contention. "And Nina."

"Of course, of course," Vera said, appearing flustered. "We have her to thank also."

Leo returned with two chairs. He placed them at the side of the bed, then motioned to Cassiani to sit down. He sat next to her.

Vera and Mrs. Lukas carried on a comfortable conversation.

"I felt the earth shaking when I was outside in the garden. When I returned to the house, I noticed a couple of pictures had fallen from the wall," Vera said. "Did you feel the earthquake?"

"It must have happened around the time that I was taking that horse pill, you know, the iron pill. The pills fell out of the bottle, and then I don't remember much after that."

"That's all right, dear," Vera said, patting her arm. "You've been through a lot lately. With a little rest, you'll be back to normal." She continued chatting with Mrs. Lukas.

Cassiani glanced at Leo, curious as to why he was so quiet. He was staring at her.

Leo flashed her a smile. "You look lovely in that dress," he said huskily.

Cassiani felt a rush of warmth spread all over her body, followed by a glorious sense of confusion. His words had touched something deep inside her that made her very uncomfortable. "Thank you," she murmured. She turned and looked towards Mrs. Lukas, as if hoping for an escape from her feelings. Mrs. Lukas was cheerfully discussing the colors and textures of Nina's interior decorating of her house.

Leo leaned towards Cassiani. "Again, I want to thank you for saving my aunt's life," he said softly. "I'll never forget it."

The room had suddenly become very quiet and the silence was louder than the chatter a minute ago. Mrs. Lukas had a pinched look on her face.

Vera arose to rummage nervously through the bags of food, as if searching for something. "Cassiani, come help me prepare the food for Mrs. Lukas," she said. "Oh, and Dr. Leo, please have some food. The boiled eggs are fresh. There's plenty for everyone."

Cassiani cracked the eggshells and cleaned the eggs. She patiently broke each morsel of bread into bite-size pieces for Mrs. Lukas, then gave them to her along with the egg.

Meanwhile, Vera took out the white tablecloth from her handbag and began to stitch a red rose, talking nonstop about her first rose she saw the other day, and if Mrs. Lukas wanted a clipping, she'd be happy to give her one. She talked about the people and their idiosyncrasies, and about the weather this time of year. She talked about anything and everything.

"Soula, I almost forgot. *Chronia Polla* for your brother and your father George!" Vera told Soula and Leo. She was followed by Cassiani's well wishes.

"Oh dear, I didn't send George a card this year for his name day," Soula muttered. "Leo, when you talk to your father, tell him *Chronia Polla* from me. I'm getting forgetful."

Leo seemed surprised. "I had forgotten all about it." His fingers drummed the table. "Wasn't there a horse race or some type of celebration to be held in Pyli for St. George's feast day?"

Vera nodded. "It is going to take place today."

"What does a horse race have to do with St. George?" Leo asked.

Cassiani nodded. "If you notice, whenever you see St. George in an icon, he is always riding a white horse. I remember reading that he was a soldier and rode in the crusades. That explains the horse. They were persecuting Christians during that time and because he was a staunch Christian, he was martyred for his belief."

"Also, don't forget, he is the patron saint of shepherds. Stories have been told about shepherds who prayed to him and received help," Vera offered. She shook her head. "If only more people had faith, like those shepherds did, we would see more miracles happening."

Cassiani thought about what her mother said. She had witnessed miracles many times in her life. "Would people recognize a miracle if it happened?" she asked.

Vera looked up from her stitching. "Only those that believe," she replied. "The unbelievers will try and rationalize it and say it was just a coincidence, or luck."

The room was quiet for a moment as everyone pondered on what had just been said.

"The average person that goes to church every Sunday may think that's enough of a reason to be called a good Christian, but it's not. We all have the capability to become saints, but very few rise to the spiritual level needed to become saints," Vera said.

"I'm amazed at how people like Saint George grow so strongly in their faith in God, to the point where they are willing to die for their belief," Leo said. "It seems so foreign to me."

"That's because you don't believe that strongly, like me." Soula shrugged her shoulders. "How can one believe in something or someone they can't see or touch? Take money, for example. I can see it and touch it. I can't see God or even touch him. Show me God."

Cassiani's eyes widened at Mrs. Lukas' statement. *Dear Lord, forgive her for not believing, and strengthen her faith in you.* She suppressed a smile when she saw her mother doing the sign of the cross, her lips moving silently as if she were saying a prayer also.

"I'm afraid I don't agree, dear Aunt," Leo admitted. "I do believe in God, and in miracles." His eyes found Cassiani's and held them there for a brief moment. "I went to church with my parents and even was an altar boy, but over the years, first with my schooling and now my job, I stopped going. I simply don't have the time now."

"It all depends on where one's priorities fall," Vera replied shakily. "My parents and the church instilled strong spiritual values in us. We did the same with our daughters. Take Cassiani, for example." She paused to take a breath, ready to continue.

Soula changed the subject. "Dear, did you make this bread?" She pointed to the morsel that Cassiani was giving her. "I've been meaning to ask you."

Without flinching at being cut in the middle of her discussion, Vera graciously began a discourse on how she made the bread. The two women continued on the topic of baking.

At one point, as Soula was chewing on a morsel of bread, she choked on it. Leo rushed to give her water to drink. After Soula swallowed the liquid, she told Cassiani that she didn't have to feed her anymore. "I think I can feed myself. Why don't you throw this away for me?" She pointed to the cracked eggshells and crumpled napkins that had accumulated on the small table.

Cassiani felt her face flush. She gathered the scraps and fled to the small bathroom. She almost bumped into Fanny who was entering the room just then. "Fanny, how are you doing?"

Fanny's tired face broke out into a wide smile when she saw her. "Oh, it's good to see you again!" she exclaimed. "We missed your help today. All the patients are asking for you."

Cassiani smiled. "I felt as if it were the right thing to do at that time." She sensed Mrs. Lukas' eyes upon her. "Here, I better not hold you up."

Fanny walked to Mrs. Lukas' bed. "So, Mrs. Lukas, how are you doing?"

Soula's mouth was covered with breadcrumbs. "How do you *think* I'm doing!" she snapped, waving a piece of bread in the air. "Every time I want to eat, I always get interrupted!"

"I promise I'll be quick." Fanny was true to her word as she took Mrs. Lukas' vital signs in the breadth of two minutes. "Enjoy the rest of your meal," she chirped, as she breezed out of the room.

Cassiani suppressed a smile at the efficiency of the nurse's performance. Fanny wasted no time chatting with her crabby patient. She did her job and left.

A short while later, Leo arose. "It looks as if you ladies have things to talk about. Mrs. Meletis … Cassiani. Again, thank you for the breakfast. It was delicious. I think I'll go out for a little break."

"I'm expecting Nina. She said that she will be coming later today," Soula said.

He nodded stiffly as he walked out the door.

Fanny returned later and did some tests. Afterwards, Cassiani repositioned Mrs. Lukas, adjusting her pillow and getting her a glass of water. It wasn't long before Mrs. Lukas was dozing off. Cassiani pulled out her nursing book from her medical bag to read, while her mother sat by her side, stitching the tablecloth, humming a soft tune.

Later in the day, others came to visit Mrs. Lukas, including Nina and her mother, the Spanos family and a few other friends. The noise level in the room rose. Cassiani moved farther away from her patient as others claimed her space.

She stood quietly against the wall, keeping an eye on Mrs. Lukas and at the same time, listening to everyone's conversations.

The news of the day was about the St. George festivities in Pyli. Cassiani was surprised to hear a starry-eyed Nina announce that Louis Kotsidas rode in the horse race.

CHAPTER 29

After Leo left the hospital, he drove to Nicko's hotel in Psalidi, needing to take a break from the hospital environment. He rubbed his sore neck, his thoughts roving around different topics. Last night he had a difficult time sleeping in the chair, so in the wee hours of the morning he had telephoned Jack at his house. Jack said he was still waiting to hear about the repairs.

"What happened to the cargo?" Leo asked.

"It's being stored in a warehouse for now. It'll be more expensive to ship by truck."

Leo then reminded him of the new grain deal with Kostis and Ben. "They're waiting to hear from us."

"I forgot about that," Jack said. "How about you telephone back here at ten, tomorrow morning. I'll have the others with me and we can discuss it then."

Leo thought about his aunt and her future. He wondered what was to become of her after he left. Then he thought about his job and how it did not allow him time for human relationships. He rarely saw his parents; they were miles away doing missionary work or he was traveling. He saw his aunt once a year for a brief time. He couldn't even take a proper vacation.

Then he thought about Cassiani. The dress, along with the pearl necklace and pulled up hair, gave her an elegant appearance. But it was her face that held his interest. It was a caring, thoughtful, face; it was a poetic face, one that easily revealed feelings.

He parked the car on the side of the street and strolled towards the hotel. It appeared that the earthquake didn't touch this part of town; it was as if nothing had changed. Yet, yesterday in the hospital he saw many people's lives affected by the earthquake, including his own. He entered the hotel and found himself walking behind a man wearing a baseball hat and toting a camera, probably a tourist. Without notice, the man bent down abruptly in front of him to pick up something. "Excuse me," Leo said in English, sidestepping him.

"Sorry, man," said Andy Andrakis, holding something in his hand. "Dropped my room key." He stuffed it into his pocket. "Much safer in there."

Leo noticed the accent. "Let me guess. *New Yohk*?"

"Yoh! Good guess," Andy said, smiling broadly. "I'm a second generation Greek, born and raised in Astoria. Andy Andrakis, and you?"

"Leo Regas," Leo said, shaking hands. *Andy seems to be a friendly guy.* "I was born here, and raised in Washington, D.C. I've been to Astoria for business, though. Lots of Greeks there." They talked a few minutes more about Astoria and its Greek inhabitants.

"Are you staying here also?" Andy asked.

"No. Just visiting an old school friend." Leo pointed to Nicko's father, Mihalis, who was standing behind the counter. "His father owns the hotel."

"Hope to see you around." Andy bid him farewell and left the building.

Leo found out from Mihalis that Nicko was having his morning coffee with Mary out in the courtyard. He stepped into the small oasis that Nicko's family built to compliment the hotel. Luscious landscaping surrounded the marble-tiled courtyard, providing seclusion and shade. In the center lay a shimmering blue swimming pool, surrounded by lounge chairs and small round tables, and beyond could be seen the sparkling blue water of the Aegean Sea.

The couple was sitting at a table, underneath the shade of a tree. Nicko was dressed in a blue shirt and blue jeans, while Mary wore a pink summer dress. Leo joined them.

"Friend, look at you," Nicko joked. "You look like you stayed up all night!"

"I did!" Leo said. He sat down. "My aunt's in the hospital. She fell and bumped her head ... and I stayed overnight with her."

"She's in the hospital?" Mary asked. "Then we must go and visit her."

"She loves company," Leo said. "Right now, Mrs. Meletis and her daughter Cassiani are keeping an eye on her. I thought I'd take a break now that they are there."

"By the way, isn't your father's name George?"

"Yes," Leo said. He smiled as Nicko and Mary expressed their good wishes for his father's name day. "Thank you." *I must remember to telephone Father later.*

"Leo, let me get you some coffee," Mary said, getting up. "Help yourself to some pastries. I helped make them." She pointed to the plate on the table as she left.

Leo took a honey-soaked finiki and chewed it silently.

"You said you slept in the hospital room with your aunt?" Nicko asked. "So tell me friend, what exactly happened?"

"It happened yesterday, around the time of the earthquake. She fell while trying to pick up some pills that dropped on the floor. She bumped her head, and they found her there on the floor. She wasn't breathing," Leo said, grimacing.

"She wasn't breathing?" Nicko asked, his eyebrows raised.

"Yes. Cassiani saved her life. She performed some kind of breathing technique. I was away when it happened." He paused. "I don't know what I would have done if I had seen my aunt like that."

"That can be something," Nicko said, stroking his chin thoughtfully. "We had some incident last year, where we were on a boat ride with a group of tourists." He paused. His face had a troubled look. "Someone fell into the water and almost drowned."

Leo's eyes flew open. "Oh?"

Nicko's face broke out into a grin. "Don't worry! Luckily I got to him in time. After I pulled him back into the boat, I pushed the water out from his chest and breathed into his mouth. After several minutes, I got him to breathe. He was so grateful; he said I saved his life."

Leo thought for a moment. "Nicko, what exactly did you do? I'd like to know how it's done, in case my aunt experiences another one of these episodes."

Nicko explained it to Leo, making the motions with his hands. "You pull back the head to help them breathe better, then take turns breathing into the mouth and then pressing on the chest, here, just below the liver, going back and forth." He finished, "Just make sure you don't press too hard because you can break the ribs and even hurt her liver."

"Thanks for the tip."

"I have an idea, Leo. After your aunt leaves the hospital, why don't you bring her here to stay for a few days? Maybe it'll do her some good. Besides, we can keep an eye on her and she'll be close to the hospital in case anything happens," Nicko said.

Leo appreciated his friend's thoughtful offer. If he brought her here, it would mean that he wouldn't have to be driving her back and forth from the mountain to the doctor's office. It also meant that if he were to leave on a last minute call, he wouldn't have to worry that she would be by herself. He nodded. "Thanks. I think it's a good idea. Could you have two rooms reserved for this Friday, no … make it three. Let's plan for her to stay a week."

"I'll do that," Nicko said, nodding. He took out a pad from his pocket and jotted down some notes. "I'll reserve a room for her on the second floor where it's more private, and she can also get a good view of the sea." He looked up at Leo. "I'll make sure you get a room next to hers. Who is the third room for?"

"For Cassiani. She's her personal nurse. Give her a room on the other side of my aunt's if you can," Leo replied. He shrugged his shoulders. "There are things that I can't do for my aunt, you know, women things."

"Cassiani?" Nicko asked, appearing surprised. He gave his friend a knowing glance. "Uh-huh. I think you better think this thing through. What will happen if Nina finds out?"

Leo stared at his friend. "What is there to think about? My aunt needs help and Cassiani is the best person to help her. Besides, what does this have to do with Nina?"

Nicko glanced around, then leaned towards him. "Look," he said with a lowered voice. "As you probably know, Mary and Nina are good friends. From what Nina told her, I hear she's interested in you. She's been making *serious plans*." He nodded knowingly.

Leo was disturbed by the news. "You must be kidding! I don't have a serious relationship with Nina, or plan to. Nina is—" he said, then stopped when he saw Mary returning with the small cup of the thick brew.

"What's this I hear about Nina?" Mary asked sweetly, placing the cup in front of Leo.

Nicko glanced quickly at Leo, appearing nervous.

Leo immediately recognized his friend's delicate situation. Nicko confided in him about Nina's affections towards him. He didn't want to expose his friend. "Ahh, thank you Mary for the coffee." He took a sip, stalling for time. "Hmmm. Nice."

"So, what were you two talking about Nina?" Mary persisted.

"We were just talking about Nina's decorating my aunt's house," Leo said nonchalantly. He glanced at Nicko. He appeared relieved.

"She did mention something about it. How's that coming along?" Mary asked.

"It appears that my aunt loves the colors."

*   *   *   *

Leo arrived at the house around twelve o'clock. He washed and shaved, then rested on the bed. He would just take a short nap and then telephone his father. Then he'll go back to the hospital before Cassiani left for the day. This way his aunt would have someone close by if she needed anything. The mattress felt exceptionally soft as he went into a deep sleep.

The telephone rang in the distance, waking him up. It was his father.

Leo groggily told him the news about Aunt Soula. "Luckily Cassiani, her nurse, saved her life." He rubbed his eyes. "I stayed overnight at the hospital with her because I didn't trust the young nurse they have on duty. She's inexperienced and was making too many mistakes."

"Hmm. It looks like your aunt is having health issues and it's not going to go away. Although this Cassiani sounds like a capable nurse, I think you should bring your aunt back with you so we can keep an eye on her. I'll see to it personally that she is taken care of."

"You know how she and mother—"

"Don't worry, Leo," George interrupted. "I've already discussed it with your mother. Here we are spending time and money helping total strangers! It's only *right* that I help my own sister!" His voice broke into a sob. He paused, as if trying to control his feelings.

Leo's eyes moistened in response to his father's sentimental statement. "You don't know how much this means to me," he said, feeling his own unexplained emotions rising to the surface. The burden of taking care of his aunt had been worrying him for several days. Just knowing that his parents would help made him feel better.

Leo's mother got on the telephone. "Dear, your father is right. Your aunt is ill and we should help her. I know what you're thinking, but we're not the same people we were years ago. We've forgiven her since then."

"You have good intentions, and I hope she reacts favorably to them."

"Son, talk to your aunt," George said. "Let her know how we feel. She'll listen to you."

"I'll try my best." *There was something Aunt Soula told you to tell Father.* "Oh, by the way, Aunt Soula wanted you to know she wishes you *Chronia Polla* for your name day, and so do I. She forgot to send you a card this year." Leo heard his father chuckle.

"She was always good about that. Thank you and tell her the same," George said. He paused. "Did you work it out with Socrates about renting the upstairs suite?"

Leo ran his fingers through his hair. "I completely forgot, what with Aunt Soula's accident. Next time I see him, I'll talk to him."

"Good. Let your aunt know I will telephone her after she gets out of the hospital. Also, that we'll be there in New York when you arrive at the airport."

"Thanks. I have some other news to tell you." Leo told his father about *The Lion* and Doukas' admission that it used to be his grandfather's ship. He could hear his father's exclamation of surprise as he told him. He continued, describing the near collision of the ship.

"Does your aunt know?"

"No. I thought it best not to tell her."

"Good. She's got enough things to worry about," George said. "Son, I didn't go into the shipping business because I saw how hard your grandfather worked. The ships were always causing problems, either breaking down, or something. Good luck with everything."

CHAPTER 30

When Cassiani and her mother arrived at the house that Wednesday afternoon, they found Bobby standing at the gate with a sheepish look on his face. He held a pastry box in his hands and was dressed in a dark blue suit, white shirt, and bright orange tie. It was apparent that he had gotten a new haircut, which made his head appear smaller than the rest of his stout body.

"Bobby! My dear, how long have you been waiting here?" Vera exclaimed dramatically, rushing to greet him.

Cassiani stifled a giggle. She knew her mother felt guilty for inviting him and was trying to make up for it by being overly nice to him.

"Oh, just a little while." Some crumbs hanging from the side of Bobby's mouth threatened to fall off as he smiled. "Hello, Cassiani." He shoved the box of pastries in Cassiani's face. "Some baklava my mother made. They're *really* good."

Cassiani took the box, thanking him. Her fingers touched something gooey underneath the box. The honey from the baklava must have seeped through the porous cardboard.

"We had an emergency and had to go to the hospital today," Vera explained. She pulled the key from her pocket and thrust it into the door. "Please, come in."

Cassiani followed them into the dark house and promptly went to wash. Vera bustled around the room, opening the windows to freshen it up.

"I heard several people got hurt from the earthquake. We were spared. Is everything all right?" Bobby asked politely.

"Oh, yes, yes," Vera said, appearing flustered. "We are fine. We were visiting a sick friend in the hospital. Please, have a seat."

Her hands washed, Cassiani proceeded to remove the baklava from the box with a fork. She placed the gooey pastries on a plate. Bobby conversed affably with Vera as she asked him questions about his job. He was pleasant enough, making jokes and laughing at them noisily. Once Cassiani realized that he wasn't showing her undue interest, she relaxed.

"Cassiani, I remember when your father used to play the violin at some events that my family went to," Bobby said, his eyes peering at her from behind the large, thick glasses. They were like two black peas, circled by a sea of glass. "You used to play the violin, too. Didn't you? One time he asked you to play with him, you were around fifteen or so."

Cassiani stared at him. She didn't remember Bobby there, but then why should she?

"Cassiani, why don't you play a little violin for us," Vera suggested. "Go on."

This was something she enjoyed doing and didn't need much pushing. In a matter of minutes, the violin was perched on her shoulders. Cassiani played a few songs while her mother sang along. Bobby decided to join them with his off-pitch, high voice. He didn't sing, he boomed. He was so loud, that it was difficult to concentrate on the music after that. Cassiani suppressed a giggle when she realized her mother's voice had also risen to a loud volume, trying to drown out his voice. He must have thought that he was supposed to sing louder, because he raised his voice even higher. It became a shouting match. Cassiani's ears were still ringing when they finished. After that song, she decided to put the instrument to rest. She had enough cacophony for one day.

Bobby was in a jovial mood and kept up a constant chatter about how well the music sounded. "Maybe we could start a music group together," he offered, smiling at Cassiani.

"Nice idea, but I don't think I have the time." Excusing herself, Cassiani grabbed the violin and retreated to her bedroom. For some reason she felt overwhelmed. This Bobby was just too noisy. She sat on her bed momentarily, her head resting in her hands, trying to calm down. Her ears picked up a faint knocking in the distance.

"Who could that be?" Vera called.

Cassiani heard a man's voice. She left for the kitchen, her curiosity spurring her forward. Her mother was talking animatedly to a man whose back was towards Cassiani. He was average height with straight brown hair. He was dressed in a casual khaki suit, with beige shoes and beige socks; everything blended together. Cassiani stopped in her tracks. *It can't be.*

"Oh, thank you!" Vera said, taking the bottle of red wine he had just given her. She gestured to Cassiani excitedly. "Cassiani! Look who's here! Andy from *America!*"

Andy turned and smiled at Cassiani. "I hope I didn't come at a bad time." His light brown eyes gazed back at her. "I tried contacting you to let you know I'd be visiting the area, and your sister gave me your address. I guess you don't have a telephone?"

Cassiani felt her face flush. "No, we don't. Please, come in and sit down."

It was an awkward few minutes as Cassiani introduced Andy to Bobby. "Andy is my nursing supervisor at the hospital where I work. Bobby is a friend of the family."

"So, Andy how did you learn to speak Greek?" Vera asked.

"I was born in America, but both my parents were originally from Crete. I grew up speaking Greek at home."

Vera's arms were folded neatly in front of her. "So your parents are Cretan. Cretans make good olive oil." She nodded. "What part of Crete?"

Cassiani poured Andy a glass of water, listening to the ensuing conversation. She then refilled Bobby's glass.

"Agios Nikolaos," Andy replied. "It is a good hour by car from Heraklion. It was my first time there and I was impressed by its beauty and particularly the large, bottomless lake."

"That's where the medical conference was to take place," Cassiani announced.

Andy nodded. "It lasted four days. I also added ten days of vacation time to the trip in order to visit relatives there."

"What made you decide to come here?" Bobby asked.

"I've always wanted to visit the island that was the birthplace of Hippocrates and also to visit the Asklepieion. It was the first medical hospital in ancient times." Andy gazed at Cassiani. "Besides, I knew that Cassiani was here. It helps to know someone when visiting an island."

"You must also visit the Hippocrates plane tree in the town," Bobby offered. "Hippocrates taught his students under the shade of that tree thousands of years ago. It's so old that its branches are being held by scaffolding."

It wasn't long before Vera ushered them all outside to sit around the small table. "Let's enjoy the nice breeze. You can also see the beautiful sunset from there."

Moments later, the drinks and refreshments followed. Both men made it a point to attract Cassiani's attention, and she found herself chatting and laughing. Vera also kept up a constant chatter, joining in, while stitching the tablecloth.

Around eight thirty Bobby stood up to leave. He grinned at Cassiani. "Thank you for your hospitality. I must be going because I have to be at work early tomorrow."

Vera wrapped a couple of round goat cheeses into a bag. "Give these to your mother, and warm regards from us," she said, handing them to him. Cassiani followed Bobby and her mother outside. They waved to him as he drove away.

Andy stayed a little while longer. He talked to Cassiani about her patients, filling her in on their conditions. "The nurses keep telling me that the patients all ask about you." The glow from the lantern made his face appear more attractive than it normally was. "We hope you return to us, Cassiani," Andy said gently.

Cassiani felt warm from the way he said those words. *What is he trying to tell me?* Her mother conveniently excused herself just then and lumbered inside. Cassiani focused her attention on Andy as he waited for her response. "I intend to return," she replied softly. "I just have to make sure my mother is well enough to travel." She explained her mother's condition.

"What medicine is she taking?" Andy asked.

Cassiani told him. "Frankly, I have my doubts about the medicine. She seems to be having side effects from it, and sometimes I wonder if it's really helping her."

They continued their conversation on her mother's health.

"By the way, what is your schedule like tomorrow? Are you free to show me around the town? I'm afraid I don't know much about Kos except for the Hippocrates connection."

Cassiani didn't feel comfortable telling him she was working for Mrs. Lukas. "I have some things to do in Kos Town in the morning, but I'll be free after three."

"Fine then. What do you say if we meet three thirty at the Hippocrates tree? Maybe we can visit a few sites, then have dinner together."

Cassiani nodded. "I can do that."

Shortly after, Andy rose to leave. They went inside. Her mother was at the table, stitching the table cloth, humming softly.

"Thank you for your kind hospitality," Andy said. "But I must be leaving."

Vera arose. "We are the ones who should be thanking you for your fine company." She gave him three goat cheeses. "It is good in the morning, with some toast."

They followed him outside and stood at the gate. "Be careful of the winding road," Cassiani said. "There are no lights, so it can be a little tricky at night."

"Don't worry," he laughed. "As long as I have my headlights I'll be fine."

After he left, Cassiani began to wash the dishes, humming.

Vera stood in the kitchen, her face glowing. "Two young men in our house in one evening. Ahhh, it reminds me of the time when Athena had suitors. First Bobby, and now Andy. He seems like a nice guy, this Andy. He looks a little like Leo Regas with his fair looks. He's a doctor, too." She grabbed a towel and began to wipe the dishes.

Cassiani stopped what she was doing and looked her mother straight in the face. "He's *not* a doctor."

Vera's eyebrow shot up. "No? Then why did he go to that medical conference?"

"He's got a master's degree in nursing, and besides, nurses go to medical conferences." Cassiani continued washing the dishes.

"Oh?" Vera appeared skeptical. "He's a *nurse*? Why would a man become a nurse?"

Cassiani laughed at her mother's frowning face. "Because he wanted to. Male nurses are not so uncommon in America, you know."

"A nurse," Vera sighed, crossing her thick arms. "What is this world coming to? I wonder if he's normal."

"What is that supposed to mean?" Cassiani asked. "He's a good human being, and he cares about his patients. Besides, he's not what you think." She rinsed a glass and gave it to her mother to dry. "He asked me out tomorrow. I'm to meet him at three thirty down at the Hippocrates tree. He wants to take me out to dinner afterwards." She suppressed a yawn.

"Oh!" Vera's eyebrows rose. "I think this Andy is interested in you. Are you interested in him?"

Cassiani didn't answer, but silently wiped her wet hands on the towel. "Mother, I had a busy day today and I'm going to sleep early." She yawned. "I didn't sleep well last night."

Vera wagged her head. "Hmmff. Here are two nice young men interested in you and all you do is yawn and want to go to sleep. If I were young again, I'd be dancing from happiness."

Cassiani fled into the bedroom, exhausted.

CHAPTER 31

The brave lion had been captured and was being led into a ship to be taken to a far away place. But the lion was strong, and it escaped its cage, and grew so large and powerful that it turned into the ship, and sailed into the sea triumphantly, but it did not know that up ahead was a terrible storm awaiting it. Cassiani was perched on the front of the ship, sent there to warn the lion. "You must turn around and go back before it's too late."

"Before it's too late," Cassiani murmured. She awoke just then with the words fresh on her lips. She looked around her room and rubbed her eyes. "I must have been dreaming." She lay in bed, her eyes wide open in the dark room. The dream had disturbed her. What did it mean … this lion? Why did it turn into a ship? What did the storm portend? Maybe it had to do with their trip to America. Maybe the storm meant trouble ahead.

Vera rapped on the door. "Cassiani." She entered the room. She was still wearing her robe, and her gray hair streamed around her, uncombed.

Cassiani sensed that something was not right. Normally her active, energetic mother would be dressed and have done a multitude of tasks by now. "Aren't you coming?"

"I can't seem to get going this morning. I didn't sleep that well last night," Vera said, yawning. "You go ahead without me. Try and put on something nice. There are doctors there."

The dresses that Cassiani washed the other day were taken out of the closet. She removed the mirror from the wall, placed it on the dresser then hopped on the bed to get a better perspective. She dressed and undressed in front of the mirror, rejecting the majority of the clothes; they were either too tight, too old, or she didn't like the style. As a result, a pile of clothes had formed on the bed. After much deliberation, she chose a pink silk dress with pearl buttons and a round white collar. It fit just right, hugging her small waist. Her hair was pulled back in a bun and pearl earrings were removed from the treasure box and put on. For the first time in a long time she dabbed pink lipstick on her lips.

Two hours later, she arrived at the hospital carrying a bulging bag of food, compliments of her mother. Cassiani had reservations about going to the hospital alone. Yesterday, her mother's constant chatter with Mrs. Lukas had made for a comfortable setting. She had the nagging thought that she wouldn't be able to maintain that type of atmosphere today. *Remember, you're not there to entertain, but to nurse.*

Today Leo was pouring water into a glass when she entered the room. She noticed his shaved face, white short-sleeve shirt, and beige cotton pants. He handed the glass to his aunt. Cassiani greeted them brightly.

Leo looked up. "Good morning." His eyes rested on her mouth.

Cassiani blushed when she saw where his gaze rested, remembering the lipstick. Did she put too much on?

"Where's your mother?" Soula asked, squinting at her from behind the glass.

"She wasn't feeling well today. Mother made you some fresh goat yogurt," Cassiani said, carefully removing the bowl of yogurt from her bag.

"She knows how to please me," Soula said, gesturing her to come to her. "I haven't eaten yet."

Cassiani positioned Mrs. Lukas so she could eat. She did not offer to feed her after the incident yesterday, but instead, sat by the side of the bed observing her savoring the creamy yogurt.

"Hmm, very good," Leo said, tasting the yogurt. "Tell your mother she makes excellent goat yogurt. I hear that it's good for you, like dandelion greens." He winked at Cassiani. "It's packed with nutrition." He went on to talk about the benefits of the calcium and the acidophilus in the yogurt. "Eating healthy foods makes for a healthy life."

Cassiani nodded. "Nutrition is one of the best ways to combat disease," she said. "If people stayed away from processed foods and tobacco, and ate more raw fruits and vegetables, they would be healthier, like most of the people here."

"You're talking about the American diet, with their fast-food and TV dinners," Soula drawled. She wiped her mouth with a napkin. "I don't know if they're healthier here now. The stuff they sell here in the grocery stores isn't better; they have canned meat, boxed foods, and canned vegetables. They're all processed." She shrugged her thin shoulders.

"I think what Cassiani is trying to say is that the majority of the people here eat locally grown foods from their fruit orchards and gardens. They make their own yogurt and cheese. All these things are more nutritious than the processed foods."

Soula then diverted the conversation by chatting with Leo about the various visitors she had yesterday. After a few minutes, she shut her eyes, as if tired of speaking. It wasn't long before she was snoring softly.

"Cassiani, can you come with me into the hallway?" Leo whispered, standing up.

"Surely." Cassiani wondered what he wanted to tell her that he didn't want his aunt to hear. She followed him, her heart racing. *Why do you always feel this way when you are alone with him?* There was no one else in the hallway at that moment.

He pulled out an envelope from his pant pocket. "This is payment for your services."

Cassiani swallowed her disappointment. "Thank you," she mumbled. She took the envelope and stuffed it into her pocket. *He's reminding you that he is your employer.*

"This covers the days you worked and extra pay for the day you took my aunt to the hospital," Leo said. There was a sparkle in his eyes. "Now, maybe we could go somewhere for coffee? There we could talk more privately, regarding my aunt."

Leo's suggestion pulled at Cassiani's heart in a pleasant way. She liked the idea, but at the same time felt a little confused by his request. She walked with him down the hallway, unable to shake off the feeling that something special was about to happen.

Fanny was coming down the hallway towards them. "How is everything today?"

"Fine, fine. We will be going out for a little while. Could you do me a favor and keep an eye on my aunt?" Leo asked. He pulled a small envelope out of his pocket and gave it to her.

"Gladly!" Fanny beamed as she took the envelope and walked into Mrs. Lukas' room.

Once outside, Cassiani and Leo strolled down Ippocratous, going towards Eleftheriou Square. Cassiani felt heady, almost as if in anticipation of something about to happen. Was this promenade among the palm trees, flowering hibiscus and irises enough to invite these feelings of promise? Or was it the fragrance in the air that intoxicated the senses? Whatever it was, it felt very good.

The square was a beautiful pedestrian zone designed years ago by the Italians. Tourists streamed by them on their bicycles. Once in a while, they'd pass a young couple holding hands. Cassiani wondered what it would feel like holding Leo's hand.

As they entered the expansive square, Leo focused on the impressive Ancient Agora to their right. "It was uncovered after the 1933 earthquake."

"I remember reading about it. The earthquake took place on April 23, which happened to be the feast day of St. George," Cassiani said.

"It looks like you have a knack for numbers." Leo nodded appreciatively. "Anyway, did you know that in ancient times it was a major trading post? The columns of the temple of Aphrodite have been estimated to have been built around the fourth century BC."

"I had read about it." Cassiani gazed at the area to their right. "I remember visiting the Agora when I was young. We lived a few blocks from here, on the other side of town."

Leo pointed to the elegant, cream colored building up ahead. "Then you probably have been to the Archaeological Museum?"

"Many times." Cassiani nodded, remembering the busts of Alexander the Great, Hercules, and the impressive mosaic showing Asklepios' arrival. Other statues included Asklepios, Hygeia, and Artemis. "It was built by the Italians years ago, and houses Greek and Roman artifacts."

"My favorite is the statue of Hippocrates, the father of modern medicine. You probably know more about him than I do," Leo teased, shading his eyes from the sun as he looked at her.

Cassiani smiled back. "My father used to tell us about Hippocrates' medical abilities, and how he believed that fresh air, clean water and exercise were important to one's health." She paused, remembering her father. "When my father was young, he wanted to become a doctor. But it didn't work out, so he ended up being a pharmacist instead. He helped quite a few people, giving them pharmaceutical advice."

They strolled by the marketplace with the different vendors. Leo stopped to look at a few vases and sculptures. "I'd like to check something, if you don't mind," he said. He studied the small marble sculptures, first one of Asklepios, then one of Hippocrates. He then picked up a female statue. "The detail on this Hebe statue is superb." He observed it some more. "It looks like the real thing. You know the story, don't you?"

Cassiani shook her head. She had seen the statue before, but never inquired about it.

"According to mythology, the goddess Hebe was the daughter of Zeus and Hera. She supposedly married Hercules." He gazed at the sculpture. "She represents youth and beauty." He glanced at Cassiani. "You know, she looks a little like you. What do you think? Do you like it?"

His question caught Cassiani off guard. She stared at the sculpture with renewed interest. "It is remarkable," she murmured.

Leo spoke to the seller, asking about the statue.

"If it's for the pretty *despinis*, I'll give it to you half price," said the seller, smiling brightly at her.

Leo laughed, then looked at Cassiani. "I'll take two, and without discount." He paid for them, then gave the wrapped gift to Cassiani. "A little gift from me. To remember this moment."

Cassiani felt her face flush with emotion. "I don't know how to thank you," she said. "I will truly cherish it." For the first time in a long time, she felt very, very special.

Leo flashed a bright smile, showing he was pleased with her response. "Just knowing you like it is my reward." He then turned and asked the seller a couple of questions about the manufacturer. He took his business card.

They continued their stroll, going towards the harbor, passing flowering hibiscus, graceful palm trees, and fragrant jasmine along the way. To their right towered the majestic castle of the Knights of St. John.

"It's amazing how there are so many architectural styles from different cultures here," Cassiani said. "The Turks built their mosques and fountains while the Romans fashioned their baths and buildings. There were Venetians, Dorians, and even Persians living here at different periods of time."

"And don't forget us Greeks," Leo said, flashing a wide smile at her.

The splendid harbor with the shimmering blue sea, decked with different colored boats, was alluring to the eye. Up ahead, they found a quaint café bordered by a plush garden that seemed to provide a private haven.

"Why don't we sit here?" Leo said, leading her to a table nestled near a flowering red hibiscus. Several pots of red geraniums sat nearby. The shade of an overhead palm tree added a refreshing respite from the sun. They ordered cold frappe coffees and vanilla ice cream.

Leo's voice was soothing and low as he talked about the picturesque harbor. "Look over there. The sea shines like millions of jewels with boundless energy that can sustain life, and at the same time destroy whole ships. The yachts are owned by people who think they are important, but in reality they are like sand in a dessert, or a drop of water in a vast ocean of humanity."

CHAPTER 32

Cassiani ate the ice cream, savoring every bit of it. "This reminds me of earlier days, when my family and I strolled along the harbor on Sundays. Afterwards, we would sit and eat ice cream, watching the boats go by. I almost feel like it's a dream." As soon as she said it, she remembered the dream she had that morning. "You know, I had a dream this morning, about a ship." A gust of wind teased the curls of hair from her tidy bun, causing them to unravel and stream in front of her face.

Leo gently removed the strands from her face, his fingers lingering over her cheek. "Do you believe in dreams, Cassiani?"

Cassiani's heart raced and her breath became shallow at his tender touch. *Why am I feeling like this? Why is he doing this to me?* Abashed at how easily this man could evoke such emotions in her, she tried to remain calm. She nodded solemnly.

"This dream about a ship," he said gently. "Would you mind telling me about it?"

She was surprised that he would want to know about her dream. He appeared sincere enough. She told him the story. "It seems so silly for a lion to turn into a ship," she finished, giggling nervously.

"It's not as silly as you might think," Leo said thoughtfully. "Cassiani, would you believe me if I told you that there is such a ship? A cargo ship called *The Lion*. My company owns it."

"The Lion?" Cassiani asked, her eyes wide open.

"Yes," Leo said. "What makes it more important is that it used to be my grandfather's ship." He had a far away look on his face. "Now it's in Turkey being repaired." He turned to Cassiani and explained what had happened. "Maybe that was what you saw in your dream."

Cassiani shook her head. "The ship was headed towards a storm and I was placed there to warn them." Her eyes widened. "It may not have happened yet."

Leo laughed. "I don't think anything's going to happen to it anytime soon. It's docked and being repaired," he teased her.

Cassiani felt her face flush. He was probably right.

Leo leaned towards her. "Now for a little different topic. What do you think about my aunt's fate? Not for the next few days, but long term."

Cassiani looked into his earnest eyes. The peaceful, romantic setting melted away and was replaced by sad reality. His aunt's health was not a light topic to discuss, particularly her eventual mortality.

"You can tell me. I can handle it," Leo said.

She weighed her words carefully, realizing that she was talking to someone who loved his aunt very much. "There was something I read not too long ago that might explain your aunt's condition. It goes like this … life is not always what it may seem and one must not take it for granted. The constant assurance of the sun rising in the morning and the moon greeting one at night lulls one into a false sense of security that all will remain the same. Not everything in life remains constant. The same goes for our health. We must not take it for granted."

Leo was silent. "Very philosophical and wise. Shall I interpret it as saying that my aunt's health is not always going to be there?"

Cassiani gazed out into the blue waters, trying to find that tranquil feeling she had a few minutes ago. "Given what happened the other day, and assuming she remains alone … yes."

"So what are the alternatives?" he asked.

"The alternatives would be to give her the best quality of life, including a good family support system and good healthcare. She will have a hard time getting all that here."

"You and my father make a good case for my taking her back to the United States with me," Leo said, laughing.

Cassiani nodded, smiling back. His laughter was music to her ears, flowing smoothly like a stream of bubbly champagne. "A strong case. You mentioned your father said the same thing?"

Leo nodded. "He feels that my aunt would be better off living there so they can keep an eye on her. They will arrange to pick us up at the airport."

"What does your father do?"

"My father is a doctor, and my mother is a nurse."

Cassiani was startled. She didn't know his parents were in the health profession. For some reason, she couldn't see Soula Lukas having a brother who helped people, but then, he was Leo's father. That explained Leo's good-natured self showing through when it came to taking care of his aunt. "Where are your parents now?"

Leo explained his parents' missionary work.

"That's quite inspiring," Cassiani said, her eyes shining. "I've always admired people who volunteer their time and talent for God. When I was young, I thought about becoming a nun."

"I'm glad you didn't," Leo said dryly, his eyebrows raised.

Cassiani blushed at his remark; unsure as to why he said that. She had never told anyone before, not even her mother, about this.

The walk back to the hospital was equally pleasant and relaxed. Cassiani did not resist when Leo slipped his hand into hers. It felt so natural. Yet an unsettling thought entered her mind and she could not let go of it. "Leo, I need to talk to you about something. It's about payment for today. I don't feel comfortable going out on this walk and being treated to a gift and refreshments, and still be paid for it."

Leo was thoughtful. "I understand. You want to keep the two things separate. At your nursing job, didn't you go out with your friends for lunch?"

Cassiani nodded. "Sometimes, but we didn't get paid for lunch."

"Then that's what we'll do. We'll remove an hour for this break," Leo said, his eyes twinkling. "It was too pleasurable to be considered business."

They had arrived at the hospital; the clock on the wall showed one o'clock. Were they gone three hours?

"I know this is short notice, but I'd like to ask you a favor." Leo paused, gazing at her intently as if he wanted to impress upon her how important this request was for him. "Could you and your mother stay at the hotel with my aunt for a week? I thought it would be good for her to be around people, and close to the hospital in case anything else happened to her."

Leo's question caught Cassiani off guard. Staying in a hotel with Mrs. Lukas for a whole week. That was quite personal and close. He didn't mention that he would also be there. "I ... I don't know if we can afford it—"

"It'll be paid for," Leo said quickly. "You and your mother will have your own room next door to hers, although I think it might be better if you slept in my aunt's room whenever the need arose. I think she needs to have a nurse close by to take care of her day-to-day needs, and I can't think of anyone better than you to do that."

"All right then. I will tell my mother."

"Good," Leo said, appearing pleased. "Now I need to leave, to do some tasks and to place a call to my office. You probably won't be here when I get back."

Cassiani bid him farewell. "Again, thank you for the gift, and the interesting conversation."

"My pleasure." Leo turned. "Could you please let my aunt know my schedule? I told her already, but she has a tendency to forget."

*   *   *   *

Later that afternoon, Cassiani met Andy by the Hippocrates plane tree. He was casually dressed in a khaki shirt and beige pants, wearing a white baseball cap and holding a camera in his hands. His eyes lit up when he saw her. She felt a little uncomfortable, the way he was gazing at her. She realized with dismay that she was overdressed for their outing; her pink dress was probably sending the wrong signals. *He might think you dressed up for him.*

They strolled along the bridge that led to the Knights' Castle. "The bridge used to go over a moat, but over time, the moat was not needed. Now, as you can see, the bridge goes over this street," she explained, pointing towards the road. They continued their walk towards the castle.

Andy glanced at the tourist book. "The Knights of St. John were on this island for over 200 years. They defended the city from the Ottomans for many decades, but in 1523 the island finally fell to the Turks." He scratched his head. "Here it says that some of the stones used to build this castle were taken from the temple of Asklepieion. Man ... can you imagine that?"

A half-hour later, with the aid of a map, Andy drove them to the Asklepieion. As they walked around the site, Cassiani shared what she knew about the ancient hospital. "It was built after Hippocrates' death in 357 BC, in his honor, but the earthquakes have destroyed much of it. The physicians were actually priests, and used Hippocrates' method of diagnosis and treatment."

Although Cassiani enjoyed the outing, the memory of the stroll with Leo earlier that day kept dominating her thoughts. A couple of times, Andy had to ask her a question twice before she answered. Afterwards, he drove them to Mastihari for dinner. He said he had heard about a good restaurant there. On their way, they saw a row of Greek army trucks.

"Those are our *modern* Knights of St. John," Cassiani remarked.

Later, as she sat and had dinner with Andy, she couldn't help wondering what it would be like if Leo were there instead. Andy must have felt comfortable, for he started opening up and talking about his family. He dropped her off at the house at eight thirty.

"My flight leaves at four tomorrow. I probably won't see you after tonight." He waved to Vera. "Keep me posted with your plans," he said to Cassiani, as he left.

"Well, what do you think?" Vera asked Cassiani.

"I don't know," Cassiani replied. "He's a nice guy, but I think of him as a brother."

"A brother?" Vera sputtered, appearing annoyed. "First Bobby, and now this one. You are too … *egoistria*!" She flounced back into the house.

CHAPTER 33

That afternoon, Leo shook hands with the travel agent, then slipped his aunt's airplane ticket into his shirt pocket. "I appreciate that you were able to help me on such short notice."

As Leo drove home, images of his aunt refusing to come to America entered his mind. He knew she could be stubborn as a mule and end up not going. How would he react to her resistance? He shook his head, thinking about it. He would just have to wait and see.

Another thought presented itself. What would happen to Cassiani and her mother once his aunt left for America? He knew that Vera Meletis could not work, at least for now. How would they manage? In addition, once he left Kos, would he see Cassiani ever again? Was she going to remain here or return to the States with her mother? He realized how little he knew about their plans. *It also means you're interested enough to want to know.*

Cassiani's image came to him, with her large, innocent eyes gazing back at him, her warm hand comfortable in his as they walked, and her wise, philosophical words. All these could not be erased from his mind. *You don't have time for any relationship. You never did.*

Once at the house, Leo focused on his task at hand. He telephoned Jack at the office.

"Leo! I have you on speakerphone. We're ready to start," Jack said.

Several issues were discussed with Carl and Stan, the two analysts. Leo discussed the pros and cons of sharing the ship with Ben's group, the costs and benefits, and the time frames of the new grain shipment. The issue not to charter the

Bali was suggested by Carl, followed by Stan's proposal of chartering it for a year instead of six months and to find products to ship back.

Jack proposed to stay with the six-month charter for the first year, and allow Ben's group to ship their products back to the United States. "This way we don't commit ourselves too much and they will help with part of the fuel costs. This will be a test run to see how well it does."

"I agree with Jack," Leo said. The others went along with it.

"Good, get a few more quotes as soon as you can. We'll go from there," Jack said.

"By the way, any news on *The Lion*?" Leo asked.

"Not yet. Call me when you get some numbers," Jack replied.

Afterwards, Leo worked steadily, calling different companies. It seemed that several were eager to do business. Two hours later, he telephoned Jack. After some discussion, Leo jotted down the final figures.

"Move quickly and get the charter contract for the *Bali* before anyone else does," were Jack's final words before hanging up.

For some reason, Leo was bothered by the new workload. It wasn't the first time that Jack gave him work to do while on vacation. *Somehow this vacation was different.* Leo had promised his aunt that he'd spend his vacation time with her and here he was working all the time. He felt an incredible weight on his shoulders as he telephoned Ben Doukas' office. "I'd like to set up a time to see him tomorrow." Leo's voice sounded heavy to his ears.

"Mr. Doukas left me a note saying he wants to meet with you Monday morning at nine. He is scheduled to fly to England at twelve thirty and will be gone for several days."

They arranged for Ben's airplane to fly Leo from Kos on Sunday, at five thirty in the afternoon, to the Athens airport. The firm's car was to pick him up from there and take him to the *Bali* so he could examine the ship. At eight thirty Monday morning the firm's car would take him to Ben's office.

Leo arrived at the hospital room half past seven. Two more vases of flowers and a basket of fruit sat on the table next to his aunt's bed; evidence that she had more visitors that day. He expected that she would be in a good mood. He was wrong. She had a mulish look on her face; her lips were pursed, and her nostrils flared. She didn't appear happy at all. *It's as if she knows about the ticket.*

"You *just* missed Dr. Vassilakis. He was here a minute ago. He told me that I have an ulcer and that is causing my anemia." Soula dabbed lotion on to her knobby fingers.

"Now that they know what you have, they can do something about it."

Soula ignored his comment. "Fanny gave me this cream for my arthritis. She said I'll be leaving tomorrow." She focused on her fingers. "You and Cassiani were gone a long time."

Leo felt annoyed. His aunt was checking up on him. He did not reply.

"Nina and her mother came shortly after you left," Soula continued. "They were here all day waiting for you. When Cassiani returned, she hardly did a thing."

"We went outside to discuss your progress. We didn't want to wake you. Afterwards, I had some work to do on a new deal. I told you that I would be busy with that."

Soula's face softened into an apologetic smile. "Tsk, tsk. I guess I forgot. You must have been exhausted," she cooed, appearing flustered. "Did everything go well?"

Leo relaxed. That was more like her normal self. "It went pretty smoothly." He wasn't about to tell her all the details of his job. He sifted his fingers through his hair, carefully weighing his words. "I need to be in Athens to sign a new contract. I'll be flying out on Sunday."

"Hmmff! You can't sit still," Soula said, pouting.

Leo became silent. *How am I going to tell her about the ticket?* "By the way, I spoke with Father yesterday and gave him your wishes for his name day. He wanted me to thank you for remembering," Leo began, then he paused, waiting to gauge her response.

"Good," Soula said, her face softening. She gazed expectantly at him, while her fingers played with the edge of the blanket. "Did he say anything else?"

Leo knew he was taking a big chance that his aunt would reject the next statement, but he had to do it. He took a deep breath. "I also told him about your condition, and we both agreed it would be a good idea for you to come back to America with me. He said that he would personally be there to receive you, and make sure you were taken care of."

A resigned look settled on Soula's face. "Today I had a long talk with Dr. Vassilakis. He also recommended that I be with family," she mumbled. "He said I'm no longer a spring chicken!" She snorted. "The old goat! Does he forget that he's almost seventy?"

A big weight lifted off of Leo's shoulders when he heard that. "He's right about being with family. You don't have anyone here to help you right now, so the logical thing would be to go to America and be with us."

Soula looked at him. "You said that your father wants to help. I know he does. He's got a good heart. What about your mother?"

Leo was pleasantly surprised by his aunt's question. As he eagerly relayed to her what his mother had told him, he noticed his aunt's eyes moistening. "She wants to help you also."

Soula's face crumpled. She grabbed a handkerchief. "All these years wasted," she muttered, wiping her reddened eyes. She blew her nose. "Do you know, after you spoke to me about your parents the other day, how many sleepless nights I've spent thinking about the past, and how things could have been different if it weren't for my pigheaded stubbornness?"

Leo sensed his aunt's sadness and it pulled at his heart.

"Don't look at me that way," Soula said, sniffling. "I deserve being lonely all these years! I earned it." She studied Leo. "So when will you be going back?"

"Two weeks," Leo declared. *Her question shows that she's interested in going.* "What do you think? We can fly back together on the same flight." He noticed her smile, then hesitation. As if reading her mind, he said, "I already bought your ticket."

"You young rascal!" Soula said, chortling. "Why doesn't that surprise me!" She fingered the edge of her collar, thinking. "Leo, now that we're making all these plans about me, what are your plans about Nina? I think she is attractive and talented, and besides, her father has money."

Leo stared at his aunt. He was surprised that she hadn't picked up the nonverbal cues he had been giving. "Nina is a charming girl, but frankly—"

"*Yiasas!*" Nina said, entering the room wearing a white knit blouse and red miniskirt. Behind her was her mother, carrying a box of chocolates.

✳   ✳   ✳   ✳

Leo awoke Friday morning in the hospital room, feeling stiff and sore. He shifted his body to the side, trying to find a comfortable position in the chair.

Fifi came cheerfully into the room. "I'll be leaving shortly and since this is your last day here, I probably won't see you again," she said sweetly. "Is there anything else I can do for you? I mean, your aunt?"

Leo shook his head. "Thank you for your help," he said dryly. As an offering, he gave her the box of untouched chocolates. *Even with her faults, she did have a good disposition and put up with his aunt's criticism.* Fifi smiled her thanks, then slipped out of the room.

A few minutes later, he stood up and leaned over to check his aunt. Her eyes were shut and she was snoring lightly, signaling she was still asleep. This was the day that she would be leaving the hospital. He stretched, then got himself a glass of water, whistling softly. His aunt awoke just then. "Good morning, Aunt Soula." He bent down to kiss her.

Soula smiled back. "Good morning!" Then she looked at his hand holding the glass of water. "I usually don't drink water, but I'd like some now. My mouth feels a little dry."

Leo slowly poured some water into her glass, then handed it to her, watching her drink it thirstily. There was something about this scene that reminded him of Cassiani, when she drank the water he gave her at the engagement party. He could not forget the girl's grateful eyes as he handed her the second drink of water.

"Fifi was just in here to say good-bye, but you were asleep. I gave her the box of chocolates," he informed her. "I know you don't like chocolates."

Soula almost choked on the water. "You did? Whatever for?" She placed the glass on the table and wiped her trembling lips. "She was all trouble, I say. Everything she did had to be undone by you or Fanny."

Leo laughed. "You forget, she was the one who rubbed lotion on your back and clipped your toenails, dear Aunt," he replied playfully. He changed the subject, talking about the statues he saw the other day at the market. His aunt's mood softened as they conversed.

CHAPTER 34

That same Friday morning, Cassiani arose at seven thirty. Today they were going to the hotel with Mrs. Lukas and Leo. Feeling somewhat anxious about the whole thing, she fidgeted with the clothes she was going to take. She folded a pair of long white cotton pants, a couple of blouses, and the flowery skirt. They were placed neatly on top of each other on the bed.

As she pulled Athena's beige dress out from the closet, she thought about the payment Leo made yesterday. When she opened the envelope at home, her mother's surprised reaction mirrored her own. There were four crisp new American fifty-dollar bills, worth much more than the few hours she worked. She gave half to her mother, who reluctantly took it after much coaxing.

Vera knocked on the door. "Cassiani, can I talk to you?" She came into the room before Cassiani could answer. "Ah, I see you are taking Athena's dress."

"We might go to church on Sunday," Cassiani explained, feeling self-conscious as she placed it on the bed. "How about you? Are you ready?"

Vera appeared skeptical. "I don't feel comfortable about going to the hotel." She crossed her arms. "What will people say?"

"What do we care about what people will say?" Cassiani challenged her mother. "I'm Mrs. Lukas' nurse. We can't be going back and forth down to the hotel. We did it for the hospital and it was too tiring and too expensive."

"You are right," Vera said.

"Also, we'll be near the hospital if anything happens to either of you. Don't forget, you've got your own health problem."

Vera pulled out a folded envelope from her pocket. "Athena's letter arrived today." Her fingers trembled as she removed the two-page letter. "It was torn at the edges by the time I got it. Can you read it for me? She wrote it in English."

Cassiani read the letter aloud, translating it in Greek. "She says that they're going on a trip to Niagara Falls. That's four hours away, in New York. They're leaving, let's see, that's yesterday. They'll be there for a week, then they plan to visit David's family in Pittsburgh." Cassiani continued reading. "Athena sent us two Olympic airline tickets with this letter, for America." She eagerly ran her fingers inside the envelope for the much-awaited tickets, but it was empty. She looked at her mother, feeling puzzled.

"The tickets aren't in there?" Vera suggested.

"I don't see them here. It's not like her to forget things." Cassiani stared at her mother. "They might have fallen out, or someone took them."

"I hope not!" Vera said hurriedly. She appeared mortified. "This has never happened before. I know the postman very well. He would *never* do such a thing!"

Cassiani bit her bottom lip. "Maybe this happened before it got to Greece."

"I will call Athena tomorrow to see what happened! She may have just forgotten to put them in."

Cassiani waved the letter in the air. "Athena's not home. She already left for her trip yesterday."

"Yesterday?" Vera echoed, pulling back silvery strands of hair from her head, appearing nervous. "What day did Athena say the tickets were for?"

"May 6." Cassiani did a quick calculation. "That's in ten days." She looked up. "Maybe we can call Olympic airlines. Maybe they can do something about it." She glanced at her watch. "Oh no! Look at the time! It's almost nine o'clock. I'm late for Mrs. Lukas!"

"Daughter, give me your clothes so I can pack them!" Vera said. She grabbed the bundle of clothes that Cassiani handed to her as she rushed out the door.

A few minutes later, a breathless Cassiani entered the kitchen, carrying her medical bag with her. Her mother was bending over the large suitcase.

Vera looked up. "Good, you chose the black skirt and white blouse to wear. They make you look professional."

"Thank you. Are you ready?"

"Yes." Vera pointed to the bulging bag. "We will be taking this."

Cassiani stared at the oversized suitcase. "There's a rope around it. What …?"

"I also added some food and … other things. It wouldn't shut, so I tied it with a rope. You never know what we'll find down there. Better to be prepared."

"Mother, it's only forty-five minutes away."

"Why spend money going back and forth for something we forgot? Come on, we're already late for the bus."

They scurried down the dusty lane. Cassiani didn't allow her mother to carry the luggage, so she ended up lugging it. The suitcase was heavier than expected and it swayed in front of Cassiani's legs, almost tripping her. As she reached the intersection, she heard the whirring sound of the tires. She turned expectantly. *Too late.* The bus sped right past them. She waved her arms desperately, hoping the driver would see her.

"Tell the bus driver to stop!" Vera roared.

"Stop!" Cassiani shouted, chasing the bus, breathing heavily. The bus squealed to a halt, causing a cloud of dust to spew into Cassiani's face as she reached it.

The bus driver got out and hoisted the suitcase into the bus. "What do you have in here? Rocks?" he asked with an annoyed look.

"Kuugh, kuugh. Please wait, my mother is coming," Cassiani said, coughing from the dust. She pointed to her mother's bulky figure hustling down the hill.

After they settled into their seats, Cassiani took her mother's pulse. "It's high. Take some deep breaths."

Vera did as she was told, fanning herself. "I can't believe we made it!"

"We should have left earlier. It puts stress on your heart to run so fast." Cassiani became silent after that, peering out the window. Everything was moving so quickly. One minute she was in America, working in a hospital and the next, she was catering to an ailing mother and an ailing employer who would rather not have her help.

Vera peered at Cassiani. "You don't seem happy."

"I don't? It's probably because I don't feel good being late, and with all the things going on with Mrs. Lukas."

"I understand, dear," Vera said, patting her hand. "Don't worry, things always have a way of working out."

*   *   *   *

Dr. Vassilakis and Nina breezed into Mrs. Lukas' room. An odd mixture of cigar and perfume surrounded the father and daughter as they greeted Leo and his aunt. "Good news, Mrs. Lukas. You are well enough to leave today!" Dr. Vassilakis announced cheerfully. He patted his patient affectionately on the arm, then began to flip through the pages of the chart.

"I have your daughter to thank." Soula smiled fondly at Nina. "She has helped me in so many ways."

Dr. Vassilakis looked surprised. "Yes," he mumbled politely, signing a few papers. "Meanwhile, I want to see you next week in my office, to follow up on that ulcer of yours." He focused on Leo. "Did your aunt talk to you about her condition?" Before Leo could reply, he rumbled on about Soula's anemia and her arthritic joints.

"As you know, Dr. Vassilakis, I am only here on vacation and will not be able to help her once I leave." Leo noticed the emphatic bobbing of the doctor's head as he spoke. "So I've made plans to take her back to America with me." Leo caught the glance that Dr. Vassilakis gave his daughter. It was as if he were checking to see her reaction.

"I have some friends that live in New York," Nina said. "They've invited me to visit them many times." She stared at Leo. "Maybe I can visit you and your family there when I go."

"Why that would be wonderful!" Soula exclaimed, clasping her hands together.

Leo's eyebrows went up. He changed the subject. "By the way, Dr. Vassilakis, the upstairs suite is available, if you're still interested." The doctor was still interested. It wasn't long before they settled on a price. Leo shook hands with Dr. Vassilakis, sealing the deal. "I'll get the key to you in a few days." Dr. Vassilakis left soon thereafter.

Nina lingered in the room. "Is there anything I can do for you, Mrs. Lukas?"

"Yes. Give me a hand. I need to get dressed," Soula said.

With much exertion, Nina's small frame managed to help Soula rise, but she couldn't hold the stance for long. In a moment of flurry, Soula lost her balance, almost falling on Nina. Leo grabbed his aunt, breaking her fall just in time; then helped lower her down on to the chair.

"I'll be all right," Soula muttered, trembling. "Nina, come help me get dressed."

Leo left for the hallway, wondering if Nina was capable of dressing his aunt. Images of his aunt falling and hurting herself spurred him to go and seek help. He found Fanny farther down in the hallway. "My aunt will be leaving today. She needs help in dressing," he explained.

"Surely!" Fanny promptly went into her room.

Leo paced the floor, his hands in his pockets. It wasn't long before Fanny returned. He looked at her expectantly.

"She's as pretty as a bride! You can go in now!" Fanny reported.

His aunt sat on a chair, dressed in a blue silk dress and white gloves. "I'd like to go to the bathroom to wash up," Soula said to Nina.

Nina appeared flustered. "Here, give me your hand." She helped her up.

"Cassiani is supposed to come shortly," Leo reminded his aunt.

"Why do you keep asking her to come? Between you and Nina, I'll be fine," Soula retorted. She leaned on Nina. "Come, my dear." They walked towards the bathroom.

"Must I remind you that Cassiani saved your life?"

Soula stopped, her body stiff as a rod. "Hah! Nina told me that she found me lying on the ground. If Nina hadn't come along, it may have been too late. Wasn't Cassiani supposed to be keeping an eye on me? What was she doing?"

Leo tensed. Cassiani had told him what happened and this is not what he heard. His eyes challenged Nina's. "Didn't you ask Cassiani to take some things into the kitchen?"

Nina's eyes avoided his. "Yes," she admitted. "While she was there, I went into the parlor and found Mrs. Lukas on the floor."

"Nina would probably have saved my life anyway." Soula reached the bathroom and flipped on the light. "She was the one who called the ambulance to come and get me." She began to wash her hands while Nina held on to her.

Leo leaned against the doorway. "It was Cassiani who resuscitated you and who realized the severity of your injury. She told Nina to call for the ambulance. She told Nina to drive you to the hospital. You may not have survived if they waited for the ambulance to come get you."

Soula stopped washing her hands and looked at Nina. "Is he right, Nina?" she asked.

"You weren't breathing, Mrs. Lukas. I thought you were...."

"That is why I appreciate what Cassiani did for you," Leo interjected. "She is a nurse. It's her job." He began to pace the room. "I want her to be by your side to watch over you. That is why I invited her and her mother to stay at the hotel with you."

Soula sniffed. "I suppose you are right. Besides, I do get along fine with Vera."

"I'll leave them a note and let them know where we'll be." As Leo scribbled the note, he realized how quiet it was. He looked up. Nina's sullen countenance was obviously the result of what he had just said, but he wasn't about to take back his words. He meant every one of them.

"Nina, I hope you weren't offended by what I said. I was just trying to get a point across." Leo placed the note on the small table. He carefully phrased his words. "I appreciate all that you and your father have done for my aunt, and I'm sure my aunt is grateful also."

CHAPTER 35

A half-hour later, Soula Lukas was finally moved into her hotel room. The flowers from the hospital were placed on the table in front of the window. After his aunt was settled, Leo excused himself and left for the lobby. A few tourists loafed around talking while others were at the counter speaking to Nicko. Nicko waved to him. "I'll be there in a minute."

Leo waited for Nicko, periodically glancing outside. *It was already ten o'clock and Cassiani and her mother hadn't shown up yet.* He stretched and yawned. His body still felt sore from a sleepless night in the chair.

"Leo. Leo," Nicko said, nudging him. "Wake up!"

"Yes," Leo laughed, rubbing his neck. "I was just thinking about a number of things, including a nice, soft bed."

Nicko chuckled. "You know, maybe what you need is a little fun and relaxation. You came here for a vacation and all you've been doing is taking care of your aunt."

How enticing were those words with their promise of youthful joy; they rang true to Leo's inner voice. "What do you propose?"

"Tomorrow the tourists are leaving. So I'll have some free time. What do you say we go for a ride then? Maybe take a stroll on a beach. I can round up Mary and a few others."

Leo thought for a moment. "I like the idea. Only I don't want to leave my aunt alone. What do you think of the Empros Thermae? The healing waters there would be good for her arthritis."

"All right, let's make it for tomorrow, at twelve. I'll be free then. We can walk around a bit, maybe take a swim. Your aunt can dip her legs into the water."

"Thanks. That means a lot to me," Leo said.

Just then Nicko's mother called him. She wore an apron and was carrying a tray of food. Her foot had propped open the pool door. Nicko hurried towards her.

Leo glanced at his watch. It was already ten past ten. Cassiani hadn't arrived yet; he would just leave her a note to let her know where they were.

A breathless Andy Andrakis cruised into the lobby just then. A big grin was plastered on his face and his nose was roasted a royal red from the sun.

Leo greeted him cheerfully. "How is my friend from New York enjoying Kos?"

"Great, man! A female colleague of mine who lives here showed me around. I would not have known where to begin if it weren't for her. Asklepieion was the best." He scratched a red spot on his elbow. "But boy did those mosquitoes bite!"

"I hear peppermint keeps them away," Leo remarked. "Just rub some on you and tuck a few behind your ears."

"Is that right?" Andy asked, appearing surprised by Leo's comment. "I am a nurse and didn't know that."

"You're a nurse?" Leo asked. He gazed at Andy with renewed interest.

*   *   *   *

When Cassiani and her mother arrived at the hospital room, they found Leo's note on the table. Cassiani read it aloud. "Cassiani, my aunt will be at the Xenoudis hotel when you read this note. Please meet us there, Leo." She tucked it into her pocket, feeling a sinking sense in her stomach. She had always been punctual in her career and it was not like her to be late. "Let's go quickly to the hotel," she said. "I don't feel comfortable that Leo paid me so much money the other day and here we are coming in so late! What will he be thinking?"

Fifteen minutes past ten, Cassiani followed her mother into the hotel lobby, carrying the suitcase. Her mother's large frame stopped abruptly in front of her.

"There's Leo," Vera said, nudging her.

Leo was wearing a white shirt that was open at the collar and light beige pants. His hands were in his pockets. There was a restrained look on his face as he nodded his greeting to them, as if he was upset about something.

"Mother," Cassiani whispered. "What are we going to tell him, about being late?"

"I'll take care of it." Vera moved towards Leo, all smiles. "Leo, a thousand apologies for being late! Poor Cassiani helped me with some health issues and before you know it ... the time passed so quickly!"

"I hope you are all right," Leo said, concern written all over his face.

"Yes, my mother is fine," Cassiani interjected, before her mother could reply. She was a little disturbed at her mother's white lie. "How is your aunt doing?"

"Aunt Soula is doing as well as expected. I think she's just glad to be out of the hospital ... like me." He paused. "Nina came early and helped. Aunt Soula is in her room, with Nina." A shadow passed over Leo's face. "So, you were busy with your mother?"

Cassiani bit her lip. She wasn't feeling good about being late. She should have been there to help his aunt. "I'm sorry that we were late. We—"

"That was nice of Nina to help. She is such a good girl," Vera interjected.

Nicko joined them, greeting the two women cheerfully. "Leo, I telephoned Mary. She can make it. She will invite Nina also," he said.

Vera fanned herself. "My dear, where is our room?" she asked Nicko. "My heart. Achh, it's beating fast and I need to sit down and rest."

"Yes. It's on the second floor," Nicko said. "Let me get you the key." He went to the counter with Vera following close behind him.

Leo told Cassiani about the plans to visit the Empros Thermae the next day. "I would like for you to come along, to keep an eye on my aunt. Your mother is invited, of course."

"Thank you," Cassiani said. The idea of going to the thermal springs was inviting.

"Cassiani! Come!" Vera waved the key in the air, signaling to her.

"I must be going," Cassiani said, bending down to pick up the luggage.

"Here. Let me give you a hand," Leo told Cassiani, lifting the roped luggage.

A loud crash was heard as the large bag spilled open its contents. Clothes, canned foods, a jar of olives, shoes, even plates smashed onto the ground. Cassiani stared dismally at the scene.

CHAPTER 36

The room next to Mrs. Lukas' room was sparsely furnished with two twin beds, a small table with chairs near the large window, and a bathroom. Cassiani's eyes rested on her mother's suitcase. It was partially stained and some of the clothes inside the suitcase had become drenched with the dark olive brine. Wrinkling her nose from the sharp smell of olives, she opened the window to freshen the room. She replayed the scene in her mind of a few minutes ago. *Oh, the humiliation of it!*

"Cassiani, please don't be angry with me," Vera pleaded. "How was I to know that the rope would break?"

"Mother! A suitcase is made to carry clothes, not a house full of things! You even brought plates and cups, and cheeses, and ... and that large jar of olives! Uugh! We were picking olives off the floor for the longest time! How many olives did you think we would need?" Cassiani exclaimed.

"They weren't just for us. I wanted to share them with Mrs. Lukas," Vera explained. "She loves olives."

"I had to get on my hands and knees, and clean everything up, with all those tourists looking on, and Leo, and Nicko watching, and then Nina walking in and laughing through the whole thing! How embarrassing!" Cassiani continued.

"I'm so sorry, dear! I wish it hadn't happened that way," Vera said, looking dejected. She wiped a reddened eye. "Maybe I shouldn't have come. All I am is trouble to you."

Cassiani stared at her mother's sad face. An overpowering sense of guilt washed over her. "Oh, Mother!" she said, hastening to her. "I'm sorry. I was just angry, just thinking about myself. You meant well and that's what counts. Who cares for a few olives that fell?"

Her mother hugged her. "You have a good heart." She got up and sighed. "Now why don't you check up on Mrs. Lukas while I start washing these clothes. I'll be in there shortly."

*   *   *   *

Cassiani found Soula sitting alone by the window. The sunlight that streamed through the window outlined her thin figure and highlighted the silky white hairs on her head. She was crouched over, appearing to be reading a newspaper. Cassiani greeted her.

"So, you finally came. What took you so long?" Soula snapped. "I've been alone for some time. Nina left over an hour ago. Leo went to the house to gather some clothes for me."

Cassiani's face fell. "I'm terribly sorry, but something unexpected came up."

Soula placed the newspaper on the table. "I can't even read this! They make the print so tiny and I left my reading glasses at home."

"I can read it for you. But first, I need to check your vital signs." As Cassiani performed the necessary tests she wasn't surprised to hear Mrs. Lukas grumbling about not needing to be tested every day. "Your blood pressure is slightly low today, though your pulse is normal." Cassiani jotted the figures down. "So what did Dr. Vassilakis tell you this morning?"

"He gave me something to take for my ulcer. He wants me to go back to see him next week. I don't know what for." Soula spoke in an irritating manner as if she were scolding a child. "If you would have been here on time, you would have been able to speak to him!"

Cassiani apologized again for the delay. She knew that Mrs. Lukas was right. Afterwards, she sat down to read her the newspaper. She was relieved when her mother came into the room a few minutes later. Vera was adept at carrying on a conversation with Mrs. Lukas, and in no time, she had her chuckling and in a good mood.

Later, when there was a lull in the conversation, Cassiani offered to take Mrs. Lukas for a walk downstairs to the pool. "It's good for your arthritis." She knew that she touched a chord of compliance when she witnessed Mrs. Lukas' face light up.

As they inched their way down the steps and into the lobby, Cassiani and her mother held on to Mrs. Lukas so she wouldn't slip on the marble floor.

"How much farther is it?" Mrs. Lukas complained. "I need to sit down somewhere."

"The door is just ahead," Cassiani said. She felt someone brush past them, followed by a scent of peppermint. "Excuse me." She turned and stared into Andy Andrakis' sunburned face. Below his baseball cap, she could see large stems of green peppermint leaves poking out from above each ear.

"Cassiani!" Andy chewed his gum noisily as he stared back at her. He was carrying two suitcases, as if he were getting ready to leave. "What brings you here?"

"I, we … are visiting a friend," she said lamely, pointing to her mother and Mrs. Lukas. They had walked ahead. Her mother turned and waved excitedly to Andy then took Mrs. Lukas out to the pool. Cassiani tried to change the subject. "Were you leaving for the airport?"

"Yoh," Andy said, blowing a bubble, then smacking it back into his mouth. "My plane doesn't leave until four, but I thought I'd leave early. You know, give myself plenty of time to beat those lines."

Cassiani smiled. "Did you get a chance to see all the sites that you were talking about?"

"Yoh!" Andy expounded on his adventures of the day. He took some more pictures of the castle, then walked to the marketplace, where he found some good deals. "My suitcase is *stuffed* with souvenirs, including your mother's great cheese!"

Just then, Cassiani saw Leo from the corner of her eye. He walked into the lobby, carrying a green satchel. When he saw her looking his way, he headed straight towards them.

"Leo!" Andy said. "Good to see you, buddy!"

Cassiani was surprised to see the two men greet each other. *They know one another.*

"Leo, this is the colleague who showed me the sites of Kos the other day," Andy said, beaming at Cassiani. "We work in the same hospital in Cleveland." He glanced at his watch. "Oh … man! Gotta go! Don't want to be late for the plane. Bye now." He shook hands with Leo and Cassiani and hurried off towards the entrance door with his luggage.

"Hello, Leo," Cassiani said. Leo nodded stiffly. He was unusually silent, his eyes lowered. For some reason, Cassiani felt that she should explain. "We were taking your aunt for a walk when we bumped into Andy. I didn't know he was staying here, or that he knew you."

"I met him a few days ago when I was visiting Nicko," Leo said. He placed the suitcase down. "You work together at the hospital?"

Leo's pointed remark caused Cassiani to feel a tinge of pleasure that he cared enough to ask. *On the other hand, I don't want him to think I have any special rela-*

tionship with Andy. She quickly explained Andy's supervisory position. "He was in Crete for a medical conference and decided to visit Kos for a few days. Since he knew I was from here, he asked me to show him the sites. So I did."

"That explains it." Leo's face relaxed. "Wait here. I'll take this bag upstairs to my aunt's room. These are her clothes from the house."

Cassiani didn't wait long. He was back quickly.

"Now that my aunt has your mother by her side, would you like to go for a walk, to discuss my aunt's health?" Leo asked.

Cassiani smiled, liking the idea. They strolled outside and walked down the street. Their conversation covered several topics, including her schooling. She described her first year in college, when she was trying to learn the English language as well as the coursework. "Math was my most difficult class because the teacher spoke broken English. So here I am with my broken English, trying to learn math from a professor with equally broken English. It was not easy trying to comprehend these complex differential formulas on the chalkboard from a teacher who talked gibberish!" She shook her head comically.

Leo told her about his own schooling and how at first he wasn't sure what to major in. "But once I took courses in business and finance, I felt that was the field for me."

They had reached the sandy beach.

"Let's stop here for a moment," Leo said, pointing to a bench. After they sat down, they gazed out at the beautiful waves. He turned towards her. "Now, regarding my aunt. You're aware of what Dr. Vassilakis said about her?"

Cassiani nodded. "She told me about her ulcer." She discussed his aunt's health, going over what kind of diet she should have and her medicine. "Arthritis is a debilitating disease. There really isn't a cure for it."

"I wanted you to know that I will be flying her back with me to America. My family plans to take care of her."

Feelings from deep within Cassiani surfaced when he said it. She could not ignore the tight knot in her chest at the news. "Oh. When are you, I mean, she leaving?" she asked, a tinge of sadness lingering on her voice. She had known all along that he was on vacation and going to leave sooner or later. *But things were different now. Would I ever see him again?*

"Close to two weeks. I wanted you to know ahead of time so you can also make necessary arrangements for employment elsewhere," Leo said solemnly.

Cassiani's eyes flew open. *He still thinks of me as his aunt's nurse.* She swallowed her pride. "Thank you for your concern. I also want you to know that we will be leaving for Cleveland soon," she said. *If we find the tickets.*

Leo turned and looked at her. "Cassiani, I hope our friendship doesn't end here. Would it be all right if I visited you in Cleveland?"

Cassiani felt that very same warm, fuzzy feeling flow through her body as his eyes bore into hers. She wanted to ask him if he was going to visit her as a friend, or something more, but she didn't have the nerve to ask. *It doesn't feel right that he would come all the way to Cleveland just as a friend. How can I agree to something like that? What will Mother think? I'm not that kind of girl.* She was silent.

"I understand. You're probably not used to something like that."

Cassiani nodded numbly, appreciating his sensitive remark. She didn't remember what else he said, just that his hand found its way to hers as he murmured words of sweet nonsense. They gazed into each other's eyes, holding hands, oblivious to the people passing by.

CHAPTER 37

Mary listened to Nina commiserating on the telephone about the way Leo treated her. "Nothing seems to be going right today! Leo made it a strong point in front of Mrs. Lukas that Cassiani saved her life as if what I did wasn't that important! So what if I forgot that I had given Cassiani some food to take to the kitchen? Was that a *crime*?" Nina asked.

Mary wasn't able to answer, because Nina continued, reliving the scene in the hospital where Leo said he was taking his aunt to America. "Although it wasn't that much of a surprise, because I already knew he was on vacation and would be going back, but what surprised me was that he didn't show *any* interest when I said I would like to visit them in New York. Nothing!"

Mary had learned from Nicko what Leo's true feelings were about Nina. *It seems that now is the right time to tell her.* "Maybe he's not interested in you, Nina," Mary said firmly.

"Mrs. Lukas kept complimenting me and telling me how much Leo liked my interior decorating. I was a fool to listen to her! My father had warned me that Leo was a hard catch, and I didn't listen to him!"

✳   ✳   ✳   ✳

Cassiani hummed as she helped Mrs. Lukas put on her robe for the afternoon nap. She was feeling exceptionally happy. Leo's image, his eyes, his hand holding hers, his words; all were replayed in her mind. She folded Mrs. Lukas' clothes and placed them to the side. Somewhere in the distance, Mrs. Lukas said something.

"What did you say?" Cassiani asked.

"I said, can you pull the curtains? The sun is too bright," Mrs. Lukas replied, reclining on the bed. "And don't come before five! I don't want to be awakened before then."

Mrs. Lukas' testy remarks dampened Cassiani's lighthearted mood. Even though she had positive feelings for Leo, Cassiani couldn't say the same for his aunt. If things were to develop with Leo, then how was she going to get around Mrs. Lukas? With a sigh, Cassiani shut the door behind her. If Mrs. Lukas didn't want her, so be it. When she slipped into their room next door, she was surprised to see her mother not resting, but sitting by the window, busy darning a blouse.

Vera looked up expectantly. "Tell me, daughter, what happened with Leo?" she asked, beaming at her. "Your face is glowing. I can tell it was something good!"

"What do you mean?" Cassiani asked. She was surprised by her mother's perceptive remark. She withdrew into the bathroom to check her face in the mirror. Was it that obvious how she felt? She knew her curious mother would not sit still until she learned the truth. *But I'm not ready to tell her about my feelings for Leo. It is too early.*

"Don't act like you don't know," Vera said, chuckling as she wagged her head. "When I took Mrs. Lukas to the pool, I expected you to join us in a few minutes after your talk with Andy. Instead, you returned an hour later, and with Leo. What did you do all that time with Leo?"

"Leo came as I was talking with Andy. He suggested we take a walk so he can talk about his aunt." Cassiani tried to speak calmly, as if things were no different, but she could not hide her true feelings. Her euphoric heart soared freely like a bird, bringing forth a big smile, causing her mother to smile at her knowingly. "We discussed her health, and he told me that they are leaving for New York in two weeks." She paused. "That's all." She resumed her humming as she released her hair from the bun and combed it.

"Hmm. I wonder why he would go for a walk just to tell you that. Did he say that he'd like to write to you, or telephone you?" Vera asked, her eyes gleaming. When she didn't get a response, she rose and put her sewing aside. She muttered to herself. "Ahh, if only you knew how much it means to me to see you happily married one day."

"What did you say?" Cassiani asked, peering at her from the bathroom.

Vera sighed. "You must be hungry. There's some tiropites on the table. I brought them with us from the house."

The cheese pies were exceptionally flaky and tasty, as Cassiani munched away. Her eyes settled on the clothes that were hanging to dry. "Thanks for washing the clothes."

Vera resumed her sewing. "It keeps me busy, like I used to be, when I worked for Soula. I even found a tear on this blouse." She lifted the blouse.

"I was thinking, whenever I have to deal with Mrs. Lukas I get anxious and nervous. She doesn't treat me like she does everyone else … like Leo, Nina, you, and Stella," Cassiani said.

Vera's eyes flew open. "How does she treat you?"

"She finds fault with me all the time and doesn't want my company. Now Leo expects me to sleep in her room tonight to keep an eye on her. I don't know how she'll feel about that."

Vera scrutinized the mended blouse, then folded it and placed it to the side. "Did you know that years ago Soula wanted to become a nurse?"

Cassiani was surprised. She couldn't picture Mrs. Lukas as a nurse, helping people. "No, I didn't know that. What does that have to do with me?"

"Wait to hear the rest," Vera said, touching her arm. "She opened up to me … and told me that she never became a nurse because her father felt that her place in life was marriage."

"That's not new around here," Cassiani said, chuckling.

"Yes, but she had fallen in love with a doctor, and her father didn't want him. So she refused to marry anyone to spite her father. When she finally did marry, she was in her forties and her husband was rich and well into his upper sixties. She became a wealthy and lonely widow in her fifties." Vera's eyes narrowed as she glanced around the room; then with lowered voice said, "There's something else. Did you know that Leo's father, George, is a doctor, and his mother, Colleen, is a nurse?"

Cassiani nodded, puzzled. "Yes, Leo mentioned it."

Vera told her about Leo's childhood and how his aunt and his parents quarreled. "It all started because Leo's mother was a nurse. Soula was plain jealous of her because she never got a chance to become a nurse. So she dislikes nurses intensely."

Cassiani stared at her mother, trying to picture these events happening. "All this time I thought it was something personal, having to do with me, but it could be anyone who is a nurse." She recalled the rude manner in which Mrs. Lukas treated Fifi and Fanny. "I think you have a good point, but how am I going to deal with her?"

Vera became quiet, as if thinking. "How would you like it if I slept in the room with her? If we need you for anything, I'll just knock on the wall."

"Thanks, Mother." Cassiani felt better. "By the way, Leo told me that his parents will take care of his aunt when they go to America. Maybe they've resolved those issues with her."

"Praise the Lord!" Vera made the sign of the cross. "There's hope yet!"

"What is *that* supposed to mean?"

CHAPTER 38

It was a cloudy Saturday morning as Cassiani rummaged through the suitcase and pulled out some clothes. Today they were supposed to go to the springs and she wanted to wear something … different. She kept remembering yesterday's unexpected walk with Leo. It felt so wonderful being with him. Yet there was a feeling of uncertainty as to where all this was going to lead her. Yesterday on the way back from their walk he told her that Sunday he was leaving for a trip to Athens. His aunt had mentioned once that he couldn't sit still, just like his grandfather. *Any woman he marries will probably have to share him with his job.*

Vera entered the room holding a brown paper bag. "Soula kept me up all night, what with her loud snoring." She massaged her back, wincing.

Cassiani suddenly felt guilty. She had a very good sleep last night. "I'm sorry about that. If you want, I can stay with her from now on."

"No, that's all right." Vera sat down at the table. "You better go to her. She's all alone."

"Not before I check you," Cassiani announced. A few minutes later, she finished her task. "You need to take your medicine. I see that you left the bottle of pills here last night."

"I have become a slave to these," Vera said, taking her medicine. "Nicko brought a tray of food up to the room and there was plenty for both of us. Soula hardly ate anything." She pointed to the paper bag on the table. "I brought you some food."

"Thanks, but I'll eat later. You said she was alone?"

Vera was unable to contain her excitement. "Nina didn't show up yesterday evening, or this morning! And Mrs. Lukas is not in the best of moods, even with me. So be prepared."

Cassiani glanced at her watch. "It's not even ten yet. Nina might come later." She went next door to take care of her patient. Cassiani coaxed her to eat more food.

"But I'm *not* hungry!" Soula protested. She clamped her mouth down and pushed the tray away. "I already ate."

"As you like," Cassiani sighed. "Shall I get you ready for the trip to the springs?"

An hour later, Cassiani returned to the room. Her mother was resting on the bed. "Mrs. Lukas thinks it's going to rain today," she informed her mother. "She doesn't think we'll go to the springs."

Vera gazed out the window at the gray day. "It does look a little cloudy to me." She brushed back stray strands of hair and yawned. "It feels so cooped up here in this tiny hotel room. I miss our house and the goats. I hope Mrs. Kalotsis will remember to give them water."

Cassiani searched her clothes. "I brought my white pants, now where are they?" She lifted them up. "It looks like they're all right." She stared at them critically.

"What about that summer dress ... the one your sister used to wear?" Vera said, heaving her body from the bed to rummage through the clothes. She pulled it out from her suitcase. "Good, it's not stained." She gave it to her daughter. "Wear this to the springs."

Cassiani did not resist, knowing that by doing so, it would probably raise her mother's blood pressure. She changed into the sleeveless gray dress. It was too large for her and fell loosely down to her ankles. Her chest felt exposed. "The front is a little low," she complained.

"It shows off your lovely neck and shoulders," Vera said proudly.

Cassiani shook her head, attempting to remove it. "I don't feel comfortable and besides, look outside." Raindrops were coming down steadily. "Mrs. Lukas was right."

Around eleven thirty Nicko came and told them that due to the weather, the plans for the outing were rescheduled for tomorrow afternoon. After he left, Vera promptly took the sleeveless gray dress and began to sew it. "I'll just make it so that it fits you better."

Cassiani and her mother visited Mrs. Lukas around five o'clock. Cassiani's hair was down and she wore her white pants and white blouse; she brought a book on nursing with her to read. It wasn't long before she was reading it, while the two women chatted about a number of things. Occasionally, Mrs. Lukas would look at her watch. "I wonder where Nina is."

When Leo arrived there a half-hour later, the small room suddenly became quite full. He went to the window and looked outside. "Still raining," he observed, settling down into a chair. "I guess even the plants need a little water." He gazed at Cassiani with an amused air.

It was difficult to talk to him while the two older women were carrying on their conversation. Cassiani glanced his way and received a special smile, which made her feel warm all over.

Later, they all walked downstairs and into the next building for dinner. Nicko and Mary joined them at their table. It was Greek night and Louis was playing his bouzouki with his band. Nicko and Leo's conversation ranged from sports, to travel, and finally to politics. Cassiani ate silently, listening to her mother's conversation with Mrs. Lukas. Mary was also silent.

Cassiani was aware of Leo's eyes periodically singling her out, but she didn't feel comfortable returning his glance, especially with her mother's hawk eyes catching every glance. "Mary, do you know what happened to Nina?" Mrs. Lukas asked, drumming her fingers on the table. "She hasn't shown up at all."

"She said she would be here later," Mary said. She peered around the room anxiously. "She told me a little about the interior design of your rooms. It sounds wonderful. How do you like it?" She began a conversation with Mrs. Lukas.

After a short while, Mrs. Lukas complained about the music, so Cassiani and her mother took her upstairs to her room to retire.

*   *   *   *

Leo gazed at Cassiani's retreating figure as she left with his aunt. He felt that she could have remained behind, but instead, like a dutiful nurse and daughter, she fulfilled her duty.

He admitted to himself that he was confused about the girl. One minute he saw her as his aunt's nurse, the next minute as a friend, and just this afternoon he felt as if he were a love struck schoolboy, wanting to visit her in Cleveland. Her silent response to his offer was a cold splash to his ego. Nina would have jumped at the idea of having him visit her.

"I'll be right back." Mary rose to go to the ladies room, leaving Nicko and Leo alone at the table.

"Friend, you look like something's troubling you," Nicko said, slapping Leo on the back.

"Is it that obvious?" Leo asked.

"Yes, as soon as Cassiani left," Nicko said, winking at him.

"Nicko, I will be leaving in a couple of weeks and so will she," Leo said. He stared out into the room. "We'll be going to different cities, leading different lives. She has her mother to take care of and I have my job. Somehow I don't want to have our friendship end here. Today I asked to visit her in Cleveland."

"Let me guess, she gave you the cold shoulder?"

Leo was silent.

"You want to hear some advice from a good old friend?"

Leo looked at Nicko expectantly.

"The girls on the island are not the same as the tourists and the American girls. Girls here don't date for the sake of dating. Nina is the exception." Nicko rolled his eyes upward. "Girls here date only if they know there's a future for them. You know … marriage. There is no such thing as a male *friend.*"

'That's it!" Leo exclaimed. "I was a complete fool! It never occurred to me that she's not comfortable with being called a friend."

Nicko nodded knowingly. "She probably thought there's no future with you, so why should she spend time with someone who just wants to dally with her? If you're interested in her, you have to let her know. She's a beautiful girl, Leo. She's not going to be single for long. I saw the way that Andy drooled over her."

*   *   *   *

Vera decided to stay with Mrs. Lukas and keep her company. "You go back. I'll stay with her. You need to have a little fun," she whispered to Cassiani. Cassiani stood there awkwardly, so Vera poked her. "Go!"

Cassiani walked resolutely downstairs. It wasn't that she did not enjoy listening to the music, she did. She wasn't sure about being in Leo's company. She was afraid that he would say or do something and her emotions would get ahead of her and reveal her true feelings towards him. *I don't want to fall in love with a man who looks at me only as another conquest, like Nina.* She saw how quickly his relationship with Nina fizzled out. She didn't want to be in the same situation down the road. Nevertheless, her heart led the way and she returned to the table, where Nicko, Mary and Leo sat. Leo particularly seemed pleased to see her.

Several people got up and formed a line dance. With a little persuasion from Mary and Nicko, Cassiani arose to dance with them. She was at the end of the line. Eventually Leo joined them, holding Cassiani's hand.

The music enveloped them in its own magic. It had a life of its own, stirring their souls from their lethargy, urging them forward towards their destiny, whatever that may be. Cassiani realized how well Leo knew his steps, his rhythm matching hers; their steps united as one. She felt light and free, her feet barely touching the floor.

Cassiani had warmed up considerably from the dance and she felt flushed as she sat back down. Leo made it a point to sit next to her. Nicko and Mary were still standing talking to some tourists.

Leo leaned towards Cassiani. "I didn't get a chance to talk to you this afternoon. When my aunt and your mother get together, they don't leave room for anyone else to talk, do they?"

Cassiani smiled knowingly, fanning herself with her hand. "That's all right. It does them both good." The waiter came by the table to take orders.

"Would you like something to drink?" Leo asked Cassiani.

She smiled and asked for a soda. Leo ordered it for her before placing his own order. "Give me the check," he told the waiter.

"Thank you," Cassiani said to Leo.

"By the way, your mother slept in my aunt's room last night. Was that her idea?" Leo asked.

Cassiani nodded. "She felt that your aunt gets along better with her. Besides, they've been friends for so many years."

Leo was silent after that.

When the band took a break, Nicko and Mary returned to the table and carried on a conversation with them about the rescheduled trip tomorrow. "Is twelve a good time?" Mary asked.

"Fine with me," Leo said. "My flight doesn't leave until five thirty."

Louis and a couple of band members joined the group. He was carrying a drink in one hand and a lit cigarette in the other. They sat down at the table.

"As usual, you gave an outstanding performance," Nicko said, slapping him on the back and nodding to the other two.

"Of course," Louis smirked. He looked around the room, waving the lit cigarette. "Nice crowd today, but someone is missing. Ahhh ... there she is." His eyes lit up as he stared at someone standing at the doorway.

Mary nudged Nicko. "Look who that someone is," she whispered to him, pointing to Nina standing at the entrance. Nina was dressed in black leather pants that hugged her body, a black halter-top, and tall heels that give her added height. Mary went to greet her.

Without Louis' bouzouki accompaniment, the remaining members of the band switched to rock and roll music. The noise level had risen as the beat of the drum and accompanying instruments filled the room with the latest in rock and roll. By now, the smell of smoke and liquor hung in the air. People were in a festive mood and several got up to dance.

Mary returned shortly with Nina, who greeted the group cheerfully.

"*Koukla mou,* come," Louis said to Nina. He gestured to the empty seat next to him.

Cassiani curiously glanced towards Leo. Apparently, he hadn't paid any attention to Nina for he was busy talking to Nicko. Nina sat next to Louis and flirted openly with him, ignoring Leo for the rest of the evening.

When the strains of a popular tango came next, Nicko and Mary promptly got up to dance. Their bodies moved gracefully together as they whispered to each other. After watching the couple for a moment, Leo leaned over and asked Cassiani if she would like to join him on the dance floor. Cassiani's heart started to race as she noticed the intent way he was looking at her. That same warm, fuzzy feeling rushed through her body. She had never danced a tango in her life. *Should I accept and take the chance of stepping on his toes, or should I say no?* Without another thought she took a deep breath and nodded.

Leo rose and took her hand. Once on the floor, he placed his arms around her waist and gazed into her eyes as they moved slowly together. Cassiani's arms hung down by her side. She was uncomfortable with her steps and kept bumping into him. She apologized. "I've never danced a tango before."

"Here," he said, gently putting her arms around his neck. "Just follow my steps."

Cassiani flushed. Her face was very close to his face. It was too personal … and too public. Her eyes focused downward. She allowed herself to be led as he moved gracefully. In no time, their steps seemed to flow together as one, fluently, effortlessly.

"You learn quickly," Leo whispered into her ear.

"You're a good teacher," Cassiani replied. She relaxed a little and found herself leaning closer to him. He felt comfortable … too comfortable. She moved slightly back.

After the dance finished, Leo's fingers lingered on hers as they walked back to the table. Cassiani felt tingly all over and yet at the same time felt confused about Leo's intentions. Her strict upbringing and years of immersion in her studies had left her inexperienced with men. *I need to leave.* "Thank you for the wonderful time," she told Leo. "But it's a little late for me and I should be going."

"Stay a little," Leo said huskily. "My aunt is a late riser. You can sleep in."

They had arrived at the table. She did not sit down. *He is making it difficult for you.* "I'm afraid I won't be sleeping in tomorrow," she said shakily. "We're planning to go to church at eight in the morning."

"Ah, then you have a good excuse," Leo said, nodding. "I've gotten away from church these past few years, what with all the traveling I do."

"Even in your travels you should be able to find *some* Greek church to visit," Cassiani admonished. She was about to continue, then paused when she realized how quiet Leo suddenly became. *Maybe I lectured him too much. Maybe he doesn't like that.*

Leo's eyes twinkled. "You have a good point there," he said. "I'll meet you in the lobby tomorrow morning. We can go together in my car ... with your mother, of course. It's more interesting when one is with good company."

Cassiani nodded, pleasantly surprised by his agreeable manner. "By the way, will your aunt be all right without us?"

"I'm pretty sure she'll be fine for a few hours," Leo said, smiling at her. "Here, let me walk back with you." He waved good-bye to Nicko and Mary, then left the room with Cassiani.

They walked toward the stairs.

"You know, you dance the Greek dances quite well," Leo said.

"Thank you, so do you," Cassiani replied appreciatively. "Where did you learn to dance so well?"

Leo grinned broadly. "My Greek school teacher pushed for me to learn Greek dancing. Before I knew it, I was leading the dances." He slipped his hand into hers as he talked.

It felt so natural for Cassiani to accept his hand as if it belonged there. She felt a sense of everything being all right as they walked up the stairs. When they arrived at her room, Cassiani noticed that he would not let go of her hand, but stood very close to her. She was afraid to look into his eyes. She didn't want him to see the emotions she was feeling.

He pulled her chin up. Cassiani gazed into his eyes, feeling an overwhelming sense of sweet nothingness, a feeling of wanting nothing more but to lean once more into his arms, to be held by him. As if he understood, he pulled her to him and they slowly danced in the hallway.

He leaned a little closer. His voice dropped to a whisper. "Now, I have a question for you."

Cassiani leaned closer to hear him. "Yes?" she whispered, gazing into his mellifluous eyes. His hand stroked her chin.

"Would it be all right if I kissed you?" he asked huskily.

She didn't know where she got the nerve, but her head nodded of its own accord. Unable to tear her eyes away from his lips, she felt his warm breath as he bent his head towards her. This time, this was not a friendship kiss, but a promise of something more. His warm lips fervently met hers, transparent in their message, sealing her heart to his. She shivered as the kiss ended.

"You can open your eyes now," Leo said softly. "That was a good-night kiss."

CHAPTER 39

The next morning, Cassiani dressed for church. She didn't tell her mother that Leo was going to take them. *Just in case he decides last minute not to come.* She went into the bathroom, humming softly as she fussed with her hair and face. Satisfied with the results, she exited the bathroom and found her mother already dressed and waiting for her.

"Cassiani, you look lovely!" Vera said. "You are glowing! Maybe we'll see Bobby at the church. That's the church his mother goes to and I know they go there *every* Sunday."

Cassiani suppressed a nervous giggle. "Thanks Mother. Maybe we will."

Leo was already in the lobby when they arrived. He was handsomely dressed in a dark blue Sunday suit with a crisp white shirt and red tie. His hair was impeccably combed.

"I wonder why Leo is up so early?" Vera whispered to her daughter.

"I didn't tell you," Cassiani whispered back nervously. "Leo said he was going to church this morning. He said he'll take us."

Vera's excitement could not be contained; she rushed forward to greet Leo excitedly.

"Good morning, Leo! Fancy you going to church!" She then looked at Cassiani with a pleased expression. "Cassiani just told me that you were going with us!"

"Yes, I think it's good to go to church, and what better way than with good company," Leo said. He greeted Cassiani. "Your mother didn't know that I was coming?"

Cassiani blushed. *He has a way of getting at the truth.* "I wasn't sure if you'd make it."

Leo laughed heartily. "I guess I deserve that. The car is parked down the street."

It was a brisk, windy Sunday morning. Although yesterday's clouds had returned, portending another gray day, Cassiani's spirits were up. It didn't matter if it was gray or raining, or sunny. She just felt wonderfully happy.

Vera chatted all the way to the church, telling Leo about how she had been married in the church and how she baptized both daughters there. It wasn't long before they arrived at the church. Cassiani noticed her mother eyeing Leo proudly throughout the church service. After the liturgy, they walked outside and found Bobby and his mother waiting for them.

Vera introduced Leo as "a friend of the family" then began catching up on news with her old friend.

"I stopped by yesterday afternoon, but you weren't home," Bobby told Cassiani.

Cassiani noticed Leo's attention was riveted upon them. She didn't want to go into detail with Bobby about Leo's aunt and she also didn't want Leo getting the wrong impression of Bobby. "My mother and I were visiting an old friend in Psalidi, who has been ill. We ended up staying there overnight," she managed to say. "Leo, her nephew brought us to church today."

Bobby eyed Leo skeptically and was awkwardly quiet afterwards.

*   *   *   *

After they returned to the hotel room, Vera insisted that Cassiani wear the gray dress for the springs. "Look, I sewed it so it fits you better." She lifted it up for her daughter to see.

The dress fit nicely in all the right places. Cassiani thanked her mother, then pulled her hair up. "I hope it's not too cold, what with all the wind." She stuck another hairpin in the bun to secure it better. "I need to be down in the lobby by twelve. What time is it?"

"Almost twelve!" Vera announced. She muttered to herself as she rummaged through the suitcase. With a flourish, she pulled out a white shawl. "Here, put this over your shoulders. It'll help a little with the wind."

Cassiani stroked the delicately laced shawl. "Aren't you afraid it will get dirty?"

"Oh, no!" Vera said. "Just try not to lose it. Your father gave it to me as a present, and it's precious to me."

"I'll be careful. Are you sure you don't want to join us? Mrs. Lukas is coming also," Cassiani said. "The spring waters will probably be good for you."

"I haven't been sleeping well these days," Vera said, suppressing a yawn. "I want to stay here and rest."

✸   ✸   ✸   ✸

Cassiani walked into the hotel lobby. Near the entrance door stood Leo, Nicko and Louis. Next to them stood Nina and Mary. The two women wore white blouses and white pants, and both held large straw bags filled with things.

Cassiani greeted everyone.

"It's very windy today," Mary warned Cassiani. "You'll need to hold on to that dress."

Leo took Mrs. Lukas and Cassiani in his car, while Nicko took the others. Cassiani sat in the back seat, gazing quietly out the window at the panoramic view unfolding before her. Leo turned the radio on, and the car was filled with soft, romantic music.

Leo began the conversation. "I remember when Father used to send patients to the springs to bathe. The minerals in the water are supposed to be therapeutic. Isn't that right, Cassiani?" He turned and looked at her.

Cassiani agreed, then talked a little about the health benefits of the springs.

After they passed Agios Fokas, the car began its climb up the hill. It wasn't long before they arrived at the thermal springs. Their car went slowly down the winding path. They parked to the side. There were very few people there. When Cassiani got out of the car, the first thing she felt was the tug of the wind on her hair and dress. She held on to her shawl as she observed the majestic gray cliffs surrounding them; the boulders jutted upward to the sky.

"Leo, take my hand," Soula ordered, as she tried to get out of the car.

Leo helped her up, then held her arm firmly as they inched their way forward on the gray sand. Cassiani strolled alongside them.

"There it is." Nicko pointed to the area to their right where the effervescent water gushed out of the fissure, spewing its therapeutic waters into the small pool area that was surrounded by boulders.

There was a momentary lapse of silence as everyone gazed out into the water. It was a majestic scene, serene and peaceful. The clear water was shallow and inviting, and the scent of sulfur that hung in the air was a reminder of the healing that took place there.

Louis pulled out a box of cigarettes from his pocket and offered them to everyone. Only Mary and Nina accepted. Cassiani shook her head when he waved the cigarette box in her face. "That's all right," Louis said, smirking. He placed them back in his pocket. "If I give them all away, then there won't be any for later." He took a cigarette lighter out of his pocket.

"You're so funny!" Nina said. Her high pitched laugh floated out into the wind. With the cigarette in her mouth, she leaned towards Louis and placed her hand over his while he lit the cigarette. She flipped her head back, her hair streaming in the wind, puffing with pleasure.

Mary looked at Nina "Did you bring your swimsuit? Nicko and I plan to swim."

"Yes I did. I'll join you." Nina flashed Louis a smile. "What about you?"

"Whatever you want, *koukla*," Louis replied, with a sly grin.

Cassiani noticed Leo eyeing the couple with an amused look.

As if Leo sensed Cassiani's glance, he turned and looked at her. "Cassiani, if you want to take a swim, I can stay with my aunt."

Cassiani shook her head. "I hadn't planned to. I didn't bring a bathing suit."

Soula sat down on a flat rock at the edge of the pool. "Cassie, help me with my shoes."

Cassiani obediently bent down to remove Mrs. Lukas' shoes.

"I'll stay here with my aunt for now," Leo said to Nicko and the group. The group continued its stroll, heading closer to the pool.

A gust of wind pulled at Cassiani's shawl, causing her to clutch it tightly to her bosom.

"Here, let me help," Leo said, laughing, bending down and removing his aunt's shoes.

Moments later, Soula inched her bare feet into the water. "Ahhh. Nice and warm."

Leo removed his shoes and sat down next to his aunt. He looked up at Cassiani. A golden lock of hair rested on his forehead. "Do you want to join us?"

"You go on ahead," Mrs. Lukas said, shooing her with an annoyed look. "I'd like to have a private talk with my nephew."

*   *   *   *

Cassiani tried to remain calm as she walked away from Mrs. Lukas and Leo. It was obvious that Mrs. Lukas did not want her. *Don't let it get to you. Leo wants you to take care of her and that is what counts.* Sounds of splashing and laughter interrupted her thoughts. Nicko had plunged into the water while the two bikini-clad women stood knee-deep in the water, splashing each other wildly, laughing, and trying to get each other wet.

Louis waded in the shallow water behind them, calling out to them. "As soon as I catch up with you, I'll make sure you both got a taste of that water!"

The excited shrieks from the two women followed as they moved quickly out of his way.

Cassiani stood there for a few moments, laughing at their merriment. Mary started to leave the group and go towards the beach. Nicko splashed Mary. "Ahh!" she shrieked. "Ooh!" She laughed and splashed him back.

Nicko splashed her once more. "Come on in, Mary! It's not so bad."

Some of that water sprayed Cassiani and she moved back instinctively, trying not to get wet. The thermal springs was a small, secluded area and not made for much walking, but mostly for swimming. Just then a gust of wind caused her dress to fly out. Without warning, it flew upwards, above her knees. Cassiani swiped at her dress, trying to keep it down.

"Cassiani. Wait."

She turned around when she heard the deep, mellow voice. Leo stood very close to her. Warm, unexplained feelings coursed through her body when their eyes locked. The previously turbulent feelings that his aunt invoked had disappeared; they were replaced by a flutter of happiness. The laughter, the splashing, the group all vanished into the background. Leo was here and nothing else mattered. They strolled up the winding rocky path, away from the group.

"So you'll be leaving this afternoon?" Cassiani asked.

Leo nodded, then talked about his trips, his work, and how time consuming it had become. "It is troubling, to say the least, when I am called away to do work while my aunt is recuperating from a serious injury," he confided.

"You did mention that you were on vacation, didn't you?" The wind teased her hair, then her dress, pulling it every which way, but she wasn't paying attention.

Leo nodded. "Yes?" he prompted, appearing interested.

"Well, to me, the definition of a vacation means to relax, to get away from work." She bent down and picked up a golden colored stone; she examined it. "Studies have shown that when people overwork they get stressed and are not as productive. And when people get stressed, that is when we start seeing them in the hospital with all kinds of diseases and illnesses. They don't take the time to notice the little things that count in life."

She placed the rock in his hand. "This simple stone is a reminder of how beautiful and perfect God has made even a mundane thing like this. It exists, along with the sky, the flowers, the sea." She smiled at him. "It is here for us to enjoy … if we take the time."

"Thank you for the gift," he said softly, gazing into her eyes. "The other day, when we walked to the harbor, I felt as if I were on vacation for the first time in many years."

"I felt the same way." She lowered her eyes as she thought about the future. *Should I tell him now?* She looked up and found him staring at her. She blushed. "By the way, I wanted to let you know that it's all right if you visit me in Cleveland."

Leo's eyes were full of compassion as he pulled her slowly towards him and kissed her tenderly. Everything fused together in one flowing, loving moment. *There was no going back.*

"Leo!" shrieked Soula Lukas.

Cassiani pulled away shakily, turning towards Mrs. Lukas' direction. She was attempting to get up. "Your aunt is calling you. I think she needs help," Cassiani said, her voice trembling. She gestured towards the older lady's direction.

Leo turned. "I think it's more than that," he muttered. His hands were clenched as he strode purposefully towards his aunt.

CHAPTER 40

Cassiani clutched her shawl tightly to her as she watched Leo walk tensely away. Just a minute ago his gentle kiss made her heart soar. Now, strong emotions threatened to turn her hopes of love into tears of discouragement. Soula Lukas was making things difficult for her. First she didn't want her to nurse her, and now she didn't want Leo to spend time talking to her.

Her eyes fell on the lapping waves below. She could no longer ignore her strong feelings for Leo. Was she experiencing this unattainable love she'd read about in love stories; or was it physiological, like her hormones running rampant? *It is too soon to be called love. We just met ... and besides, he hasn't said that he loves me.* She continued her stroll, going away from the thermal springs to an unpopulated area. For some reason, she wanted to be alone.

Everything seemed more vivid and beautiful here. She bent down to pick up a small flat stone, remembering the stone she gave Leo, staring at its golden color. Etched on its surface was the shape of a plant. Even the plant was once alive, *like us*. Now it's a fossil, imprinted forever on this stone. Like a chapter in a book, it has its own story to tell. *If time reveals my story, will it be a happy one?* Cassiani looked long and hard at the stone. She blinked back her tears as the answer came to her. *Not if Leo's aunt stays the way she is.*

The wind pulled and tugged her dress, her shawl, and even her hair. Just then, her hair toppled out of its bun. She removed the hairpins and shook her head; her hair danced all around her face. She took a deep breath. She didn't feel like fighting the wind.

Suddenly, a gust of wind ripped the shawl from her hands. "The shawl!" she yelled, her one arm stretched out. She ran after it. She could not let it out of her sight; the white shawl that belonged to her mother; the precious shawl that her father gave to her mother.

Like a skittish white kite, the shawl flitted every which way, then flew upwards to her right, up the craggy slope, following some invisible path designed by the wind. At some point, it fluttered behind a group of large gray boulders, vanishing out of sight. She combed the area with her eyes but couldn't find it. "The shawl must be here somewhere!"

Willfully, she climbed the steep slope of craggy boulders. Reaching the top, her eyes combed the rocks. There it was, a piece of white lace hanging over the edge, just beyond her reach. She looked around desperately for a stick. Nothing could be found. In a frantic attempt, Cassiani leaned over the jagged rock, feeling its jab, as she stretched her arm forward. Her fingers grazed the tip of the shawl. *Just a little closer.*

She touched the tip and yanked the shawl with all her might. "Yes!" she shouted triumphantly, clutching the shawl to her. Her victorious moment was brief, as the rock underneath her foot slipped out of place and fell below. Unable to get her balance, she careened backwards, falling, falling into the rocky terrain below and into a state of unconsciousness.

Cassiani felt a powerful light pulling her upward. She began to float towards its source. It was so bright, so peaceful here. She felt as if she were in a dream. She could see far and wide around her; she could see the whole world. It was an incredibly serene feeling.

Below her, a woman was lying still on the rocks. Who was that woman and why was she down there? The wind wound itself around the woman, teasing her dress, her hair, as if by its very force it could help her get up. A bruise had formed on the side of the woman's head and the white shawl was clutched in her hand. Cassiani was amazed at the resemblance of the woman to herself. Why did she look like me? How could it be me? I am here … but where is here?

*   *   *   *

While talking to his aunt, Leo had kept a watchful eye on Cassiani. He saw her walking away from the group. He saw her running after her shawl. Her frantic chase reminded him of the time when he was a young boy and his favorite kite had blown away. He chased it madly down the beach, just like she did with her shawl; only in his case, his kite was smashed when it plummeted into the jagged rocks. He also remembered the feeling of being out of control when he chased the kite, oblivious to everything around him.

When Cassiani disappeared out of sight, the fear of something happening to her was too great to ignore. He bolted up. "I'll be right back." Not waiting to hear his aunt's response, he hastened towards Cassiani, leaving his aunt behind.

Leo followed the path he saw her take, calling out her name. "Cassiani, are you there?" He sensed that something was not right when he got no reply. She had disappeared without a trace. He searched everywhere for her, continuing to call out her name, but there was no reply.

*   *   *   *

Cassiani looked around her dazed, trying to decipher what happened. "Where am I? How did I get here?"

As if sensing a presence, she turned and saw her father. He was walking towards her. He appeared exactly as she remembered him. Handsome in a dark suit and with a kind face. He stretched out his arms. "Father!" she said joyfully running to him. "Oh, Father!" She hugged him. He smiled and she could read his thoughts.

"It is all right," he said. "Follow me."

They walked down a path filled with beautiful flowers and trees; their colors were splendidly vivid. Ahead, several people were waiting, watching, with smiles on their faces. She recognized her paternal grandparents and waved to them, calling out. Next to them stood her grandmother and another man. "Why that's Yiayia Athena!" She waved to her. "Who is that man next to her?"

"That's your grandfather Nicholas, your mother's father," her father said, pointing to the tall man next to Grandmother Athena. "You never met him. He died before you were born."

"Let's go tell Mother!" Cassiani exclaimed, feeling excited.

"I'm sorry, dear. But I have to remain here," Father said gently. "I cannot go back. Do you want to stay here?"

"Oh," said Cassiani, feeling confused. She felt so peaceful and serene here. It was a beautiful world. All her relatives were here and there was no feeling of wanting anything. But Mother needs me ... and what about Leo?

"Do you want to stay here?" her father repeated.

Cassiani hesitated before responding. "It feels so good here ... as if there is no need for anything."

"Look down there," he said, pointing downward. "Maybe someone needs you down there. Someone dear to you?"

*   *   *   *

Leo was about to turn back and retrace his path. Just then the wind's loud sigh, busy hewing the jagged rocks, replied back: "Leo … I'm here!" it said. The sound came from all around him. Did he hear Cassiani in the wind? She must be here somewhere. Leo blinked, looking upward, trying to hear those words again. This time there was nothing. Then he spied the shawl. His heart leapt when he saw Cassiani lying there, motionless. She had been there all this time and he had not seen her. Her gray dress blended into the gray rocks, hiding her momentarily from the undiscerning eye. He scrambled towards her, feeling the wind pulling him upwards, towards the boulders. In a short time, he had reached her.

*   *   *   *

Cassiani looked below at the man with the golden brown hair. He was walking around the area where the woman lay, calling out Cassiani's name. Her heart sailed. It was Leo, and he had come looking for her. Apparently he did not see Cassiani's body, but turned around to go in the other direction.

"Leo! Leo!" Cassiani cried out, waving to him. "Leo, I'm here! I'm here!"

He stopped and looked upward, his face appearing puzzled, as if he heard her; then he froze when he spied Cassiani's body. In a matter of moments, he had scrambled his way up the rocks to her. He bent his face towards her as if to kiss her, then sprang back, as if appearing surprised. His fingers found their way to her wrist for a pulse. Cassiani could see the shock on his face. She heard him emit a loud groan, followed by, "Cassiani, please live!"

*   *   *   *

Leo was so relieved to see Cassiani that he couldn't help kissing her beautiful face with its large, dreamy eyes that were now closed, those glowing cheeks, and curly hair, wild and free, cascading all around her. When he realized she wasn't breathing, he desperately cried out to her, but there was no response. A black pit of nothingness threatened to overtake him. He had never felt so helpless before in his life.

Somewhere deep in the back of his mind, he heard Nicko's words "… take turns breathing in the mouth, then pressing down on the chest." With sweat on his brow, his heart pumping, he pulled her gently on to flat turf, and began the resuscitation process. After what seemed like a long time, he stopped. She still wasn't breathing. In his anguish he cried out to God. Then with desperate conviction he resumed the arduous, rhythmic task of helping her to reclaim her life.

It seemed like a long time that he was there. At one point, he stopped his efforts; his shoulders were slumped forward. "I was too late."

*   *   *   *

"Don't stop Leo! Don't stop!" Cassiani shouted, hoping he would hear her. "I want to live! I want to come back!"

In a fit of anguish, Leo stood up, his fists in the air, shouting in the wind. "Oh, God! Why did you let her leave me? Why?"

"I must go back! I don't want to die!" Cassiani cried, pulling away from her father. She sobbed. "I must go back! Leo needs me!"

CHAPTER 41

Cassiani gave a big gasp, then began to breathe shallowly.

Leo sat back, letting the tears of relief flow down his face. "Cassiani, Cassiani," he cried, yearning to hear her sweet voice respond. There was no reply, no lovely eyes looking into his. He gently touched her head for bumps. On the side of her head, he felt something wet and sticky. He moaned when he saw the blood on his hand. *I must move fast.* He removed his shirt and ripped it into strips, then tied them together. He wound them around her head, trying to stop the bleeding.

Leo gently picked her up and carried her, climbing down the rocky hill and retracing his steps back to the group. "Dear God, you helped me find her and helped her breathe. You have helped me so far. In Jesus' name, I pray to you, heal her, and let her get well enough to live a normal life."

The walk back was slow and arduous as he carried Cassiani along the winding path. The leisurely walk before had now become a tortuous, rocky path. He could not see where his feet landed. When he almost slipped, he was forced to stop and regain his balance. Just then he heard Cassiani moaning softly. He pressed forward, knowing that every step brought her closer to recovery. *I must get her quickly to the hospital.*

By the time Leo arrived at his car, he was out of breath and his arms were aching. He realized that it would be difficult to get Cassiani into the car without help; he could not open the door. He desperately looked around. Below, he could see Nicko on the beach, talking to Mary and the others. He summoned as much energy as he could and called out loudly. "Nicko! Come!"

Nicko and the others rushed to his side, their faces showing concern and surprise. Leo quickly told them what happened. With the help of Nicko and Louis,

Leo placed Cassiani in the back seat of the car. His heart leaped when her eyes fluttered open just then, focusing on him. "Leo," she whispered. She seemed as if she wanted to say something.

"Shh, it'll be all right," Leo said, his finger touching her lips. "Just rest for now."

Cassiani gave a hint of a smile before drifting off again.

Mary's face was pale as she peered into the car at Cassiani. "Is she all right? Do you suppose I should go with you to the hospital?"

"I think she needs you," Nicko said.

Mary entered the car and held on to Cassiani.

"What's going on?" Mrs. Lukas called out in a high pitched voice. She was sitting at the edge of the thermal springs, waving to them excitedly, her feet still soaking in the water.

"Nina, please go tell her," Mary said. "The poor lady is frantic from worry."

Nina sullenly walked towards Mrs. Lukas.

"Nicko, could you take care of my aunt?" Leo asked, as he sped away to the hospital.

*   *   *   *

The sun was setting when Nicko and Mary drove Cassiani back to the hotel. There was barely any talking as Cassiani slept along the way. When they entered the lobby, Cassiani groggily noticed it was only six o'clock. It seemed as if she had been in the hospital much longer. She turned to Nicko and Mary. "Thank you for all your help. It means a lot to me."

"That's what friends are for," Mary replied. "You should go and rest."

"I'm planning to do that." Cassiani walked slowly towards the stairwell, trying to keep herself from falling. She felt a little weak in the knees. *Maybe I shouldn't have left so soon from the hospital.* Mary rushed to her side.

"Here, let me help you," Mary said. "You look a little shaky."

Cassiani thankfully held on to Mary's arm as she escorted her to her room. When they reached the door, she turned and said, "I've been meaning to ask you about Leo—"

"Why don't you go ahead and rest now?" Mary interjected. "We'll talk about him when you're feeling better. Meanwhile, we promised Leo we'd keep an eye on his aunt."

Cassiani sighed with relief when she entered the room and didn't find her mother. She wasn't ready to talk about her mishap. A few wet clothes were scattered around the room, hanging to dry; signs of her mother's washing. Cassiani placed the shawl on the chair and went into the bathroom. She leaned on the bathroom sink and looked in the mirror. She removed the bandage from the side of her face, running over the bruised area with her fingers, examining the cut. It was not a deep cut and did not need stitches. *The doctor said that Leo had brought me to the hospital, but when I woke up, he was gone.*

After they cleaned up her injury, they ran a few tests on her. Two hours later, the doctor returned. "You were very lucky, young lady," Dr. Vassilakis said. "No broken bones or ribs, and your heart is pumping strongly. I don't see why you can't go home today."

Cassiani remembered being amazed at his words. She knew that a miracle had occurred. She remembered seeing her father in the dream. "Was it really a dream?" she asked, staring in the mirror. "Was it?" She was afraid to say it wasn't a dream. That it was real. That she had died and the reason she came back from her near-death experience was for Leo. *But he was not there when you woke up.* When she stepped out of the bathroom, she found her mother entering the room. *Should I tell her what happened?*

Vera greeted her. "I was down at the pool. How did it go with you?" She looked at her eagerly.

Cassiani's voice shook slightly as she replied, "We went to the Thermal springs but it was quite windy. Your shawl came in handy." She went to the chair, picked up the shawl and gave it to her. "The wind took it but I managed to catch it."

Vera studied Cassiani's face. "What happened to your face? You have a few bruises."

Cassiani tried to remain calm. Her mother had an uncanny way of getting to the truth right away, yet she didn't want to excite her. She carefully phrased her words. She told her about the ride to the spring, the spring water, the walk, and the run-away shawl. "Next thing I knew, I slipped and fell. I must have hit my head because then I blacked out." She continued, informing her that Leo had revived her, then drove her to the hospital with Mary.

"Oh, poor girl," Vera said, the tears glistening in her eyes, her hands clutching the shawl. "Thank the Lord that Leo was there."

Should I tell her? "Mother, I got to see Father. He looked just like I remembered him."

"You saw your *father?*" Vera looked at her incredulously, as if she had just seen a ghost.

Cassiani took a deep breath, trying to keep her voice from shaking as she relived that dreamlike moment. "Yes, and all my grandparents and relatives." She swallowed, telling her about her near-death experience, almost afraid to say the next words. "*I think I had died and gone to heaven*," she whispered.

Unable to control her emotions, Vera wailed. "Ooh! My baby!" She embraced Cassiani, hugging her tightly, her body swaying and rocking her daughter back and forth as if she were a small, hurt child. She crooned softly. "Oh, my baby. I almost lost you. I almost *lost* you."

Cassiani didn't know how long she was in her mother's arms, just that it was as if they had reached a higher plateau of love that transcended the moment of time.

After a few minutes, Vera released her daughter and took a handkerchief from her pocket and blew noisily. "I shouldn't have given you that shawl. I'm to blame for what happened."

Cassiani looked earnestly at her mother. "Mother, it's not your fault. How did you know that the shawl would fly away?" She paused. "We can't see it, but there's a whole world out there, a spiritual world. It was so peaceful. I feel that it was meant for me to *go there*, for some reason, but it wasn't my time to stay."

Vera silently made the sign of the cross, nodding her head solemnly.

Cassiani arose and paced the room. "There *is* an afterlife. It's a beautiful world, just waiting for us." She turned and smiled at her mother. "You know ... although I'm not afraid of death anymore, I'm very glad that I came back."

CHAPTER 42

Leo sat in the hospital waiting room, talking with Nicko and Mary. They were waiting to hear the results from Cassiani's tests.

Dr. Vassilakis entered the room, smiling at them. "Good news. Cassiani's tests show that she will be all right." He paused. "We expected a lot worse. It was a miracle, that's all I can say," he mumbled.

Leo felt relieved as he thanked him. "Will she be able to leave today?"

"We gave her a small dose of pain reliever, so she's sleeping lightly. When she wakes up, she's ready to go home," Dr. Vassilakis said, walking away.

Leo turned to his friend. "Can I talk to you for a moment?" They went outside to talk. "I've got a dilemma on my hands. I don't know what to do." Leo clasped his hands together. "I've got my boss expecting me to close a deal that should have happened a few days ago. I have my aunt who just got out of the hospital and wants me by her side twenty-four hours a day, and now there's Cassiani …" he paused, trying to control the emotions that swept over him.

"Whom you love and whom your aunt can't stand," Nicko finished.

Leo gazed at his friend, nodding slowly. "You're very perceptive." He stared out on to the road. "The only thing is, that my heart says one thing, but my mind says another."

"If you follow your heart?" Nicko prodded.

"If I follow my heart then I would stay here, to be by her side when she wakes up," Leo said. He turned and looked at his friend sadly. "But you see, Nicko, it is not so simple. It wouldn't be fair to Cassiani to make a promise I may not be able to keep. With my hectic schedule, where can I find the time for a relationship?

Many people are counting on me right now to close this deal, and I can't let them down."

"Yes, you do have a problem," Nicko said thoughtfully. There was a twinkle in his eye as he took out a set of worry beads from his pocket and gave them to him. "You might need these."

Leo broke out laughing. "Thanks." He took them and flipped them.

Nicko patted him on the back. "Don't worry, my friend. I've witnessed love and if it's strong enough, it can and will conquer all obstacles. Mary and I will keep an eye on Cassiani for you."

*   *   *   *

Later that afternoon, Leo flew to Athens in Ben's private airplane. He gazed out the window, retrieving the worry beads from his pocket. There was something soothing about the clicking sound of the worry beads as he played with them. It was windy and had started to rain. The small airplane rocked occasionally along the way, but his mind was traveling fast in other directions. Several things had happened since he came to Kos: first, the degradation of his ailing aunt's health; then the grounding of the ship; and now Cassiani's accident. It was as if negative forces beyond his control were unleashed all at once.

Initially, he wanted to stay behind and tend to Cassiani, but he knew that if he stayed behind, what would she expect … a long-term commitment? And what about her mother? He had never allowed his emotions to take over and rule his actions. Was he ready for a long-term commitment? *Not at this time. Not with this job.*

His hopes of having her take care of his aunt were now nonexistent. His aunt made it clear today at the springs that she did not want Cassiani "following me everywhere I go." Even more importantly, after the fall, Cassiani herself was incapable of watching his aunt. Luckily, Nicko and Mary were there to help. *But for how long?*

As soon as he got a chance, he would call Nicko to find out how things fared with Cassiani … and his aunt.

*   *   *   *

Ben's driver picked Leo up at the airport and drove him to the Piraeus harbor. The windows were fogged, and it was difficult to see outside. The harbor was empty of signs of life; there were no people, not even a stray cat or dog. Beyond the heavy rain and fine mist loomed the dark shapes of the freighters. Docked in rows, these massive ships were eerily motionless and difficult to identify. The cargo ship could barely be seen, and the driver drove around, trying to find it. It took quite a bit of maneuvering, but he managed to find it.

"There it is. The one with the lights," the driver said, pointing.

Leo thanked him, opened his umbrella and walked purposefully towards the ship. He carried his briefcase with him. He spent almost two hours there, reviewing everything with Christos, the ship manager.

Satisfied with the results, Leo left around eight o'clock that evening. The rain had become a light drizzle as he walked alongside the dimly lit harbor, thinking. The smell of the rain hung in the air, as the heavy fog settled around him like a thick blanket. He stopped to gaze at the ships anchored there; his mind was on other things.

He was about to make a deal worth hundreds of thousands of dollars of merchandise, yet it wasn't that important to him. He couldn't wait to get back to Kos, to Cassiani, and to his aunt. He admitted that his priorities had shifted these past few days.

Cassiani had told him about her dream of the ship. It was as if she had a premonition about the ship going into a storm. *But what could happen to it now? It is still in Turkey being repaired.*

His thoughts shifted to Jack Finch. Although he was a widower, he had lived a full life. He held an MBA, had been married, raised a family, and now was enjoying his grandchildren. Leo thought about his own parents and their years of happiness together. All his life he did not have to work. He grew up in an upper class neighborhood in a suburb of Washington, D.C., attended a private school, and studied at an Ivy League college. Although his father inherited wealth from his grandfather, money wasn't handed down to Leo that easily. His father believed that by being given money, one didn't learn how to manage it. So everyone worked in his family, while the savings accounts grew each year into millions by the time Leo graduated from college.

One day when Leo was still in high school, he asked his father, "Since we are rich, why do you work? Aunt Soula hasn't worked a day in her life."

"Your aunt and I are different. I like being a doctor and I'm happy," his father said. "She likes being rich, yet she is unhappy. Don't let money dictate your choices in life, son. Money comes and goes and if not well managed, can bring sorrow to a family. It's your character and the decisions you make that are important and will last for a lifetime. When I retire one day, I want to know that I will have made a difference in someone's life, by saving people's lives rather than by counting to see how much money I have in the bank."

Leo continued his walk. After a few minutes, he stopped and looked around; he realized that he was lost. A man bumped into him just then. He was short, of dark complexion, and wearing a raincoat. "Excuse me," Leo said, "could you tell me which way are the taxis?"

When the man saw Leo, he appeared startled, showing the whites of his eyes. He hobbled quickly away without saying anything, his head bent forward. Leo stared at him. There was something familiar about him. He watched the man disappear into a ship. Leo walked closer to have a good look. Even that ship seemed familiar; its color was the same as that of *The Lion*. It was labeled *The Lady*. Leo shook his head. He must be seeing things. Their ship was in Turkey, being repaired. The captain and crew were there, not here.

Leo eventually found a taxi. After he settled into the seat, he looked out the window. He couldn't let go of the scene. *Where have I seen that man before?*

*   *   *   *

The sound of heavy winds and the drumming of rain against the tall window-pane awakened Leo in the middle of the night. He could not go back to sleep but instead lay in bed thinking about a number if things. He recalled the telephone conversation he had with his aunt last night. She was upset about his leaving without talking to her. Leo apologized and explained the urgency of Cassiani's situation. "I didn't know how bad her injuries were. She was breathing, but not conscious. Then I had to leave for the airport."

"Hmmff," Soula said. "From what I heard from Mary, Cassiani got out of the hospital quickly. If she was that bad off, why didn't they keep her in the hospital, like they kept me? Besides, what is she doing now? I haven't seen her all day."

Leo did not argue with his aunt. He was too tired. He ended the telephone conversation with the excuse that he had work to do. He wanted to tell her that Cassiani would no longer be her nurse, not only because his aunt wanted it that way, but also for Cassiani's welfare. The poor girl had fallen and almost died and the last thing he wanted was to burden her with an unwilling patient. He needed to talk to Cassiani but it would have to wait until after the meeting.

*   *   *   *

When Cassiani awoke in the hotel room, it was already nine thirty Monday morning. Usually her mother was there to wake her, but not today; she had slept another night in Mrs. Lukas' room. *What use am I to Leo's aunt, or my mother? I'm supposed to be helping Mrs. Lukas and my mother, and now my poor, sick mother ended up helping Mrs. Lukas.*

The guilt feelings continued to taunt her, pushing her to move, to get up, but her sore and fatigued body resisted. She felt pain radiating down her legs, and in an attempt to curb the discomfort, curled up into a ball; that helped a little. Bruises had formed on her arms and legs from the fall. Cassiani lay in bed, trying to will herself to move. She said a prayer to get her going. It was no use. Her body was not cooperating.

Mrs. Lukas wakes up late anyway, so I'll probably not be needed for at least another half-hour. She began to daydream, her thoughts filled with Leo's image. She relived all the moments spent with him, including the scene where she fell on the rocks. It was love that drew her back to Leo, to earth, to live once more. She just knew that she came back for him.

The sun was shining through the window as Cassiani arose and went to the bathroom to wash. This was one time she appreciated not having to go outside to get water. As she washed her face, she studied it in the mirror, gingerly touching the bruises on the side of her forehead. It was a miracle that she didn't sustain worse injuries. The sound of a door shutting alerted her that her mother had returned. Cassiani went to greet her mother. "How did it go with Mrs. Lukas?"

"She's already washed and combed. When I left her she was eating her breakfast and that can take all morning." Vera placed the bag of food on the table. "Here, I brought you some food."

Cassiani peeked inside the bag. There was a small carton of milk, a straw, two toasts, a packet of cream cheese, and an apple. "I'm not that hungry. I'll eat after I finish checking Mrs. Lukas."

"Don't be in a hurry. You're still a little weak," Vera said. She removed the food from the bag. "Eat something to get strength. You didn't eat at all since yesterday morning."

Cassiani obliged her mother and sat down to eat. She bit into the toast. Short stabs of pain shot from her jaw to the side of her head as she chewed. Swallowing slowly, she set the toast back down. "I'll stay with liquids and a straw for now."

She watched as her mother pulled the small milk carton from the bag and stuck the straw into it.

Cassiani thanked her and sipped quietly. "So how was it last night? Was everything all right?" she asked, trying not to think about the throbbing pain.

Vera told her about the way Mrs. Lukas fussed over the fact that Leo left yesterday for the hospital in a hurry, leaving her behind at the thermal springs. "She also complained that Nicko was a fast driver and she had to hold on to her seat. She said that ride back to the hotel aged her ten more years!"

"At least she's well enough to complain," Cassiani said.

CHAPTER 43

At eight thirty, Leo was dressed and ready to go when Ben's chauffeur buzzed the apartment. The rain was still coming down strong and pounded the cars, making visibility poor. The ride to the meeting was very slow due to the traffic, and they arrived at Ben's office an hour later. When Leo entered Ben's office, he found several people waiting for him. He greeted Ben and Kostis, then looked around.

"Leo, you know Christos," Ben said, gesturing to the ship manager seated to his left. He then pointed to the other two seated next to Christos. "This is Steve Psilos, our accountant, and Mihalis Mavrakis, our attorney."

Leo nodded his greeting. After an hour of discussing the mechanics of the cargo, the charter, the legalities, the funding, and the insurance options, Ben handed Leo the contract papers. "As you know, we keep our ships well maintained," Ben said. "You don't have to worry about the crew. Christos will take care of that. I assure you that he will find the best men for the job."

Leo nodded, reviewing the documents. "What did we say about customs?" he asked the attorney, leafing through the papers.

"We'll take care of the legalities of the Greek customs," Mihalis said.

Around ten thirty, the papers were signed and they were shaking hands. Leo peeked outside the window. "I don't know how long this rain is going to keep up. I had planned to leave here in the afternoon."

"Our small plane will not be able to fly out in this weather. It is not that easy to maneuver in bad weather," Ben said apologetically. "Even I had to reschedule my meeting later today. You can try flying back tomorrow. Just call the office to make the necessary arrangements."

Leo wasn't surprised to hear the news. He thanked him and left. As soon as he entered the apartment, he telephoned his travel agent. The flights were fully booked for the next couple of days. He then telephoned Jack at his house and told him about the finished deal with Ben and Kostis.

"Good work! If you were here, we would celebrate!" Jack said. "If only we had better luck with *The Lion*."

"By the way, Jack. I wanted to ask you something. Do you recall what the captain of *The Lion* looked like?" They had chosen a hiring agency for the captain and the crew. Leo had never set eyes on the captain before the near-collision in the Turkish straits.

"It was dark when I arrived in Turkey, and I couldn't see him that well. I don't remember much, just that he was dark, either Indian or South American, and he favored his leg. I think he had a limp."

Leo bolted up. He was sure now that the man had recognized him and vanished out of sight so Leo wouldn't see him. "That man was the captain and he was going back to *The Lion!*"

"What?" Jack asked, sounding puzzled.

"Jack ... I think our ship has been hijacked! I'll talk to you later!" Leo hung up the telephone, grabbed his raincoat, and rushed out the door.

$$* \quad * \quad * \quad *$$

Cassiani began to dress, fussing with the hairpins for her hair. She was wondering if she should leave her hair down to hide the purplish bruises that had formed on the side of her face. "Did Mrs. Lukas say when she was expecting Leo back?"

"No. There was no mention of Leo at all," Vera replied.

Cassiani was surprised to hear that. She opted to leave her hair up. "I feel sorry for her."

"Don't feel sorry for her," Vera scoffed. "She's had a full life, the old prune! And at her age, shouldn't be jealous of a mere girl like you, and more importantly, you being my daughter! I've given the best years of my life serving her!"

Cassiani was puzzled by her mother's criticism of Mrs. Lukas. This was the first time she heard her mother say anything negative about her. *Was it due to the conversation we had yesterday about the way Mrs. Lukas treated me? If so, I better keep quiet on that score.*

She found Mrs. Lukas sitting in an armchair napping, which was fine with her. She sat by the window, gazing out at the beautiful view of the splendid water, waiting for her to awaken.

Mrs. Lukas didn't have much to say when she woke up, and was stubbornly quiet even after Cassiani tried conversing a few times with her. Cassiani diligently performed the tests, carefully jotting everything down, noting that everything was unchanged. "Your numbers are good," Cassiani said, putting her instruments away.

"Of course they are! I don't know why Leo wants all these tests to be done all the time!" Soula snapped. "I'm perfectly fine … just a little ulcer and arthritis, which the doctor said is not anything to worry about for my age." She stared at her sullenly. "By the way, can't you do something about those ugly marks on your face?"

Cassiani turned crimson. Her hand flew up to her bruises. She had forgotten all about them. She wasn't sure if she should explain how they occurred. It seemed as if Mrs. Lukas was not in a state of mind to listen.

There was a tapping on the door. "Mrs. Lukas. Mary here."

"Come in, my dear Mary!" Soula gushed.

Mary greeted them. She wore a creamy white sundress that contrasted well with her suntan and matching sandals. "I brought you those magazines I told you about."

"Cassiani, now that Mary is here, I won't be needing you," Soula said, dismissing her with a flourish of her hand.

Cassiani fled from the room, feeling unusually flushed. She could not forget the way Mrs. Lukas callously commented on her injury, as if it were some beauty mark that could be erased. Cassiani's frustration was building up. How could she justify her services to Mrs. Lukas if the woman didn't want her around? *I'll have a talk with Leo as soon as he gets back. Maybe I can convince him that his aunt will be fine without me. I'd rather not spend another minute with her!*

Cassiani found her mother sitting at the table, stitching the tablecloth. As she entered, she saw her mother pressing her hand on her chest. "What is it, Mother?"

"My heart. I don't like the way it's beating," Vera said. "Come. Do my readings."

Cassiani wasted no time in taking her vital signs. She didn't like what she saw. "Your blood pressure is high and so is your pulse. Did you take your medicine?"

"Oh, dear! Thanks for reminding me. I forgot it again," Vera said, appearing anxious. She quickly retrieved her bottle of medicine and promptly took her pill.

Cassiani sat near the window, trying to calm down from Mrs. Lukas' comments. At the same time, she also felt guilty for sitting there and doing nothing. Leo's image felt so distant from this morning. It was changing so rapidly, from a beautiful image, to one associated with an ogre of a woman. How could Cassiani have feelings for someone who not only was related to this woman, but loved her very much? Maybe she should just forget about Leo. She didn't want to compete with his aunt for his affection.

Vera studied her daughter. "Daughter, you look unhappy. Is it because she sent you away again?"

Cassiani didn't want to aggravate her mother or excite her heart. "Mary just came and brought her some magazines, so I wasn't needed." She saw her mother's skeptical face. "I don't mind, really, because after my fall yesterday, I do need to rest." She gazed out the window wistfully. "What bothers me is that I'm being paid to help her, and I'm not doing much of that these days."

"Maybe we shouldn't be here," Vera said, looking worried. "Maybe we should go home so you can get well. You are doing exactly what I did when I had my heart attack. You aren't allowing your body to get the rest it needs."

Cassiani was silent. Her mother had a good point. She could hear distant strains of Greek music coming from somewhere outside the window, but the thought of humming felt so foreign to her now. *If only we could go home.*

*   *   *   *

Mr. Makris, the supervisor at the port, leafed through the papers in a tired manner, then shuffled them together. "I'm sorry Dr. Regas, but we have no record of *The Lion*. There is no such ship in the Piraeus harbor." He shrugged his shoulders. "If you saw it a few days ago, it is no longer there."

"No, no. I saw it yesterday evening as I was walking in the harbor," Leo insisted. "It couldn't have left so quickly."

Mr. Makris frowned. "Maybe you *thought* you saw the ship. With weather like this, it's easy to make a mistake." His bushy eyebrows twitched nervously, as if trying to convince Leo of the truth.

"I'm sure it was our ship! I recognized the color. I even saw our captain entering it, although the flag was different. It was Malaysian ..." Leo stopped, shaking his head, trying to recall the colors of the flag in the fog. "Actually I'm not sure. But it used to be a Greek flag and the ship used to be named *The Lion*. They may have painted over that name ... that is why it now has the name *The Lady*," Leo rambled.

Mr. Makris appeared exasperated. "You are not making any sense! Are you trying to tell me that your ship *The Lion* was in *our* harbor without your knowledge, and without our knowledge, and that it was wandering around with a different flag and name? What do you take me for?" he said with raised voice.

Leo's jaw clenched at the man's disbelief. He did not know how the ship bypassed port authority, but somehow it did. He could not rest. "I'd like to make a telephone call, please."

Mr. Makris made a tired gesture towards the telephone. "Go ahead." He then proceeded to bury himself in the papers on his desk, ignoring Leo.

Leo telephoned Matt Doran at the embassy in Turkey and told him the news. "I want you to check up on our ship. I think it was hijacked. I saw it in Piraeus this morning but the port authority here says that there is no such ship." He then gave him his phone number at the Athens apartment. "Call me as soon as you get any information."

Later that afternoon Leo talked to Jack at length about *The Lion*, including seeing the ship at the harbor. Jack's words mirrored Mr. Makris' words. "Maybe you *thought* you saw it. Besides, it was going through repairs. How could a damaged ship travel?"

"This is one time that I don't mind being wrong." After Leo hung up, he thought about Jack's words. *Maybe he was right about the repairs. Maybe I am seeing things.* Then Leo remembered Cassiani's dream about the ship and the nagging thought that she was right could not be shaken off.

CHAPTER 44

The rest of the day was unusually subdued. Even Vera did not talk as usual or offer to go and visit Mrs. Lukas. She did not even sing, but quietly stitched the tablecloth. Around lunchtime she went downstairs and brought back some food, including yogurt for Cassiani. "It's not homemade, but at least it'll do," she said.

After lunch, Vera yawned, saying she was tired and wanted to sleep. Cassiani got herself ready to visit Mrs. Lukas once more. This time she let her hair down to hide the bruises on the side of her face. When she closed the door behind her, she noticed that her mother had already dozed off. Cassiani realized how little sleep her mother must be getting with Mrs. Lukas. She was strongly beginning to question the wisdom of coming here.

To her surprise, Cassiani found Mary still with Mrs. Lukas, talking animatedly to her. A new tray of food sat on her table. It was untouched.

"Will you be needing anything Mrs. Lukas?" Cassiani asked stiffly, standing at the door. As long as Mary was there, she did not care to enter the room. *If Mrs. Lukas criticizes me in front of Mary, I know what I will do. I will quit.*

"No," Soula barked. "We are doing fine."

Cassiani almost slammed the door behind her, but at the last minute decided not to. She was ready to quit. She had never experienced such an unfeeling, unsympathetic patient before. All her patients at the hospital where she worked gave her satisfaction, and the one person that she loved had to have such a despicable aunt. How was she ever going to overcome this?

Listless and dejected, Cassiani went to her room to cry, but when she saw her mother sleeping on the bed she didn't want to wake her up. Instead, she held back her tears and quietly shut the door. She walked downstairs. Every bone in her body felt sore as she inched her way down each step. She wandered around the hotel grounds, taking in the atmosphere of the bustling place, trying to forget her feelings of hopelessness. Tourists were coming and going, all ages and nationalities. They all appeared to be peaceful and content as if they had found paradise here on earth.

Cassiani was beginning to get tired but didn't feel comfortable going back up the steps just yet. She entered the pool area, hoping to find a lounge chair to rest on. Although several chairs were taken, there were a few available. She lay on a chair, her face tilted upwards, absorbing the sun. She promised herself that she would only think of positive, uplifting thoughts. To her consternation, she was unable to accomplish this. Even thoughts about Leo were elusive. Her mind was totally blank and in that place of nothingness, she finally found peace. In a short while, she felt drowsy and began to drift off.

"Cassiani!"

Mary and Nicko were coming towards her. She sat up and greeted them. Mary was in a good mood.

"I was so worried about you," Mary said, hugging Cassiani. "It was hard to talk to you with Mrs. Lukas being so grumpy! How are you doing?"

"Still a little sore," Cassiani admitted. She pointed to the bruises on her face.

Mary stared at her face. "Ugh." She wrinkled her face as if she had just seen a spider.

Cassiani winced. "It looks worse than it is. It will go away in a few days. Again, I wanted to thank you and Nicko for helping me. That really meant a lot to me."

"Don't thank us. Thank Leo," Nicko said, grinning. "He organized everything before he left. I just told him we'd take care of you."

"You should have seen him." Mary's eyes shone with admiration. "He carried you all the way to the car and drove you to the hospital."

"But he didn't stay at the hospital," Cassiani said.

"He couldn't. He had to leave for his trip," Nicko said, shrugging his shoulders. "He's called a couple of times, asking about you."

"Nicko, you're needed inside," Mihalis said, gesturing to him from the door. Nicko excused himself and left.

Cassiani continued conversing with Mary. They chatted about a number of things, from fashion, to hairstyles, to wedding dresses. Cassiani was surprised at the change in Mary. A few days ago Mary hardly paid attention to her, but now she was acting like she was her best friend. *Like it used to be.*

"I hope you can make it to my wedding," Mary said.

Cassiani thanked her, surprised by the request. It was difficult to plan so far ahead. There was so much unpredictability in her life right now. "The wedding is in the first week of September?"

Mary nodded. "Just to let you know, Leo's going to be our best man."

Cassiani was surprised to hear the news. "I've signed up for a college course in September. I'll let you know if I can make it." She glanced at her watch. Her eyes flew open; it was almost six o'clock. "I need to be going. Mrs. Lukas is probably awake by now." She stood up, wincing from the soreness in her body.

"Good luck with her. I noticed how she talked to you."

"She treats all nurses like that. She doesn't like nurses," Cassiani said, walking away.

*   *   *   *

Cassiani found her mother frantically pacing their room.

"Cassiani, where were you? It's six o'clock and I've been looking all over for you!"

Cassiani eyed her mother. "Mother, you're out of breath again," she warned.

Vera ignored her daughter's remark. "Nina knocked on the door an hour ago, and woke me up. Said Mrs. Lukas was asking for you. So I went next door to find out what she wanted."

"She was asking for me?" Cassiani asked incredulously. "When I went to check up on her earlier, Mary was visiting her, and she said she didn't need me, so I left."

Vera wagged her head, appearing upset. "I figured that much! That snake, Nina, had gone there to collect her pay, and Soula didn't have her checkbook with her. Soula wanted you to go to the house to get it, along with a few other things!" She sat down on the bed, fanning herself with her hand. Vera took a deep breath. "Where were you all this time, young lady?"

"After she sent me away, I returned to the room but you were sleeping. I didn't want to awaken you, so I went for a walk down by the pool," Cassiani replied.

Appearing satisfied with the answer, Vera seemed to calm down a little. "While I was there, Leo called … and he asked for you." Her eyes were wide as saucers as she leaned towards Cassiani. "What got me angry was that she complained to him that you were never around!"

Cassiani sighed. It was a matter of time before her mother would finally see the way Mrs. Lukas had been treating her.

"I reminded her that she sent you away earlier and Leo must have heard me say it, because he asked her about it. They got into an argument over you."

"Oh, dear."

Vera smirked. "After she was done talking to him, I demanded to find out what Leo had told her."

"You did?" Cassiani whispered, picturing her emotional mother huffing and puffing angrily at Mrs. Lukas, and all the commotion that probably took place. She knew she had a staunch supporter in her mother.

"I sure did!" Vera crowed. "He said that she shouldn't have sent you away and since she didn't want you, then so be it; you weren't going to spend any more time with her! Come on. We're going home!" She moved around the room with astonishing speed, grabbing clothes from everywhere and stuffing them into the luggage.

Cassiani's knees were shaking and her hands felt clammy. "We are?"

"Yes! She had that coming to her!" Vera wagged a pointed finger at her daughter. "You should hear the things she said about you, in front of Nina, but I won't go into that. I don't want you to see her again! Do you hear me? Come, let's get ready."

Cassiani followed her mother numbly, shocked at the turn of events. Everything had happened so quickly; one minute everything was quiet, and the next, chaotic.

Vera continued ranting about the ingratitude of Soula Lukas. "After saving her life! Huh!" she snorted, shutting the suitcase. Then she spied something else in the room and went to get it. "After what I did for her, now that's another story! She forgets that you're my daughter and anyone that insults my daughter, insults me! All the foods, the yogurts that I took to her, the … oh … my heart!" Vera sat down, holding her chest.

Cassiani rushed to her side, realizing her mother's overreaction was affecting her heart. She took her vital signs. "You need to relax, Mother. We'll leave, but you first need to calm down." She monitored her mother's heart until she felt she was stabilized. Every time her mother would start a tirade, she would ask her to be quiet. "It's not good for your heart," she would remind her.

The suitcase did not need a rope this time, as several items had been removed and it could be closed without problems. Cassiani attempted to lift it, but it slipped from her weak hands and landed on the ground. "Oh! I think I'm still too weak."

"I'll carry it." Vera lifted the bag. "I'm glad I didn't bring the good China," she muttered.

"But what about your heart?"

"You can't even walk, how are you going to carry this?" Vera retorted.

As they left the room, Cassiani wondered what Soula Lukas was doing or thinking. Although the lobby was bustling with people, Mr. Mihalis and Nicko noticed them immediately. Cassiani and her mother stopped briefly at the counter.

Vera waved her hand in the air. "We have to leave." She touched her chest. "My heart. We need to get it checked. Please check up on Mrs. Lukas. She is by herself."

Cassiani didn't like that her mother hid the truth. She placed the room key on the counter. "We won't be coming back." She followed her mother out the door, carrying the suitcase.

Nicko followed them outside, appearing concerned. "Was there anything wrong with the room?"

"Everything was all right," Cassiani said, reassuring him. "It's just that Mrs. Lukas doesn't want me to nurse her anymore, and Leo agrees."

*   *   *   *

Leo sat there fuming. He placed his head in his hands. The last thing he wanted was to be angry, and this was the first time he had ever been so angry with his aunt in all his life. He had done the best he could to have nursing care for his aunt, but her ungrateful remarks were what pushed him over the edge. How could she say those things about Cassiani? How could she treat Cassiani so callously? *She didn't want the girl at all.*

"I had it coming to me and I was blind to it!" he mumbled. "She gave me signals all along that she didn't want Cassiani, and I didn't pay attention." Why was he so oblivious to his aunt's messages? Did his aunt think he liked Cassiani and that he was using the excuse for her to nurse his aunt as a means to have her close by? Was his aunt using Nina as a decoy, as a means to push Cassiani away? He had never seen the scheming side of his aunt until now. *My aunt has become an ornery old woman and I'm not about to get embroiled in her small world.*

"Now I know why my parents kept away from her all these years," he muttered aloud.

He paced the room, trying to decide what to do next. One thing for sure, he had promised his father that he would take care of his aunt until they returned to the United States. He needed to keep that promise. He had calmed down considerably by the time he picked up the telephone and called Nicko.

"Nicko? Yes, Leo here. I wanted to let you know that I have to stay an extra day in Athens due to the weather. Meanwhile, I need to ask you a favor. Could you keep an eye on my aunt, just make sure she's all right? Cassiani is no longer going to take care of her. She doesn't want to be nursed."

"I know, Cassiani told us," Nicko said. "Mary went and spent time with your aunt after Cassiani and her mother left. She brought her out to the pool. That's where she is now. She's doing fine."

"You're a good friend. By the way, what did Cassiani say? How did she look?"

"Cassiani looked sad, and walked as if she were still sore. I asked her if everything was all right with the room. She just said that your aunt didn't want to be nursed anymore, and that you agreed. Oh, and her mother was breathing hard … said her heart was bothering her."

Leo was quiet. "Thank you for telling me. I'll see you tomorrow."

✴   ✴   ✴   ✴

Nina stared at Mrs. Lukas as she hung up the telephone, her eyes wide with wonder. "Mrs. Lukas, I hope I didn't cause …"

"No, you didn't," Mrs. Lukas said, appearing dejected. "It's not your fault. It's mine. I stubbornly refused my nephew's advice, and I got what was coming to me."

Nina proceeded cautiously. "Does Leo get angry a lot?"

"Oh, no! This is the first time I've seen him so angry," Soula muttered, staring out into the room.

"I'll leave you sleep, then," Nina said, standing up. "Don't worry about the payment for the decorating. I can get it later."

Nina went to the pool area, looking for Mary. Louis Kotsidas ambled towards her, wearing an opened shirt, khaki shorts, and slippers. His thin, hairy legs begged to be covered.

"So what are you doing tonight?" Louis asked Nina. "I'm playing at the club …"

CHAPTER 45

Later that evening, Leo turned on the television to watch the news and to hear the weather report for tomorrow. The telephone rang just then. He answered it.

"Matt here. Sorry to be the bearer of bad news, but you were right. Your ship is missing."

Leo couldn't believe his ears. A tight feeling in his chest caused him to sit down. His grandfather's ship was stolen. He was sure now that the ship he had seen at the dock today was his ship, and that man who avoided him was the captain. *But why were they there? Who were they doing business with?*

"What about the repairs? Wasn't it going through repairs?" Leo asked.

"Apparently they were fixed.. or—" Matt paused.

"Or what?" Leo prodded.

"We think there may have been a pretense in the severity of the damage to the ship. It may not have needed the repairs. How else was it able to travel so quickly? We do not know. What we do know is that it is nowhere to be found. The captain and crew vanished with it. We think they played a part in its disappearance."

"Hmmm. I see. I appreciate you finding out for me," Leo said. "Please let me know if you get anymore information about the ship." His jaw was clenched as he hung up the telephone. *Everything is going wrong today.* He sat there, staring at the television. Not one to get depressed over things, he typically would rationalize through difficult situations. But this was the first time in his life that he felt hopeless. *How will they ever find the ship?*

Bored with the news, he arose to turn the television set off. He stopped when he suddenly heard the announcer talking about a ship that was caught in the storm earlier that morning and had to call for help. His fingers trembled as he turned the volume up.

"*The Lady* was rescued in the Aegean Sea, a few miles from the Piraeus harbor, and was brought to the harbor with the help of tugboats," the announcer said. "Her captain and crew are all right. We'd like to ask the captain a few questions."

Leo tensed when he saw the captain's face. Sure enough, it was the captain of *The Lion.* He was scowling at the reporters, and instead of answering their questions, he turned his back on them. "That's him!" Leo shouted at the television, swearing aloud. That was the captain of *The Lion!* In a few strides, he reached the telephone. He was going to get to the bottom of this.

✻   ✻   ✻   ✻

Several hours later, Leo called Jack Finch and told him the news. "I notified the police, and with much explanation and a telephone call to Matt Doran, they were convinced that the ship was our ship. The captain and his crew were questioned and arrested."

Jack swore when he heard the news. "I'm getting too old for this. How did they manage to do this?"

"They were part of some organized group. They set everything up ... from the feigned near-collision and the grounded ship, to their engineers pretending that the ship had sustained damages. The captain and crew hijacked the ship and renamed it so they could move unsuspecting people's cargo!"

"What happened to the ship?"

"It's at the Piraeus harbor for now. It was caught in a storm, and this time, has real damages that need to be taken care of before it embarks. I'm having independent engineers come in to look at it tomorrow."

"Can you take care of the repairs? We also need to hire a new crew to send her back on track. The stored steel in Turkey is costing us money and we need to move it to its destination. Make sure we don't go with the previous hiring agency."

"The agency no longer exists. The police investigated it and told me that the agency has disbanded. They have left no trace."

After he hung up the telephone, he realized that Jack Finch was close to retirement and had been depending more and more on him over the years to do the traveling. He also realized that Jack's dependency was causing Leo to work more than he cared to. Did Leo want this type of responsibility full time? He would have to remain in Athens a few more days to take care of the ship and the manning of its crew.

*   *   *   *

Cassiani and her mother arrived home at six thirty that evening. Cassiani was exhausted and went straight to bed. When she awoke two hours later, she found her mother in the living room, stitching the tablecloth. Her mother's pinched face and reddened eyes revealed that she had been crying.

Vera placed the tablecloth to the side and arose when she saw her. "Let me fix us something to eat," she said, going to the kitchen. "You must be hungry."

"I'll help." Cassiani followed her mother mechanically. She had to move, just do something, to forget the mind-numbing events of that day.

"Oh, dear," Vera said, gazing sadly into the refrigerator. "I didn't do any shopping because we were going to stay at the hotel. I have a little cheese left and some dry biscuits. Let's see what else I can find."

A somber feeling descended upon Cassiani as she watched her mother go through the cupboards. She didn't have any energy to help. "I feel tired, and a little thirsty." After she drank some water, she went to rest on the sofa.

Just then, there was knocking on the door. It was Mrs. Kalotsis.

"Vera! I didn't know you had returned!" Mrs. Kalotsis exclaimed. "You said you'd be gone for a week and I heard some voices, so of course I had to come and check."

"I would ask you to join us for dinner, but we hardly have anything to eat. We weren't planning to return so quickly."

"I'll be right back," Mrs. Kalotsis said before Vera could respond. She returned quickly with a plate of food. "I made this fresh today. Where's Cassiani?"

Cassiani joined them. A plate full of stuffed cabbage leaves basking in a lemon sauce was sitting on the table. Her stomach lurched at the scent of the food. Mrs. Kalotsis kept them company as they ate the warm food. "These are wonderful!" Cassiani said. The soft cabbage leaves and equally soft rice filling were easy on her sore jaw. "Thank you!"

"You're welcome! So why did you come so quickly, my Verula? Is everything all right?" Mrs. Kalotsis asked Vera, her warm eyes showing concern.

Cassiani tensed. She stopped eating and looked at her mother, unsure as to how she felt and how much she was going to say. This was not the right time to discuss this issue.

"It was simple," Vera said, her mouth filled with food. "Mrs. Lukas didn't want us there."

Cassiani relaxed. Her mother appeared calm. Maybe she had gotten over it.

"She didn't? Whatever for?" Mrs. Kalotsis asked, with bated breath.

Vera wiped her mouth. "Let's say she has Nina and others watching over her. After Leo left, she didn't think Cassiani was needed."

"Really!" Mrs. Kalotsis exclaimed.

Vera stabbed the stuffed cabbage with her fork. "Yes! I don't ever want to see her again!"

"Mother. Please calm down," Cassiani said.

"I thought you were friends ..." Mrs. Kalotsis began, appearing puzzled.

"Not anymore! Anyone who insults my daughter, insults me!" Vera exclaimed dramatically, flourishing her fork in the air.

"Oh! I'm so sorry to hear it."

That's all Vera needed to hear. Her words spilled out in a torrent, her eyes glistening from unshed tears. "Would you believe it, after all these years of toiling by her side, cleaning her bathrooms, her dirty, smelly underwear, and her dishes ... feeding her and singing to her, the old *you know what*! She had the nerve to talk about my daughter—"

"Slow down, Mother. Remember your heart condition," Cassiani admonished.

"See! I can't even have a proper fit anymore! I have to think about my heart!" Vera pulled out a handkerchief from her pocket and blew her nose.

Mrs. Kalotsis arose to leave. "You'll be leaving soon for America anyway, and all this will be behind you."

Vera walked with her to the door. "Nina was there to witness everything! I saw her smug face just gloating over what Mrs. Lukas said to Leo about Cassiani. Leo can have Nina for all I care!"

"Mother!" Cassiani arose, infuriated. Her mother had gone too far. She stormed into her room, sobbing. The thought of not seeing Leo again was too much to handle.

*   *   *   *

Vera and Mrs. Kalotsis stood outside talking softly in the dark.

"What do you suppose made Cassiani upset?" Mrs. Kalotsis asked, appearing concerned.

"Because of what I said about Leo and Nina." Vera sighed. "You know, Leo saved Cassiani's life. My daughter almost died," she choked on her words, gave a great sob and buried her head in her handkerchief. "God was with her." She told her the story.

With reddened eyes, Mrs. Kalotsis solemnly made the sign of the cross. "That was truly a miracle!"

"Yes." Vera sniffled loudly. "She would have died if he hadn't come in time."

"Do you suppose Cassiani has fallen in love with Leo because he saved her life?"

Vera nodded emphatically. "It would have been such a nice match, but with a monster of an aunt ... I don't want my daughter mixing with such a family." She shuddered at the thought. "As long as Leo is close to his aunt, she'll torture Cassiani for the rest of her life."

"*Ola einai tihera,*" Mrs. Kalotsis said before leaving. "If it is meant to be, Leo will find a way to get together with Cassiani. Even with an aunt like that."

"Yes, all depends on fate," Vera repeated, walking with her to the gate.

After Mrs. Kalotsis left, Vera went into Cassiani's room. She found Cassiani on her bed, sobbing. She stroked her head tenderly. "I'm so sorry, daughter. It feels like a bad dream today."

"I'm sorry also. I wish things were different," Cassiani said, sniffling. "I did want to earn some money ... to help—"

"Don't worry about the money," Vera smiled, sitting on the bed. "I'm just thankful that you're alive and that we're rid of that terrible woman! I get heart palpitations just thinking of what she said!"

"What did she say?"

Vera cocked an eye, hesitating. "Let's say, it wasn't complimentary."

"What did she *say*?" Cassiani insisted. "I really want to know."

Vera sighed. "She said that she couldn't stand you. That you bored her to death, and that you were the sorriest looking person who came her way!" Vera choked on the last words, sobbing. "My beautiful daughter, the sorriest looking person coming her way? How dare she!"

Cassiani regretted asking her. "Mother. Please calm down."

Vera stared at her daughter. "You almost died yesterday and so what if your lovely face was bruised from the fall ... you're alive. That's what matters." She arose, going to the door. "And, and instead of being compassionate about it, she criticized you. I'm glad she didn't become a nurse. She would have been *lousy!*"

"Mother, please calm down," Cassiani repeated.

Vera was too angry to listen. "I want to leave here! I don't want to see her face again!" She left the room and returned, clutching two tickets in her hands. "Here they are! The tickets! We're leaving!"

Cassiani's mouth dropped open. "The airplane tickets for America?"

Vera wiped her tear-stained face and sat down on the bed. "Yes, the tickets. I admit it. I hid them," she said heavily.

"But why?" Cassiani asked. "Why hide them?"

"I didn't want Athena paying all that money. I was going to tell her they were lost so she could get her money back."

Cassiani's eyes challenged her mother's eyes. "Is that the only reason, Mother?"

"I didn't want to go. I wanted to stay here." Vera arose and swept out of the room, saying, "But now, we're going!"

CHAPTER 46

The days flew quickly by as Cassiani and her mother prepared for their impending trip. By keeping herself busy, Cassiani didn't find the time to think about anything else. They went through the closets, drawers, everything that held anything, to see what to take.

There was an unspoken agreement not to mention Leo or his aunt. It was as if a door had closed on everything dealing with them. But that didn't keep Cassiani from thinking about Leo. Just when she admitted to herself that she loved him, just when he showed his own love for her, the rift between her mother and his aunt had to happen.

Cassiani felt a strong urge to talk to Leo, to thank him for saving her life, but how could she get in touch with him? He and his aunt were staying at the hotel. It would be too public a display for her to go back there and try to find him. The problem was too complex for her to solve.

Friday morning, Vera brought her luggage into the kitchen to show Cassiani. "What do you think? I can put a rope around it," she told Cassiani, as she eyed the bulging bag.

"We don't want anything spilling out at the airport," Cassiani warned. "When they open it up at customs, we'll have to close it up again."

Vera reluctantly removed several items from the luggage, including a jar full of olives. Determined to take every last piece with her, she went back into her bedroom to search for a smaller bag. A half-hour later, she showed Cassiani a bulging tote bag. "I put the rest of the things in here. This bag will go on the airplane with me," she explained.

Later that morning, they went to the bank to withdraw money for the trip. Bobby happened to be the only teller there; he chatted with them for a couple of minutes. He was his usual congenial self, and it wasn't long before he asked if he could stop over on Sunday for a visit. When they told him of their trip, his jaw dropped. He stuttered his congratulations, unable to hide his disappointment. "Hope you have a good trip," he muttered.

"Thank you. Maybe you can visit us sometime," Vera said sweetly.

Cassiani nudged her mother. *How could she be inviting him to America? When will she realize I'm not interested in him?*

"What?" Vera said to Cassiani, but Cassiani did not reply.

Bobby seemed to like the invitation and smiled broadly. "Thank you very much!"

"Now I'd like to withdraw some money," Vera said.

"From which account?" Bobby asked.

Cassiani's eyes flew open. She was surprised by his question. She knew of no other account. *Unless Mother hid it from me ... just like the tickets.* She looked at her mother sideways, her eyebrows raised.

Vera giggled sheepishly, as if what he said was a joke. She handed him the savings book. "This one, of course."

After they left the bank, they walked down the street. Cassiani asked her mother about the other account. "I didn't know there was a second account." Her mother did not reply immediately. "Is there?"

After a moment of silence, Vera stopped and nodded. "I'm sorry, daughter that I didn't tell you sooner. That second one is for your dowry." She took out the savings book from her purse and showed her the balance. "I didn't want you to know until the time was right. When you are ready to get married, you can hold up your head high, and be married like your sister was, and like a Meletis should."

Cassiani's eyes moistened at her mother's thoughtful gesture. Her mother had made many sacrifices for her. She hugged her. "Mother, I love you! You're so wonderful."

"I love you, too! But I sometimes ask myself if all this was worth it. Here I was working for this, this woman ... to make a measly drachma. Here you were, constantly being criticized by her and then almost dying, and—"

"We can use some of the money for the trip," Cassiani interjected. "I don't need that much. That is more than plenty for a dowry."

"No, no. We'll be fine. I still have the money you gave me last week," Vera said firmly. "Let this get some more interest in the account."

*   *   *   *

Sunday arrived quickly. It was a whirlwind of activity that morning, as this was the day they were taking the ferry to Piraeus. Cassiani made sure that her mother did not overload her luggage. "Remember what happened at the hotel," she warned her.

This was also church day, and they made plans to attend the liturgy services.

As Cassiani prepared to dress for church, she couldn't find her gold cross. She looked everywhere for it. "Mother, have you seen my cross?" she asked.

"No. When was the last time you wore it?" Vera asked.

Cassiani thought and thought. "The day I went to the springs with the group. I think I was wearing it then."

"Maybe it broke off when you fell," Vera said.

"Oh, Mother! I'll never find it now," Cassiani groaned.

"We'll get you another one," Vera said.

A half-hour later, Cassiani was bent down in church, praying. She prayed for several things, including finding her cross. She prayed that Leo was all right and maybe one day that they could see each other again. She prayed for a safe trip. She felt peaceful after she finished.

After the church service ended, she followed her mother outside. Her mother spoke to a few people, telling them about their trip. Stella Spanos and her husband passed by for a few minutes and spoke to them, wishing them a safe journey, then left. Cassiani stood to the side waiting for her mother to finish. She didn't feel like talking to anyone.

As she gazed around the courtyard, Cassiani was surprised to see Leo standing to the side. He was just as handsome as ever, dressed in his navy blue Sunday suit. He was staring pointedly at her, almost brooding. Her heart leapt when she saw him. He was the last person in the world that she expected to see here. She wanted to run to him, to talk to him. But instead, she stood there, unable to move. The joy of seeing him lifted her up and she smiled the brightest smile at him. *He saved my life. I could never forget it.*

Her smile must have sparked some comfort, for Leo's somber face lit up in return. As if sensing her unspoken feelings, he came swiftly to her side and took her hand. "Cassiani," he said, gazing intently into her eyes. "How are you doing?"

"I'm doing fine. I wasn't expecting to see you here today," Cassiani said, her voice shaking from emotion. She didn't wait for an explanation but rushed into the next words, her eyes lowered. "Thank you for saving my life. If you hadn't come, I don't know what would have happened." He didn't answer. She looked up to witness his moistened eyes. They were the most beautiful eyes in the world. "I'm sorry for all that happened afterwards."

"I should be the one apologizing," Leo said. "My aunt was wrong in what she said and did." He sighed and looked out into the distance. "I would have come by sooner but I was away. I didn't get back until Friday evening." He told her about what happened with their ship, and how he had to take care of everything, including the legalities and the hiring of a new crew.

"The dream, it came true," she whispered.

Leo squeezed her hand. "Yes, the ship did go into a storm after all. You do have a gift, Cassiani. Try and cherish it, and use it wisely."

"Cassiani, we must be going! We have to take the ferry shortly," Vera called to her. She nodded a stiff greeting to Leo, then turned her back, resuming her conversation with the women she was with.

Cassiani blushed at her mother's behavior. "Now *I* have to apologize for my mother's behavior. We are leaving today and she's a little nervous."

"I understand," Leo said. "You are leaving for America?"

"Yes. We'll take the ferry to Piraeus, then catch the plane tomorrow evening from Athens," she explained.

"So the time has come to say good-bye." Leo continued to hold her hand. He paused as if he wanted to say something. "Cassiani, if things were different between our families. If I didn't have all the responsibilities I have, then I would be free to tell you how I feel about you." Strong emotions played on his face. "Let's say that I have feelings much deeper than friendship for you. But the time is not right. I need to take care of a few things first. Do you understand me?"

Cassiani nodded, lowering her eyes, hiding her own emotions. "Yes." She felt somewhat disappointed that he didn't speak the words of love that she wanted to hear. He gripped her hand. *I love you, but this isn't the right time to tell you. If it's true love, it'll find the right time.*

Leo seemed relieved. "Before you go, I want to give this to you." He took an envelope out of his pocket and handed it to her. "It contains payment for the days you worked at the hotel."

"That's all right," she mumbled. "I shouldn't accept this. I didn't do much."

Leo pressed the envelope in her hand. "I want you to take it." He then pulled out another envelope from his other pocket. "I found this yesterday when I went to the springs for a walk. Let's say that I went and had a heart-to-heart talk with God." He lifted the gold cross and chain from the envelope, and placed it in her hand "It must have broken off the day that you fell."

Cassiani stared joyfully at her cross. "I'm so glad you found it! This means a lot to me! And the chain, you replaced it." She clutched it to her bosom.

"That's the least I could do," Leo said, smiling wistfully. He pulled out a little black notebook and a pen. "One more thing. Could you give me an address and a telephone number where I could reach you?"

Cassiani gave him the information, watching him jot down her sister's address and telephone number, spellbound by the image of him contacting her in the near future.

"Cassiani!" Vera called out.

"I have to go." Cassiani's eyes met his in a moment of unspoken sadness. "Good-bye." She turned to go to her mother's side, when she felt his arm pull her back.

Leo leaned towards her and whispered into her ear. "Remember. We'll see each other again. Soon!" He left before she could reply.

CHAPTER 47

It was a Wednesday afternoon in June when Cassiani left the University hospital. It had rained all day, and she got drenched going to the bus stop, having forgotten her umbrella behind at work. It was an exceptionally busy day, with an emergency that sent one of her patients to the intensive care unit. The tense event had drained her physically and emotionally, and she was glad when the bus finally arrived in Cleveland Heights. All she wanted to do was rest.

The bus rolled to a stop and she got out. With shoulders hunched, she dashed towards the house. Her sister lived in an old brick house with three small bedrooms. Cassiani and her mother shared the second bedroom, while Verula slept in the third and smallest bedroom. Although larger than the house in Kos, it housed four adults and a young, lively child—which meant there was no privacy.

The sound of her mother's hearty singing as she entered the house signaled that she was feeling well again. When they arrived a few weeks ago, Cassiani promptly took her to a prominent cardiologist at the nearby Cleveland Clinic. She had heard about their excellent cardiology department. Although her mother did not have health insurance, Cassiani paid for her mother's healthcare. It was worth it. The doctor changed her mother's medicine and her mother seemed to be doing better with it. Several tests later, he adjusted her mother's medicine even more. After a few follow-ups and subsequent tweaking of the medicine, her mother began to feel more comfortable.

Verula came running to greet her. "Aunt Candy! Let's play! Let's play!" Her angelic face was flushed and her brown ringlets flew in the air, as she jumped up and down, tugging at her aunt's white uniform.

Cassiani laughed at her four-year-old niece's antics. She enjoyed coming home to this loving reception. She picked her up and swung her high up in the air, then gave her a big kiss on her chubby cheek. "So, you want to play! Heh?" She proceeded to tickle her. The room erupted in shrieks of laughter.

"There's a letter for you!" Athena announced. She was a younger version of her mother, with the same attractive features and temperament, and the same resounding voice. Her belly protruded like a beach ball in front of her as she helped her mother make dinner in the kitchen. With flour dusted hands, she pointed to the envelope on the table.

Cassiani noticed that it was postmarked from Japan. There was no return address. She placed Veroula down and with trembling hands she opened the letter. Her mother was eyeing her nervously. Cassiani read the letter silently, thrilled that Leo had written to her.

> *"Dear Cassiani, I hope my letter finds you well. My work is keeping me very busy travelling here and there. I am writing to you from Tokyo, where I am attending a trade show. I tried calling you once, but whoever picked up the phone hung up on me. Anyway, I do think about you often, and the stone you gave me has come in handy. Regarding my future plans, I plan to be in Cleveland the end of June. I will telephone you when I arrive. I hope to see you then. With warmest regards, Leo*

Cassiani's heart soared as she reread the letter. She could feel her lips curving into a smile at the thought that she would see him soon. She tried to appear calm as she folded the letter and put it back in the envelope. She wanted to share her news, but she wasn't sure how her mother would handle it. Ever since they left Greece and came here, her mother never mentioned Leo's name or his aunt's name, making it clear that she did not want to deal with that family. Athena was another matter. She was receptive when Cassiani confided in her about Leo, including his aunt's behavior towards her and her near-death experience.

Athena glanced at her excitedly. "Cassiani, who is it from?" she asked. "Is it from Leo?"

Cassiani's excitement could not be contained. "Yes! He wrote to me from Japan!"

Athena rushed to her. "Tell me," she said eagerly. "What did he say?"

"He is at a trade show in Tokyo. He said he tried calling but someone hung up on him," Cassiani replied, staring at her mother, searching for any cues.

"Hmmf!" Vera said, slapping the meat on the table and pounding it vigorously with a meat pounder.

Cassiani sensed her mother's irritation. "We'll talk later," she said softly to Athena. "I think Mother doesn't want to hear his name."

"She'll get over it! It shows he's thinking about you!" Athena whispered fiercely to Cassiani, then resumed her task of making the biscuits.

It was the topic of discussion with her sister for several days. Cassiani's thoughts fluctuated each time she thought about Leo. First came the warm, loving thoughts, followed by the anxiety and dread of having to deal with his aunt in the future; yet the satisfaction of seeing him in the near future overrode any of her hesitations. Cassiani's only frustration was that she could not write back because he did not include a return address.

*   *   *   *

That same day, Soula was enjoying her afternoon tea with George and Colleen in the family room. Since her arrival at Potomac, Maryland, a couple of months ago, George had promptly taken charge of her care. At first, Soula had been skeptical about the whole thing, but over time, she found their companionship delightfully pleasing and comforting. Her health had stabilized, and she had regained strength with Colleen's home-cooked meals, along with the vitamins and supplements she was taking.

"Colleen, look at this," George said, pointing to a newsletter he was reading. "They finally got the materials for the new church in the Dominican Republic."

"That's good, dear," Colleen said. She turned to Soula and explained the project. "We were hoping to be involved with the building of that church, but the supplies were on back order, so we thought it would be better to return here, to be with you."

"I'm glad you did," Soula cackled. She took a sip of the green tea, then picked up a slice of pasta flora to try. This time, her hand did not tremble as it brought the pastry to her mouth. She had just returned from walking around the grounds alone, and felt full of energy and zest.

"They have enough people," George said, scrutinizing the paper. "It looks like Basile and his wife are now in charge of the project."

Soula gazed at them with renewed eyes, marveling at the way the couple had matured and the way they worked well together in such a loving manner. "Any news from Leo?"

"Yes, he called while you were taking your walk," George said. "He'll be here in a few days. He won't stay long. Has plans to drive to Cleveland the end of the month."

"Cleveland?" Soula's eyebrows went up. "Whatever for?"

CHAPTER 48

The days sped by. Cassiani became very good friends with Lisa Brenner, another nurse on her floor. Lisa was a petite blonde, two years younger, single, and always finding humor in the slightest things. Lisa had become her confidante those summer days. Many times, during lunch breaks, the discussion would lead inevitably to Leo.

Occasionally, Andy Andrakis would stop by the nursing station when Cassiani was there and chat with her. Often she'd feel his eyes upon her, as she'd breeze in and out of a patient's room. Her instinct told her that he was interested in her, but she didn't want to go beyond friendship with him.

The fourth week of June arrived. Cassiani felt a mounting excitement about seeing Leo again. She would rise each day, humming a cheerful tune, wondering if that would be the day he would telephone and tell her he was in town. By the end of the week, Cassiani's humming had stopped; she was feeling discouraged. There had been no telephone call from Leo.

The following Monday, Andy came by while Cassiani was alone at the nurse's station and told her that a friend gave him extra tickets to a Cleveland Orchestra concert for that evening. "I know it's last minute, but would you like to go?" Andy asked.

Although tempted, Cassiani refused politely with the excuse that she had other plans. *What if Leo comes? I don't want to be tied up with Andy.*

Later that morning, while assisting a patient with a breakfast tray, Cassiani was called to the nurse's station by Lisa.

Lisa handed her the telephone. "It's a long distance call for you. I think it's *him*," she whispered, her eyes large with excitement.

Trembling with anticipation, Cassiani spoke into the telephone. At first she didn't hear anyone. She was about to hang up when she heard Leo's voice in the distance.

"Cassiani?"

Cassiani's heart soared at the sound of the deep, male voice. "Leo, is that you?"

"Cassiani, how are you? I tried calling your house and this time a little girl picked it up and then hung up on me. So I looked up the telephone number to your hospital and asked for you."

"That must have been Verula, my niece! Where are you? Will you be coming to Cleveland?" Cassiani asked excitedly. She wanted to talk and talk, to not let go of this moment.

"I'm afraid not. I'm sorry." He was silent. "That's why I am calling. I am in California. It's an emergency ... something to do with a shortage of wheat. We're scrambling to find a supplier and I need to fly to Italy later today. I'm sorry that I couldn't make it."

"Oh." Cassiani had forgotten how demanding his job could be. Her disappointment at his not coming could not be openly expressed. Lisa was hovering around her. Even Andy came by, looking curiously at her. She rarely got personal calls here at work. Cassiani felt frustrated; there were too many people around her to talk to him. She stared at her shoes in stoic silence.

"I hope you understand," Leo said.

Cassiani wanted to cry, but being a nurse, she had learned to hold her emotions in check. "I understand," she murmured, chewing her lip nervously. Lisa tapped her on the shoulder.

She pointed to a patient's room, whispering to her. Cassiani nodded to her. "Leo, I have to go now. A patient is asking for me and it's urgent. Thank you for calling." A part of her was disappointed in him and yet another part of her didn't want to hang up, even if he had let her down. *I came back to life for him, remember?* She thought she heard a faint sigh on the other end of the telephone as she hung up. She stiffly walked to the patient's room.

Later in the day when she arrived home, Cassiani didn't feel like eating. She gave the excuse that she was tired and went early to bed. There, in the privacy of her bedroom she finally allowed her bottled up feelings to flow freely, crying into her pillow. All those days thinking about Leo, waiting to see him face to face, to talk to him, were wasted. All that time thinking he loved her. He only loved his job, and his aunt.

At one point, when her crying had slowed down, she wiped away the tears. She turned around, her nose stuffed, staring up at the ceiling, trying to find logic somewhere in all of this. She realized that her expectations had gotten the better of her, and because things didn't work out the way she expected them to, it had turned out to be a let down. Her eyes fell on the Hebe statue on the dresser. It seemed so long ago since he gave it to her.

Just then she heard people whispering outside her room. She knew it was her sister and mother trying to figure out what happened. She turned over quickly and reburied her face in the pillow, trying to act as if she were sleeping. She didn't want anyone to see her red eyes. Like a violin tuning a high string came the whining sound from the hinge on the door as it slowly opened. She knew it was her mother even before she saw her, from the heavy breathing and the creaking of the wood floor. Her mother always seemed to find the beams that creaked the loudest. Cassiani suppressed a nervous giggle.

"Cassiani, is everything all right?" Vera asked, sitting down by her side, patting Cassiani fondly on the back.

"I'm just a little tired. It was a long day," Cassiani mumbled into her pillow, trying not to sink from the weight of her mother's body on the edge of the bed. She knew her mother wasn't too fond of Leo and his aunt, and she didn't feel comfortable telling her what happened. Her mother sat there, as if waiting for Cassiani to say more. After a few minutes, she heard her mother sighing, followed by the sound of the whining door as she shut it behind her. A few minutes later, Cassiani heard the door open again. This time it was Athena.

A scent of perfume filled the room as Athena glided to the side of the bed and sat down.

"Cassiani, what's the matter?" Athena asked. "Everyone's at the table ready to eat. Verula won't eat without you. Even David is asking about you. Why don't you join us?"

"Tell Verula I'm not feeling well," Cassiani mumbled. "I'll eat with her tomorrow." She didn't feel like talking. She didn't feel like doing anything.

Athena was silent. "Wasn't Leo supposed to come around these days?" she ventured. "I remember that's what he said in his letter." When she didn't get a response, she leaned over and touched Cassiani's arm. "Did something happen today? You can tell me."

Cassiani turned and gazed sadly at her sister. She knew that Athena was sincere. She was also uncanny, like Mother, in uncovering the truth quickly from her. Cassiani sniffled; she also knew that if she didn't say anything, Athena would sit there and tease it out of her. *Might as well tell her.* "Leo called me at work today." She looked up at her sister. "He had promised he'd be here, but he called instead ... long distance."

"Oh, you poor thing!" Athena said, appearing dismayed. "He called you *long distance*? How *could* he?"

The tears welled up in Cassiani's eyes. "Said he's in Californiaaah!" she wailed, letting her feelings spill out. "He lied to me! I can't trust him ever again!" She buried her head into the pillow sobbing and didn't hear the door shut this time.

✳   ✳   ✳   ✳

After dinner, David went into the living room to play with Verula while Vera and Athena cleaned up in the kitchen.

"What did she tell you?" Vera asked her daughter.

"Who?" Athena asked innocently.

"Cassiani, of course!" Vera said exasperated. "She was crying when I went into the room earlier. I could see. Did something happen with Leo?"

Athena eyed her mother, wondering how much she could confide in her. "How much do you want to know?" When she saw her mother's worried face, she told her.

"Ahh, so Leo didn't come," Vera said sadly. "Deep down I always thought he had a good heart. Too bad." She was quiet as she wiped the counter top. "So Cassiani *does* love him. I thought there was something there, although she hadn't mentioned anything all this time." She looked at her daughter. "You know, he saved her life, don't you?"

Athena nodded.

Vera's eyes narrowed in distaste. "Maybe his crazy aunt had something to do with this."

"I don't think it's that," Athena said, shaking her head. "It's in Leo's hands. From what Cassiani has told me, his job is very demanding and he travels all the time."

"Just like his grandfather," Vera muttered.

✳   ✳   ✳   ✳

The days flew by like sparrows in the wind. Athena and David had begun house hunting. They were eager to move into a larger house, now that Athena was expecting. Evenings were filled with lively discussions on the different houses they visited.

Cassiani kept herself busy at work, at church, and at home, trying hard not to think about Leo. Whenever it was a sunny day, she would take a different route to the bus to get home. Her stroll would lead her through the campus of Case Western Reserve University, across Euclid Avenue, passing by Severance Hall, and towards the Art Museum. There, she would sit on one of the benches by the pond, relaxing under the shade of a tree, enjoying the ducks floating by. On one such occasion when she had a particularly busy day at work, she impulsively entered the museum and wandered around the different art exhibits and paintings, enjoying it immensely. It was as if time stood still in these paintings. *I should do this more often.*

One day during lunch, Lisa asked her about Leo. "You haven't mentioned him in a while. Has he had a chance to visit you?"

Cassiani shook her head. She gazed sadly out the window. "He's too busy."

"Do you love him?" Lisa asked.

Cassiani stared at her friend. She nodded slowly.

Lisa flashed her a bright smile. "Don't worry. Things will work out."

On the first day in July, Andy approached Cassiani about attending a Fourth of July fireworks concert on Sunday. This time she accepted. The days flew by and on Sunday, to her surprise, when Andy came to pick her up for the concert, Lisa was also in the car with him. The sun was already setting when they arrived downtown. Several streets had been closed off for the event. They had brought their chairs, as did other people. They set them down on the road, waiting for the concert, given by the Cleveland chamber orchestra, to begin. Cassiani and Lisa talked comfortably with Andy. Cassiani noticed one time when Lisa and Andy got into a deep discussion about baseball, something she could never get interested in. *They seem to be in their own little world.*

As the darkness descended, the concert began; lively, drum-rolling music was piped through large speakers. Big screens positioned in a couple of places revealed the spectacular laser show that accompanied the music.

Much later, as Andy drove Cassiani back to the house, he chatted about a number of issues, about the music, his love for baseball, his family, and his ordeals at the hospital. Cassiani sat in the back and listened, while Lisa, who sat up front, nodded periodically to show him she was listening, then would enter a word here or there. When they arrived at her house, Cassiani politely asked them in.

"It's nine already. Have to be up early tomorrow. You know how it is," Andy said, chuckling. He gazed at Lisa fondly. "I also have to take Lisa home."

Cassiani smiled knowingly. She sensed there was something developing between Lisa and Andy. Although she was happy for her two friends, a feeling of loneliness tugged at her heart. "Thank you for everything. I had a very nice time."

When Cassiani entered the house, the noise from the family greeted her. Athena and David were playing a game with Verula in the living room. Verula was shrieking with laughter as her father chased her. Vera was sitting in the small dining room, her head bent down, engrossed in what she was doing; she was stitching the tablecloth.

Cassiani greeted her mother. Athena joined them. They asked her excitedly how the date went with Andy. "It was nice." She told them about the music and the event.

"Why didn't he want to come in?" Vera asked. "He could have stopped in for a minute to say hello."

"He has to get up early tomorrow, for work. Besides, he had to take Lisa home," Cassiani said, her voice faltering. She noticed her mother's eyes widen when she heard Lisa's name. She continued. "Andy's like a brother I never had. Although he's fun to be with, and has a steady job—"

"Those are the types that make good husbands!" Vera interjected. "See what happens? You didn't show interest in him and now he's going after Lisa! You're going to remain on the shelf! An old maid!"

"Now, *Mother*," Athena said. "You can't force Candy to marry someone she's not in love with. There has to be chemistry between them. Besides, the fact that he brought Lisa along shows he never was serious about Candy in the first place. If someone's serious about someone, they wouldn't be so quick to form a relationship with another person."

Cassiani nodded appreciatively. Her sister always had a way of saying just the right thing.

Verula must have finished her game with her father, because she came charging into the kitchen just then to greet Cassiani. "Let's play! Let's play!"

Cassiani laughed and swung her niece in the air. David ambled into the kitchen just then and greeted her. He was above average height, lanky, with chestnut brown curly hair and dark brown eyes, and always had a ready smile.

"Time for night-night," David said, gently taking his daughter from Cassiani. "You've had enough playing for tonight."

Athena busied herself helping put Verula to sleep while David took his nightly shower.

"Did I get any mail?" Cassiani asked her mother. It had become a daily habit for her to ask. Her eyes grew large as her mother ambled to the counter and gave her a letter postmarked from Greece.

"It's from Mary. What does it say?" Vera asked.

Cassiani read it. "Mary asks about the family and your health. She also writes about her wedding date being set for Saturday, September the eighth. She asks if I'd be able to come."

"Isn't that the time that I'll be going back to Greece?" Vera asked. "Maybe you can come with me then. There might be some nice young men at her wedding."

"I'll think about it," Cassiani said, marching away. She knew that she wanted to share her friend's happiness, but she also knew that Leo was going to be there. He was Nicko's best man. In her heart she wanted to see him again, but the memory of his telephone call a few days ago was still a bittersweet one. *Maybe he'll cancel that event, the way he cancelled his trip to Cleveland.*

*   *   *   *

A week later, Athena gave birth to a healthy, eight-pound baby boy. It was an exciting day for the whole family. They named him John, after his paternal grandfather. When Athena came home with the baby, everyone hovered around him. That night, the baby's crying kept Cassiani awake. This continued for several nights. She learned to sleep with cotton in her ears.

By the end of July, David and Athena had closed on a new house. Everyone was enthusiastic about the move. It was located in Parma Heights on the opposite side of town.

The house was a brick colonial, and much larger than the previous house. It had four large bedrooms, two bathrooms, and a spacious back yard.

Athena was still nursing the baby so Vera and David took charge, preparing the boxes and coordinating the move. Cassiani helped during her free time. They rented a truck and with the help of a few friends, hauled the furniture to the new house. The new house was close to everything; the shopping mall, the community college, the Parma library, and the local hospital. Yet one rarely saw people walking anywhere. Everyone drove cars.

The well-manicured lawns and accompanying sidewalks were empty except for two times a day, first in the morning when the children ran down the street to catch the school bus; then early afternoon, when they walked back to their homes, sometimes cutting through people's lawns to get home more quickly. It rained most of the time, so whenever there was a chance of sunshine, it was enough of a reason for people to drop everything and go outside.

A few days after their move to Parma Heights, Cassiani agreed to go to a Cleveland Orchestra concert with Andy and Lisa. It was an all Beethoven concert. Afterwards, they went to the German restaurant located near the concert hall. Cassiani felt once more that little tug in her heart when she saw the way Andy spent all evening talking and joking with Lisa. She remembered how he did that with her just a few months ago in Kos. *Why does it bother me?* Cassiani secretly wondered whether they were seeing each other. She got her answer when Lisa confided in her the next day during their lunch break.

"Guess what?" Lisa showed her the engagement ring on her finger. She excitedly told her that she had been going out with Andy the past few weeks. "He proposed to me last night after the concert. Oh, Cassiani! I'm so in love!" she declared, her face glowing.

"That's wonderful!" Cassiani exclaimed, smiling at her friend's happiness. *Why am I feeling the same way as I felt for Mary's engagement ... anxious?* "I wish you both the best of luck."

✻   ✻   ✻   ✻

The hot and humid summer brought torrential rains in the evenings, cooling everything down. Cassiani's daily commute was even more taxing as she had to travel over an hour each way to and from work, which meant getting up earlier and coming home later. It did not bother her because she enjoyed her job. But a week after Lisa's engagement, Andy was promoted to an administrative position. The whole staff on that floor was talking about it when Cassiani arrived for work. As soon as she found out, she went and talked to Lisa.

"Now that we're getting married, he wants to make more money," Lisa explained proudly to Cassiani. "Isn't that grand?"

"That's great! Have they found a replacement for him?"

"Mrs. Farroll is her name. Andy told me she's very set in her ways."

Mrs. Farroll turned out to be an older, heavyset woman who had an abrupt and abrasive behavior towards her staff. This caused two nurses to quit within two days of her arrival. To make matters worse, because of the shortage in nurses, Mrs. Farroll wanted everyone to take turns working evening and night shifts as well as day shifts. As a result, Cassiani's schedule became erratic.

The first time she worked evening shift, Cassiani returned half past midnight to her house, and found her mother anxiously waiting up for her.

Vera was upset. "What decent girl would be traveling so late at night, all by herself!" she scolded. "If your father were alive, he wouldn't allow it! You must look for another job!"

The next day, Cassiani began her search for another job. She bought a newspaper and started reading the job ads. One day, at lunch break, while she was perusing the job ads, Lisa joined her at the table.

"What are you up to?" Lisa asked, sitting down and opening her bag of food.

"I'm looking for work," Cassiani said. She pointed to a section in the newspaper. "Look at this one. They're hiring at the Parma hospital. It's much closer to home and is a morning shift. Even more importantly, it pays more."

"Are you going to apply?" Lisa asked.

"You better believe it!"

*   *   *   *

The next day, while in London on a business trip, Leo tried calling Cassiani's home. To his consternation, the line was disconnected. The letter he sent her a couple of weeks ago had been returned. Feeling determined to contact her, he telephoned the hospital where she worked. It was around two thirty Cleveland time. A nurse named Lisa answered the telephone. He asked for Cassiani.

"Sorry, but she's not in. You wouldn't happen to be Leo?"

"Yes." Leo was pleasantly surprised that she knew his name.

"I've been hearing so much about you from Andy and Candy! I mean Cassiani!" Lisa exclaimed.

"Andy?" Leo asked. He wondered why she said Andy's name in the same sentence as Cassiani's. *Was there something between Andy and Cassiani?*

"Andy is my fiancé," Lisa said proudly. "When he talks about Kos, he fondly recalls how you saved him from the mosquitoes with your peppermint. If he were here, I'd have him speak to you, but he no longer works here. He's been promoted." She lowered her voice. "The new supervisor is *awful*. She has us working different shifts every day."

"Do you know when Cassiani is expected to work?"

"Let me check the schedule." She shuffled through papers. "Let's see, today is Friday, so she has the evening shift today. Cassiani doesn't like having to work evenings because she has to travel over an hour to get here."

"Over an hour?" Leo asked. He knew Cassiani lived close to the hospital. *Did she move?*

"Ever since she moved to Parma, she has to take a bus and the metro to get here. I hear she applied for a nursing position at the Parma Hospital. I think she'll get it."

"Could you leave her a message that I called?" Leo asked. "I won't be able to leave a phone number because I'll be leaving shortly for Italy."

After he hung up, Leo telephoned his father. "Remember that nurse, Cassiani Meletis?"

"The one you were going to visit in Cleveland, but couldn't," George replied.

"Her new supervisor has her working evening shifts, and she has to commute over an hour by bus. She's applied for a nursing job at Parma Hospital." Leo paused, waiting to hear what his father would say.

"I'll see what I can do."

*   *   *   *

Later that day, when Cassiani arrived at work, she found Leo's message. She read it with mixed feelings. He had called while she was away. He didn't leave a phone number.

When she returned home late that evening, she did not feel like facing her family. She didn't want to talk to anyone but instead went straight to bed. She felt frustrated that she couldn't speak to Leo.

Athena came into the bedroom, trying to find out what happened.

"Is it that Leo again?" Athena asked.

Cassiani sat up. "He called today," she said, her nose stuffed. "I wasn't in, and he didn't leave a phone number!"

The next morning, Cassiani received a telephone call at home from the supervisor at the Parma hospital. They were interested in setting up an interview Wednesday at ten in the morning. The interview went smoothly and the following week, Cassiani was hired on the new job. The hospital was much closer to her home and the commute was much less, giving her more spare time.

CHAPTER 49

September

Cassiani left the Cuyahoga Community College auditorium, feeling exhilarated. She had just finished playing in the Cleveland Philharmonic's first concert of the season. She even played a solo violin part that went exceptionally well. The auditorium had been filled and the concert had been well received. Her only remorse was that no one from her family was there to enjoy the concert. Her mother had left for Greece a week ago. Her six-month visa was going to expire soon and she needed to go back. Athena and David went to Pittsburgh to visit his parents for two weeks and to show them their grandson.

As Cassiani left the auditorium, she saw Lisa and Andy coming towards her. Cassiani had invited them to the concert and was happy to see that they made it all the way over to this side of town. She smiled at her two friends, glad to see them. They beamed back at her and congratulated her for her fine playing. Cassiani couldn't help noticing how well Andy and Lisa matched as a couple. They were about the same height, with similar outgoing personalities. They seemed to finish each other's sentences. *Like Stella and Panos Spanos.*

"Would you ladies care to go out for a bite?" Andy asked charmingly.

"Thank you," Cassiani began. His question caught her off guard. She didn't have a car and that meant he would have to drive her to the restaurant and back home. "I didn't drive."

"Oh, don't worry," Andy said. "We'll take you home later."

They decided to go to a nearby restaurant. The meal was exceptionally tasty for Cassiani, who hadn't eaten much that day.

On their way back home, Cassiani gazed out into the blackness, the reflection of her face solemn as she realized she was going to an empty house. It was something she did not look forward to.

"I forgot to tell you, Cassiani. Leo Regas telephoned again last week asking about you," Lisa offered. "I told him about your new job and he seemed pleased." She turned around and looked at Cassiani. "Did he get in touch with you?"

Cassiani nodded. "He left a message, but I wasn't in at the time," she mumbled. She could see Lisa's questioning eyes. She knew what her friend was thinking. She shook her head. *No, he didn't call back either.*

✳   ✳   ✳   ✳

The house was empty when Cassiani arrived. She turned on the lights and walked through the marble tiled foyer and down the hallway. It was very quiet and lonely. She still had to get used to being by herself in this big house.

Usually on Sundays, the house would be bustling with activity; beginning with Athena's boisterous voice, followed by the two children's high-pitched voices clamoring for attention, along with her mother's singing, and even David's occasional comment. Now all Cassiani could hear was the slow ticking of the clock on the kitchen wall as she turned on the light in the kitchen. The answering machine showed two blinking lights. She pressed the button.

"Cassiani, this is your mother … Cassiani, are you there? She's not there." It sounded as if the last sentence was spoken to someone. "Cassiani, I am not doing well. It's my heart. Please come."

"Not again!" Cassiani felt the blood rush to her head. Her mother's voice sounded very weak. Now that her mother was on her own again, she was asking for help once more. Cassiani had reservations when her mother left for Greece. She wasn't sure if her mother could handle being there by herself and taking her medicine faithfully. It seemed as if Cassiani had been right.

With shaky finger she pressed the button for the second message. "Cassiani, are you there? It's your mother. *Please* pick up the phone." There was a pause. "I am not well, daughter. I may not make it."

Cassiani groaned as she heard her mother's heavy breathing. Her mother sounded even worse. She took deep breaths. "Now calm down."

She went upstairs to her bedroom, her knees feeling weak. She wondered from where her mother telephoned her. *Was it from the hospital?* How could Cassiani call her back if there was not a telephone? Her lips felt dry and her hands clammy. *You must do something.*

Her mind raced ahead. She had saved close to three thousand dollars. One thousand of that went towards paying her mother's trip and three hundred for her mother's expenses. She had promised her that she'd mail her money. "Whenever you need it."

"Thank you, daughter," Vera said. "May the good Lord pay you back three times over."

Cassiani had enough savings in the bank to pay for her roundtrip ticket, plus some extra cash. The only problem was that she hadn't had time to earn her vacation yet. *I'm pretty sure that if I needed it, I could take advance vacation, or family sick leave.*

She changed, glancing at the mirror. Her cheeks were unusually flushed. She nervously undid the pins in her bun. Her eyes settled on the folded tablecloth that sat on her dresser. Before leaving for the trip, her mother gave it to her. It was finally finished, and very beautiful, with its tightly stitched bright red roses and green stem border contrasting well with the white linen.

"Cassiani, here is your tablecloth. Keep it in a safe place. It is part of your dowry."

✳   ✳   ✳   ✳

It was a sunny afternoon on Kos Island. The sunlight was streaming through the parlor as Vera finished leaving her message on the telephone. She gazed out the window at the unkempt garden. *The roses need to be pruned.*

"My dear, did you find her this time?" Soula asked, placing her cup of tea down.

"I'm afraid not," Vera said, sighing. "I know that she had a concert to go to today." She nervously pulled back strands of hair from her face. "Did I sound weak enough?"

Soula cackled. "Positively sick!"

"I hope I didn't overdo it. She might be frustrated that she couldn't reach me." Vera planted herself down on the sofa and resumed her stitching. "So tell me about Leo. You said he was coming for Nicko's wedding?"

"Yes," Soula said. She leaned excitedly towards her friend. "George and Colleen are also coming. They took such good care of me, that we became very good friends. I already miss them and I've only been gone two weeks." Her eyes glistened with unshed tears. She patted Vera's hand fondly. "I'm also glad that you are back in my life. There's nothing like having a good friend like you."

"Me too," Vera said, beaming. "I have to hand it to you. When you came over to the house a few days ago, I was ready to chase you out the door with the broom."

They both broke out laughing.

"Like I said," Soula began. "I had no idea how much my nephew loved your daughter until I saw that his anger kept him away from me. I had a long talk with his parents, and then with him. The boy has good intentions for your daughter and I'm not one to get in the way." She shuddered. "My father did that to me and I don't ever want to have someone say that about me!"

"Speaking of your father," Vera said. "Does Leo intend to stay with his job?"

"Oh, no!" Soula exclaimed, gesturing in the air. "He's already left that firm over a month ago. He's working for himself now. He's a consultant." She said it with a proud manner. "I knew he had it in him to be his own boss."

"Ahh," Vera said, nodding. "Whatever happened to Nina?"

"Huh! That girl is something else!" Soula said, frowning. "Can you imagine the nerve of her marrying that ... that ... bouzouki player? And all along I thought she was interested in Leo. I paid her a pretty penny for all the decorating she did." She sniffed as if offended. She peered around the room. "Do you like it?"

"Yeeesss," Vera said, trying to find something good out of a totally beige room. "With a few cut roses, it'll look even better."

CHAPTER 50

Cassiani walked into the Kos airport, tired and anxious about her mother. It was six thirty Wednesday evening. She had slept on the airplane and still felt a little groggy. It had been a whirlwind of activity since Sunday, trying to get all her things in order. She bought her ticket, made arrangements for time off from work, and had the mail held at the post office. She also telephoned Athena. Athena appeared surprised to learn the news about their mother.

"But Mother was in very good condition when she left," Athena insisted.

"Yes, but knowing Mother, she probably stopped taking her medicine now that she's by herself. Remember how many times we had to remind her?" Cassiani answered. "I think it's better that I go and see how she's faring."

"When will you be leaving?" Athena asked, her voice sounding worried.

"Tomorrow afternoon. I should be in Kos by Wednesday evening. Wish me luck."

"I will. If Mother calls here, what should I tell her?"

"Tell her.. tell her ... anything you like."

Cassiani had even telephoned Lisa at her house and given her Athena's phone number in Pittsburgh. "Just in case you need to contact me," she told her. "I will be in touch with her."

"You mean, in case Leo calls again?" Lisa said impishly. "I hope he does call. Good luck with everything."

It took over an hour for Cassiani to get her luggage. Tired, she walked outside the airport and into the balmy evening. The island breeze felt nice on her skin, waking her up. She took a deep breath of the fresh air. The memories of Kos a few months ago flooded her thoughts; her mother's health, then the earthquake, then the visits to the hospital; the tense moments with Mrs. Lukas' snide remarks; and the beautiful realization of love when Leo saved her life. There was a bittersweet feeling associated with the island. It was the very first time she fell in love and the very first time she died. She pushed the memories aside and focused on the task at hand. She looked for a taxi.

"Would you like a ride, Miss?"

Cassiani froze. She knew that deep voice anywhere, in her dreams, her thoughts, even in heaven. She took a deep breath, trying to calm her emotions. How could she ignore the feelings coursing through her like electricity? How could she ignore that she still loved him? She turned and faced him. "Leo. What brings you here?"

Leo smiled. "I came to take you home." He handed her a bouquet of bright red roses. "I would have brought you daffodils, but they're not in season."

"They're beautiful!" Cassiani exclaimed, smelling the flowers. "Thank you."

Leo seemed pleased. "They're not the only ones that are beautiful to look at," he said softly. He lifted her luggage and they walked slowly to the car. "I tried contacting you a few weeks ago."

Cassiani nodded. "I heard." She flushed at the memory. He hadn't left a telephone number or called back. She thought he had forgotten about her, but he was here, in front of her, enticing her with his smile, his looks, his whole being. "How did you know I'd be here today?"

Leo was silent as they walked. "It's a long story."

Cassiani's mind was racing and so was her heart. They had reached the car. She watched as he placed her luggage in the trunk. He took the flowers from her and placed them in the back seat. She didn't know where to begin, or what to say to him. "I'd like to hear it."

"It started many months ago." Leo came towards her and held her hands. "When I came to Kos last April, all I was thinking about was to visit my aunt and try and coax her to health. Then you entered into my life in an unexpected way, and left, the same way." He had a rueful look on his face. "How did I know that nothing was going to be the same for me after that? No matter how many trips I took, no matter how many people I saw, I kept seeing your face in front of me."

Cassiani was silent. "If that's how you felt, then why didn't you come to see me?"

"I know I disappointed you, and I'm sorry. I usually keep my promises." He became silent after that as he looked out into the distance. "I knew that if I continued working at this job, that I might lose you. So I quit my job and formed my own consulting company."

Cassiani looked at him in amazement. "You quit your job?"

"With my own business, I can arrange my time better." His eyes probed her eyes. "We can see each other more often. Would you like that, Cassiani?"

Cassiani nodded; she was pleasantly surprised by the news. Then she remembered that it wasn't just his job that got in the way of their happiness. *Go ahead, don't be afraid to ask him one more thing.* "And your aunt? How is *she* doing?" she asked, her voice wavering.

"Fine. She sends her love." Leo bent his head down and kissed her slowly, passionately. He wrapped his arms around her and held her close to him. "By the way, the story hasn't ended."

Cassiani's tears began to flow uncontrollably. "Why did you do that?" she asked, her face buried in his shoulder.

He murmured into her ear. "I did it because I love you." He sensed something was wrong when she didn't reply. He moved back to study her. When he saw her tears, he wiped them gently. "I'm sorry about everything, about my aunt, about my not keeping my promises. I wish I could have done this months ago. I love you. I couldn't get you out of my mind all these months."

Cassiani gazed into his eyes, searching for the truth. She found it in his liquid eyes that shimmered with love's golden glow; they promised of moonlit strolls along the beach, of Sunday afternoons filled with love, Vivaldi, and roses. A smile lit up her face. "I love you too," she whispered. She was rewarded by the relieved look on his face followed by a passionate kiss.

Cassiani rested her head on his shoulder afterward, embraced by his arms. "I've been meaning to tell you something," she said.

"Hmm."

Cassiani told him about the near-death experience, about what she saw and heard, and about how she came back for him. She could see the wonder in his eyes. "I could hear you calling," she said, the tears streaming down her face. "I didn't want to die. I wanted to live … for you."

Leo hugged her tightly. "I don't know what I would have done if you didn't make it. All these months since then, I've played that scene over and over again in my mind." He moved slightly back and gazed in her eyes. "Will you forgive me for not staying by your side at the hospital?"

"You saved my life and arranged for my care," Cassiani repeated. "You *wanted* me to live and I came back because of that. That counted more than anything else." She saw the wonder in his eyes. "I know you had your job to do. I know how difficult it was for you to stay. There is nothing to forgive."

Leo kissed her once more, sealing their love even more. "You know, Nicko and Mary are getting married in a few days," he whispered into her ear.

Cassiani nodded. "I know."

"Hmmm. Maybe we should do the same one day," he murmured.

"Oh, Leo!" Cassiani said, moving back and seeing his smiling eyes. "That would be wonderful!"

They stood there talking for a long time about their future. There was no trace of tears on Cassiani's face by the time they entered the car.

"We better be going," Leo said. "Your mother is probably wondering why you're taking so long."

"Oh!" Cassiani exclaimed, feeling guilty. She had forgotten all about her mother. "I wonder how she's doing."

"Last time I saw her, she was sipping tea with Aunt Soula and talking about the latest news," Leo said. He winked.

THE END

978-0-595-46793-8
0-595-46793-8

Printed in the United States
200216BV00003B/250-267/A